Sign up for our newsletter to hear
about new and upcoming releases.

www.ylva-publishing.com

Rewriting the Ending

by hp tune

Acknowledgements

As time has passed, I have found gratitude in the losses and loves from which this book grew its roots. I am appreciative of the opportunity to share the end product with others, and should a few readers find connection or enjoyment within these pages, then that, too, is a bonus.

Although this was a work of midnight chapters, it wouldn't have made it this far without a few important people.

For Gabs: a million thank yous for the year of shared late-night motivation, brainstorming, and wine.

For Michelle: your endless patience with my fluid timeline and tolerance of my humour is so appreciated and valued.

And for Laura: for whom I will always stay.

CHAPTER 1

It had been an absolute battle to get to the expansive entrance of the Emirates Lounge at Los Angeles International Airport. Or, rather, to get to their partner lounge in LAX run by Korean Air. All Juliet wanted now was to slip through the glass doors, pour herself a glass of white wine, and sit down. A chair, a bed, a lounge—she wasn't fussy. She just wanted to be off her tired and sore feet.

Not that it mattered what she wanted as the immaculately dressed young man behind the counter turned her business class ticket over and over in his hands. His face was deadpan as he peered over and ran his eyes up and down her slim body. It was barely perceptible, but his eyebrows rose slightly before his face went politely blank again.

Juliet scowled. She was pretty sure he was judging her faded yoga pants and slightly stretched cap sleeve T-shirt unworthy. Her matted blonde hair was probably not helping her cause either, nor were the Merrells on her feet.

"I'm sorry, ma'am, but all business class boarding passes must be stamped for lounge entry unless you have your Skywards membership card with you."

Juliet swallowed heavily. She cast her gaze to the print on the wall of the Los Angeles skyline and sighed.

"Right, ah, *Jeremy* is it?" She squinted at the name badge pinned to the left side of his chest, scowling at how she had to lean forward to make out the small font.

"Yes, ma'am," he said, raising his left hand in front of him as if to protect himself from her using his name again. "However, I cannot allow you access on this boarding card."

"Yes, Jeremy, you have made your policy very clear. *However,* let me just tell you a little bit about how I've come to be standing here in front of your delightful tone. We have to thank for this intimate moment not one but two cancelled connecting flights on a codeshare ticket, followed by an absolute string of expletives being screamed next to my ear by another passenger, grossly intoxicated, by the way. And to cap it all off, one of your employees used me as a protective shield, earning me a significant bruise to my shoulder when I body-blocked a flying laptop bag thrown at her by another irate passenger. Add to that not having slept in the last thirty-eight hours since my journey began in Arizona, three security checks, and two hours of waiting for the privilege of standing in front of this lounge, not to mention the five hours I will now have to wait for a very long flight to Dubai. By the way, Dubai will still not be my final destination. Believe it or not, that will be Brussels!"

Although to his credit, he gave her a fleeting look of disbelief, Jeremy mostly maintained an air of quiet confidence mixed with a petulant toddler's resolve.

"I understand that you have had a difficult day," he said. "However, I am still not able to approve your entry."

Juliet tipped her head back and raked her fingers through her greasy hair, exhausted and fuming. "You have my original ticket, you have my boarding pass, and I'm sure there is record of my upgrade in the system. I strongly suggest you work your magic, sir, before I make my third consecutive complaint." She carefully disguised the term *asshole* under her breath as he shuffled a few papers on the desk, his only attempt at appeasement.

"Perhaps I can be of some help."

Juliet turned around at the sudden interruption. Another passenger stood queued behind her, waiting in a calm, patient stance. "Your name?" the woman asked, her deep brown eyes sparkling as she smiled widely. She tucked her thick, dark hair behind her ear.

"Ah, Juliet. Juliet Taylor." Her body shrunk into itself as her stuttered response left her mouth slightly ajar.

This earned a nod and a wink from the woman before she pressed herself over the counter. Her ample breasts were exposed by her plunging neckline, and a thick gold chain and pendant had fallen into the hollowed space within her cleavage.

"My card, Jeremy—Skywards Gold. And my boarding pass. Now, Ms Taylor will be joining me as one of my permitted guests while you go about sorting out this unnecessary debacle. It sounds as if Ms Taylor has been through enough today, and I would appreciate you contacting John, my Emirates consultant, who will ensure that she is adequately compensated. I suggest you look me up."

Coughing and with a slight blush to his cheeks, Jeremy handed the card back to the woman and glanced at his computer screen. His eyes dilated slightly, and his demeanour immediately altered. "Of course, Mrs Revira, go ahead. I will find you inside and advise you of the outcome. I apologise for the inconvenience."

Eyes falling and hands reaching down to her hips, the woman smoothed the skirt over her thighs and toyed briefly with the silk belt tied just over the right of her pelvis. "It's 'Ms,' thank you, but 'Mia' is fine."

Handbag over her shoulder, Mia Revira took the handle of her Louis Vuitton cabin bag and nodded at Juliet to follow. Juliet felt slightly stunned as she trailed wordlessly behind, laptop bag across her chest and faded Mont daypack over her shoulders.

"Thank you," she said as Mia led them to a quiet corner where two excessively large lounge chairs sat with a low white coffee table between them.

"Oh, of course, not a problem; the kid is a waste of space."

Leaving her wheeled case in the walkway next to her, Mia slumped down on the chair and moved her fingers through her straightened hair. "He once told my, ah…" She hesitated a moment before shaking her head. A smile pressed at her lips. "My sister…He told my sister she wasn't appropriately dressed—something ridiculous about exposed toes. I mean, she was wearing Jimmy Choos."

Juliet politely laughed, and a quick search of her few memories of the name *Jimmy Choos* recalled some fancy heels that she would never be caught wearing. Well, certainly she would never be skilled enough to walk in them, anyway. "Well, thank you again. I'm just desperate for a shower and some food and to finally sit in something more comfortable than a plastic airport chair."

"Yeah, sounds like you've had an absolute *shit* of a day," Mia said.

Juliet could see how her own surprise provoked another smile in Mia, and it made Juliet laugh again, more genuinely this time.

"Leave whatever you don't need here, and I'll have a wine waiting for you after your shower," Mia said. "Red or white?"

"Umm, yeah okay, sure. I would love a white wine. As long as you don't mind my company."

"Not at all. On long-haul flights, it's always nice to have someone sane to make conversation with."

"I could be a serial killer," Juliet said. She let just the corner of her mouth turn up.

"Ah, a serial killer who can't manage a power-hungry but very juvenile desk boy?"

"Fair call, thanks. Get me that white wine, then."

"Blend?"

"Sorry?"

"Do you want a blend? You know, what kind of white wine is your drink of choice?"

Juliet felt herself blush slightly. "I don't mind. A sauv blanc, if they have it, but at this stage, I would take whatever was offered."

"Go shower," Mia said as she gave the smallest of waves to a staff member who rushed over in the middle of wiping another table with a damp dishcloth.

Juliet dropped her laptop onto the chair opposite her and wandered off, suddenly grateful for the clean clothes, hairbrush and travel-sized perfume she had stuffed down the bottom of her backpack. She couldn't wait to stand for at least ten minutes under steaming hot water. And if she ever successfully arrived in Belgium, she told herself with a certainty she already knew was pretty delusional that she was never stepping foot on another plane again.

As she walked back from her shower, manoeuvring past tables and the occasional briefcase, Juliet's first sight of Mia was her discarded heels, neatly paired together on the floor by her chair. Her feet rested on the edge of the coffee table, primly crossed at the ankles, with toenails perfectly manicured and polished. Her elbow sat propped on the side of the chair. She was nibbling at a small piece of bread. Her long dark hair—past her shoulders and halfway down her back—was cut with a fringe that was brushed across her forehead and styled towards her temple. She had the most incredible figure that Juliet had ever seen, beautiful curves and a strong posture, and delicately smooth dark skin. Latino heritage, maybe, given her surname. But then, she could just be married to a Latino, given how Jeremy had called her Mrs Revira. Although it was intriguing that she had corrected him on that. The way she had played with her belt had made it seem like the moment had somehow bothered her.

"Hi," Mia said when Juliet placed her backpack on the floor, sliding slowly into the soft seat opposite. "You look a little more refreshed."

Again, Juliet felt her cheeks warm. "I never expect to use my emergency change of clothes, but I just discovered a good reason why I should pack them."

"I'm not beyond doing a bit of airport shopping just so I can change, I must admit."

"True," Juliet said. "Always an option."

"Well, you look good," Mia said. As Juliet repositioned her fitted, long-sleeved shirt over the waist of her jeans, she thought she caught Mia glimpsing at her white skin. "And so ready for a wine."

"Absolutely exactly what I need after today." She took a long sip and dropped a few macadamia nuts into her mouth as she settled back into the chair. "So I'm sorry I didn't quite introduce myself properly. I'm Juliet, and I'm completely indebted to you for saving me from young dictator Jeremy."

Mia grinned and handed her boarding pass to her. "I know, Ms Juliet Danielle Taylor," she said. "Always a good way to find out someone's full name: just look at their boarding pass or passport."

"And it's only fair to share, then." The banter came easy to Juliet, and she relaxed as she lifted herself slightly off the chair to grasp Mia's passport on the table.

"A fellow American," she said. "And oh, it's not Mia." Her eyebrows rose as she read. At Mia's audible groan, she added, "Mallania…That's gorgeous. I like it."

"Yeah, yeah. Unless you're my father yelling at me, it's not really used. So I haven't heard it in a long while."

"Well, you should use it. It's unusual, nice."

"Yeah, right," Mia said. "On a different note, you're sorted for the rest of your trip, a little upgrade to first class."

"Really?"

"The downside is that you're stuck next to me until Heathrow, but you can always block yourself off. These flights have the dividers in them."

"You organised this?"

"I called in a favour, no big deal. My family have a pretty hefty account with Emirates. The airline wouldn't like to upset me."

"So, for the second time today, I owe you a thank-you."

Mia shook her head. "Really not a drama at all."

5

"I haven't even left the States, and this has already been a crazy trip. It's just surreal. I started the trip in cattle class and have ended up in first. Nothing like a silver lining."

"Oh yeah. I heard you mention the person throwing a laptop bag at you… What the hell?"

"I know!" Juliet shrugged. "Makes a good story, I suppose, presuming I actually get to Belgium to tell it. Anyway, how about you? Where are you off to? Where did you start?"

"Hold that thought. We need a top-up while I'm standing." She soon returned from the bar with two fresh glasses on a tray, along with two plates of various canapés. "I had one of these smoked salmon pastries before—divine."

Juliet took one and emitted soft murmurs of satisfaction.

"I haven't come far today, just drove from Vegas," Mia said. "I caught up with a friend there for a few days 'cause I'm headed to Scotland for a while. Not really sure when I'll be back."

"Really?" Juliet asked, licking her lips and sitting herself up a little straighter. "That's a long way to go for an indefinite amount of time. What's over there?"

Mia hesitated, breathing deeply in a clearly deliberate way and using what Juliet guessed was a calm expression perfected over years for use when she was feeling anything but calm. She had learned such techniques herself the hard way.

"Just a family property over there," Mia said. "So I'm having a bit of a break and checking up on things. I thought I may as well do some relaxing and getting back to nature."

"It's meant to be beautiful in Scotland. I haven't seen a lot, just spent some time in Edinburgh when I was younger. Or rather, I drank my way around Edinburgh, which is the way I spent most of my youth in the UK and Europe."

"It really is beautiful. I've spent a couple of summers there, and it's just stunning. Can't say I've done the backpacking and drinking gig, though. Not that I'm not partial to the odd bottle or two." She flashed Juliet a slight grin and a sheepish glance at her glass. "Obviously."

"There's a point where you definitely outgrow sharing a room with fifteen other equally irresponsible young people. Though seriously, it's not so summery in Scotland at the moment…"

"No, I think *freakin' freezing* is what you're looking for. Though Brussels won't be any better!"

"I know, no idea what I'm thinking, actually. I'm not a huge one for the cold."

"So, what sends you over there?"

Juliet sighed heavily, though she smiled. "My editor. I've missed a crapload of deadlines, and if I don't finish this book, I'm going to have to pay back my advance and lose my contract. We're calling it a sabbatical, and if he hears that I'm recapturing my backpacking youth, I'm in trouble."

"A book? You're an author?"

"Well..." Juliet's eyes cast briefly to the ceiling. "If that's what you call writing one book and then failing to produce another...then I guess so."

Mia laughed. "I can't see why that would possibly not count, and what better place to focus on your next one than in a European city?"

"You sound like my editor, a little cheer squad. I'm actually heading to Bruges, a bit quieter and cheaper too. My budget isn't quite first class."

"And what's the plan? How long will it take?"

Juliet scoffed, dramatically dropping her head back. "Honestly, I have no idea. I've said six months, but I'm not sure...I'm not convinced it will ever get written."

She heard the hint of sadness edging into her own voice. She stretched out her neck, reaching across the table and letting her hand linger over the remaining appetizers, trying to choose. "Was that good?" she asked quietly, nodding towards the small piece of quiche remaining in Mia's fingers.

"Yeah, good. It has bacon, though, so only if you're not a vegetarian..."

"Definitely not. And bacon...Everything is better with bacon."

"Thank God for that. I might have had to get you kicked out of this lounge if you were one of those vege types.

Juliet yawned, rubbing at the bridge of her nose. She checked her watch, working hard to mentally calculate their time until boarding. "Still three hours." She screwed up her nose.

"Why don't you sleep a little? I won't let you miss the boarding call."

"Sorry, I'm not great company after all. It's been a long day—or two days."

Jumping up, Mia padded barefooted to an adjacent chair, gripping a cushion by the corner. The pendant around her neck bounced against her chest as she bent over the chair, and the silk top that she wore rode slightly up her back, exposing a muscular lumbar. Juliet allowed herself a prolonged, self-indulgent stare. It had been a long time since she had permitted herself an unfiltered fantasy. And this woman was perfect stimuli for her imagination—robust and with lips that she could devour in seconds. She felt a wry smile on her face when Mia was suddenly standing over her looking perplexed.

"Here," she said. "Put this under your head; you're dazing out. Get some shut-eye." Juliet found it intriguing that someone clearly as wealthy and no doubt educated as Mia could slip into colloquial phrasing that wouldn't have been out of place in Juliet's own family home when she was growing up.

"Ah, thanks. Yeah, thanks." Taking a final sip of her half-finished glass of wine, Juliet pushed it back towards the centre of the coffee table and smiled as she took the grey-coloured cushion from Mia. "Make sure you wake me. And I'll apologise in advance if I start snoring. Just throw something at me."

"I promise I'll be gentler than that." Mia grinned as she withdrew an iPad out of her handbag. It was the last thing Juliet remembered seeing before she fell into unconsciousness.

By the time Mia checked her e-mails and glanced over, Juliet was sleeping soundly, mouth slightly ajar and face utterly relaxed. Her hands were tucked up under her chin, and her knees were drawn towards her chest. Mia's hands stilled over the sides of her iPad as she watched Juliet slowly breathing in and out. She could see the edges of a tattoo on the inside of Juliet's wrist, a slightly faded blue colour, though she couldn't quite make out what the tattoo was. The same wrist had a handmade bracelet around it, black and red braided thread with some small patterned beads; it was dull and clearly worn. It combined well with the fraying jeans. Clearly, Juliet lived a very different life than Mia. Her clothes had no visible label, and despite a clear lip gloss, her face was makeup free.

Mia, in comparison, had black eyeliner carefully applied, and her mascara brush had grazed her eyelashes twice. A deep blush highlighted her cheekbones, and an illuminating powder had been the final touch to multiple layers of various foundations and powders. Her lips wore a frequently applied bright red lipstick.

Even now, she was still playing her role in upholding the family name and all the expectations that came with that.

There was something very appealing in the way Juliet was casually dressed and the lived-in look she carried. She appeared genuine—authentic. Nothing about Mia screamed façade, though she suspected that everything about her own presentation yelled false pretences. Maybe one day she could buy an old backpack and disappear, leave the Chanel wardrobe behind and don a pair of yoga pants. Maybe she could meditate in Indonesia or attend a Hindu retreat in the crowds of India. Maybe she could write a novel too, hiding away in an apartment in Bruges.

Juliet had the luxury of making independent decisions—booking economy-class tickets and blending into the hordes, going wherever whenever she wanted. Mia was suddenly insanely jealous of the stranger in front of her snoozing her way through a stopover after fate had pulled her into a first-class lounge. She hadn't planned it, hadn't even expected it, yet Juliet was just going along with no idea of what was next, bar a loose plan to end up in Belgium with her backpack and laptop. How freeing it must be.

Slowly, Mia smiled. She gave a silent laugh as Juliet released the softest of tiny snores. How incredible it was that Juliet trusted a stranger enough to fall asleep in her presence with all of her belongings on the floor and her boarding pass on the table.

Maybe this was the push Mia was looking for, this blonde-haired vision of mystery in front of her. She had a day to figure out how to be someone new, someone less like the person she had been born to become.

And more like this hauntingly stunning woman that had literally fallen across her path.

CHAPTER 2

"Juliet, it's time to wake up." Mia placed her handbag where she had been sitting. Juliet didn't move. Glancing at the monitors, Mia located their flight with a nod to herself. "They're boarding," she said. "We need to make our way to the gate."

Juliet released a soft moan, her eyelids shivering a little but staying stubbornly closed. Relocating Juliet's bags next to her own, Mia crouched by Juliet's side. "Hey. Jules, honey, we need to move. It's time to board."

"Huh?" Juliet gasped, eyes shooting open when Mia tugged at her forearm.

"Our flight. We have to go."

"Flight?" Juliet's eyes darted from Mia to their surroundings. "Oh, yeah, flight."

"Sorry. You can sleep more on the plane…"

"Agh, I feel like a train wreck."

"Well, you don't look like one." Mia hoisted Juliet's daypack onto her own back before holding the laptop bag out as Juliet slowly rose to her feet, rubbing her eyes and stretching her back. "Here. They won't go without us, but I really hate having my name called out over the loudspeaker."

"Thanks, yeah. Umm, do you know our gate?"

"Yes, all organised. Just follow me. Grab that water if you want it. I've got an extra bottle."

Juliet just nodded, again rubbing her eyes and clearly trying to orientate herself. "Hey, I can take my bag." Her words were slurred with sleep as she blindly followed Mia towards the exit and towards the first travelator.

Mia shrugged. "I've got everything. You just concentrate on staying on your feet."

"I don't really know you, but you seem to be enjoying this far too much." Juliet stood in barely an upright slouch on the travelator as she inspected Mia with narrowed, suspicious eyes.

"Me? I'm just helping you out, remember? Without me, you would have snoozed those hours away in a very uncomfortable sterilised chair or, worse, on a patch of revolting carpet."

"Have I mentioned that I owe you one, Mallania? Because I do."

Mia scowled. "Just because you saw my passport does not mean you get to throw my full name around, you know."

"Oh, crap." With a loud gasp, Juliet patted her pockets repeatedly. "My boarding pass…"

"Relax, I got it. It was on the table the whole time. I have it in my document wallet, don't stress."

Juliet finally returned Mia's smile. "I swear I've travelled around the world and have never once lost a passport or boarding pass or missed a flight."

"That's what happens when you have no sleep for a couple of days. It's not great for your cognitive abilities."

There was a long moment of silence.

"Next gate," said Mia. Juliet fell in step next to her. Their height was dramatically different as they stood side by side, she noticed, though if Mia were to slip off her heels, they would only differ by an inch or so. "But don't worry. You'll have plenty of time to sleep over the next eighteen hours."

"Which reminds me," Juliet said, her expression looking perplexed. "I know why I'm flying this ridiculous route to Europe, but what about you? I was just saving money, and then they completely screwed up."

Mia shrugged. "It was booked for me, sort of. I didn't really mind. I was originally going to spend a few nights in Dubai, to go…umm, yeah, to go and ah…what is it? Ah, do some shopping." Her cheeks flushed red. She wondered for a paranoid moment if Juliet knew she was lying, knowingly allowing her to indulge in the appearance of truth-telling.

"Sorry, I'm getting tired too," Mia tried to allay her discomfort with a kernel of truth. "I ended up changing my flight instead. I quite like flying."

"Really? I hate it."

"That's because you're always cramped at the back of the plane."

Juliet laughed and rolled her shoulders. "Maybe. I mean, I do fly. It's not like I don't, but I don't really like it. The whole take-off and landing, the idea that we're all stuck in this little tiny cylinder in the middle of the sky."

"You want to take something? I've got a relaxant in my purse." Mia kept her tone casual, as if everyone in the world carried a supply of Diazepam. She didn't want Juliet thinking she was some kind of drug addict. Then she wondered why she cared what Juliet thought.

But Juliet merely laughed and shook her head. "No, no, I'm good, thank you. You shouldn't take that crap, you know. It's not good for you."

Mia glanced sideways. No one in her circle would ever have cared enough to make such a comment. Not to mention, Diazepam was the just a drop in the ocean, along with the boutique party pills and lines of cocaine that were occasionally brought out after the wine flow slowed. "Yeah, worse things, though, I suppose."

"Of course. There always is." Juliet fell behind Mia as they headed directly past the economy queue and onto the aircraft. Juliet's eyes went visibly wide as Mia stopped and deposited the backpack onto Juliet's expansive seat and her own case was placed in the overhead compartment.

"You need anything out of that?" Mia asked.

"Umm, I might just get out the book I'm reading…" Her fingers scurried beneath the zipper as an attendant waited.

"Anything good?" Mia plopped herself down in her seat across the aisle.

"An oldie but a goodie—*Wuthering Heights*. I thought it might get me feeling nostalgic and in the writing mood."

"Is it working?"

Juliet laughed loudly, and it elicited a chuckle from Mia. Juliet had the most incredulous, infectious laugh. "Not even remotely."

"I'm sure once you arrive, you'll be writing nonstop."

"Hmmm," Juliet said, smirking as she sat down and opened various compartments, exploring the seat and the controls. "I appreciate your confidence."

"Something tells me that you could do anything you set your mind to."

"Really? You think? You've made a quick assessment of me, Mia."

Mia nodded. "I do, and I'll have you know that I'm seldom wrong."

"We'll see." Juliet cocked her head. "We'll see."

To Juliet, long-haul flights felt like an unending, special kind of torture. She had been on enough flights to know they were always filled with people experiencing some kind of emotion. Some were devastated by their reasons for needing to board the plane—funerals, a bad breakup, a forced work transfer.

Others were ecstatic, brimming with nervous excitement at a long-planned trip or a return home to see family or attend a wedding. A smaller number seemed quieter, reflective, lost. God knew she had probably been all of those things at some point.

Juliet wasn't sure what she was on this trip, though. Possibly she was none of these things. Mia, too, seemed to be something hard to pinpoint, a traveller that couldn't be stereotyped into clichéd groups. She was obviously on her way somewhere, for a reason that Juliet wondered if Mia even knew herself.

The only thing she knew was that it had taken forever to get there.

"Ladies and Gentlemen, this is your captain speaking. As you may have noticed, we have begun our descent into Dubai, where the local time is seven p.m. and the temperature is a balmy thirty degrees Celsius…"

Juliet sighed heavily and kicked at her bag as the usual flight announcement commenced. She squeezed her bag into a small cupboard at her feet. Her seatbelt was firm at her hips, and her fingers twisted the blanket that was still extended over her legs. She cast a sideways glance at Mia, surprised to find her watching her movements intently.

They had both slept the first eight hours of the flight, though Mia was watching a movie by the time Juliet fully awakened. For the remainder of the flight, they had alternated between chatting and watching television, reading magazines and newspapers, and sharing comments on everything from current affairs and politics to the latest celebrity gossip. It was smooth and surprisingly easy, simple.

"Best part of the flight, right? The landing?" Mia joked.

Juliet emitted a half-hearted sort of chuckle.

"Come on, relax," Mia said. "We'll be on the ground in a half hour, and after a small amount of duty-free shopping, we'll be sipping champagne in the best lounge."

"*You'll* be duty-free shopping."

"True."

"In one of the worst airports in the world."

"Oh, that's harsh. Surely there's worse. I mean, you were saying you've been to some of those small and smelly airports in India."

Juliet screwed up her nose. "Yeah, but even they're not as busy. Dubai is like Grand Central Station. I don't really do crowds."

"You don't do crowds, and you hate take-offs and landings. I'm learning so much about you, Juliet."

"Hey, you shouldn't pick on me when I'm stressing out. At least save it until I can give as good as I get."

Holding her hands up in front of her, Mia made a show of conceding defeat. "Okay," she whispered. "I'll wait until we're firmly on the ground, at which time I will endlessly tease." Suddenly, she paused and frowned. "Sorry," she said, "I just presumed then. Completely."

Juliet glanced to her side and raised her eyebrows. She had no idea what Mia was presuming.

"That we would stay, you know, together during the stopover." Mia licked her lips and cocked her head. Juliet wondered if she was nervous. "I know I'm probably not your usual type."

Juliet shook her head before the plane jerked, and she gave a small, barely audible cry. Recovering her composure, her eyes returned to meet Mia's, but found them fixed on the flight path screen in front of her. The infallible confidence that Mia had been emanating since their meeting had disappeared. Mia's silence and zoned-out stare confused her.

"We have over seven hours in this godforsaken airport we're about to land in and then yet another flight that's eight odd hours long. So the answer is, 'No, I'll save my own company for the months I have ahead of me.'"

Mia nodded and offered a small smile, but her shoulders remained hunched as she folded in on herself.

"But back up a little," Juliet said. "What's this crap about my *usual type*?"

"I just thought that you probably only socialise with arty types…"

"Mmm," Juliet said. "Like, other authors, artists, musicians, that kind of thing?"

"Umm, yeah?"

"And free spirits, save-the-forest types…"

"Exactly."

"You're right. I usually just sit around campfires and pass around bongs."

Mia's glance jerked up suddenly, eyes wide and mouth slightly ajar. "You're joking, obviously."

Juliet grinned back at her. "Yes, yes, I am. I don't have a type, Mia. I like meeting people from all different backgrounds, and I don't judge a book by its cover. As a supposedly decent writer, the concept of superficially judging people just annoys me. Although something tells me that you probably haven't spent your life talking to people like me."

"I'm not that interested in being who I've always been," Mia said softly, scooping her hair away from her neck. She secured it in a bun by a gold clip as the plane again shuddered through a change in atmospheric pressure.

Juliet's hands gripped the armrests. The seatbelt sign flicked on, and the attendants rushed past them to finalise their pre-landing tasks.

"You good?" Mia asked.

"I hate flying."

"I can see that. Should I ask why you continue to fly when you clearly don't enjoy it?"

Juliet rolled her eyes and didn't bother responding. She was completely dumfounded that people would allow fear to stop them from doing anything.

"Ten minutes," Mia said, "fifteen tops, we'll be on the ground."

"This is why I never travel with anyone. People feel compelled to try and make me feel better."

"Does it work?"

"Never."

"You poor thing." Mia reached across to offer a friendly squeeze of her shoulder, while Juliet managed only a tortured expression in return. "All right, distraction. Does distraction work?"

"Nope."

"What if I told you that while you were sleeping, I saw those two over there, in 2A and 2D, sneak into the bathroom together?" Her forced, low whisper made Juliet perk up.

"What?" She raised her eyes, though her hands maintained their death grip. "Who?"

"Over there, 2A." With a nod towards a window, she cast her eyes to the right, adding, "and 2D."

"Oh my God, really?"

"Yes."

"She, ah, she has to be twice his age?"

"Our flight attendant Jamie thinks at least twice."

"That's…that's pretty horrific, actually. I used that restroom afterwards." Juliet shuddered. "I mean, those bathrooms are small."

"Maybe she's more flexible than she looks."

"Mia!"

"What? It's possible—sit on the toilet or do it against the wall."

"Are you about to tell me that you've done it?"

Mia coughed, and a glimmer of a scowl crossed her face. "No, definitely not. She is at least twice his age, and my guess is that he's more our age than that teenager sitting back there."

"Okay, that's enough distracting. My eyes are burning with just the thought of it, so no more talking." As if on cue, the wheels of the plane dropped, and the engines slowed with another jerk and uneven dip of the aircraft. "Oh God, just land already. I need my feet on solid ground for a few hours."

"Almost. Just think of *Abuela* over there and her toyboy if you're feeling uncomfortable."

Juliet laughed and nodded. "Yeah, thanks for that." They shared a glance and laughed slightly louder before Mia turned her gaze to the view out the window. Juliet continued to softly giggle as she closed her eyes, knuckles white.

They approached unsteadily towards the runway.

"You know," Juliet said as she tried to keep up with Mia. They weaved through crowds of rushing people inside Dubai International Airport. "That lip gloss you bought, it pretty much cost...ouch!" She shot a middle-aged man a disgusted look after absorbing an elbow to her stomach. "That lip gloss costs more than my weekly rent in Bruges is going to be."

"What?" Disbelief seemed to settle in Mia's eyes.

"Yep."

"Where the hell are you staying?"

Juliet looked upward. "Details... I don't really know yet. I'm sure it's okay. It has a bathroom and heating. What more do I need?"

"Umm, safety? Cleanliness?"

"You haven't lived, Mia, until you've swatted cockroaches in your kitchen and kicked the front door three times to get it to close. Or stepped over roommates having sex on the lounge room floor when you get home from a twelve-hour waitressing shift with finals the next day."

Reaching the desired elevator, they waited, Mia looking lost in thought. "You really lived like that?" she asked.

"Mmm-hmm, absolutely. And that was a good day."

"Oh, what did the worst ones look like?"

"You really don't want to know."

"I do. I so do."

"I might put you off the Moët that you're craving…"

Mia laughed, pushing the elevator *up* button multiple times, as if expecting it to arrive faster. "You know what I really feel like now?"

"Please say 'coffee'?" Juliet had been craving quality caffeine for the last six hours of their flight.

"Nope. I want a chocolate bar, some fries and a Coke. A real Coke, none of that diet, aspartame-filled crap. And I want to drink it out of the can—not a straw or a glass or a glass with a straw." She opened her mouth to continue the diatribe but stopped at Juliet's amused look. "What?"

"That's unusual for you?"

"Are you kidding me? Everywhere I go, there's someone watching, waiting for me to screw up so they can tell their wives and have it spread around the freakin' trophy wives club. I once bought a chicken from the store, one of those cooked ones, and a friend of my sister saw me go through the checkout. Seriously, by the time I got home, there was a personal trainer, diet consultant, and a brand new treadmill waiting for me." Mia's hands gestured wildly, and her lips pressed tightly together.

"Bullshit," said Juliet. "There is no way that happened."

"Oh it happened, and that's only one example. So, while you were using your shoe to kill insects, I had a drawer full of stomach control pantyhose before I even finished high school."

Juliet softened. There was a real look of pain across Mia's expression. "Well," she said as the doors opened and they slipped inside, "*we* are going to go upstairs, which is completely your world, and I'm going to introduce you to my world. Are you game?"

"I have no idea what that means. Do I get to drink a Coke?"

"Do you trust me, Mallania Revira?"

"Ah, you remember that I barely know you, right? We met yesterday at the airport…" she trailed off.

"Do you trust me?"

Mia hesitated, and her eyes met Juliet's unblinking.

For a moment, Juliet expected a *no*. "Come on, I'm not asking you to base jump off a building with me! I promise it will be completely safe, and it may just change your life."

"Big call. 'Change my life,' hey?"

"Yep, absolutely."

"All right. I'm game. What are you going to make me do?"

"Make you?" Juliet chuckled as she pushed Mia out of the elevator in a manner that screamed *lifelong friends*. It was one of those small moments of relaxed interaction only possible when friends had crossed certain boundaries not readily crossed with strangers or acquaintances.

"Ah-huh. What are you going to make me do?"

"That all depends. What do you have in that ridiculously inconvenient suitcase?"

"It's not inconvenient, it's useful. It's easy. It's part of a set."

"What's inside of it, Mia?" Juliet took a step back as Mia handed over her card to the lounge attendant and confirmed their onward flights. It took barely a minute before they were inside the first-class lounge and standing to the side of the elaborate food buffet.

"I don't know what you're looking for," Mia said, "but I have some clothes, a few toiletries, some jewellery that I didn't want to check in, and a few magazines."

"I don't suppose you have a pair of jeans in there?"

Giving Juliet a perplexed look, Mia nodded. "Yeah, I've got two pairs."

"Two?"

"One dark blue and one faded blue so that I had, well, options." Mia blushed again. Mia had yet to exhibit that suave confidence Juliet had first been introduced to in the Emirates lounge.

"Okay, faded blue out and heels off, and take off all of that gold while you're at it."

Mia nodded slowly, hand slowly tracing over the thick chain around her neck, a number of bracelets bouncing against her wrist. "Right," she said, lifting her bag onto a chair and unzipping it. Her belongings were profoundly ordered, folded and placed in a jigsaw arrangement. Mesh zippered bags held various toiletries, power cables, and adapters in each corner of her case.

Juliet reached blindly into her backpack, pulling out and tossing aside a rolled-up hoodie over the back of the chair. A hairbrush fell to the floor. "What's your foot size—like, an eight?"

"And a half," Mia said. "Are you dressing me like a…umm…like ah, *you*?"

"Yep. You are going to spend the next, what, twenty hours, being more pleb-like. Consider it a social experiment. Take note of how people treat you. How they don't treat you. How no one, and I mean no one, looks twice if you shove a double cheeseburger and fries down your throat."

"Be anonymous?"

"Exactly. You never know. You might like it."

"Why? Why would you do this?"

Juliet shrugged. "Maybe it'll help my book." She offered Mia a light-hearted, wide grin she knew wasn't believable for a moment.

"So go on," Juliet continued. "Go get changed, and I'll be right here."

Mia turned to go when Juliet added, "Oh, wait." She gave a slight cheer as she tugged a pair of flip-flops from her bag. "These don't even remotely match this shirt, but that's half the fun." She held out the items to Mia and indicated with her head towards the restrooms. "Oh, and you just use the shampoo and conditioner they have in the shower cubicles. You don't take your own travel-sized organic hair and body products in."

"How did you know I have organic products?"

"Just a guess. And hey, I'm all for saving the environment and treating the body well, but hell, that stuff is expensive."

Mia rolled her eyes and disappeared, leaving Juliet to reorder her backpack and find a fresh shirt to change into. She kept her hoodie out; the blasting air conditioning was making her shiver. By the time Mia returned, Juliet had jotted down almost two pages of notes in her Moleskine—reflections and ideas for her novel. "Oh, now you look awesome!"

Mia rolled on the balls of her feet, looking down at her manicured toes with their deep-red polish. "I feel…ridiculous, but comfy."

"You look good! Come on, sit down and relax. The next plan is food."

"There's no way this shirt fits you. Is it from the ex-boyfriend pile?"

Juliet laughed immediately, shaking her head. "No," she said. "No. My brother's, actually. It's an Army football team shirt."

"It's loose and light. I don't have to suck in my stomach."

"As if you do anyway. But yes, it's a few years old and pretty well worn."

"I'm not so sure on the shoes. They make me short, really short."

"You're my height. That's not short. And look around: who cares? No one is even looking at you, and so what if they do?"

Mia nodded slowly as Juliet cast her eyes around their surrounds. No one was looking at Mia. There were just businessmen reading newspapers and couples sitting at laptops or eating soup. "I guess so," Mia said.

"Why don't you put that necklace in your purse too?" Juliet watched Mia's fingers curl around the pendant until it was clasped inside a closed fist.

"No," Mia said simply, giving no room for negotiation.

Juliet watched her silently as Mia went about putting her belongings back with meticulous precision into their carefully designated spaces. Finally, Mia stood back up and exposed her smile, and Juliet couldn't help but think that the casual brown-haired woman standing in front of her could have been a woman she had met at a bar or the supermarket. She was makeup-free, and the natural glow of her skin, even after a long-haul flight, was beautiful. Her physique beneath the loose three-quarter-sleeve jersey looked fit and strong and healthy, belonging to someone with whom she wanted to walk down the street and share a meal. She suddenly didn't look like she belonged somewhere a world away.

"Next?" Mia said.

"Oh, this is where I get to have a quick shower and you get to go to the buffet and get whatever food and drink you want. Not what is healthy or good for jetlag and not what some bitch from LA would expect you to eat. And so definitely not a carrot or celery stick with a small dollop of hummus. And when I get back, I expect you to have a few delicious options for me as well."

"Now this sounds like fun."

"It should be. Meals shouldn't be a trauma, Mia."

"Mmm. Anything you want in particular? Drink?"

"I would like a coffee and a beer, please."

"A beer?"

"Yep, ice cold beer, preferably out of a bottle. But they might kick us out if we get too carried away, so a glass is okay." Juliet grinned, standing up and taking a few steps before turning back. "Hey, make sure you wait for me. There are some instructions to go with the food. You want to enjoy eating."

Mia laughed and nodded. "Yes, Juliet."

By the time Juliet returned, wet hair half caught in the neck of her hoodie, Mia had a range of decadent treats on the table and two tall glasses of beer waiting. She had spent part of the time Juliet was away staring at the food and salivating. The rest of the time, she had been preoccupied with managing the rising anxiety in her gut. Lifelong habits were hard to break.

"Nice choices." Juliet raised her eyebrows as she examined the items before her. "And that looks suspiciously like a tumbler of soda?"

Mia shrugged. "It may be diet. I was going to lie and say I got that Coke, but the truth is I caved."

Laughing, Juliet slumped down on the other end of the two-seater sofa and tucked one leg up underneath herself so that her body was tilted towards Mia. "You're excused. To tell you the truth, I drink diet soda too. Sugar *and* caffeine? I'd never sleep."

"From what I've seen, you could sleep through an earthquake."

Juliet's grin fell to a weak smile, and she gave Mia a fleeting, defeated look. "I wish." A moment later, the expression was gone. "Anyway, the point is that if you want to have a Coke occasionally, then you can."

"Yeah, yeah, easy for you to say…I mean, you're all skinny and, you know, hot."

"I don't pretend to know everything about well, anything, actually. But if you think the most important thing in life is what size jeans you fit into, then I've overestimated you, Mia. I took you as someone with much more substance than that kind of shit, as if it matters at the end of the day. Being a reasonable person? Treating people well and with respect and kindness? That is what you want to go home to. Not some false size zero who can't form an independent thought."

"I didn't mean that it's the most important thing." Mia hesitated briefly. "I just meant it as a compliment."

"It's the hoodie that does it," Juliet said seriously, narrowing her eyes and nodding.

"What?" Mia stared at Juliet.

"The hoodie makes me hot. I mean, what's not to love about the Gap logo that draws attention to my very awesome cleavage?"

Mia laughed, and Juliet gave a soft snicker.

"All right, I'm starving." Juliet took two fries first and then dropped a brownie square into her mouth. "Mmm. That *is* good." She licked her fingers slowly in a clearly deliberate performance for Mia. With a swipe of the back of her fingers against Mia's shoulder, she silently prodded her.

Mia slowly leaned forward, deliberating momentarily, and then picked up a fork.

"Hey, put down the fork," Juliet said. "We're using our fingers. It's all part of the fun. And what did you even *get* a knife for?"

Laughing, Mia dropped the fork onto the table. It clipped the side of a plate and bounced noisily. Juliet curled her fingers around Mia's forearm.

"Wait. What are you eating, Mia?"

"Ah, cheesecake, Juliet."

"Are you going to enjoy it?"

"Yeah, of course."

Juliet sat tall and squared her shoulders. "Then bite it in half, taste it. Finish it. Lick your fingers." Her tone was passionate.

"You're nuts."

"More like genetically flawed," Juliet said. Her tongue peeked out of her lips as she smiled.

It seemed so simple, eating and not thinking, but everything Mia did, every item she bought, every word that came out of her mouth was considered. She was used to analysing the outcome of every single one of her choices, anticipating the complex domino effect that could result from something seemingly insignificant. Food was just one example.

"Mmm," Mia purred, eyes fluttering closed. She dipped the end of her thumb and index finger into her mouth and sucked on them with a loud pop. "I so need another one of those."

She heard Juliet emit a childish giggle, and it made her open her eyes. Mia's foot had started tapping over and over. Her knee jiggled as Juliet's knuckles grazed her thigh, and Mia cursed the sudden burning behind her eyes. Juliet would think her crazy if she started to cry for no reason. "Thank you," she said, a perceptible catch to her voice.

Juliet smiled. "I'm going to try the passionfruit one," she said and held Mia's stare for just a moment too long for Mia's comfort.

Yet, when Juliet averted her eyes, it still felt a little too soon.

CHAPTER 3

"You know what? I just realised that I have no idea what day it is or what day I left home," Juliet said, sitting next to Mia in a hard plastic chair in Heathrow Airport, with her face in her hands.

Mia felt conflicted. Despite the lengthy flights, she had enjoyed getting to know Juliet and spending time in her company. It had been too long since she had had the opportunity to enjoy someone's company without expectations. She wasn't that ready to say goodbye; not that she thought Juliet probably cared. "I so hope this apartment you've organised in Brussels has a bed."

"I'm wrecked. I literally feel like I've been run over by a truck."

"It's potentially your last flight for six months, so just relax and enjoy the… Oh, wait, maybe don't enjoy the flight. But enjoy the fact that you are so close now." Mia smiled.

Her feet were crossed out in front of her with Juliet's red flip-flops on display. She still wore Juliet's shirt, and her jeans had stretched slightly over the course of the flight, loose now around the legs and waist. Flicking her toes so that the flip-flops tapped against her heels, she said, "You know, I should own up. It was me that was once refused entry for my inappropriate footwear that time. I'm not sure why I pretended it wasn't."

Juliet didn't comment, just smiled and shrugged.

"Hey, are you sure you don't want your shirt and shoes back? I feel bad for taking them."

Juliet shook her head vehemently, eyes bloodshot and tired-looking when she raised her face. "Definitely not. I hope you wear more of them, actually, though it'll be a little cold for flip-flops right now. So you probably don't need to worry about not being allowed into airport lounges over winter."

Mia felt her cheeks warm. "True, but I think I might just do that, wear more comfortable clothes. It's been kind of amazing. When I bought our coffee before, no revolting old men accidently touched my ass. Or my breasts."

"Well, that would be disappointing." Juliet's voice dripped with sarcasm.

"If you come and visit me after you've finished your book, I'll hook you up with a new shirt. Apparently the Scottish rugby jersey is pretty good. Or the team is good? I'm not actually clear on that. But either way, I'll get you something socially appropriate."

Juliet laughed. "Sounds like a good deal to me. So you'll still be there in five years when I eventually get this manuscript done?"

"I have more faith in you than that, Juliet." Mia wished she knew what to say to let Juliet know that she wanted to get acquainted more. Why she couldn't just say that, she didn't know. Was it crazy to expect Juliet to do it, just because she couldn't?

"Yeah, well, you're the only one," Juliet said. She seemed to have missed the serious undertone Mia intended. "You realise that when I actually get to Brussels, I'm going to have to write? I won't be able to procrastinate any longer."

"Please take a couple of days to relax and recover." Mia had already gotten the impression over the past two days that Juliet wasn't anywhere near as kind and gentle with herself as she was with other people.

"I might need a reminder of that."

"Well, consider it done. Are e-mail and text okay, or will I also need to leave long and detailed messages on your cell?"

"Probably e-mail and text will have the effect needed. You know, it feels kind of weird: we've spent just about every minute of the last forty-eight hours together, and now we just go in different directions."

Mia propped her head up on her hand, elbow on the armrest next to her. "I was just thinking that earlier. You'll stay in contact? I'm really excited to hear how the book goes."

"Absolutely." Juliet glanced at the *go to gate* message sitting next to her flight number on the departures information screen nearby. "And I want to be kept up to date with how the change of scenery is treating you."

They shared a look for a few prolonged seconds before Mia finally broke the silence. "Are you okay?" She tried to keep her tone gentle, helplessly watching tears well in Juliet's eyes, blue irises glazing over.

Juliet coughed. "Yeah." She shook her head as if flinging the emotion away. "Just being silly." Her smile looked forced to Mia, although really it appeared more a hybrid grimace than anything remotely close to an expression of happiness. "You, umm, have to change terminals, right?"

"Afraid so. You ready to go through?" Mia reached out for Juliet but was halted when Juliet jolted upright.

"I'd better be."

"Sure," Mia said, taking her handbag off her lap and dropping it onto the chair as she stood. "So I just want to thank you. I've actually had a great couple of days. And I'm really glad that I saved your butt with Jeremy in LAX."

Juliet scuffed her feet slightly, fingers toying with the hip pockets of her jeans. "Me too. It was really nice to meet you, Mia." She took a step to the side, eyeing the screen again.

"Hey," Mia said. "I at least want a hug. I mean, you've seen me eat cheesecake and fries, after all."

It was enough to elicit a weak laugh from Juliet, and she met Mia with a tight embrace. "Thanks for keeping me sane."

"You're welcome." Mia leaned back and pressed a kiss to Juliet's cheek. "I hope this flight goes okay, and I look forward to your e-mails."

"You too." Juliet stepped away and towards the security point before turning back. "Don't forget: do what makes you feel good, Mia. Okay?"

Mia felt a smile spread across her cheeks. "Okay."

And with a brief wave, Juliet disappeared, and Mia walked in the opposite direction. She carried with her a few contact details of a stranger, a stranger to whom she felt strangely close to. But that shouldn't make sense. She was being irrational and childish, everything she had been accused of her whole life. There was no way that a normal person could imagine a relationship was possible with some random woman she had met two days ago in an airport.

The further they drove, the more snow Mia observed out the window from the backseat of the black Bentley that had picked her up from Edinburgh Airport with its wheel rims carefully polished and tyres meticulously shined. The snow-capped hills far off in the distance signalled winter long before the small pockets of white ice usually began appearing at the side of the road and on the grassy fields. She checked her watch and phone. Juliet would hopefully be settling into her apartment by now, and with any luck, she'd manage to stay awake through the afternoon.

When Mia's driver Martin had picked her up, she had greeted him with a warm smile and a shake of his hand, even a light peck to his cheek. She knew him relatively well, and he had a cheeky, wicked sense of humour, although it only appeared occasionally, when he was sure it was appropriate. Mia had always appreciated the wink that he would give her when everyone else was oblivious to his humour.

Still, Mia knew after she had left Juliet in Heathrow Airport that not even Martin would call her by her first name or joke with her completely without filter. Anyone at the house would be walking on eggshells, doing whatever they could to keep her happy and content, for with just one bad word from Mia to the employment agency in London, their jobs could be lost or their company's contracts could be cancelled.

But Juliet didn't know about any of that and presumably wouldn't care. Mia had the impression that Juliet didn't need to be liked by Mia or anyone else. Mia was just someone with whom she crossed paths for twenty-four hours, nothing more and nothing less.

The estate in Overscaig, in the Highlands, had been staffed for a month pending her arrival, and so the kitchen would be brimming, the grass would be trimmed, and the horses would be groomed. Three boxes of belongings would be awaiting her arrival, just a range of necessities she had shipped a few weeks ago.

As expected, Martin had a small cooler in the backseat stocked with two small bottles of white wine, freshly squeezed orange juice, and a can of traditional lemonade. Mia avoided the wine and sipped occasionally on the juice, unscrewing the top and drinking out of the bottle, thinking about Juliet.

They had been travelling for almost four hours when the window between the backseat and the front slowly descended; she met Martin's eyes in the rear-view mirror.

"Ms Revira, we are coming up to a service centre, would you like a comfort stop?"

Mia smiled and nodded. "Please," she said softly. "Thanks, Martin."

"You're most welcome. After this, we leave the dual carriage way, and it's mostly single lane from here. We'll be travelling a little slower."

"The view is beautiful, I can hardly complain."

He smiled again. "It is nice to have you again, Ms Revira," he said after a moment. "And, may I say, I was sorry to hear about…" He paused. "Well, I was sorry to hear about *things*."

Mia swallowed. "Thank you," she said. "I appreciate that, but please, I'm here on my own, so what I would really like is for you to call me Mia."

"Of course. It's a beautiful name."

Martin's compliment came out more like a distant, neutral observation, but Mia blushed a little anyway and tucked some loose strands of matted and messy hair behind her ears. "Is Jasmine still there? She used to make the most incredible risotto."

Martin shook his head as he took a short exit off the main road. "No, she met a young man in Glasgow, and he is in his final year at Dundee, about to become a doctor. They married not long ago, I heard, just a few weeks ago."

"A doctor?" Mia asked, eyes widening and mouth opening. "How lucky."

"To marry a doctor? With all those long hours, I'm not sure I would want my daughter marrying a young doctor." Mia observed his head shake in the rear-view mirror, and he waved his hand in the air.

"No, I meant to be studying medicine," Mia said. "Who would want to marry, right, Martin?"

Martin rested his elbow on the centre console and Mia met his eyes in the mirror. "You're a wise girl, Mia. A wise, wise girl."

Having successfully negotiated the train from Brussels to Bruges without uttering a word of mispronounced, grossly incorrect Flemish, Juliet was stuffed—completely, utterly, and deliriously exhausted. And it was highly possible that not one of the four locks on her apartment door actually fastened adequately.

The kitchen she had been promised housed no more than a small fridge and a microwave on a bench. The apartment did have a bed with an oddly sized double mattress that was a few inches too short for the frame. But at least it had clean, crisp, white sheets and two new pillows. And the bathroom, the glorious bathroom, was no larger than a closet, but it had hot running water. Scalding hot. Which was good, because the heater seemed to rumble loudly but barely emanate warmth.

She literally stumbled from the bathroom to the bed, catching her shoulder on the corner of the door and feeling her knee buckle slightly. She'd never had a knee injury, never even had so much as a twinge, but even her knee was begging her to stop moving at this point, with the implied threat that it soon would prevent her from walking at all if she did not comply.

And it was only six in the evening. Pulling out her cell phone, she double-checked the settings and time zones, then examined her watch to make sure everything matched. Blinking heavily and rubbing her eyes, she tried to focus on the screen.

Made it to the apartment, and it even has a bed. Thank fuck. Have you made it too?

She had to read the message four times and go back and correct the typos, but eventually she got it readable and pressed *send*. She made a mental note to get her hands on a local SIM card in the morning, or whenever she regained consciousness.

Only a couple of minutes passed before her phone beeped, though it was loud enough to make her jump. She was sprawled across the bed, freshly showered and dressed in sweats, but she had yet to slide under the warm covers, as she was trying to maintain an illusion of alertness. Who was she kidding? She was already half dozing.

Getting close. So pleased you've made it. Is the apartment up to standard?

Juliet couldn't help but laugh.

Mine or yours?

Quickly, her old Nokia chimed.

Somewhere in between? :-) I hope you sleep well tonight. I know I will.

The apartment is fine and has a bed, which is all I care about right now. Sleep well too, and take care.

Juliet kept her phone in her hand and curled onto her side, reaching across the bed to tug the blankets down. They were thick and heavy, and she could already feel her eyelids sporadically closing against her will as she manoeuvred herself underneath the covers without having to get herself up.

After a few minutes, her phone again received a message, and it jerked her back awake.

You too.

It may have taken five days, but the sun finally came out and the clear blue sky above Overscaig was stunning as Mia settled into the driver's seat of a 2010 Jeep Wrangler. It wouldn't last, and even in the best conditions at that time of year, she would only have six hours or so of light. It was bitingly cold, thanks to a seasonal wind that cut through layers of clothing. She had taken a few days to get her energy back after the lengthy trip, just lazing by the fire and drinking cups of steaming soup until she had begun venturing outside on a few occasions, walking through the snow to the stables that sat almost nine hundred feet from the main house. The horses had relished her attention and had accommodated her on short rides as she tried to rebuild her confidence with the skill. They seemed far taller than she remembered from her last ride, just under two years ago. Or perhaps it was that her sense of invincibility was progressively vanishing with every month and year.

She had a specific destination in mind, a one-hundred-mile return trip that in the midst of summer would only take three hours but with her cautiousness in winter would take her close to four or five. Add in a coffee and lunch, and she would easily be out each minute of sunlight. Despite her need for vigilant awareness of ice patches and other cars on the narrow country roads, the driving was relaxing. She loved the view, the stone fences that ran along the shoulder of the roads, and the sweeping, rock-filled fields.

And she was alone. There was no one checking on her or offering her food and drinks. Although the maid Janet had relaxed since her arrival, Mia still felt smothered. Even her insistence that she travel alone to Durness had elicited an hour of concerned banter and eventually a survival package, which she was fairly sure had enough supplies to keep her alive in the car until the end of winter. She appreciated the concern, but she wasn't made of glass and wasn't about to shatter at any given moment. She was not useless.

So the drive was a pleasant reprieve and essentially drama free, if she didn't count the small, furry, and unidentified animal that may have had a misfortunate run-in with one of the all-terrain tyres. Which she didn't: some things were a little different in the country.

Eventually, she pulled into a small parking space outside a bed and breakfast that doubled as the local café. There was a fairly well-stocked Spar just up the road and a hotel just a few hundred yards in the other direction. In the warmer months, it had the most delicious sight of the ocean—the North Atlantic with a view towards the Norwegian Sea. Making a quick run between the car and the café entrance, her fingers curled inside the pockets of her knee-length woollen coat and she hurried into the building, looking forward to and the warm comfort of a log fire and gas heating that she knew was inside.

Just one other patron sat quietly in the corner, focussed intently on the laptop that he had in front of him. It took a few moments for staff to respond to the old-fashioned bell hooked on the front door. "Hi," Mia said, blowing into her hands to warm them.

"Good morning," the middle-aged woman said, apron tied around her waist. "Can I get you anything?"

"Mmm, please." Mia scanned the laminated menu on the counter. "Could I have, umm, a skinny latte and the Caesar salad?"

The woman chuckled. "I can do the salad," she said politely, "but the ingredients aren't the freshest around here at this time of year. I can recommend the soup, though. It comes with a crusty bread that is to die for. The lasagne and chips are popular with the locals."

Mia's face ducked down an inch, and she returned to the menu, feeling the heat rush to her cheeks. "Of course, I didn't even think. Sorry…" Contemplating, Mia suddenly heard Juliet's voice in her mind and she smiled. "Actually, the lasagne and chips sounds spectacular. Thank you."

"Not a problem. Just take a seat, and I'll have it out in twenty minutes or so. Help yourself to the magazines or newspapers."

"I heard that you have a bookstore here, is that right?" Mia asked, taking a step back and peering around the corner.

"Ah-huh, just around there. Go ahead and browse, I'll give you a call when your lunch is ready."

"Thanks."

Stepping around the corner, Mia walked past a small line of tables next to the wide windows until floor-to-ceiling shelves appeared. The narrow corridor opened into a large expansive room. Bookshelves lined the walls and were in tightly squeezed rows in the middle. She picked up a small calico bag and worked her way through the sections. Although her goal was to try and find Juliet's novel, she didn't particularly expect it to be stocked and so went about selecting a range of reading material, something to keep her busy for a few weeks. Her eclectic tastes meant she chose two autobiographies and a thick crime book and then another last-minute inclusion by an Australian comedian she had once seen at a women's health fundraiser in Los Angeles. Focussing her attention then, she started scanning the spines for Juliet's book and working her way through different genres. Juliet had been incredibly inept at disclosing to Mia anything about the content, and Mia sensed it was more a book of self-discovery and philosophy than anything fiction.

She was wrong. There, in the middle of the fiction section, under *T* on the bottom shelf, were two copies of a novel by Juliet Taylor. Mia tugged at one of them from the tightly packed shelf, and sat back on her feet where she had knelt down.

Things My Mother Should Have Told Me:

A story of being anyone but who you were raised to be.

Mia was grinning widely when she earned a tap on her shoulder, and she jumped slightly at the contact. "Found anything you like?"

"Yes, actually. I'll take these five…and the bag." She still couldn't believe she had found Juliet's book.

"I've just put out your lunch. Go ahead. We'll fix these up when you're done."

"Thank you. Is it all right with you if I start reading? I'm keen to start this one."

"Absolutely, you go ahead, love. And a fabulous choice. That's up for a few awards this year, one of the best written, bravest literary fictions that I've read in a long time. I hope it does win an award or two. It might get the publicity it deserves. Actually, a media release that we got from the publisher a few months ago said the author had another book in the works and that it was due out this Christmas. Guess it didn't happen."

Mia nodded slowly and gave a half smile. "I know the author, actually. Juliet. Well, met her recently."

"You did?"

"Ah-huh. I did."

"Well, lucky you. If you can ever get me a signed copy, there's a week-long stay here in it for you."

Mia laughed quietly. "I'll have to work on that."

Blank.

It didn't matter how many times Juliet closed her laptop and reopened it. The document was still glaringly blank. Empty. Void of anything profound, thought provoking, or insightfully brave. It was even absent of something crap, grammatically flawed, and sickeningly clichéd.

Juliet let her forehead drop. Her computer emitted a familiar rapid-paced buzzing sound, of a computer key being struck and then held down. When she raised her head, biscuit crumbs were pressed to her right eyebrow, and the screen was no longer a mocking white but had two and a half lines of a lower case *c* across the top of the page.

That was never going to win her a Pulitzer.

Most of the people in Overscaig both dreaded dealing with the Revira family and yet had, at some point, relied on them for a decent chunk of their income. Janet, who had only recently begun working as a maid at the estate in advance of the black sheep daughter Mia returning to the fold, was no different. The Revira family reputation preceded them, and just the mention of one of them returning to stay had sent the small local towns into a flurry. It seemed as if most had a story to tell of conflict at some point with one of the family members, everyone from the local produce suppliers through to the Royal Mail outlet.

Janet herself had experienced some anxiety at the thought of coming to work here, but she'd needed the money, and for all that they were difficult to deal with, the Reviras tended to pay their victims well for their trouble.

However, Mia Revira was turning out to be something quite unexpected. Janet had grown up in this town, and when she had told her father that she would be working for the Reviras, he had repeatedly warned her not to expect too much. She remembered being a young girl and how her father would return home from delivering supplies and lecture them. *It doesn't cost anything to be respectful, but those people still can't afford it,* he'd say. It didn't make any sense to Janet until she was much older.

She couldn't quite recall when Mia and her husband had purchased the adjacent estate, but at some point, the Revira family had had less presence in the area and then had disappeared completely. The gossip that went around for months when Mia and her husband divorced was that it couldn't have happened to a nicer family.

Yet, although Mia was a grown woman with her mother's infamous ease at telling servants what to do, this current lady of the house had not grown up with Mrs Revira's equally infamous disdain for them. At the moment, Mia reminded Janet of a girl, actually, curled up in the corner of a long sofa, a hand-knitted wool blanket over her lap.

"Can I ask you a question, Janet?" Mia asked quietly. The sofa's wide seat and deep cushions seemed to almost swallow her.

"Of course." Janet hid her surprise, returning a polishing cloth to the bucket she was carrying as she worked her way around the wooden furniture. She even smiled at Mia as she sat down on a recliner across from Mia, having finally started to relax while on the property, thanks to Mia's cues. "Do you need something?"

"No, not at all. I'm good, really good."

A knee-jerk panic overcame her. "Have I, done something? Have I done something incorrectly?"

"No, no. I didn't mean anything like that. Relax," Mia said quickly. "I just wondered…Well, I'm reading this book, and I suppose it's making me think a little. Do you still have parents?"

"Oh." Janet squirmed back on the single recliner and crossed her legs. "I do, yes. My parents live in Ireland now, not far from Galway."

"Do you have a good relationship with them?"

"Yes, I do. I always have, and it would be great to see them more often, but it's a way to go, and it takes time and money."

"Do you think that people either become…someone, I suppose, because of their parents or despite them? That's what this book is talking about at the moment, the idea that although there are so many variables and different aspects, that essentially, who we are is because either we were supported, encouraged, and directed by our parents or because we looked at who they were and resolved to become someone entirely different."

The concept came out a little disjoined and unclear, and Janet guessed that Mia was thinking about the meaning of what she said even as she tried to articulate it. She gave her a nod and another small smile. "That's a reflective book that you're reading," she said. "It makes some sense, I suppose. How can we not be influenced by the people who raised us—whether that's a negative or positive thing?"

"I was raised to be a very specific person, to have the opinions that I was told to have, to believe what I was told to, and to live within the rules that were already established for me. And when I couldn't really do that, it all fell apart."

Janet's eyebrows rose. It was the most frank Mia had been with her since she'd arrived. In fact, it might also be the greatest number of words Mia had said to her at one time. She felt herself take a sharp little intake of breath as she decided what to say.

"From what I've seen," she said hesitantly, "the world gets a little bit of a shock when someone acts a certain way for a long time and then suddenly draws a line that they can't cross. It's like someone suddenly saying 'no' when they've spent their life saying 'yes.'"

"I was meant to be a trophy wife who withstood whatever was thrown my way."

Janet cocked her head. "And what happened when you didn't?"

Mia sighed heavily and drew her bottom lip into her mouth. "It all fucked up."

Though the language surprised Janet, she didn't show it and just nodded slowly. "The way I see it, for what it's worth, things will always..." She hesitated almost imperceptibly. "*fuck* up—to everyone everywhere. It's what you do next that counts."

"I'm trying," Mia whispered, a stray tear tracking down the side of her nose until it curved in over her lip.

Janet gave a sad smile, although Mia was oblivious, eyes focussed on the closed book in her lap. She'd heard stories from a still-furious Martin about the things that had happened here to Mia. She had an inclination to tell her, *You got fucked over is what happened.* But Janet needed this job, and it was perhaps safest to pretend for now that she didn't know.

"Yes, you are," was all she let herself say. "I can tell."

Wandering through the centre square of Bruges for the fourth time since she arrived, Juliet kept an open umbrella close over her head. She was wrapped from head to toe in a number of layers—gloves, scarf and boots all included—and it was doing a fine job keeping away the slight drizzle of rain. Her internal dialogue as she dragged her feet from puddle to puddle was edging on a panicked self-criticism. The idea that she would arrive in Europe and be inundated with great ideas and a fluidity of writing had been spectacularly destroyed. Over the past two weeks, it had exploded into a mass of miniscule pieces. Just remnants of her hopes and dreams now lay discarded around her messy, barely secure apartment.

But she had to somehow keep herself trying. She didn't have a choice. She no longer had a home to return to, no job to reinstate. Failure wasn't an option. Yet, she felt as if she were precariously close to a complete meltdown. She would probably end up in a mental health facility, rambling incoherently about a book she had to write, about the writer she once was.

Juliet shuddered and forced the thought away; it was just a little too close to home.

So she stopped at a corner pub, with its promise of mashed potato and German sausages and a bottled Duvel. The facility was warm and dry, though filled with an odd combination of loud tourists and seemingly quiet locals.

She happily settled into a small booth by a window and peeled off a few outer layers. She shouldn't be eating out; she knew that. She should be skimping on money, making cheap meals at the apartment, and focussing on writing. She should be keeping herself alive with instant coffee and marmalade on bread, the fantasy she'd had when making her plans. The thought that she would arrive and literally not be able to write hadn't really occurred to her other than as a running joke with her editor and with Mia. The idea hadn't been *real*.

At the thought of Mia, Juliet withdrew her phone. She'd texted Mia her new number a few days ago but hadn't heard much from her. Her finger lingered over the keys, yet she put the phone away before she typed anything. Mia needed her space, to have her time out from the world and do whatever it was she planned to do. She didn't need Juliet, the crazy nomad that she had accidentally stumbled across in an airport for two days, texting and complaining at her.

Juliet sighed and shook her head. She needed to get a grip and fast.

Curled up on her side near the edge of the king-size bed, Mia was buried deep beneath sheets and heavy blankets. If she rolled onto her back, she would be precariously balanced on the mattress, risking a two-foot fall to the plush white carpet below. She was enthralled in Juliet's book, tears steadily flowing over the bridge of her nose and falling to the feather pillows she was propped against.

She finally released a shuddering breath when she found herself staring at the blank inside page of the back cover. Slowly, she closed the book and tucked it under her arm, squeezing her eyes shut and crying.

The book had remained loosely held in one arm when she awoke later that night, the lamp still on and illuminating the large room with an eerie glow. Placing the book on her bedside table, she gave it a tired, lingering glance before she switched the lamp off.

She had questions for Juliet.

CHAPTER 4

Such an intense action movie should have succeeded in distracting Mia. The scenes played across the flat-screen television mounted on the wall in the lounge room, but even the brilliance of Quentin Tarantino couldn't manage to hold her focus.

Flicking at the screen of her iPad, Mia started a game of spider solitaire but quit after two minutes. She tried looking through her photos, but they were nothing that she hadn't spent hours staring at over the past few months, and she eventually returned to her mail. She was thrilled that Pamela Anderson wanted to offer her diet secrets, and couldn't be more pleased that a long-lost relative from an oil reserve in Saudi Arabia had left her a trillion dollars. Thrilled.

Juliet had sent her a short e-mail the day before, and it was simple and polite but lacking in the kind of connection that they had seemed to form while travelling together. So Mia hadn't responded straightaway, just waiting as she pondered what it was that Juliet's novel had created in her and how she would go about asking Juliet about it. It had stirred so much in her, but she had to stop herself from inundating Juliet with her unfiltered reaction.

She cast her eyes over the e-mailed text, rereading.

Hi Mia,

I'm trying to trick myself into thinking that if I'm e-mailing you, than it's not actually an avoidance strategy. Because obviously, I'm on my computer, so I'm being productive. Right?

How are you? How are things going in Scotland? Freezing cold?

Things are fine here, nothing too exciting to report. I can't say I've managed to get the writing happening, but I'm not panicking yet. Any news to report from your side?

:-) Juliet

Mia's fingers lingered over the keyboard imagery. She had to admit that one of the better skills she had learned throughout her thirteen years of private school education was an ability to touch-type, although her aptitude in multiplying matrices and using vector products were slightly less useful. She was sure she had managed to acquire other useful knowledge; it was just that nothing else was coming to mind. She had certainly developed an ability to be an absolute conniving bitch if she needed to, and in that environment, with a school of spoiled girls who were immeasurably talented at creating havoc, that skill was needed. Wearing the wrong nail polish in eighth grade had cost Mia a place on the equestrian team. Or, rather, it was her invective retort to the teasing echoing throughout the classroom that had cost her the spot.

Now she could smile at the memory. Impassioned was one thing she had always been, though she had probably learned to contain the feeling—or had been forced to learn to contain it.

Hello Juliet,

It's great to hear from you! You can't just e-mail and say that things are "fine." Tell me about Belgium. Have you eaten some chocolate and had at least a pint or two of beer? I know you told me that your apartment had a bed, but what's it like? Is it okay?

I could just keep firing questions at you, but you probably wouldn't find that too enjoyable! So I'll be good.

Things are pretty good here, though it's taking me some time to get used to the weather. I forgot how crazy making barely any sunlight and just constant drizzle is, not to mention the snow and sleet and ice. No wonder people get that depression thing over here, what's it called? Seasonal Depression or something?

I've been focussing on relaxing, long soaks in the bath and watching movies. And I've been doing heaps of reading, picked up some new stuff to get stuck into. Actually, I picked up your book...I think I've almost stopped crying. :-) Where was my heads-up?

Amazing, by the way. Oh, and there's a lovely owner of a B&B a couple of hours from here who is quite the fan. She's promised us a week-long break there if I can get her a signed copy. What do you think? Up for a mini-break in the snow? It's an incredible spot, actually—by the water...Not great for swimming, but views to die for. I'm not really making it sound appealing, am I? :-)

Hope to hear from you soon.

M xo

With her fingernail tapping the screen, Mia pressed *send.*

Juliet slumped in the makeshift desk chair, shoulder blades draping themselves over its black plastic frame as her head dropped back and her eyes closed. She groaned loudly and then again. She couldn't figure out why she hadn't even considered the possibility that Mia would seek out her book. And not for the first time since she wrote the thing, Juliet cursed the fact that she hadn't used a pseudonym. Her editor had told her it was silly and unnecessary, and that in this age of the Internet and YouTube, she would never be able to do an interview or media tours if she really didn't want people to ever find out who she was. The publisher would have pulled its deal or reduced the number of copies printed if she'd insisted on it.

She should have lied to Mia. She should have said she was an administration officer or worked in publishing. Her fallback fictitious job was always that of a non-specific office worker, but then Mia had asked, and the truth had flowed from her mouth without a second thought. She had no idea why that was. She hadn't had any difficulty making up inconsequential lies to any other woman she had taken home. And she had never seen them again, so it hardly mattered.

But she didn't sleep with Mia.

And she wanted to see her again at some point.

She grunted—a long, varying noise, drawn out until she had no breath left. She wanted to see Mia again.

Now, where the hell had that thought just come from?

Motionless for a few minutes, Juliet stood up and walked to the corner of the living area where the small kitchen was. She stood at the two small benches in the corner that made up the entirety of the kitchen and switched the kettle on. It hummed into life. Once, it was possibly an automatic device, but now it just whistled until she came over and switched it off. She supposed if left alone, it would eventually burn off the water and then blow up in a display of smoke and, potentially, fire. It would probably burn the entire apartment block down, including her computer, which had nothing useful on it anyway. Maybe that wouldn't be so disastrous?

"Just make your tea, a nice peppermint and relax," Juliet told herself, directing her words at the white plastic kettle. "And stop talking to yourself," she added, finally laughing at her idiosyncrasies and tendency to panic. Not about anything major, though. With huge life dramas and disruptions to travel or health issues, she would barely bat an eyelid. But come to anything resembling emotional connectivity or someone having access to the part of her she kept in a tight vault, or someone seeing her faults, her failures? Well, that elicited the craziest of thoughts.

Screwing up her face at the kettle's offensively loud whistle, she turned it off and poured the boiling water into a large mug. She toyed with the teabag for a minute, tugging it up and down through the water until a pleasant odour started to permeate her senses. She tossed it into the trashcan under the sink.

Returning to her laptop, she sat the mug aside to cool and contemplated Mia's e-mail again. She had to respond, and she wanted to. But she wasn't going to sit around for two days trying to figure out what to write.

You slipped that in nicely, Mia. Very sneaky. Having someone you know read your book is a bit like standing naked in front of your greatest enemy. Awful. ;-)

Sounds like things are going really well for you, though? You're sounding kind of relaxed, and I have to say, I'm fairly jealous of the bath. There's nothing better than a few candles, some music, and soaking in a steaming bath for an hour. I don't know if I ever quite got the essence of this six-month break? Is relaxation the big goal?

I'm with you on the weather thing. Cold weather always seems like a better idea in theory than in reality. It's pretty cold here too, although I wouldn't think anywhere near as chilly as you have it. And to answer your questions—I have, as a matter of fact, had a number of beers, classic Belgium, of course, and a few chocolates. There's this little shop in town, and the chocolatier makes the absolute best white chocolate pralines. They are...Well, I'm not sure I have the words. Melt-in-your-mouth orgasmic bliss.

The apartment is okay. I mean, it's not the Taj Mahal or anything, but it's quiet and clean. I really need to get out and buy a decent desk chair, though; I'm just using one of these plastic seats from a dining setting, which is about as comfortable as sitting on a line of pins. I think that's my only complaint, really. I'm in Europe—what's not to like, right?

I might try and do a few days of writing and then catch the train down to Paris for the day as my reward. I can go and buy a coffee and stare at the Tour Eiffel. I've never actually seen it with snow, so I should try and time it for that. I'll make sure I send you a photo! :-) Jealous? You may have a bath, but...

Okay, I better get back to 'work'. (Can you read my non-verbals from there?)
Take care, Juliet :-)

It was late in the afternoon when Mia read Juliet's e-mail, though she worked her way through every word three times before she set her iPad aside. The e-mail was positive enough and polite, while somewhat casual, but it lacked an authenticity Mia couldn't quite put her finger on. Juliet had skilfully avoided Mia's subtle hint to bring up some talk about the book, and she supposed it wasn't surprising. Juliet hadn't been particularly forthcoming with details about her life, and neither had Mia. With time, Mia could see herself telling her entire life story to Juliet, but she wasn't sure that was reciprocated. And maybe she was just reading too much into an e-mail. It was a crappy form of communication at the best of times. Still, it was all they had. She left the reply until the following morning.

When she awoke the next day, curled up in bed and not at all interested in facing the cold, Mia thought briefly about the vivid dreams she'd had throughout the night— bright images and loud noises that had awakened her multiple times, her subconscious playing tricks on her. In one dream, she had been running at full speed and effort down a long corridor, checking every wall for a gap, and frantically turning door handles, each one locked. And still the infant's crying she could hear in the distance had become louder and more distressed, even as she felt herself pulling further and further away.

Pushing an extra pillow up behind her, Mia shifted herself on the bed, covers pulled up to just above her waist. She wore a thigh-length black camisole, bought not long after her marriage had ended, a rebellious act almost. He had always wanted her to wear one for him, and she never would. Wearing it made her feel empowered now.

Good morning Juliet, it's great to hear from you!
I have to confess that though it's nine in the morning here, I'm still in bed. And I only really just woke up—crazy! I don't think I've ever slept in this long; I'm loving it. Had some super-crazy dreams last night, and I hadn't even had a nightcap. Bizarre!

Relaxation is pretty much the goal, to answer your question. Things have been...Hmmm, how should I phrase this? I've been through a bit of a rough time. Lots of stuff has been happening, and I had the opportunity to do this. So I thought, why not? It's gotten me away from things, given me some space, and for the first time in ages, I feel like I can breathe again.

I'm not sure why you would think that someone reading your book is awful? I mean, Juliet, it was incredible. You should be standing on street corners and selling it—I don't know how these things work, but you should somehow tell the world that this is a book they need to read. And I hear it's up for some awards. When do you hear if it's been shortlisted?

I did wonder when I was reading it how much of your own life influenced the storyline? You mentioned when we were jetlagged and exhausted that you had been to a few specific places, and I noticed them in there. I know it's fiction, but still, I wanted to ask. The character just seemed so alone and haunted, and there was no one in the world that had her back. And it ended that way, with a defeated realisation that there was nothing else.

Do you believe that? Is that what you think? Is that you? I thought maybe it was me too, but it's not. Tomorrow is...tomorrow. There has to be hope.

I know that all probably sounds crazy, but I've done hardly anything except think about it for days. And I wanted to ask you questions straightaway, but I wasn't sure if that was okay. I don't want to offend you or upset you, so please don't be. I've got this overwhelming need to just delete this e-mail and send something that is just drab and boring, but I'm trying to be this new person. Or at least a different person, someone who doesn't just keep their mouth shut and toe the line, someone who takes risks when the risk is worth it; and you seem worth it. And I don't know why, and it doesn't all make sense, but yeah, it is what it is.

Sorry, I know that probably reads like someone on acid...Please let me know if I've offended you, I really haven't meant to.

Hope to hear from you soon.

Mia xo

Taking a breath, Mia pressed *send* before she could second-guess herself. Immediately, a sense of regret filled her. She had no right to be questioning Juliet; they barely knew each other. But she felt compelled to. She felt something,

something unidentifiable, but it was there between the two of them. She wasn't imagining it. She was sure of it. Wasn't she?

Gathering together her notebook, ballpoint, and granola bar into a satchel on the kitchen bench, Juliet grabbed her laptop and was about to slam it shut when, acting on habit, she first clicked on the mail icon to the bottom left of the screen, balancing the computer precariously in her palm. Mia's e-mail stared at her as Juliet slumped back into the chair and put the computer back down on her desk. She raked a hand through air-dried curls, tumbling them into each other so they twisted over the crown of her head.

Finally closing the laptop, Juliet decided to leave it behind after all and collected her satchel. It was a bag she had bought in India, where she spent a few weeks backpacking after several months at a Buddhist retreat in Cambodia. She'd gone with her hostel manager to an orphanage outside of Siem Reap, where the owners of the hostel provided some financial aid to the facility as well as leftover food. Some of the older children learned skills at the in-house school and made bags, purses, tapestries, and jewellery. So Juliet had bought a bag for herself, a brightly coloured across-the-body satchel with a single large pocket design with a zippered opening and a flap that hung loosely. She had picked up her brother a bracelet too, black and red, the most masculine she could find, and it matched the tokenistic Cambodian beer shirt she had picked up for him.

Plucking her thick jacket off the back of a chair, Juliet slid into it and knotted a scarf around her neck. Glancing back at the computer, Juliet hesitated, unzipping her bag and reaching into it. She fumbled blindly, and with her forehead burrowed, she eventually withdrew her phone. Quickly, she typed a text to Mia, knowing that she was feeling a whole lot of something, but it definitely wasn't anger. She needed to tell Mia that.

Hi, just got your e-mail and about to head out. I just wanted to say I'll reply later, not offended at all. Hope you're okay.

She was standing at the bus stop before a reply came through.

I'm so relieved. I was worried. Enjoy your day and stay safe.

Much later that afternoon, and with several afternoon drinks under her belt, Juliet finally sat down to write her e-mail to Mia.

Hey Mia,

I should warn you first up, I've had a few drinks this afternoon, so hopefully I'll make sense in this e-mail. I had to celebrate: I actually got some ideas on paper today. Yes, I did say paper, but they're actually down in black and white; or blue and white. I was using a blue pen.

I'm not sure where to start with the things you wrote, but I'll give it a go. I'm sorry to hear you've been having a crappy time, and I guess that's probably an understatement. The break is a good idea, and it takes some guts to do that too. If I can help at all, let me know. I've been told that I'm not a bad listener...Any time you want to talk about things, or if you want to tell me anything, you can. I'm yet to be shocked, and I've seen a thing or two over the years. So don't feel like you can't talk to me.

You've probably got all these great friends that you talk to, and that just ended up sounding stalker-like, right? Damn.

Hmmm, and on to your questions about the book. That fucking book. Sometimes I wish I never wrote it. I could still be at college or teaching or something. It is a fiction, you're right, and that's what it is—fiction. I know there are some parallels that can be drawn, and I definitely used places that I've been to and experiences I've had, or ones that others have had, but it's mostly a complete mix of real and exaggerated and completely made up. That's how I write, I just take something small that is familiar and then I build on it. Sometimes it becomes unrecognisable, and at other times, it becomes the opposite—too close.

I'm not sure if that answers your questions well enough, but yeah, that's kind of it. You really didn't offend me, so don't be worried. You shouldn't ever stress about bothering me. I'm pretty resilient. It takes much more than that to annoy or hurt me. :-)

Correct me if I'm wrong, but it seems a bit like the themes upset you?
Sending a virtual hug your way...
Juliet :-)

Woollen hat pulled low over her forehead, Mia sat atop a white mare. Its hooves and speckled black ankles sank into the thin layer of snow. Mia rode slowly, distracted as she headed towards the corner of their first paddock, a few bare trees in her peripheral vision. She felt unsettled, anxious. Christmas was only two days away, and it was just another anniversary that she despised, yet another reminder of the life she'd lost, the future that seemed certain yet fell spectacularly apart.

And she still hadn't replied to Juliet's e-mail.

Juliet had quite the skill of saying something whilst not saying a lot at all. She was oddly neutral, and Mia wondered if she ever fired up in anger or dissolved in hysterical tears. This was another similarity to her book's character, who seemed just void of emotion and fight. Mia felt suitably dramatic and unstable in comparison. Yet, Juliet invited her to share and communicate. It was confusing.

Loosely holding the reins, she allowed the horse to idly walk at will, only mildly correcting her direction when she moved towards the stream that weaved from past the west boundary to a loch that was miles away. Mia reluctantly returned to the barn when a drizzle of rain began to fall, realising then that her nose was icy cold and her lips were chapped. A glance at her watch told her she had been out for just shy of two hours, and she was grateful when Janet interrupted her shaky hands from trying to unbuckle the billet straps.

"There's some soup on the stove." Janet softly rubbed the horse's neck. "You should take off that wet jacket and warm up."

Mia shivered, wrapping her arms around her middle. "Thanks," she said, shoulders trembling with cold.

"Go on." Glancing sideways at Mia standing motionless a few steps away, Janet told her, "I've got this."

Silently, Mia slipped away back to the house, careful not to slip in the slush. She went straight to the shower, using the steaming water to slowly warm herself. When she emerged half an hour later, her face was pale, though her cheeks were tinged with pink, a combination of the cold from outside and the too-hot shower. She had applied a clear hydrating lip gloss, though the chapped skin still stung when she spooned some thick pumpkin soup into her mouth.

Cloaked in a blanket, she finished a cup of soup before refilling it again and sitting on the floor, close to the fireplace.

She opened her iPad and sighed.

Hi Juliet,

Thanks for your e-mail, and sorry for not getting back to you sooner. I've been trying to get my head together, but it probably hasn't been going quite as well as I would like. I tried to phone you yesterday, thought we could talk over the phone, but I get that you're a little busier than I am—all my relaxation.

Great to hear that you've been able to get some writing done; I knew you would. And you deserve to reward yourself with some drinks.

So what I'm getting from what you said about the book is that you put some of your own experiences in there. The book had an incredible effect on me. I would really like to hear more about it. What do you think?

If you can picture it, I'm sighing right now. I'm sitting on the floor by the fireplace, and I've just regained feeling in my fingers (seemed like a good idea at the time to go for a ride in freezing temperatures.) I have no idea how to say what I want to say. I don't have all these people in my life to talk to. And I'm only just realising that I never really have, but you probably figured that out two minutes after you met me. You're good at reading people, aren't you? I don't know what makes me say that, I just think your book is all about saying the things that people don't say. Or don't even think about.

Do you hate that? People telling you what your book is about? Feel free to throw something at me—virtually, that is.

I think I mentioned to you that I have a sister, Daniela. I'm only eighteen months older, and we spent our entire childhood together, constantly playing and talking, doing everything together. We even had some of the same friends when we were going through high school. We still talked heaps, even when we lived in different places, went to different colleges. I was her bridesmaid when she got married.

When I was seventeen, she caught me in bed with a woman. But she also found me smoking weed on at least five occasions, cigarettes in my school bag, major dents in my car—you get the idea. So we didn't really talk about it again; it was as if it didn't happen. Six months ago, she arrived at a jazz bar, where I was meant to be meeting my husband for a drink and dinner and to try and agree on our financial settlement, although there's a bit more to that story. Anyway, I was standing in the corner, kissing the female violin player. Daniela walked over, dragged me to the door and asked me what the fuck I was doing with a woman (my sister, by the way, has a husband and various other male suitors).

I had a long prepared speech, should the need ever arise, though I won't bore you with that five-minute diatribe. But the main point is that I told my sister that I was bisexual. She didn't say a word, just gave me this look of disgust and walked away. And I haven't heard from her since. She even changed her phone numbers, e-mail addresses. I heard that she moved too. Who does that?

We were always different. She was really into the high-profile socialite scene, but I wasn't; I did it, but I wasn't into it. Still, we always got along. We never fought or argued, always stayed in touch. And then suddenly, the one single person who had actually been around for my entire life was gone. Because of what? Because I...

I don't know what I should have done. Lied? Lived an entire life that was a lie? I don't know.

I'm sorry. That seems to be a theme for my e-mails. I end them with an apology. And it's Christmas in two days. I hate Christmas. But I feel like I should wish you a Merry Christmas and holiday season and all of that. But then, doing that would make me want to cry, and I'm trying to not be a crazy person right now.

I'm sorry.

She didn't sign off; she just closed her eyes and sent the e-mail. Then she curled up against the foot of the recliner and stared at gentle flames until the room was cloaked in darkness.

CHAPTER 5

One hand to her chest, Juliet reread Mia's e-mail. Her stomach somersaulted, and a lump swelled in her throat. She felt disbelief and uncertainty at the awareness of what Mia had lost. And Juliet assumed it was only the tip of the iceberg. She was strangely envious of Mia, envious of the openness and the honesty. Juliet could barely conceptualise the anxiety she would feel if she were to attempt the same.

A big part of her wanted to attempt it. She had never wanted to be honest like that before, and she doubted she would ever want to again, or to anyone else. But to Mia, there was the distinct hint of a possibility.

Life had been a slow progression into isolation for Juliet. She hadn't always been so closed off. She had always been close to her family, and she'd had a range of friends during her childhood and youth. She'd even had a string of relatively stable relationships in her early twenties, none of which ended particularly traumatically. In reflection, though, she had never been as open and communicative as her partners had been. She had always been the listener, the supportive one.

Her tight fists slammed onto the desk with a loud bang to try and make herself feel more alive. The laptop bounced slightly, and the desk groaned at the unexpected impact. Squeezing her eyes shut, she bolted upright, stumbling as the chair flipped back and crashed to the floor. Ignoring it, she paced around the small living area, back and forth and into the kitchen. She walked into her bedroom, stood at the foot of her bed with her hands on her hips, and shook her head. She was frustrated at her own insecurities, at her inability to be who she wanted to be. After a few minutes, she walked purposely into the bathroom and stilled herself, gripping the chipped basin, head bowed with her weight on her arms. Slowly, she raised her face to the mirror, staring at her own reflection.

Her eyes looked sullen and ringed with darkness underneath the lower lids. They almost looked bruised, but it was only tiredness that had evoked the telltale sign of exhaustion. She hadn't been sleeping that well, just a few hours here and there, with intermittent periods of staring at the ceiling or listening to the wind outside.

She shook her head at her mirrored image, briefly distracting herself with a promise to eat more and better. She had only been in Belgium less than two weeks, though it had been more since she had started her trip from the United States. She guessed she had lost a couple of pounds, maybe a few.

Her eyes had a few laugh lines. She didn't mind that; they told the story of the life she had lived, or at least they provided evidence that she had lived. She had always liked her eyes for being clear and bright. Though even she could tell that they were no longer the highlight of her looks that they once were, they seemed even duller and greyer now since she'd arrived. The lack of sunlight wasn't helping her pale complexion either, but if she blamed it solely on the cold European winter, than she was deluding herself. Her appearance told of long hours spent staring and thinking rather than living.

Taking one hand off the basin, she turned on the hot water, fingertips trailing under the flow as she waited for it to warm. She cupped both hands and repeatedly splashed the water onto her face. She stopped when the water became too hot, reaching for a hand towel.

Instead of returning to her computer, she slumped to the floor of the bathroom, shivering slightly on contact with the cool tiles.

It was dark before she moved again.

"Ready for Christmas, Mia?" Martin walked through the doorway and stopped a few steps away from where Mia reclined, open book on her lap.

Offering a half smile, Mia shrugged. "Just another day, I suppose. How about you? Shouldn't you be leaving earlier than Christmas morning?"

"No, not at all. With all of the kids spread out, there's no real reason to rush. My son and his wife will be home by lunchtime, so I'll make sure I arrive around then."

"And they have children, right?" Mia asked, knowing that Martin had a couple of grandchildren at least.

"Just the one, a very boisterous toddler. My daughter in London has an older boy who just started school in summer and another one on the way."

"Oh, that's right, the pilots, yes? How are they possibly going to manage two children?" Mia laughed.

Chuckling, Martin rubbed his hands together and nodded. "Apparently, Grandpa will be required for the occasional school holidays—babysitting duty, although hopefully not until this next one is a little older. It's been a long time since I changed a nappy. That said, I don't think my daughter is too thrilled about taking another year off work. She had only just started training on the direct London-to-Sydney route when she found out. She loved doing the Dubai-to-Sydney leg because she got to catch up with Amy, my youngest, who is studying there. They were always so close."

Mia shook her head, amazed. She had known that Martin's children were spread out, but she had no idea how he stayed so connected to them all given his long hours and only occasional holidays. "Lucky you're skilled at Skype, by the sounds of it!"

Martin laughed, throwing his hands in the air. "Oh you sound like Amy. I don't understand the Skype."

"Remind me to teach you one day. Your kids will love it."

"That they would. Their tolerance for my lack of technology skill has at least improved in recent years. Their mother was much more apt at that. She would be laughing in her grave at me attempting anything on the Internet, I suspect."

"How long has it been now, Martin?" Mia asked.

Rubbing the side of his jaw, Martin squinted and moved his head side to side as he appeared to count. "Uhhh, must be sixteen years. Amy was six when El passed away, and she's twenty-two now. How the years go."

Mia nodded and drew in a long inhalation through her nose. "Sometimes. Other times they seem to drag."

"There's never enough time, Mia. I learnt that very young: make the most of every minute." He grinned. "And that means when your youngest up and takes herself off to Australia, you just smile and book yourself a flight to see those kangaroos at the opera house."

Laughing, Mia shook her head. "You know, people really believe that there are kangaroos running around in cities in Australia, don't you?"

"Unfortunately, yes. Oh well. Good for a laugh, I suppose."

"Are you heading back soon?"

"To Australia?" Martin asked and Mia nodded. "No, maybe late next year if there's some time. I would like to get my boy over there, but he hasn't had much of a chance to travel yet. Maybe I'll talk about it with him this Christmas."

"Great idea." Mia smiled. She knew that Martin had single-handedly raised his children after his wife's death from cancer. She also knew that despite his reluctance to use Skype, he phoned them religiously twice a week and memorised every birthday and anniversary. He spoke about them proudly when given the opportunity. He was certainly nothing like her own father.

She wondered briefly what her family would be doing this Christmas. But she knew there would be no cards or gifts in the mail, no phone calls. Not now.

The bedside clock flashed bright red digits when Mia rolled over and opened one eye. *07:55.* Mia shuddered. She had last glanced at the clock at five in the morning, having lain awake mostly all night. Her head pounded with a horrific headache. She felt as if she had consumed two bottles of champagne, but she hadn't touched a drop. She wasn't game to, no matter how much she wanted to numb herself.

Her phone next to her on the bed flashed suddenly and she reached blindly for it. She had four new messages.

The first three were generic, mass-sent "Merry Christmas" texts from people she hadn't spoken to in years. They were like New Year messages, sent on the eve of midnight, alcohol fuelled, as if it was the perfect time to touch base with friends and enemies. The most recent was from Juliet, and Mia released a sigh of relief. She hadn't heard from her since she had sent the e-mail.

I'm reluctant to wish you a Merry Christmas, but I wanted to check in on you. How are you doing?

Mia closed her eyes in a prolonged blink; her chest ached.

Merry Christmas, Juliet. How are you? I'm okay, thanks.

The reply was quick, and if Mia were to guess, Juliet was curled up in bed just as she was. And words couldn't describe how much she wished to have Juliet's company, someone gentle and smiling here with her, to get her through the day.

Snug in bed! Are you really okay? I know today is tough without family, and I wanted to say that I'm thinking of you.

Shrugging at the vacant room, Mia deliberated for a few moments. She stared at the screen and lingered with her thumb over the letters.

Not really, but it's just a day. Thank you, though.

You should be here. We could have started with a champagne breakfast, followed by a beer lunch, and then a cocktail finish.

A single chuckle rushed air through Mia's nose, and her shoulders briefly moved with the exhalation.

That would have been better.

A few minutes passed before Juliet responded.

Is there anything that you need? Anything I can do?

No, not at all. I'm just wallowing in my own misery. I'll try not to share.

Mia swallowed heavily, waiting for a response.

Oh honey, you share as much as you like.

Mia burrowed further into her pillow, tugging the duvet as high as she could, just one hand poking out the top as she held her phone. She squeezed her eyes shut, determined not to spend the entire day in tears. Some of it, yes, but not all of it.

Maybe I'll come see you for a few days soon. Would that be okay?

Yes! Of course. Book some flights today, maybe that'll help. Hey, we could go to Paris when you're here.

Was Juliet's enthusiasm real, or was she just being her usual nurturing self, trying to coax Mia out of her sadness?

Only if it snows, right?

Ha ha. I'll make an exception. Take care today, and call me anytime, k?

Not crying was easier said than done.

Thanks, J. Can I call you that? :-) You have a good day.

I won't complain today; you're having a rough day already. :-) Talk soon.

When Mia made her way out of the bedroom, wet hair tied back in a twisted bun and a designer V-neck sweater over the shirt Juliet had given her, she found a row of gifts awaiting her on the coffee table. She cast her eyes over them briefly, fingering the tags before heading into the kitchen and making herself a cup of strong coffee. Her instinct was not to bother with breakfast—she wasn't in the least bit motivated—but ended up spooning herself a bowl of cut-up fruit from the fridge and tossing a handful of toasted granola over the top. She flopped herself down onto the sofa, flicking the television on and changing channels until she fixed upon the world news, anything to avoid a carol, a Christmas tree, or an oversized Santa.

She reached first to the delivered item, obvious by its clear cellophane, company sticker, and small card poking out at the top. There was a large box beneath the extensive gathering of cellophane. She withdrew the card, and a sad smile caught the side of her lips; it was a gift from Juliet.

Dear Mia,
Just a little collection to indulge in and cheer up your day—maybe this one won't be so bad. I hope this aids the relaxation. These are a few of my favourite things and hopefully yours too.
Happy 'look after yourself' Day,
Juliet

PS. I'm not sure there's a person in Durness that doesn't know the Revira family; you were super easy to track down. Oh, and we have that accommodation by the sea whenever we like.

Rechecking the sticker, Mia was surprised to see that it had been made by the same place where she had stopped to buy Juliet's book, the one that had wanted a signed copy. She figured Juliet had quickly worked some magic, and this added to the confusion Mia felt about her. Her e-mails seemed caring but detached, and her text messages were almost to the point of worrying about Mia, yet she seldom mentioned herself. Mia had no idea what Juliet was doing for the day or even if she celebrated Christmas. Did she hate the holidays as much as Mia? She had no idea at all. Yet, she was someone who obviously made a range of phone calls from a separate continent, just to have a gift delivered to Mia, whom she seemed to care about, but not really connect with. It was odd… or complex. Juliet was complex.

The gift box had a range of items in it, a small number of handmade chocolates, including some white chocolate-covered coffee beans and dark truffles. There was an early edition Kahlil Gibran book—*Sand and Foam*, not *The Prophet*, his most well-known volume. Also in the box were a few bath products—a milk soak and body scrub to go with the two half carafes of French champagne. The final item was a beautifully handcrafted leather notebook, a deep red colour that had two long leather ties to secure it shut. A pen was clipped on the top, and embossed on the cover were two eagles, wingspans wide.

And now Mia was crying.

Sniffling, she opened the other two gifts, a pair of earrings from Martin, which probably cost a third of the Christmas bonus Mia had transferred into his account as a surprise. She had done a similar thing for Janet as well, although the flights home had been the focus. Janet had bought Mia a voucher for a full-day treatment at a day spa in Edinburgh. They seemed to have really taken a shine to her: she couldn't remember a time when any of the staff, in her childhood home or later on, had ever bought them gifts, except the nanny that had raised her and Daniela. She had always given them the doll or toy they wanted when their parents didn't get it right.

It should have made her feel better, but it didn't.

Barely able to move with the number of layers she had on, Mia worked at saddling her horse. It took longer than it should have, her fingers numbing quickly without gloves on as the snow fell softly outside the barn. Before mounting, she double-checked her coat pocket, two folded-up pieces of A5 notepaper still securely inside. She settled into the saddle, and after tugging gloves onto her hands, she took the reins and tapped her heels to the horse, walking it out into the elements.

Mia had spent most of the day wallowing, agitated as she restlessly moved from the lounge room to her bedroom, pacing through the kitchen or distractedly looking out the window. She couldn't concentrate to sit in front of a movie, and when she tried to read a book, she kept having to reread paragraphs and flick back a few pages, unable to absorb the words. Usually the quietness didn't bother her, and having the place to herself was enjoyable. But she was feeling uneasy and locked in.

Riding across a postcard-perfect paddock, her back rounded, she slumped slightly forward, her chin frequently falling to her chest. She kept casting her eyes to the dimly gray sky and sobbing, before dropping her head back down. Her shoulders trembled. The horse walked at a slow, calm pace, as if cautious, protective of its fractured rider.

Slipping down to the undisturbed snow after just over an hour of riding, Mia's knees and shins were wet as she crawled forward. Snow melted with her body's heat and soaked into her jeans. She was shivering intensely, though she wasn't really feeling the cold.

Momentarily, she was tear free, edging down a small embankment until her fingertips could reach the freezing flow of a freshwater stream. If she followed the current for sixty or seventy miles, she would hit a beautiful loch, surrounded by small log cabins and old wooden jetties. Fumbling, she sat back on her feet, legs folding under her as she unzipped the pocket of her jacket.

She withdrew the two pages of lined paper, filled with her own cursive writing. The pages had been torn out of the notebook that Juliet had given her. Mia had spent thirty minutes earlier this morning penning a tearful goodbye. It had been in the back of her mind ever since her therapist had suggested letter writing as a way to deal with the grief. But she hadn't been able to bring herself to actually do it. The words had run around her head at will, coalescing into different phrases and thoughts, but she hadn't put any of it onto paper. Until now. And that was the idea behind what she was doing. Well, that was what her therapist had insisted was a key task in her journey, her recovery.

It had all sounded like a load of bullshit to Mia, yet she had gone back to the idea time and again, in hope of some sudden epiphany. But epiphanies weren't something that happened in real life, and when she had relented and reluctantly committed herself to writing a goodbye, she had found that she couldn't do it.

She had thought it would be easy, fluid, and simple, a sarcastic and purposeless task. It wasn't.

It was downright difficult—impossible and unpleasant, actually. It hurt. It made her entire body ache until she felt like she might disappear under the pressure.

Her hand trembled. The words seemed superficial and hollow, completely inadequate for what she was trying to describe. She wanted to represent the depth and complexity, and everything she thought of seemed clichéd or insincere.

And now that she had written it, she couldn't let it go.

So she grasped the thin pages to her chest, and they wrinkled under her tight hold. The lightly falling snow caught the edges of the paper, and it wilted. A few words on the first line began to run.

She had to do it before they disappeared.

Juliet poured her first glass of wine, a room temperature Merlot that was still a little too chilled for her liking. The microwave was heating some frozen mini-pizzas, and leaning back in front of it, she fished her phone out of her back pocket. Tossing it around in her fingertips for a moment, she briefly debated whether or not to text Mia. Juliet hadn't heard from her since that morning, and it concerned her. It was instinctual rather than anything specific—a little niggle in the back of her mind despite her attempts to distract herself.

Hey! How are you coping with the day?

After half a bottle of wine and numerous pizzas consumed, when Juliet still hadn't received a message back to that deceptively simple text, she gave a shrug at the television and then gave herself an internal talking to about becoming too close. She was not just attracted to Mia. She wanted more than just fleeting desire. Juliet hadn't felt that way about someone for a long time, and it wasn't comfortable.

She couldn't do it. She wasn't willing to put it all on the line. The outcome had never been particularly traumatic, but it never had been particularly worth it either, and it had always eventually made her feel like the walls were closing in.

She had her writing and her travel. She could work her way around the world again, meet people, and have casual unattached flings. She wasn't made for relationships, and she had long ago made her peace that a life alone, filled with adventures and experiences, was her purpose.

Until she found herself continually checking her phone. Until she was worrying herself through three more glasses of wine, and Mia still hadn't replied.

Almost a full bottle, and not a single word from Mia.

Not even an "all good" or "fine" response, no response at all. Juliet found herself desperate for her phone to beep, just that little message jingle that would tell her that Mia was fine and she could go about moving on.

Moving on from what, she wasn't sure, but she assumed sobriety would bring some clarity. She was certain that her perceived connection with Mia was exactly that—a perceived one. Her self-delusion was just a symptom of being alone without a safety net. She wasn't specifically attracted to Mia. She was attracted to the illusion of someone stable and supportive in her life—the kind of person that could rescue her in an airport. But that's all it was, an illusion of some happy-ever-after story.

Juliet had apparently, despite her better judgement, subconsciously created Mia into the person that she had always assured herself that she would one day settle down for. Her travel and independence, as strong and fulfilling as it was, wasn't something she had planned for forever.

She would one day meet the woman that was worth making sacrifices for and who would make sacrifices for her. The reciprocity was important; this person would be her partner and her equal.

But that wasn't Mia; equal they were not.

Juliet took another long drink from her glass, the liquid sliding down her throat now with barely a warm burn.

If only Mia would respond so Juliet could go about forgetting her.

Flicking the small blue lighter she had brought with her, Mia tried to blink through her tears. The snow was starting to turn into a sleety rain, and cold droplets of water sneaked against her neck and into her scarf.

Trying again to quickly turn the thumbwheel, a small flame jutted up before fading; it flickered at the page before the dampness extinguished it. Her hand was stinging, and each digit felt oversized and weak. She had written the letter, and now she couldn't burn it.

How cruel was this world?

Using the paper as a shield for one final attempt, Mia forced her thumb down hard, teeth gritting as a sharp pain ran through the palm of her hand. The flame appeared and held, catching the long edge of the letter and burning quickly. Mia breathed a sigh of relief and stumbled to her feet.

She tried to keep the smouldering object close until she was forced to hold just the corner as the red line became closer and the paper disintegrated. It was almost done. Holding it out in front of her, arm outstretched, she watched tiny pieces of ash drift and then disappear. They were too tiny, and the afternoon was too dark and wet to keep track of them.

She wasn't meant to anyway.

And then it was gone. Her words, her goodbye, everything she felt was now a part of the landscape. Some of the scraps drifted into the stream and were carried away, while others flew into the rocky edge or landed atop snowflakes on blades of grass.

Her apology, the desperate request for forgiveness from somewhere it would never and could never come.

An endless flow of repentance.

She couldn't bring herself to do what she had been instructed to do, though— to forgive herself.

Mia wasn't sure how she negotiated the path back to the stables, though she suspected her horse had protectively carried her home. He stood unmoving next to her when she slumped onto a bale of hay, phone loosely held in her hand. She stared at the screen through tears, repeatedly talking herself in and out of using it. She was filled with trepidation at the thought of baring her wounds again. Yet she was immobilised at the alternatives. Selecting the most recent number on the phone's log, Mia closed her eyes and pressed the green call button.

Three rings and a muffled voice answered. "Mia?"

CHAPTER 6

"Mia, is that you?" Juliet quickly tore the phone from her ear and checked the caller identification; it was definitely Mia's number.

"I'm sorry." Mia's voice was a muffled murmur through the phone.

Rolling onto her back and scooting up the bed, Juliet leant back against the wall, knees up in front of her. "No, no, it's fine. It's okay. What's wrong?"

"I'm sorry. I didn't mean to call."

"Hey, it's fine. Honestly, what is it? What's going on?"

Juliet's pace was a little faster than she would have liked, her pitch higher too. She took a slow breath and rubbed her eyes. Panicking would not help Mia.

"I fucking hate this day," Mia said. "I can't keep doing this all the time. It's making me crazy."

"Okay," Juliet said softly.

"I fucking hate it. I hate this day, Juliet. I really hate it."

"You want to talk me through it?" This earned Juliet a shuddering cry over the line. "Or we can go with distraction if you like."

"I'm sorry I called." Juliet could hear the strain in her voice, the effort to articulate words through her breathlessness. "I just needed to hear someone. There's no one else here, and I…"

Juliet held the phone, waiting with patient silence.

"I'm not always like this." Mia's voice was a whisper.

"Hey, don't worry. We're all sometimes like this."

Mia hiccupped a laugh. "Yeah?"

"Yeah, seriously." Juliet could imagine her blotchy skin and the tears coursing down her face.

"I don't…I don't know what to say."

"It's okay. If you want me to just stay on the phone while you cry, I'm good with that. Or we can talk, whatever might make you feel a bit better."

"Are you this nice to every girl you meet in an airport?"

"Only the hot ones." Squeezing the bridge of her nose, Juliet cursed at how the words had rolled unfiltered off her tongue. She should never have had that bottle of wine.

She heard a short, sharp bark of amusement over the line. "Is that right?"

"Was that a laugh?" Juliet asked. "Because if that's all it takes, then the rest of this phone call should be pretty easy." She heard Mia sniffle and the distinct sound of skin on skin, likely the sound of Mia wiping tears from her cheeks.

"If it makes you feel any better, I don't phone every blonde I meet in a flood of tears, Juliet."

"Just a select few, hey?"

"Just the mysterious cute ones."

Juliet smiled. Mia's changed tone seemed to suggest Juliet was helping her mood. "Hmmm, so they have to be not just cute, but mysterious too. You've got standards."

They fell into a brief silence until Mia asked, "Were you doing something when I phoned? I hope I didn't interrupt you."

Juliet smiled and shook her head at her empty room. "Not at all. I may have just polished off a bottle of wine and was contemplating getting under the blankets rather than where I had collapsed on top of them. Are you at home? You're not in some dark alley somewhere?"

"I don't think a drink would have helped me tonight. And yeah, I'm at home. A dark alley? I'm not in London, you know."

Juliet laughed. "That's right, you're in the middle of nowhere. So, you're at home and what—curled up on the sofa having a meltdown?"

"Pretty much. I'll umm...I'll explain properly sometime. Tomorrow, even, but I just really need to not be thinking about this. So, to answer your earlier question, distraction would be great."

Juliet hesitated only momentarily. "I get that." She kicked at the sheets underneath her until she could slide down the bed to lie down. She tried to spread the duvet over herself. "And I promise I won't talk about the weather, but I just have to say that it is freezing over here. I'm going to have to sort out some better heating, because this is insane."

"Tell me about it—the weather anyway. It's been snowing on and off here most of the day, in between rain and sleet. Although now I'm back inside, I've got the heat high, so it's more like summer in here."

"Oh that's cruel! I need more clothes on inside than I do outside."

"You need a better apartment, Juliet."

"Nah, it's all right for the moment. It'll do, anyway. Speaking of, have you given some more thought to coming to visit? Or have I successfully put you off my apartment?"

Mia seemed to have settled, her voice more stable and her breathing even. "I would like to, but only if that's actually okay with you. I mean, I can come whenever suits; it's not like I have a schedule."

"And clearly I have a whole heap of structure too! Come whenever you like, no stress at all. You can fly into Brussels or Paris. Even Amsterdam isn't far. And I can show you the sights of Bruges or the best pub. I'm trying several of them to make sure I know the best one."

Mia laughed again. "It's a tough job to try them all out. Do you just go on your own, or have you met some people?" Her mood did seem to be improving, Juliet thought.

"I just go in on my own—a few drinks and I end up talking to anyone. Not much different than back in the States."

There was a pause over the line. "I could never go into a bar or club on my own for a night out, I don't think."

"What?" Juliet asked loudly, laughing. "Where are those feminist principles? It's empowering. I'll show you the ropes."

"I would to a café or restaurant, maybe, even a movie—and I do. But I don't know about a bar."

"What's the worst that could happen?" Juliet asked.

"I don't know," Mia said. "Someone takes advantage of you."

"Maybe I'm the one taking advantage of others," Juliet teased. "I'm kidding. I know what you're getting at. I just figure that anything can happen anytime I walk out the door, so some risks are worth taking."

"True, fair call. So, how has the writing been going?"

Juliet groaned, palm of her hand smacking lightly against her forehead. "Did you have to ask?"

Mia laughed. "That good, huh?"

"Worse. I have written some, a little you know. Maybe a chapter, but it's shit. It really is."

"I'm sure it's not."

"Oh it is," Juliet said firmly. "I should delete it and start again, but I just can't bring myself to do it. I'll delete it and then have nothing. I have no idea what I'm going to do."

"Do you think you're just stressing too much and so there's too much pressure?"

"Thanks, Doctor Phil. Probably. Who knows, actually? Either way, I don't have anything decent written. I keep thinking that maybe I should just phone my editor and call it quits, try and figure out a way to pay back my advance."

"No, don't," Mia said. "Not yet. Just give yourself some time. You've got six months, right?"

"With days ticking away..."

"Well, wait until the end of the six months, and if it's still all out of the question, I'll take care of that advance for you."

Juliet quickly laughed, a mix of awkwardness and amazement, until she absorbed the genuineness in Mia's voice. "I couldn't let you do that."

"We'll argue about that in six months' time."

Juliet couldn't place the unsettled feeling in her stomach. Six months? Mia and her would still be talking in six months?

"Got that?" Mia asked after a long moment of silence between them.

"Yeah." She needed to move the conversation away from the security of their friendship, though it seemed ridiculous that they couldn't talk about what had made Mia phone her for the first time and in a flood of tears. Meanwhile, Juliet could only talk so much about herself in the interest of distraction before she started to feel conflicted and uncomfortable. The topics edged past superficial without her even realising it.

"So, what's your plan for the rest of the night? Straight to bed? I'm a little concerned that I'll hang up and you'll just curl back up on the sofa crying."

"I'd like to say that won't happen," Mia said, her breath sounding heavy to Juliet all of a sudden. "But there's no guarantee. I'm not quite as foetal as I was a little while ago, though."

"I'd kind of prefer that not to happen. Can I help?"

"You have, trust me. I probably should have phoned you when I didn't sound completely suicidal, sorry about that."

"You really need to stop apologising to me, and I mean really, *really* need to stop." Juliet chuckled. "So, have you eaten tonight? Showered?"

"Ah, no and no to that."

"Right. So when you're ready, you're going to get up and walk into the kitchen. You're going to open the fridge and tell me what's in there." Juliet made her tone authoritarian and her pace slow, serious.

"Mmm?" Mia asked, and Juliet could almost hear the small smile.

"Yep, that's right."

"I've got it sorted. Really, I'm okay."

"I know," Juliet said. "This isn't about you, it's about me. I have no food, so I'm living vicariously through you. So go on, onto your feet, and tell me what you have to eat."

"I know what you're doing."

"Then get on with it. You need to eat, Mia, and I bet you haven't had a thing most of the day."

"I had breakfast."

"And now it's eight thirty at night."

"Okay, okay." The sound of the seal breaking on the fridge met Juliet's ear. "There's heaps of food."

"Awesome. What looks good?"

"Umm, there's a pasta salad, which is good, some cut-up fruit, yogurt, juice, soda. Ah, some cold meats, cheese, eggs, a few jars of…something—olives, maybe." Despite the breadth of options, Mia sounded positively uninterested.

"Talk about well stocked. This definitely isn't a game we should both play, because I think I've got an old loaf of bread and some cheese—and a shitload of wine, of course. Well, what do you think? Some pasta salad and a juice are probably good—no preparation and all."

"Yeah, I guess. I'm really not hungry though."

"So grab a bowl and a glass, or you can eat straight out of the containers if you like. I won't tell anyone."

"Nah," Mia said. "I think I'll go get a bowl. You're not going to need photographic evidence of this, are you?"

"I expect that I'll be able to tell when you're actually chewing."

"Juliet!" They both laughed simultaneously. "You are quite insane, you know that?"

"What? It's hard. I'm all the way over here, and you're all crying and upset and not telling me what it's about. What am I supposed to do?"

"I have never met anyone like you," Mia said. Over the line, Juliet heard the clanking of a bowl on something, wood perhaps, and the sound of liquid filling a glass. "Where have you been my entire life?"

"Ha ha, running amok. You know that."

"I find that hard to believe. Surely you haven't spent your whole life going from place to place."

"For the most part, bar a few attempts at settling down."

"Didn't work out?" Mia asked.

"Not so much." Juliet's shoulders rolled forward, and she bit on her lower lip before continuing. "My choice in women, not so great. Or maybe their choice in women is not so great. I'm not sure I'm a great catch."

"Maybe you just haven't met the right person…yet."

"Yeah." Juliet shrugged to an empty room. "Sounds like a good excuse to me."

"Sometimes we run for a reason, right? It doesn't have to always be our fault. There are reasons, contributing factors. It's hard to not blame ourselves."

"What makes you think I've run, Mia?"

"Hmmm oh, I don't know. You don't talk about anyone or anything like it belongs somewhere, so I'm just guessing. Sorry."

"I didn't say you were wrong," Juliet said. "And I'm obviously more transparent than I like."

"Are you kidding me? You're like a puzzle, and the pieces are spread all over the globe. Don't be less transparent; I won't stand a chance then."

Juliet laughed. "How's that dinner going?"

"Nice segue. Dinner is fine. How much do I have to eat, Boss?"

"Just a little. I'm happy as long as you've had something."

"Are you going to direct me to the shower as well? 'Cause this conversation could take a whole new turn."

"That sounds suspiciously seductive." Juliet grinned. The conversation was finishing with a completely different tone from where it had started, thankfully.

"You know what I said about mysterious blondes."

"Now I'm not mistaken: that is actually flirtatious, right?"

"Maybe a little," Mia laughed. "Which is *clearly* effective, given I'm in a different country."

"True. And you really do need to shower and get into bed and sleep. Sleep is good."

"You need to sleep as well. You were in bed when I called, weren't you?"

"Still am. I would have gotten up, but I was hoping the slight drunkenness that I was feeling wouldn't be obvious through the phone if I just stayed in bed and didn't move. Did it work?"

"Very well. I never would have been able to tell."

"Too kind. I have to back up, actually. Some of my neighbours are insisting on drinks tomorrow afternoon or night. Apparently the gossip mill says I'm some lonely chick that needs buddies to show her around."

"Oh, you'll have to call me and tell me how it goes. That sounds like a great distraction for me."

"Ack. They'll probably try and set me up with some guy or do shots off the table."

"As I was saying, that would make a great story; perfect distraction."

"I'll keep that in mind—try and get some material for you. Hey, are you in your bathroom yet?"

"And if that was flirting, you need to do some work on your skills," Mia said. "I should let you go."

"You going to be okay?"

"Yeah, thank you—so much. You got me back to sane."

"Anytime. I'll touch base with you tomorrow, okay?"

"Thanks. And hey, before you go, Juliet…" Mia's voice dropped back down to barely a whisper.

"Mmm?"

Mia's sharp intake of breath whistled down the phone line. "Today, umm, today was, is, the anniversary of a death. Someone really important, it was a…a big thing."

"Oh Mia, I'm sorry. I'm so sorry. I had no idea."

"I know. I just wanted you to know that…I'm not crazy. I'm just…"

"You're sad. I know. I really do understand. Today sucks for you."

"It does. Thanks."

"All right, take your shower and get into bed and try and get some sleep."

"You too," Mia replied, seeming unsure as to how to end the call.

Juliet smiled. "Yep, and just so you know, I'm looking awesome in jeans and a hoodie and socks too. And my hair hasn't been brushed. Still think I'm hot?"

"You can't wear jeans to bed!"

"No such thing as can't. It's definitely not the first time."

"Thanks for making me laugh," Mia said. "Talk to you soon, okay? Keep me up to date with how your drinks go tomorrow."

"Will do. Night, Mia."

"See you."

Juliet sunk back and scooted down the bed, covers up to her neck. She rolled onto her side and curled the duvet into her fists, tugging it close. Maybe she owed it to herself to try just one more time. Maybe Mia was worth one more risk.

When five young people knocked on her apartment door the next day, Juliet had picked up her bag with great reluctance and left with them. She laughed and she smiled, chatted idly, and tolerated the introductions. All the while, her mind wandered, contemplating when it was that she had gotten old, and when seemingly intelligent people in their mid-twenties had changed their approach to fashion.

Short skirts and knee-high UGG boots didn't make a winter's outfit in any universe.

Aided by a number of wines and one unfortunate tequila shot, Juliet lasted a few hours, listening to tales of their last "huge" night and their declarations on what the going rates for various drugs were, all oral of course. Intravenous was apparently for the young and stupid. And addicted, Juliet had managed to contribute.

She texted Mia after a few hours, needing a break from the perfectly nice but somewhat immature group.

Hi, out with the youth of today. Odd. How are you doing tonight?

Doing okay, thanks to you. Any setups yet?

Juliet smiled, though her neighbours had gone oblivious, disappearing in pairs to the bathroom and returning with pinpoint pupils.

"You want?" one asked Juliet, and she politely turned down the offer. She quickly texted Mia back.

Not yet, just got offered an unidentified tablet though—score.

Don't take unknown substances!!! You'll end up in the hospital.

Don't worry, turned it down. The tequila was rough enough for me.

Easy on the tequila; that crap is harsh.

"Juliet, you kicking on? We're going to move, got some dancin' to do."
There was a brief display of uncoordinated movement, supposedly dancing.
"No, no thanks, actually. I'm good. I'm thinking of heading back home."
"Oh come on, come on girl! You look like the dancing type."
Juliet shook her head, the British couple reaching for her hands in an attempt
to tug her to her feet. The other three were from Belgium, perpetual students at
the nearby college.
"Nah, honestly I'm exhausted. You guys go ahead. I've had a great night.
Dank uwel."
"Oh, Flemish!" One of the male students bent to kiss Juliet's cheek. *"Het is
niks, graag gedaan."*
Juliet laughed. "Say what?"
His friend explained. "He said, 'You're welcome.'"
"Oh, right. I need to learn a few more phrases! Have a good night. Don't do
anything too crazy."
"Are you right to get home?"
"Yeah, I'll just finish this drink and take off. I'm fine."
"Nice to meet you, Juliet. We should do it again some time." A few more
choruses of the same sentiment rounded, and they disappeared out the door in a
range of cheers and loud comments. She was definitely feeling old.
Picking her phone back up again off the sticky table, she wiped it on her
jeans and tapped a reply to Mia.

*The kids have gone. Just finishing my drink, and I'm heading home to bed.
I think the tequila went to my head.*

Go home and go to bed. Drink lots of water.

Getting there. How many hours spent crying on the couch/bed/floor today?

A few moments passed, and Juliet sipped on her wine, enjoying her time
people watching as the bar seemed to swell with a wave of patrons.

None at all, actually, just some quiet reflection. You must have fixed me.

I doubt that, but I'm glad you had a better day. You deserved a reprieve. All right, I'm going to head home. Talk to you later?

Let me know how you pull up tomorrow. :-)

Will do.

Juliet pushed her wine glass across the table before pocketing the phone in her jeans and grabbing her bag sitting next to her hip on the seat. She weaved through the crowd, tucking some strands of curled hair behind her ears as she secured the bag across her body. She reached the door and stepped out, groaning as a rush of freezing air met her. Tugging her coat closer around her body, Juliet shoved her hands into her pockets and with her head down, started to make her way along the sidewalk. It was only a fifteen-minute walk back to her apartment. Or if she wanted, she would come across a taxi rank just a bit further up the street and on the other side of the road.

She didn't get a chance to decide, feeling a rough and calloused hand wrap around her mouth and a tight arm grip her around the middle. She managed only a muffled cry and a slight struggle before she was pulled down the side of a closed shop. She couldn't understand a single one of the range of harsh words spoken into her ear, but the tone of the coarse voice was clear enough, as was the intentions of the large body controlling her struggling limbs.

She arched her back and tried to shake her head to rid herself of the palm pressed over her mouth, failing as her face met the corner of the building, bricks tearing at the skin over her cheekbone. A wave of nausea spread through her as she was turned and forced back, shoulders and head taking the brunt of the force. A knee connected with her abdomen, and she doubled over, crying out as the hand dropped from her face to her neck.

The bag across her body was being forcibly tugged, caught around her as the man tried in clear desperation to tear it from her. She fell towards the ground, and, again, she found his knee connecting with her ribs and stomach as he crushed on top of her. He pulled so hard on her bag that the strap tore, but not before the cotton material ripped across her neck, burning the soft skin.

"Just take it, please." If the man understood what she was saying, he didn't acknowledge it. He stared at her, one hand lingering at her neck, then pulled her up a few inches off the ground. When he slammed her back down, the grey light from the street front dulled and her vision tunnelled, slowly fading to black as she lost consciousness.

CHAPTER 7

Blinking, Juliet tried to orientate herself as her surroundings slowly came into focus. She groaned and tried to move, elbow grating along the cement. A sharp pain pierced her side and wrapped around her abdomen. She slumped backwards, her head cushioned where she had expected to meet the hard ground.

A gentle hand gripped her shoulder, and she looked up: a middle-aged man talked at her, voice slow and gentle, though she couldn't make out any words. Realisation dawned upon her. She wasn't in America. She was in Belgium, and she was supposed to be walking back to her apartment. A flash crossed her vision—the tall, strong male ripping the bag from across her body. She whimpered again, and her eyes drifted to a woman standing a few steps away, cell phone to her ear. She murmured a few soft words at Juliet.

"Engels…" Juliet whispered, bringing a hand up to tap her cheek and forehead. "Engels."

The woman, dressed elegantly in long black slacks and a thick red coat, muttered something to the man and crouched down to Juliet. "English, you speak English?"

"Yes," Juliet said, bringing blood tinged fingertips in front of her eyes. She tried again to move.

"Lie there, I've called an ambulance."

"My bag?"

The man coughed and repositioned the rolled-up coat under Juliet's head, dabbing at her forehead with the sleeve. "He ran off with it," he said, throwing a hand back over his shoulder to indicate towards the street. "Don't try to move."

"Thanks," Juliet said. "I think I'm okay."

"The ambulance will be here soon, they'll take you to the hospital."

"I don't think I need…" She tried to tug her legs up, but her hip flexing sent another sharp pain across her stomach.

"You need the hospital." The woman scooped her long, dark hair to fall over one shoulder and sat down next to Juliet, a soothing hand resting on her forearm. "What's your name?"

"Juliet."

"You need the hospital. Is there someone we can call?"

"No, thank you. I'm here…" She moaned again. "I'm here on my own."

The woman's soft fingers wrapped around Juliet's forearm and squeezed gently. "We'll wait with you until the ambulance arrives, you'll be fine."

Tears burned her eyes as Juliet gave an awkward nod. She closed them. Her entire body hurt.

A few hours later, Juliet was sitting up on a gurney with its back raised and with a pillow behind her head. She had been treated exceptionally well, from the kind strangers that had found her and called the paramedics to the hospital staff that went out of their way to communicate with her in English and calm her. Being in an emergency room in a country where she didn't speak the language was frightening. It made Juliet wonder for the first time what it would be like to be a foreigner back home in this situation. They would probably just call in an interpreter for a few minutes and get frustrated that their visitor couldn't speak English.

Juliet couldn't praise the staff enough.

As she had been patiently told a number of times, the scans of her head were clear, no bleeding of the brain or skull fractures. Her eye socket and mandible were heavily bruised, but not broken, and the two lacerations on her face had required only a few stitches.

Her ribs were the most damaged, with multiple fractures, and she was lucky to not have had one of those ribs puncture her lung. Scans did show some bruising and a small laceration to her liver, but thankfully it required only conservative management. They were insisting on keeping her overnight, and if Juliet was honest, she was in no rush to leave the safety and warmth of the hospital.

She was moved to a short stay ward, an area for observation for patients not being admitted to the hospital. It was quieter than the emergency department, and she was fortunate to get her own room. Juliet deduced that her insurance must have been more than adequate. Again, they made sure she had a nurse whose English-speaking skills probably surpassed many in the States.

"How are you feeling, Juliet?" The scrub-clad nurse graced her with a genuine grin.

"I'm okay, thank you." Juliet offered the young woman a smile in return.

"Do you need some pain relief?"

Juliet shook her head.

"All right, then. I'm just going to get some water, see if we can't clean some of this blood off you. Is that all right?"

"Yes, please. Umm, can you tell me what time it is?"

"Mmm." She looked at her watch. "It's two thirty in the morning."

Juliet's eyes widened. "Oh, I had no idea."

"Do you need to make some calls? I can arrange a phone if you need to contact someone back home."

Again, she shook her head, tensing her shoulders and relaxing them. She was starting to feel stiff and uncomfortable, quite in pain, probably from a combination of the analgesia and lack of movement. "Did I have a cell phone when I came in?" she asked, aware that her clothes had been quickly removed and replaced with a thin gown on her arrival. Only her plain cotton panties remained on.

Squatting to the floor, the nurse reached under her bed and beneath her rolled up jeans and jacket. As she rose, she handed Juliet her phone that had been hiding underneath the clothes. "That's all you had on you."

"Yeah, my bag got taken."

"Police were here earlier. They'll come back tomorrow and take you back to your apartment. Your keys were in your bag, right?"

"Yeah, keys and wallet. Nothing else really, everything else I left back in my apartment."

"Passport?"

"Ah, in my backpack in the closet, thankfully. It's such a hassle to get a new one."

"Well, if you need to make some calls, just let me know and I'll step out."

"It's a little late to be phoning at this hour."

"People don't mind being woken for things like this, I assure you. I've never once had someone get upset for being woken to come in."

Juliet smiled. "She's in Scotland, can't exactly come in; it would just worry her. I'll message her at a better hour."

"Okay." She smiled, hands on her hips. "I'll be back in a few minutes, see if we can't make that hair of yours blonde again."

Sighing, Juliet pulled the sheets higher until they reached over her chest and tucked under her armpits. She pulled a few strands of hair away from her head. She hadn't glanced in a mirror yet, but she assumed she was quite the sight, bloody and bruised. The bruising would only get worse too. They had mentioned that the stuff on her face wouldn't fade for a week or so and that her ribs would take just under two months to fully heal. She should be able to move more freely in a few weeks though, cough without agony in a couple.

She should have stayed home and worked on her book; what had she been thinking?

Returning with a round green bowl, a number of wash cloths, and a packet of wipes, the nurse placed it all on the meal tray table and wheeled it closer to Juliet's bedside. She sat gently on the edge of her bed and surveyed her face. "Pretty bad, huh?" Juliet asked.

"It'll look better once I've finished."

Juliet offered a sad smile. "You've all been amazing to me, really lovely. I can't really complain."

"Will your friend from Scotland come over? Look after you for a bit?"

Shrugging, Juliet pondered the question. "I don't know, maybe. We don't know each other that well, but she was planning a trip over here soon. Maybe she can bring it forward, I'm not sure. It's not so bad. I can look after myself."

"You're probably looking forward to some sleep."

"Kind of, I don't know if I can sleep, but I'm tired—exhausted, actually."

"It's been a big night."

"Yeah, big night."

She allowed the nurse to finish cleaning her up in silence. "Thank you," she said when the tugging on her hair ceased and the nurse moved away from her bed.

"It'll do until you can shower. You feeling all right?"

"Yeah."

"The doctor has written up something to help you sleep, would you like it?"

Juliet considered it briefly. "No, thank you. I'm fine." She could probably manage for a few hours, and figured she would wake up sore enough without the added fatigue from a sedative.

"All right. Well, you're due for some more pain medication, so that should help a little. It's important you get some rest, Juliet."

When the woman returned, Juliet took the two white capsule-shaped tablets offered to her with water. "Thank you," she murmured, for what felt like the one hundredth time that evening.

"Rest. It's nurse's orders."

Juliet smiled and obliged her by closing her eyes, waiting until the door was closed before opening them again. She sighed heavily and grazed her fingers over her face and through her hair. There was just a small amount of artificial light coming through the glass window on the door to her room. Despite her efforts to push the evening's events out of her mind, her eyes continued to close, and she replayed the moment a rough hand had appeared from nowhere and covered her mouth. She felt the involuntary push of her legs as she was dragged from the sidewalk.

She forced her eyes open and looked around the room, feeling how her heart rate had raised. Sleep would be a nice reprieve from the horrific memories that seemed intent on preoccupying her every thought.

Forcing her mind to concentrate, Juliet focussed on the phone call she'd had with Mia, the sob that had half caught in Mia's throat, and the way she had tearfully laughed. If she could trick herself into concentrating on Mia for a few moments, perhaps sleep would find her.

And aided by the slow absorption of the pills, she did slip into sleep. Slowly and sporadically, back and forth from being fully awake, but eventually she dozed.

She didn't wake up until a blood pressure cuff started swelling on her upper arm and a peg-like device was placed on her index finger. She blinked twice in quick succession as a tall older female in the same familiar green scrubs smiled at her.

"Just taking vitals," she said, chart held against her hip as she jotted some readings into the small squares on a form. "How are you feeling?"

"Umm, fine, I think." Juliet felt sleepy, confused. "Ah, what time is it?"

"It's ten in the morning. We held off for as long as we could."

"That's okay. That's fine." Juliet rushed to appease, because not only had she slept, but she had slept for longer than she would usually.

"You take your time," the woman said. "The doctor will be around later on. I expect he will discharge you. The police and your insurance company have already been on the phone." Juliet nodded, placing a hand on the mattress by her hip and trying to slide herself up the bed. "I'll put the back up a little, is that better?"

"Yeah, thanks. Can I have a shower at all?"

"Of course, don't rush up, just wait a few minutes. I'll get you some soap and a toothbrush, a towel. Were your clothes cut off? We have some supplies to get you home if you need another top or sweatshirt."

Juliet shrugged. "I don't know."

Reaching underneath the bed, she pulled out the ball of rolled-up clothes and placed them onto Juliet's lap. She went about untangling them. The jeans were still okay, and the top was fine. The jacket she had been wearing was splattered with blood.

"Don't worry, I'll get you something warm. It's cold out there today."

Nodding absentmindedly, Juliet waited silently until the nurse returned with a sweatshirt, towel, and a few toiletries. With Juliet's hand on the nurse's arm, Juliet allowed her to slowly guide her off the bed, her grip still firm.

"I'm okay," Juliet said.

"Nice and slowly. I'll show you to the bathroom. Don't be too enthusiastic with the washing, all right?"

Left alone in the bathroom, Juliet used the toilet first, gasping as she tried to lower herself smoothly onto the seat. Every muscle pulled with the effort, and her ribs seemed to emanate waves of pain with every twist that was slightly outside a straight position. Nausea swept through her with the exertion.

When she finally stood in front of the mirror above the basin, she slowly untied the gown and let it fall to the floor. She wasn't sure if she had convinced herself that it would be worse, but she didn't react to the image that stared back at her. She just worked her way methodically from her face and down to her hips, the rest of her body hidden from the reflection. Her face was swollen and mostly red. The bruising would appear shortly, and the stitches were just visible behind the clear sticky plasters that covered them. The side of her chest was a dull red, and there were dots of blue that signalled the first signs of bruising. Her neck was splattered with specks and lines from where her bag had been torn from her.

Turning back to the shower in the corner of the room, she turned the water on and let it wash over her chest and stomach down to her legs. It stung in places as the warm water met exposed skin lacerations. She would never complain about a shaving cut again. It took her almost ten minutes, but she managed to work some shampoo unevenly through her hair.

By the time she left the bathroom in jeans, a top from the night before, and an oversized sweater, she at least felt slightly more human. And she was moving a little easier too, not quite as afraid of every turn and flex; she could manage the pain. When she returned to her room, a breakfast tray with food sat on the wheeled table and her phone next to it had a message from Mia.

Hey, so how did the night end up? You didn't end up going out with them did you?

She took a sip of juice. The liquid felt good in her mouth, and her stomach didn't jolt at the sudden intrusion. There was an unknown but agreeable flavour of marmalade spread over her toast.

Turns out not so great. I'm in a hospital.(!!!)

Her phone rang instantaneously, and she debated whether or not to answer it. As she stared at the silent ringing, the option was taken out of her hands as the call ended. A text followed seconds later.

What happened? Are you okay? Can you talk?

Juliet was halfway through typing a reply when her phone rang again; she answered it this time. "Hey," she said softly, too exhausted to manage much of a façade.

"Juliet? What happened?"

"I'm all right, Mia, don't stress out." She tried to swallow the emotion in her voice. She had underappreciated the value of a familiar voice. Mia was emanating a stressed tone, though, whereas Juliet had been calm and controlled when Mia had phoned her upset.

"Were you in a car accident? Are you hurt?" Mia asked. "I thought you were heading home after we messaged last night?"

"Not exactly. I'm okay. I was just walking home and got mugged. Some guy took my bag."

Mia gasped. "What?"

"I know. Fucked, right?"

"Are you really okay? I mean, you're in the hospital. Of course you're not actually okay." Juliet could hear Mia's pacing through the phone, the hasty steps that she was taking and the slight breathlessness.

"Ah, I'm a little beat up. I'll survive."

"Juliet, can you not do that?" Mia huffed out an impatient-sounding breath. "I'm worried, and you're being all vague."

Juliet sighed, trying to blink away the tears before they threatened to fall. "I've got some bruises, a few stitches in my face and head." She hesitated, throat tingling with a slight burn, and her voice caught as she tried to elaborate. "A couple of fractured ribs. I kind of look like I've gone a few rounds." She squeezed her eyes shut, and tears gathered on her lower lashes.

There was a long exhalation from the other end of the line. "Sweetie," Mia murmured softly.

Juliet clenched her teeth, a precarious hold on control. "You'll make me cry," she managed to say, with even a slight scoff mixed in.

"You want me to come?"

Shaking her head, Juliet took a moment to respond. "No, no, not right now. I have to see the police and get back to my apartment. I might need your help to sort out replacement cards and stuff, though, if that's okay."

"Of course, whatever I can do. There's a fax and Internet and everything here. I can phone places and pretend to be you. You'll need some money to tide you over. I can get some sent to the manager of your block or to the local bank. But we can sort that later. You sure you're all right to be discharged?"

"Yeah, there's a doctor that will come around soon. I suppose they do ward rounds or something. Apparently, the police have already phoned. I don't even have my keys. Everything was in my bag. This is just a hassle as much as anything else."

"Yeah, well, the logistics we can sort. You have to look after yourself, though. That's more important."

Juliet chuckled. "Says the girl who hasn't just had all of her cards and shit stolen."

"Great point. But you have broken bones and stitches. Priorities, okay? You need to take it easy."

"I know I do. Hey, the doctor is here. Can I call you back later?"

"Anytime. Or I'll call you."

"I'll let you know what's happening. Thanks, Mia."

"Bye."

"Bye."

Juliet's eyes fixed on the team of doctors standing at the end of her bed. "Hello." Her gaze dropped to the barely touched meal still on her table.

There was some brief communication between them, presumably in Flemish, before they focussed on Juliet. One stepped forward, and Juliet guessed he was one of the senior doctors by how he had dominated the previous conversation. "How are you feeling?"

Forcing a smile, Juliet nodded, though if one more person asked her how she was feeling, she might just walk herself out of the hospital. "Okay, thank you."

"Pain?"

"Only a little, manageable," she said.

"Would you like to leave?"

Juliet raised her eyebrows. Was it up to her if she left the hospital or not? "Umm, yeah, I guess so. Yes."

"You can be discharged with some pain management, and you'll need the stitches removed in a week. Here or a local practitioner is fine. You have some papers in your chart, and I will sign those for your insurance company."

"Okay." She was somewhat awestruck and immensely appreciative of the English communication. "Umm, the nurse was going to redress the stitches," she said, tapping her face, just above her eyebrow, and they all nodded in unison at her. "And the police are coming back?"

"Yes, they are outside waiting. No rush. You should eat breakfast." He checked his watch and smiled. "Or lunch."

"Thank you so much. You have all been wonderful to me."

As if on cue, the nurse from earlier returned, a few sealed dressings in her hands. She had a brief conversation with the team before they all filed out of her room.

"Teaching hospital," she explained to Juliet. "That's why there's so many of them. Only trust the ones in scrubs. The others are interns and students."

"They're the bosses?"

"Yes, and blue are the trainees."

"I remember the black scrubs from last night."

"They probably checked you over first, ordered some scans and X-rays. A loss of consciousness means you come in as a high priority."

Juliet nodded slowly. She hadn't spent much time around hospitals, just the occasional visit. "So we'll just change these, and you can head off."

Reaching over to the table, Juliet took a couple of bites of cold toast as the nurse went about putting gloves on and peeling back the plastic dressing covers. "I gave a statement to the police last night, didn't I?" She stared quietly at the wall as she tried to place all the pieces together in some sort of chronological order.

"There are notes in your chart. You spoke to police before they moved you around here. They might have some more questions for you, though."

Juliet shrugged. "If it's anything like home, these people don't get caught anyway."

"You never know."

Rolling her eyes, Juliet stilled as the adhesive was peeled from her skin, then some antiseptic applied. "Any doctor can take the stitches out in a week?"

"Yes, there are plenty of local doctors around, and I've got some discharge papers for you to take, so they can just be given to them. Any new pain or any changes or concerns, you should come back."

"Thanks."

"I wish all my patients were as polite as you. Now stay and finish what you can and stop at the nurses' station on your way out. I'll have your papers and some analgesia ready for you."

When she was left alone, Juliet finished the slice of bread and recovered the plate, reaching for her phone as it vibrated next to her on the bed. Another message from Mia.

Sending you a virtual hug xo.

Almost the exact words Juliet had typed in an e-mail to Mia a week or so earlier. Pushing her feet into shoes, Juliet sat on the edge of the bed and tapped at her phone.

The hug made me feel so much better. :-) Just about to leave hospital, talk to you soon. xo

A kiss and a hug, right there for the first time, in black and white.

It took Juliet three attempts before her key card lit green and she could open the door to the hotel room. At the huge king-size bed and the folded fluffy white towels, she breathed a heavy sigh of relief and could already imagine collapsing onto it while watching some terrible cable show.

She hobbled to the opposite side of the room, leaning on the doorway and poking her head into the bathroom. There was a large bath, and given that her knee had only just started aching, the idea of a soak in soapy water was deliciously appealing.

The day had been long and generally crap despite the support and understanding everyone had shown her. When the police had taken her back to her apartment, they found that it had been entered and her belongings ransacked. The only saving grace was that her passport, still held securely inside a zippered side compartment in her backpack, and her clothes too were still all there despite everything having been tossed around her bedroom. Her laptop and cables, however, were nowhere to be seen. She had given a minor cheer of excitement when she found a small USB stick on the floor of the kitchen. Whether it had been deliberately discarded or had just fallen out of her computer, she wasn't sure, but she was endlessly grateful.

She was surprisingly ordered and calm, just going about collecting her gear and liaising with the police. She made sure that she had the police reports and had them scan and e-mail a copy to her and to Mia's e-mail addresses as well. Mia, at Juliet's hesitant request, had taken care of some of the insurance side of things. Within a few hours, Mia had had the insurance company arrange more than adequate accommodation for Juliet; in fact it was perfect.

However, it was somewhat ironic that the best accommodation she had managed to have in years was a result of a traumatic assault. Her life was nothing but absurdities.

Not unexpectedly, her phone started ringing. It was at least the fourth time that day she had spoken with Mia. And Juliet was starting to want to answer each call. If she was being honest, she waited for them. "I owe you," Juliet said immediately as she answered.

"You do?"

"Yep, this place is incredible. What did you do, threaten the insurance company?"

Mia laughed. "Would I do that? No, not at all. It fails the PR test if they put you up in some dive, so it definitely didn't take much convincing. Those med reports you had sent through also helped guilt them into things."

"I can't wait to sleep," Juliet murmured, "and the bed looks awesome."

"You must be exhausted."

"Yeah, pretty much. It's been quite the day."

"How goes the pain level and stuff?"

Juliet muttered a nonsensical sound. "All right I suppose," she said. "Not great. Trying to pack my bag and just moving in and out of cars…bit rough on the ribs. I'm starting to look delightful too. My eye can barely open with the swelling."

"Ack, that's awful. You poor thing."

"Oh, don't be too sympathetic. You've just about organised my life today; not sure how it would have gone without you."

A snigger drifted through the phone.

"What?" Juliet asked.

"Nothing," Mia said. "I'm just happy to hear you're okay with me helping you out."

"Oh, have I not been grateful? God, because I am. So much."

"I know. I'm only kidding. There are a few more things I need to organise for you, though, so you have to put up with me a little longer. Your insurance company…Oh, by the way, I'm now best mates with your file manager, Jerry. He's oddly chipper. Anyway, they want to move you tomorrow to somewhere different for a week. I don't really get why, something about vacancies with their usual motel chain, I think. So you'll need to be sorted around ten. They'll arrange transport and all that jazz."

"Are you kidding? I just want to hide in the one place for at least a week. I really shouldn't be seen in public."

"Have you thought anything about what you're going to do? This wasn't really part of the plan."

Juliet sighed, and she felt her chest tighten. She hadn't really expressed it, but the idea of continuing with her initial sabbatical idea was frightening. "I really don't know. Can you just stay in touch, though? I mean, you don't have to, and I know that you're going through…something…something too…"

"Yes, of course, Juliet." Mia made a point of interrupting her before she could talk herself out of the simple yet cautious request. "It's okay to be scared, you know."

"I'm not *scared*." She was, however, embarrassed and vulnerable, she thought.

"Yeah. And I'm not grieving."

"We're a pair, huh?"

"Absolutely. So, are you going to take a shower and get some rest?"

"I think I'm going to run a bath, actually, soak for a little while. I thanked you, right, for sorting my insurance stuff? I really couldn't have done it today. I don't know what I would have done."

"We're just even now. I owed you for my Christmas…thing."

"Thanks. We'll talk tomorrow?"

"We'll talk tomorrow," Mia confirmed. "And hey, I'm giving you a hug right now, kind of gentle though. Wouldn't want to hurt you."

Juliet laughed lightly, open palm protecting her ribs. "Don't make me laugh."

"Bye, Juliet. Get some sleep."

"Will do. See ya, Mia."

Hanging up, Juliet tossed her phone onto the bed. She turned on the faucets over the bath and padded back across the room. Peeling her clothes off, she left them on the floor, not sure she wanted to keep them. But she would make that decision in the morning. The closet held two robes on wooden hangers, so she withdrew one and carried it to the bathroom, testing the temperature of the water before lowering herself in. Slowly, she stretched back until her shoulders rested against the porcelain with a towel wrapped into a ball that she stuffed under her neck as a pillow. The water lapped over her bruised stomach and up over her breasts, not quite reaching her neck, where the two-inch-wide material burn wrapped over her shoulder and collarbone.

Juliet closed her eyes and locked her damaged body out of her vision. And in the silence of the bathroom, the isolation of the hotel room, she cried thick, heavy tears that didn't stop until her shoulders shuddered and her side protested with a painful throbbing.

CHAPTER 8

Taking a deep breath, Juliet flexed her bicep and lifted her backpack, weighed down with clothes, books, some emptying toiletries, cables, and a few food items that she had collected from her apartment's pantry. She audibly cried out in pain and doubled over at the attempt, bag falling to the floor and toppling on its side. Bending over, she placed two open palms on her thighs and tried to ease air into her lungs. She opened her eyes and stared at the offending object. It was probably only thirty-five pounds, but it was thirty-five pounds she couldn't lift.

She fished around for a stray bill in her pockets, disappointed when she didn't find a random euro. Tapping her thumbs together, Juliet checked the side zippers on her large backpack before digging inside her daypack and around the messy main compartment. When her fingers withdrew with a collection of discarded breath mints, she threw them in the trashcan before returning to scavenge further. Eventually she drew out a rolled up collection of US bills, secured with an elastic hair tie. She figured there must have been some logic in her doing that when she left the States, but for the life of her, she couldn't remember what that was. It would have to do.

A cursory glance at the clock indicated that it was ten fifteen. She was meant to be out by ten.

"Hello," she said into the handset to reception, "could I have someone collect my bags please? I'm in room 1210."

She opened the door a few minutes later, guarding her ribs. "Thank you," Juliet said warmly, holding out four dollars. "I'm so sorry, it's all I have." The porter waved away her offer. She insisted again, and he took the tip, though not before staring openly at her battered face.

"Go ahead," he said, "and I will bring."

The woman behind the check-in desk downstairs did not manage to completely hide her second glance behind a neutral smile as she looked up from the computer monitor.

"I'm checking out of room 1210," Juliet said. "My travel insurer should have arranged payment."

"Yes." She scanned the notes on her file with her index finger. "Yes, all done. There is a gentleman by the chair over there waiting for you. Your bags won't be a moment."

The invisible line in the direction the woman indicated led her gaze to a man standing alone in long black slacks, a white collared shirt, and double-breasted jacket. "Hello," she said as she walked toward him, "I'm Juliet Taylor."

He gently shook Juliet's limp hand. "Ma'am, your bags are on their way down, and then we can get on our way."

"On our way?" Juliet asked.

"Yes, ma'am. Your flight is at ten past three from Brussels. I'll have you there in plenty of time."

"My flight?" The words were out of her mouth before Juliet realised. She repeated them with significant disbelief. "My flight?"

Reaching inside his jacket, he withdrew a folded-up piece of paper. "My instructions state SN 2063 with Brussels Airlines, departure time at three ten. Is that correct?"

Juliet shook her head. "Ah, no, I don't understand. My insurance company was arranging alternative accommodation, umm, a change in hotels. There must be a mix-up, and you're here for someone else."

He pressed a number of keys on his cell phone and held the phone to his ear, jotting down some notes as he carried on a quick conversation. Disconnecting, he met Juliet's expectant look.

"The flight is from Brussels to Edinburgh and booked by a Ms Mia Revira. Is that familiar?"

Juliet opened her mouth to speak and then closed her lips again. "Ah." Her facial muscles tensed, spreading a dull ache into her temples. "Can you wait a moment?"

Stunned, she drew from her hip pocket her phone, the only thing of value that she still owned. The driver stepped back, indicating to the single lounge chair for Juliet to sit. He walked over to the lobby counter to collect Juliet's bags as she hastily dialled Mia, cutting off Mia's soft greeting.

"So there's this man here who thinks he's driving me to the airport to get on a flight to Scotland?"

A prolonged silence drifted between them, and Mia asked quietly, "You're mad?"

"I'm not mad, but I thought I was changing hotels. I mean, you said last night that they were arranging another hotel." The spontaneity was eliciting some panic, given the trauma of the previous thirty-six hours. She softened. "You organised this?"

"It was all starting to get a bit crazy. The insurance will only cover you for so long, and you were going to have to do all this running around to get new cards. I just thought that if you come here, you could get some rest and I could help get everything organised." Mia paused, and Juliet heard her draw in a quick breath. "And then you can go back when you feel better. I have a guest room here, and there's heaps of space."

Again, Mia stopped momentarily. It gave Juliet an opportunity to interrupt, but she was still frozen with disbelief.

"I'm sorry. I should have discussed it with you. I just thought that if I gave you time, you would not want to do it or would want to sort everything out yourself. I didn't mean to just make the decision for you."

"Okay," Juliet said. "Okay."

"Okay? So you'll come? I mean, if you really want to stay, I can sort something else out for you there…"

Juliet glanced around the hotel lobby, eyes scanning from the revolving glass door and across to the restaurant where she'd had a buffet breakfast. She looked at the driver Mia had arranged, who was chatting idly to the staff and a couple of guests.

"I have nothing," she said, "and I've never been in this position before. I have nowhere to go and no money and no one to turn to."

Mia took a moment to answer. "It's not conditional, Juliet. If you want to stay, I'll get back on to Jerry and abuse the crap out of him, if that's what it takes. But you do have someone, okay? You hear me? I know it feels strange, but I'm right here."

"I really don't want to stay." Her whisper came out shaky.

"Then you have a flight to catch."

"I do."

"You do. Okay?"

"How do I…I mean, I can catch a train or something from Edinburgh?"

"I'll be there. I'm not putting you on a train." Mia laughed. "Now go on. You've got an hour-or-two drive ahead of you. Have you got some water?

Something to eat? The guy driving you should have your flight details. Just check in with your passport. But if you need any of the paperwork, let me know. I have it all here."

A slight smile tugged at one corner of Juliet's mouth. "Yeah, I got a bottle from the room, and I may have taken a muffin and apple from breakfast this morning. They're in my bag."

"Nicely done. I'll see you in sunny Scotland, 'kay?"

"Sunny?"

"Shhhh, that's your only job—bring some bloody sunlight with you."

"Mia?"

"Mmmm?"

"Thank you."

"See you soon."

Juliet stared at the floor for a moment. With one eye mostly closed and her head pounding, she slowly leveraged herself into a standing position and nodded at the driver, smiling as much as she could. She was ready to leave.

Of course, Mia had booked her to Edinburgh Airport in priority business class. Juliet shuddered to think how much the fare and the transport Mia had arranged for her was. She would find a way to pay her back. Somehow.

The paracetamol had kept her residual pain to a reasonable level on the short flight as long as she didn't move, but she relied on the random kindness of a woman with long dreadlocks down her back who picked her pack up off the luggage belt and placed it on a trolley for her. The woman was gone as quickly as she appeared, gathering her own backpack as it arrived in front of her and hoisting it easily onto her back. Just another person for Juliet to be grateful to, and she could hardly believe the care everyone around her had provided her—strangers in lines and staff in hospitals, on aircraft. It was all a bit surreal. Perhaps humanity wasn't at all as bad as she had come to believe.

Walking straight through customs at Edinburgh Airport without being given a second glance, Juliet found herself pushing the cart through a relatively thick crowd and bowed her head as she walked until she felt an open palm to the small of her back and she jumped.

"Juliet," Mia said, falling into stride next to her and reaching across to take control of the luggage with one hand. She led them towards the end of the corridor, stopping next to a bundle of long chairs outside the restrooms and a small café. "Let me look at you," she said gently, placing both hands on Juliet's shoulders.

"Hi," Juliet said, raising her dramatically bruised and swollen face. Juliet felt her lips tremble, and she couldn't help but swallow loudly to keep the bile from rising in her throat.

Mia smiled. "You're a mess," she said, fingertips lightly travelling up Juliet's neck until they tenderly touched where Juliet remembered the edge of red and blue coloured over her cheek. The coverings over Juliet's stitches had been peeling just at the corners too, and when she had taken a last look in her hotel room mirror this morning, she'd noticed how the whole effect had given her a slight roughness in contrast to the soft, clean hair that was tied at her neck.

She nodded at Mia, and Juliet's eyes unexpectedly filled with tears. She didn't resist when Mia gently stepped closer and placed her arm around Juliet. Juliet relaxed immediately, propping her chin on Mia's shoulder.

"I'm so glad to see you," Juliet said. It was all she could manage without completely dissolving. She hadn't known just how alone she had felt until Mia's arm had wrapped around her without question.

"Me too," Mia said. "I had no idea what to expect."

Another few moments passed, and Juliet made no effort to move, trying to blink away her tears before stepping backwards. "You look good," she said, changing focus, "and I like the hoodie." Juliet bundled the thick fleecy material in a fist.

"I told you I would do a little shopping."

"It was a good choice."

Mia's glazed dark brown irises betrayed her happiness as Juliet released Mia's hand to carefully wipe at her swollen eye, unable to successfully blink away her emotion.

Mia said, "All right, so I figure we should get moving. It's going to be dark for most of the drive back. But I desperately need a coffee to go and something to eat. You'll have a coffee, right?"

"Ah…" Juliet hesitated, and Mia immediately headed them towards the café queue.

"Skinny latte, right? No, a caramel latte? Espresso? Damn, I swear I knew your coffee order when I was driving here."

Juliet gave Mia an incredulous look. She could barely believe that they were in front of each other again and that things were anything but awkward. "Latte," she answered.

Mia raised her hands up in the air as if wondering what the delay was.

"With one sugar," Juliet added.

"Mmm-hmm, and what else? One of these packaged sandwiches maybe?"

Juliet shook her head quickly. "I'm not really a sandwich fan."

"Oh, thank God, me either."

"I could go for a Thorntons Bar."

With her fingers grazing the counter, Mia collected a few different chocolate bars. "Can you eat crackers, or does it hurt to chew?"

"Sort of. I had some granola for breakfast and had to take really small bites."

Mia added a cylinder of Pringles and requested a tub of grapes and two bottles of water as she withdrew her purse. Who knew where the grapes had been imported from in the middle of winter, Juliet thought, but she supposed that something nutritious to balance out the chocolate was probably important.

"Now, just so you know, I will probably ask multiple times a day, and I don't want to be rude or to smother, but I genuinely care…" Mia handed over some money and took the plastic carry bag of items. They stepped to the side to wait for their coffee order.

"And?"

"Can we have a deal that you answer honestly?"

"Umm, can I know the question before I make that deal?"

"I just want to know how you're feeling and if you are in pain or needing space or whatever. I want you to feel like you can tell me."

"Of course," Juliet said, probably a little too quickly.

"So, well, *that* was genuine!" She affectionately rubbed Juliet's forearm.

"Sorry." Juliet felt sheepish. "I will. I'll make you that deal."

"Okay, so how are you?"

"Not really one to just brush over things, are you?"

Mia shook her head.

"Well, to answer your question, I'm sore and stiff, but thanks to some painkillers earlier, I'm okay if I'm not bending or lifting. And I kind of can't believe how relieved I am to see you."

"Relieved?"

"Yeah, I wasn't so sure. I know I wanted to come, but it just felt weird that we have only known each other what? A couple of weeks, three maybe?"

"That's not exactly crazy," Mia said slowly. "But I promise you I'm not a maniac that has a car full of axes."

Juliet laughed softly, wincing at the painful tug to her ribs. "Besides, I trust you more than some people I've known for most of my life."

Head dropping slightly to the side, she smiled. "I'm trustworthy," she said slowly and clearly.

They were interrupted by the announcement of their coffee order. Mia collected two large paper cups with black lids. "If you can handle these, I've got your bags."

"Easy," Juliet said.

"It's not far to the car; this airport is hardly massive. There's a multistorey car park just across the walkway, maybe only a few minutes. Is that okay?"

"Yeah, I'm good." Juliet watched Mia hoist her backpack onto her shoulders. "What are you doing? We can probably push the trolley through."

Mia gave her a wide grin and a small wink. "I have always wanted to do this," she explained.

"Carry a pack?"

"Be a backpacker!"

"You're insane, Mia," Juliet said, watching in amusement as Mia started to walk, day pack in one hand and large handbag in the other.

She wasn't quite sure how to articulate her gratitude to Mia, so she didn't and just fell into a comfortable silence. She needed to find the words, and she would at some point, but for the moment, she was content to just ride out the day. It all felt like a blur, as clichéd as it sounded, but she still wasn't entirely sure how she went from having a few casual drinks to standing bruised and battered in Edinburgh Airport with Mia protectively looking her over.

"The car is just over here," Mia said, breaking the silence as she led Juliet from the elevator. "It's the black Jeep." She used the remote lock, and the parking lights flashed in front of them. Depositing Juliet's belongings in the trunk, she then opened the passenger door, tossing in her handbag and their bag of snacks. The coffees went into the centre cup holders up front, and she held the passenger door open for Juliet.

"It's a bit high," she said. "Sorry."

"It's fine." Juliet quickly dropped her arm when she went to reach for the handle just above the doorframe. "Ouch."

Juliet turned her back to the seat and slid, using her foot to step up and shuffle backwards. "Graceless, but effective," she said, smiling.

"Looked good from here," Mia said as she closed Juliet's door and walked around the car to climb into the driver's seat. She took multiple long gulps of her coffee before releasing a satisfied-sounding sigh. "God, that's good for airport coffee." Juliet nodded her agreement, sipping from her cup. "Okay, you good to go?"

"Yep, ready when you are."

Pulling out of the parking space, Mia waved her hand towards the back seat. "I put an extra jacket back there, if you get cold. Or else it works well as a rolled-up pillow."

"You thought of everything, hey?"

"That one's for me, actually. I know how much you can ramble on. If you're napping, I get some quiet time!"

Juliet's stomach involuntarily moved as she tried to stifle a laugh.

"Don't," she pleaded. "Don't make me laugh. Now I realise I'm looking a little fragile, but why don't you fill me in with how you've been doing since Christmas?"

Mia cast a quick sideways glance at her before placing the parking ticket and her credit card in the machine and exiting. "Jeez, that took you at least five seconds to ask. Impressive."

"What can I say? You're a captive audience and there's only so long I can wait for you to bring it up. I've learnt through the years that if you don't ask, you don't find out."

"I'm not sure I've seen that on a greeting card." Mia easily negotiated the city bypass to meet the M90.

"Mmmm," Juliet said eventually, not buying into the misdirection, nor Mia's supposed road focus. "And?"

"Shitty things happen to a lot of people, right? I mean, look at how you've spent the last couple of days. I'm just crap at anniversaries. I turn into a mess. I get all...miserable, and it all spirals until I'm kind of...fucked."

"So every Christmas it's the same?"

"Well, if *every* Christmas equals the last two, then I suppose so."

"Shit, you're hard on yourself. That's not long."

"You sound like the therapist I had. She told me the second year was the hardest. I threw some annoying little ornament across her room when she said that. She's lucky it wasn't the Zen garden, all that sand and crap. But who the hell tells some traumatised person—don't worry, it'll get worse? She was, like, a three hundred and fifty bucks an hour waste of space."

Juliet nodded, rolling her eyes. "I had therapy once, and by once, I mean literally once. I never went back. He asked me my thoughts on God and the afterlife, though I'm still not sure what that had to do with my relationship breakup. I think he might have been Catholic and not so keen on counselling *my type*." Her last words were emphasised with air quotes.

"Oh, don't talk to me about Catholics. My family is…devout. As in, able to quote Bible passages devout."

"You're kidding?" Juliet asked. "How did they feel about…" she trailed off, mouth slightly ajar.

Mia's expression, still staring at the road, had visibly tensed.

"Sorry, none of my business."

Mia sighed. "No, not at all. They're not…keen. That's probably an understatement. Your family doesn't mind?"

Juliet shrugged. "Not particularly. My family is a bit complex in plenty of other ways, though. Can't have everything, I suppose. So, how long is this drive?"

"About or just under five hours, if we only stop once and don't hit any ice or snow. The weather hasn't been as bad today, thankfully."

"I really could have caught a train, you know. I feel bad for everything you've done."

"Life of leisure, remember? Besides, it was good for me to get out of the house. Misery and all."

Tentatively bending forward, Juliet reached for the snack bag. "Do you mind if I open something?"

"Mmm, please."

"Go me halves in a chocolate bar?"

Mia nodded eagerly. "Caramel good with you?"

"Perfect." Juliet halved the chocolate and handed a piece to Mia, licking dripping caramel off her fingers and smiling with her good cheek. In any other time and place, Juliet probably would have done it slow and sexy in an attempt to flirt with Mia. In the current environment though, the adrenalin that she had been running on left her, and her knotted stomach felt settled.

She had made the right decision.

When they pulled up next to the main house, Juliet was sound asleep, head propped up against the window with Mia's rolled-up jacket under her neck and ear. She had probably been asleep for almost an hour, though they had chatted constantly up until that point.

Mia left the car running, quietly taking Juliet's bags from the back and placing them just inside the front door. It was dark and cold out, and a wind that cut right through her had picked up throughout the day. Mia shivered, returning to the car with her hands inside her sleeves.

"Juliet," she said softly with the driver's side door half-open, taken back to the moment she had to awaken Juliet in the airport lounge. "We're home," she added in a lyrical tone.

Juliet stirred, lifting her head and blinking in confusion as the jacket fell down her shoulder and onto her lap. "I fell asleep." She looked around the car as Mia moved to close the door and reappear at the door on Juliet's side "Thanks," she said quietly. "I didn't keep you much company there at the end."

Mia shrugged and held out an arm for Juliet to use if she needed it getting out of the car. "No problem. I was concentrating on the road, and you were snoozing like a baby."

Sliding out, Juliet landed on her feet with a slight jerk and lingered with her open palm above Mia's forearm, as if ready to grab it if she lost her balance.

"Come on." Mia waved her into the house. "I'll give you a very quick tour around and then leave you to settle in for the night."

"Thanks. You must be exhausted, aren't you? It's kind of late, and you have driven over ten hours today."

"I really am. I'm pretty sure my bed is calling me, actually. I can put you out some dinner if you want, though."

"Thanks for the offer, but I'm fine. Just ready for some meds and bed."

"Oh, you're sore?"

Juliet nodded.

"Okay, quick tour then, just so you know where to find anything you need throughout the night. So, kitchen is here—there's heaps of food in the fridge and the pantry. Cups and mugs are up there. Eat and drink anything you find, it's all good. Janet and Martin are back soon-ish, so everything will be restocked. Or we can always pick up anything we need."

"Janet and Martin?"

"Oh, staff. They've gone to visit family for Christmas. Janet is mostly around the house cooking and cleaning, that kind of thing. Martin is a driver, but he also manages the property and does general maintenance or, you know, problems with the horses."

"Yeah," Juliet said. "Of course."

"They're really nice. You can chat to them or ask them for anything, it's no issue. Ah, through here is a sitting room. The fireplace is usually going. It's really nice to read a book or magazine out here. There's a television both here and in the lounge room, which is through those double doors. The other way out of the kitchen is the dining room, but I never eat there. Feels a bit weird sitting by myself at a setting for eight. Now through this way is my room, so if you need anything, just knock."

"Beautiful," Juliet whispered, poking her head through the door but respectfully not walking in. It was an impressive room, with the large king-size bed in the middle and its intricately designed dark wooden frame. Mia smiled to herself at the familiar sight of the bedside tables matched with carved-wood lamps atop, with just a couple of her favourite books sitting on one. To the side of the room, the two single reading recliners were positioned with a glossy table between. Mia imagined for a moment her and Juliet seated in them, overseen by the large piece of artwork that adorned the nearest wall.

Walking further down the corridor, Mia pointed to another room. "That's set up as a study or an office. There's a desktop computer, and there's also a laptop—feel free to use them. There are no passwords set up or anything. That over there is just a spare room, a bit of a day room type thing."

At the end of the corridor, Mia opened the last door and stepped through. "This is your room," she said.

Juliet's eyes lit up instantly at the sight of the guest bedroom. "This is amazing," she said, "just stunning. I might never leave here."

"I hope everything is okay. I've put some towels in your bathroom, and there are toiletries and things there. This place is mostly stocked for me right now, so unfortunately you get my shampoo and conditioner, face scrub, body wash, et cetera. But we can get whatever you like when we go out. Umm, what else? I've got the heat pretty high, but there's a control just next to your bed. Ah, phone is on the table, and there's a small fridge underneath the TV cabinet with water, juice, fruit, and yogurt in there, but like I said, just grab whatever from the kitchen. What am I forgetting? Oh, there are extra blankets in the closet. I put them on a bottom shelf. There's also a bathrobe and a few spare shirts and things if you need them."

Juliet spun around, voice unsteady as she stepped back toward Mia. "Mia, I...Just, thank you."

"Oh, no drama. I'll just go grab your bags while you have a quick poke around and see if I've forgotten anything."

Juliet slowly eased herself to sit on the bed and remained perched on the edge when Mia returned with her bags.

"You might not need to unpack if you're tired. Just grab a shirt, and there's a toothbrush and all that kind of stuff in the bathroom."

"Perfect."

"Did you think of anything else?" Mia stood in front of Juliet, who was still on the edge of the bed, gaping at everything.

"No...nothing. There's nothing more I could possibly need."

"Okay. So your pain meds are easy to get?"

Juliet nodded.

"In that case, I'll leave you to it. Just remember, I'm right down the hall. Just knock and wake me or give me a sharp jab."

"Hey," Juliet said, using one hand on the mattress to push herself to stand. "I'm completely overwhelmed, thank you." She stiffly leant forward and lightly pecked Mia's cheek. Mia just smiled, tucking her loose brown hair behind her ears. "Completely overwhelmed," Juliet repeated.

Running her thumb over Juliet's upper arm, Mia said, "I hope you sleep well."

Juliet looked like it took a moment for her to register the touch. After a prolonged moment, she smiled. "You too. Good night."

"Good night, Juliet." Mia slowly pulled the door closed until the latch clicked.

CHAPTER 9

Waking to the sound of dishes clanking, Juliet rolled from her back to her side and tried to clear her sleep-filled vision to check the time. It took her a few attempts, the digits slowly coming into focus. It was almost ten. She had slept undisturbed throughout the night.

She lay there for a few minutes, eventually working herself into a sitting position and drawing the covers back as her feet hit the carpet. She was even stiffer that morning, but the pain was still the same, jabbing at her side and catching her with the slightest of twisted movements.

Taking her time in the shower, she seized the opportunity to sit on the edge of the tub and shave her legs and armpits. Winter didn't bring out the best in her self-maintenance. It was too easy to don the multiple layers and forget about what was underneath. The mirror didn't lie, though, revealing her face's blue bruises that were purple in the centre and yellowed towards the edge. She turned away, not wanting to see her reflection.

Back in the bedroom, she pulled the sheets and duvet up, returning the colourful throw cushions to the centre. Dressing carefully, Juliet pulled on a pair of yoga pants from the top of her pack, though they could probably do with a wash. She chose one of Mia's shirts, a V-neck striped Tommy Hilfiger tee that was a little too big and hung off one of her shoulders. It exposed the faded grey bra strap underneath. The heat was high enough that she didn't need another layer for the moment. Taking a water bottle from the fridge, she broke the seal and opened the door to the hallway.

She followed the corridor until it opened up into the living area. She could make out Mia's deliberately low and soft voice emanating from the kitchen. Juliet was almost at the breakfast bar when she heard the distinct sound of a male voice, and she self-consciously untucked damp hair from her ears and smoothed it across her forehead and eyebrow.

"Good morning," she said softly, and both Mia and the tall, middle-aged man turned to face her.

"Oh, hi, good morning," Mia said, watching Juliet gingerly slide onto a stool and place both hands on the bench before she exhaled. "How did you sleep?"

"Well, thank you." One of her eyes widened, a request for an introduction.

"This," Mia said, leaning back against the sink, "is Doctor Swinn. I thought it might be good to get you checked out, see how everything is healing."

"Lucas, actually," he said. "Lucas is fine."

"Umm, sure," Juliet said softly. "Sorry, you do house calls?"

"Sure do. I do three half days a week at the hospital, and then the rest of the time, I'm out doing visits. I've done the odd callout here over the years."

"I'm sorry to keep you waiting. Mia, you could have woken me."

"Oh no, not at all," Doctor Swinn—*Lucas*—said. "Sounds as if you needed your rest, and I did get a very nice cup of tea."

Juliet shrugged, sharing a glance with Mia before her gaze fell back to the bench. She was uncomfortable at the attention. Mia cleared her throat and said, "I'll make you a coffee and then leave you to it."

"It's all right," Juliet said. "You can stay."

"Good," Lucas said quickly, turning to Mia. "I'll show you how to change these dressings. I'm assuming there's a few stitches under there."

Juliet nodded.

"And did they tell you it's a week or ten days before you need them out?"

"Ah, a week, I think. I was a bit dazed, but yeah, I'm pretty sure a week."

"All right." He crouched and reached into an open backpack; it almost looked like a camera bag crossed with a first-aid kit. With gloves on, he stepped up to Juliet and slowly peeled off the half-stuck dressings. "Did they give you antibiotics?"

Juliet shook her head. "No, should they have?"

His forehead burrowed, and Mia stilled by the percolator, one hand holding a white mug. "Mmm," he said, "not necessarily. They're a little red, but not too bad. I'll leave some topical antiseptic; just put it on each day." He waved at Mia to come closer. "See this?" he instructed, fingertip at the edge of a small line of stitches on Juliet's forehead.

"What am I looking at?" Mia asked, and Juliet tried to breathe slowly, struggling with the awareness of two bodies crowded just inches from her face.

"You can just make out the line where the cut is. See how it looks a little red and irritated? You're looking for a white discharge. That's what we don't want. So, if you notice even a couple of speckles of a white paste, your job is to call me straight away."

"Yep, got it," Mia said.

Juliet tracked her, watching as she crossed back around to the kitchen and poured her a coffee.

"Changing the coverings is easy." Lucas spoke in a matter-of-fact tone as he went about dressing the wound. "Just peel them off, leave the wound exposed for a few minutes so that it dries out, and then just cut these to size, although these pre-cut ones should be pretty right. Just a few dabs of this red antiseptic will do the trick—careful of your clothes. Think you can handle that, Mia?"

"Don't get it on clothing, okay?"

Juliet smirked. "What can go wrong, right?"

"Exactly. It's hardly surgery." Lucas placed the pads of two fingers over her cheekbone and palpated it lightly as he bantered with them. "All right, so how's the pain level? That mandible wasn't fractured?"

"No, just bruised."

"And the eye socket?"

"Same." Juliet's head drew back slightly as he went about tugging her lower eyelid down to glimpse at the surface of her eye. "Ow."

"When was the assault?" he asked.

"A couple of days ago. Boxing Day."

"Ah. The swelling should start going down tomorrow. You might actually get to see out of that eye."

"That would be good." Mia leaned across the counter and kept Juliet's coffee between her hands, watching intently.

"Mia said you have a couple of fractured ribs?"

Juliet nodded. "Yeah, on the right side. A couple at the front were broken and I think one at the back. Others were just bruised."

"I fractured one playing rugby league when I was at med school—worst injury I ever had."

"Yeah, it doesn't exactly tickle."

"Make sure you take your prescribed pain meds. Don't wait until you're in agony before you take them."

Juliet gave a guilty nod. Taking care of herself wasn't one of her strong points. She did this with her life too, waited until it all fell apart before she started fixing things. Who needs to be proactive, right?

Lucas wrapped a stethoscope around his neck and moved around behind her. She felt her shirt being slowly drawn up. She knew from having inspected herself in the mirror that her back looked like a kaleidoscope of colour, but that her abdomen were not quite as bad.

"Now I want you to rest all right?" he said strongly. "No lifting or twisting, just plenty of time lying on a bed or a lounge." Juliet felt the base of his palm pressing against various areas and heard him murmur something unintelligible whenever Juliet's body guarded against his pressure. "Breathe in and out," he said. He repeated the same pattern standing in front of Juliet. "Still sounds clear."

"Yeah, I can breathe fine."

"No blood in your urine or stools?" She shook her head. "You haven't felt lightheaded? Heart palpitations?"

"Nope."

Checking her blood pressure, he finally lowered his instruments back to his bag and peeled his gloves off. "Everything looks okay, but you need to take some time to rest. Don't push yourself. You need to heal."

Juliet nodded.

"Was there anything else mentioned when you were discharged?"

"Oh, I did have discharge papers if you needed them. Sorry, I forgot about that. They mentioned something about my liver too, a small tear or laceration. They weren't worried, though."

"Even more reason to take it particularly easy. Any stomach pain or cramping, give me a call. And I'll cast my eyes over that letter when I'm back in a few days to take those stitches out."

"Thank you." Juliet adjusted the shirt she was wearing to fall back over her hips and indicated to Mia to slide the coffee across. "Thanks," she whispered.

"You're more than welcome," Lucas said warmly, looking up from where he crouched on the floor and packed his bag. "I'll see you again in a few days, say Tuesday or Wednesday. I'll have my receptionist call you with a time, okay?"

Mia left the room with Lucas. By the time she padded back into the kitchen, Juliet had made her way to standing in front of the open fridge, taking out one item at a time and placing it on the bench.

"Can I get it for you?" Mia asked.

Juliet shook her head. "Nah, I'm gonna have some of this fruit and yogurt. Is that okay?"

"Oh don't ask, just go for it. It's probably the last day for the fruit, so we should definitely eat it. I'll go to the supermarket tomorrow or the next day."

Juliet finished preparing her breakfast and followed Mia into the lounge room, settling slowly into the soft sofa. Mia turned on the television, leaning back with her slipper-clad feet on the coffee table.

"Hey thanks for organising the doctor this morning," Juliet said. "I hadn't even given that a thought."

"No problem. I just phoned and was sussing out what days he was doing home visits this week. Made me feel better to have you checked out, even if you didn't really need it."

"Well it's one thing ticked off the list. Pity there's a few more to sort. The idea of phoning my bank is about as appealing as stabbing myself in the eyeballs. Or make that *an* eyeball. I can't wait for this swelling to go down."

Mia laughed, sliding her elbow up on the back of the sofa, hand supporting her head. "You cancelled your cards, didn't you?"

Juliet nodded. She had been given the relevant number at the hospital and had managed to get it done quite easily. She suspected that having them replaced wouldn't be quite so simple.

"So there's no huge rush," Mia said. "I think today should just be relaxing for you."

"I'm not sure I've got the strength to do anything but that." Juliet spooned yogurt into her mouth, pushing the hard pieces of melon she found to the side of the plate. Despite the long sleep, Juliet still felt incredibly tired and run-down. In just a couple of weeks, she had lost her strong, fit, and energetic appearance, and she couldn't imagine what Mia thought. The same yoga pants Juliet had worn in the airport were now loose around her waist and thighs; the fabric pooled under the heels of her feet now, sitting lower on her hips than they had back then.

"Pretty uncomfortable today, huh?"

"Yeah, kind of. Everything hurts, and all the time. I could cope with the ribs if everything else didn't ache too—my legs, arms, face. Even my neck and shoulders are annoying me this morning. Guess I tensed up when I was trying to get away."

"Ack, you poor thing. Drugs…The answer is always drugs." She offered Juliet a smile. "Do you remember much about it?"

"The mugging?"

"Yeah. You didn't really say much on the phone."

Juliet grimaced. "I was knocked out at the end, but he had my bag then, so he just took off, I guess. Fuckwit."

"So you were just walking home?"

"Yeah, I had just left the bar we were at. The young guys that lived in my block had kicked on. I'm not sure where they went, but I stayed and finished my drink and then just wandered out, I didn't even think about it. Where the bar is, there's a cab stand kind of up along the road and down a side street. Or if I kept walking, I would have hit my apartment in ten or fifteen. It really wasn't far. I suppose I should have had someone walk me to a cab, but I don't know. Why would I?"

"Exactly," Mia said. "And it's not something I've done heaps, walked through a city alone or from a club, but I figure that's kind of what you do? Why would you even think twice about it?"

"I know, and my first thought when he put a hand around my mouth was that it was one of the guys I was drinking with. They were trying to get me to go out dancing. I just figured one of them had spotted me and was messing with me. Stupid, hey?"

With an emphatic shake of her head, Mia stretched her hand out into the space between them to emphasise the *no*. "How is that stupid?"

"I probably wouldn't have even gotten hurt if I had just given him my bag."

"Agh, twenty-twenty hindsight. Surely you were just acting on instincts? How do you think in the middle of that?"

"He landed with his knees on me," Juliet said, caught in the flash of memory. "On my stomach."

Head bowed slightly, she focussed on the bowl in her hands resting on her lap. It was the first time since it had happened that she had thought through the attack step by step. She had been remembering bits and pieces, even waking herself up when she dreamt of parts. But trying to piece it together in order was hard. It was confronting, and she found herself struggling for air, just like she had that night.

"Shit." That one word, which came out of Mia more like an exhaled breath than anything else, lingered in the heavy silence between them.

Juliet scoffed. "Yeah, shit. It didn't hurt, but I couldn't breathe. It was like one of those drowning dreams, where you can't get to the surface or you're stuck under waves. I don't know if you've ever had that one."

"I've had it a few times," Mia said. "It's an awful feeling, not being able to get air in. But this wasn't a dream. You didn't get to wake up."

"I thought it would be better when he got off my chest. It seemed to take ages. He was trying to get my bag. I don't know why he didn't just threaten me. I would have given the bag to him. That's what I've been taught about travelling—they always say just give it, it's not worth it. But then again, I don't know. I can't remember if he was yelling at me in Flemish."

Drawing in a slow, shallow breath, Juliet said, "Anyway, he tugged until my bag broke. I thought he was going to rip my fucking neck off, he was pulling so hard."

"Weren't there people around?"

Juliet shrugged. "Mustn't have been. I mean, people came. There was this lovely couple who called the paramedics. But I blacked out. The next thing I knew was this guy was leaning over me, trying to get me to stay still, and a woman was on the phone."

"You're lucky they found you."

"I know. I really was. And they were wonderful. Once they figured out that I spoke English, they talked to me and then told the paramedics and even the driver at least five times that I only understood English."

Mia rubbed at the sleeve of her shirt that Juliet wore and slowly repositioned her weight. "Scary, hey?"

Forcing a smile, Juliet nodded but then shrugged. She just felt ambivalent for the moment, as if nothing could elicit positive or negative emotions. "You don't really know me, but the idea that I'm even here with barely a protest, that I got on a plane that you booked…" She dropped her voice low. "That's scary."

The admission lingered in the air.

"With some rest, and letting your body heal, you'll feel better."

"I hope so."

"I know you will. This place is pretty amazing. I'm sure it has healing properties in the water or something."

"Healing properties? You know I've been on a Buddhist retreat in Cambodia, spent some time in India learning about Hindu religious practices? I even once learnt the death and dying rituals of the Greenlandic Inuit."

Juliet watched a careful giggle surfacing.

"Well, this place," Mia said, "as in this house, has absolutely no traditional religious or…dying beliefs. Unless you count the odd crucifix that you might find shoved in a cupboard. And apparently, some previous owners have their ashes scattered in one of the far paddocks. But you want healing? Take all the yoga and meditation you like, but how awesome would it be to go for a horse ride and not see a single person? Or even stare at the fireplace for hours without interruption? Seriously, that's healing."

"Who needs the four noble truths when you have a fireplace!" Juliet teased.

Mia gave her a perplexed look. "Are you taking the piss, and I have no idea?"

"Oh, how very British of you to say that," Juliet teased her. "No, Mia, I'm just messing with you." Juliet dropped a hand to push lightly against Mia's knee before her hand fell back to the sofa fabric between them.

"Well," Mia said, grinning, "it's hard to tell when you can't laugh." Standing up, Mia collected the remote controls from below the television, holding them out to Juliet. "There's quite the movie collection, what's your veg out genre? A revolting romantic comedy? Violent thriller? Lesbian sex romp?"

Juliet rolled her eyes at the last one. "Oh yeah, made for every man's enjoyment. So definitely my choice."

Shuddering, Mia nodded. "Makes me nauseated…"

"Tell me about it. Nah, my choice would be maybe something that doesn't require much thinking. Not a drama. Our lives are dramatic enough. Oh, sorry, you probably have things you want to be doing rather than watching movies with me."

"Nah-ah. I'm settling in for the morning. Then I might do something productive, like start collecting forms for you to fill out to get your cards replaced. But this morning, I'm taking up at least a little of this sofa."

"Well, I don't mind then. Why don't you choose? I trust your tastes."

"Really?" Mia's eyes twinkled with mischief. "No one ever says that to me. I could be obsessed with supernatural thrillers or something."

"Are you?"

"No," Mia said quickly, "not at all. How about something upbeat, a musical? You can hear me sing along." She started humming a tune Juliet immediately recognized.

"Oh now that sounds like something I'd like to experience!" she said. "We're watching *Mamma Mia*, aren't we?"

"How did you guess?" Mia asked innocently.

"That's 'Dancing Queen' you're humming—don't deny it." Juliet chuckled. "I'm a fan from way back. But go ahead and bring it, even if I'm going to have ABBA songs in my head for a week." Mia grinned as she found the DVD on her shelves and put it into the player. As she did, she sang loudly with her back to Juliet, swaying her hips and shoulders, releasing the most incredible voice.

Juliet watched in admiration, fishing out two capsules from her pocket and dropping them into the small amount of yogurt in her plate. Mia was still singing as the menu screen appeared.

Juliet had met a lot of amazing people in her travels, most of whom she learned something from—practical advice or important life lessons. But Mia... Mia was something entirely different.

Juliet could hardly believe that two days passed quickly and in much the same way, the two of them watching movies and reading books and quietly talking and getting to know more and more about each other's lives. Or not so quietly sometimes, as Mia would encourage Juliet into debates about current policy decisions and petitions for law reforms back home. They had started to move around each other with familiarity.

The third morning was no exception. Juliet made her way into the kitchen, her wide-leg flannelette pyjama pants and a plain, long-sleeved top slightly askew. She pulled the milk from the fridge and two cups from the cupboard and stood back watching as Mia poured their coffee.

"Morning," Juliet murmured, her voice husky with sleep.

"Oh, she speaks pre-coffee this morning."

"Mean." Juliet slid onto a stool and took a mouthful of the deliciously bitter liquid.

"Better?"

"Much." Juliet rubbed a little at her eye, now opening almost as wide as the other with the swelling going down. "How did you sleep?"

"Okay I think. You?" Mia opened the freezer and withdrew two apple-and-cinnamon muffins, placing them in the microwave. She pressed a few digits, and the appliance hummed to life.

Juliet nodded. "Good, I can finally move my head without it hurting, which is a big help for sleeping."

"Your eye is looking better today," Mia said, leaning across the bench and placing her fingers under Juliet's chin. She tugged slightly, drawing Juliet's face towards her, examining the faded purple and yellow skin. "Is your vision okay?"

"Ah-huh, I can see peripherally, which is also a big bonus. Maybe I won't walk into furniture now."

Mia smiled, using her thumb to move the area slightly under Juliet's eye, checking the sclera for specks of blood. She pressed at the side of Juliet's nose and nodded when Juliet didn't react, other than her eyes tracking Mia's hand movements. "Heaps better," Mia confirmed.

"You playing doctor?"

Laughing, Mia nodded. "I'll have you know, I was pre-med at Harvard, so not such a stretch."

"What?" Juliet gasped, swiping at Mia's wrist and gripping it. "You were what?"

"Yep. Did pre-med and went straight into their med school afterwards."

"And you dropped out?" Juliet asked, shocked. "No one drops out of Harvard."

"Not exactly."

"Really? What did you do? Oooo, tell me you slept with a professor?"

Mia shook her head with what looked like a rueful smile. "No, though there was the hottest anatomy professor with legs that literally went on forever. She was hot. I definitely would have slept with her."

"Mmm, Juliet murmured, cocking her head to the side as if processing a delightful mental image. She grinned and waved a hand in front of her. "So what happened?"

Drawing her hand away from Juliet's grasp, Mia took a sip of her coffee. "It wasn't so much my choice."

Juliet blinked once and stared at her, waiting for more.

"Being a doctor," Mia said. "Not quite the life my parents had mapped out for me."

"Are you kidding? What parent wouldn't want their child to be a successful doctor?" She paused. "So, what happened?"

"Oh, they just refused to pay my tuition and threatened to cut me off. They had a plan for me, and that wasn't it, not even close."

"I don't get it. They pay for you to do pre-med and then just..."

"Yeah, kind of. I was expected to go to college. It filled in some of the time between high school and everything else. My father's executive assistant even filled out all my college applications for me. I just had to write the admissions essays and sign off on them."

"I was to be smart but not too smart, mature but not too mature, have some life experience, but not too much. You get the idea. I chose to do pre-med. They would have preferred maybe history studies or some sort of English literature degree, even creative arts. And when I didn't, they were kind of okay with it, but then I just got almost too good."

"Too good?"

"Yeah," Mia said, exhaling loudly. "I was in the top ten per cent, walked straight into the med school program with no problems. My undergraduate advisor saw I was smart enough but absolutely hopeless with the paperwork, so she helped me fill out all the med school application forms. I didn't even involve my parents. She told me where and when the exams were, everything. Pathetic, really, looking back. If I was more invested, more motivated, I might have found a way to make it all work.

"But once I was in med school, I was living my life, forming my own opinions, and starting to not want what my parents had planned for me. They slowly realized that. So they withdrew their support, made sure I didn't have much of a choice."

"Shit," Juliet muttered, shaking her head. "You couldn't have transferred? Gone to a different school and worked?"

Mia laughed, turning back to wait as the microwave ticked down the last few seconds. "In theory, I suppose, but that's not so easy when your reputation precedes you. Not to mention, I was raised to think that my father was godlike. He wanted me to fear him. It gave him power. My father would have blocked any college application just by sending an email to his colleagues, the boys' club, calling in a favour. I can only imagine the stories he told about me—his out of control, feminist daughter. They all would have worried that their own daughters could turn out like me. And how could I have done it on my own? Where would I work? I was a spoiled kid who hadn't ever even made a bed or a meal. What was I meant to do? People have no idea the power he holds."

"So what was their idea?" Juliet asked as she took a warm muffin from Mia. She broke a piece off straightaway, dropping it in her mouth and relishing the fact that she could now chew without issue. "That you would get married, be a trophy wife and pop out some kids?"

Mia stood very still. "Yes, that's exactly what they wanted. And look, it's easier now to look back and wonder why I didn't apply for financial aid or a huge student loan, but I just didn't know. I was book smart, but I wasn't life smart. I thought that money in a bank was the only path possible."

Juliet blinked, mouth slightly ajar. She licked her lips and closed her mouth before opening it again. After three times of repeating the same process, Mia laughed.

"Sorry," Juliet said.

"Don't be. Do it a few more thousand times and you might be where I am when I look back at that nice stage of my life."

"So you did what your parents wanted?"

"I did." Mia turned her back and hoisted herself to sit up on the countertop, resting against the wall, a large round analogue clock above her head. "I married the guy. They had him set up for me from before I was in elementary school. We both knew it too."

"But you…"

"My parents didn't know back then, and I've never talked to them explicitly about my sexuality. Why would it have even occurred to them? It's against their religion, their beliefs. It's all very 'under wraps' in their world. My father's business partner has a wife, and they both have mistresses. No one cares about what happens behind the scenes, just keep up the fucking façade."

Juliet shook her head incredulously. "What about your sister? Daniela? She knew."

"I don't think she believed it was real at first, just a one-time youthful experimentation. My sister thinks I should have spent my life with my mouth shut and played the part. She cares only about her image and little else these days."

"Shit, Mia. I had no idea."

"Nothing like having some baggage, huh?"

"Oh, honey, we've all got baggage. Craploads, most of us. So what happened in the end? You're obviously here alone, no rings…" Juliet's index finger grazed over the place where a diamond would sit.

"Divorced." Mia cast her eyes to the ceiling with a sigh. "Yet another way I've brought the family into disrepute. But at least I had a good lawyer and a financial settlement."

"I can imagine they were impressed."

"Another understatement. It's like a cult, and I've been excommunicated. Apparently, there's some story that I've gone mad, but it's as if I no longer exist. I hear nothing from them."

"Delightful people. Really nice. Sorry, I know they're your family, and I'm probably not supposed to say what I think, but fuck, that's just disgusting behaviour."

"Yeah." Mia offered her a sad smile. "I can do what I want now, though, right? Silver lining and all."

"You can, absolutely. You can make decisions that are only about you, no one else. Just you."

Mia rubbed her hands over her thighs and leant forward. "Speaking of," she said after a small silence, "do you feel up to going out for a while today?"

"Umm, yeah. Where to?" Juliet couldn't quite keep up with the sudden change in the conversation. One thing she was learning about Mia was that she would always share only what she was willing to and at a time when she felt comfortable.

"I just thought we could go into town and pick up a few things. We need to let the post office know about your replacement cards and stuff coming through, since they'll be registered mail. And we need some food. Martin's back the day after tomorrow, but Janet arrives still a few days after that, I think. I don't know. She sent me an e-mail to check on me."

"Okay, I definitely feel up to it. I just… Well, I still look pretty awesome."

"Who cares? We'll just ignore anyone staring. Besides, I want to take you out to lunch."

"Out to lunch?"

"Yep, you know that meal in the middle of the day? That's lunch. We can sit down, order, have a wine. What do you think?"

"Sounds great, Mia. I probably can't wear my pyjamas, though, hey?"

Peering over the side of the bench, Mia laughed. "Well, I like them. How you managed to find pyjamas for adults with ducks on them is beyond me, but I think they're very cute."

Juliet rolled her eyes, tipping the mug to her lips and drawing out the last drops of coffee. "Cute is exactly what I'm going for in bed. Just let me shower, and I'll be right out, okay?"

"Take your time."

Juliet grinned at her and then slowly walked down the hall with her coffee.

CHAPTER 10

They would be delusional to think that the day was warm, but it was *warmer*, and just a few degrees made the difference between walking along the street and driving the few hundred yards. It wasn't snowing or raining, and the sun would at times peek out behind white clouds, just not quite regularly enough to earn the use of sunglasses.

Mia found the hour-long drive to town enjoyable. The roads were dry, and there was only the occasional car to wave at. The snow-covered mountains looked particularly spectacular when the sun reflected a glistening white layer. Juliet had murmured at one point that the view alone was healing, which earned an eager nod from Mia.

Throughout the drive, Mia had talked a little more about her family, and the relationship she no longer had with them. She still felt betrayed, and especially now as she started to talk about it, she couldn't believe that people could just walk away from their children, the very people they're meant to love unconditionally. In an academic or rational sense, Mia understood people making the choice to be someone who others perceive as important rather than actually be someone of importance. But emotionally, that choice no longer made sense to her. It was becoming so clear to her that she was no longer interested in the disguise that everyone wore. She wanted to know what was underneath. Who someone was suddenly meant more than *what* they were.

And Juliet did more than pique her interest. She had to read between the lines with Juliet. It wasn't as simple as just listening to her words, which were right now about her mother and generally flowing in a relatively carefree manner. But there was something more in what she *wasn't* saying. She spoke about relationships as if they were necessarily by definition filled with heartache and tragedy, but then she also seemed envious of the concept of marriage, or at least willing to be open to that kind of risky connection. It was as if her head and heart were constantly in battle, more so than in most people, and Mia found herself gathering questions that she was waiting for the right time to ask.

"Kansas," Juliet said, apropos of nothing in the middle of the journey. "My mother lives in Kansas."

Mia turned to glance at Juliet, who had turned slightly to face the side window. The occasional house or property they had seen along the drive was now replaced with shop fronts as they drove into a park. "Oh," Mia said, "I didn't realise. I mean, the way you were talking, I thought maybe she had died."

"Sometimes I think that would be easier."

"Than your mom being alive?"

Juliet shrugged. "Sounds awful, I know."

Mia didn't respond straightaway, but she shook her head. It didn't sound awful, and it fit with Juliet's book, but then it didn't: the story ended with the character having never made peace with her mother for the things she should have done, the things she should have taught her daughter. Mia couldn't conceptualise why Juliet talked with such sadness and loss when her mother was so accessible.

She put the car into park and shut it off. "I guess it's complicated."

"It wasn't always like that," Juliet said, and Mia wondered if she was concerned that Mia was judging her. As they got out of the car, Juliet kept her chin dipped, face towards her feet.

"You don't have to explain, really." There was no reason for Mia to think that Juliet wouldn't tell her when she was ready. It wasn't easy to trust, and Mia hoped that as she shared more of her life, Juliet would do the same. Trust was something that was earned over time, and it shouldn't just be handed over, Mia thought. It was no wonder people got hurt by other people if they threw their trust around like it was a cheap baseball.

Mia wasn't quite sure where the baseball analogy came from; she didn't even like baseball. She squinted her left eye and raised her right eyebrow and could feel the smile on her face when Juliet asked, "Do I even want to know what you're thinking about?"

"Whoops," Mia said, chuckling. "I was just ranting about baseball in my head."

"Baseball?"

"I know, hence the laugh. I don't even like baseball. Don't worry, just cracking myself up. I'm that sad." Mia led Juliet to a post office and pushed her key into a post box. She withdrew a pile of envelopes and placed them in her bag. "You're not too cold?"

"Nope," Juliet said, shaking her head. "It's not exactly super warm, but I'm not ready to sit on a fire either."

Happy to see Juliet's gaze rising up to meet hers, Mia nodded. "Well, down the end of this road is a pretty good pub, or we can get back in the car and drive to the next town, which is maybe twenty miles away. There's a funky café there."

"I don't mind," Juliet said, shrugging. And she didn't seem fazed either way; she seemed more confronted by the stares that had fixed upon her, random strangers that couldn't draw their eyes away from her visible bruises.

"Ahhh," Mia hesitated, drawing the sound out as she looked along the road and at their surrounds. There were a number of people about, the clear weather having drawn everyone from their homes for supplies and top-ups and a change of scenery. "If you're okay with it, how about we walk down to the end and have a look? If you think it's okay, than we can go in and have a late lunch. Otherwise, we'll wander back and go for a drive. Sound like a plan?"

"Sure," Juliet agreed, smiling as she looked down at the sidewalk, not meeting anyone's gaze on the street. They walked slowly and carefully, Juliet on the cemented path and Mia stepping onto the grass whenever the path narrowed or a tree branch intruded upon their space. After a few hundred yards and a number of gasps and muttered observations from strangers, Juliet shook her head.

"Do they have to all have something to say?" she asked Mia pointedly.

"People are rude, no social skills whatsoever."

Widening her scarf, Juliet pushed her hands into her pockets and dropped her head, lifting her eyes occasionally to keep track of where they were going.

Mia dropped an arm around Juliet's shoulders. "Fuck 'em," she muttered. "Just ignore them. Who cares if they stare?"

"I care." Mia could barely hear her.

"Wasn't it you that made me get changed at an airport just to prove some point about opinions?"

"Maybe...but this is different. They probably think I'm some weakling who...I don't know."

"Mmm? Who does what?" She knew by Juliet's tone that she had no real argument to validate the way she was feeling. She kept her arm in position, and Juliet slowly closed the small gap between them, pressing into Mia's side.

"I just wish they wouldn't stare."

Mia nodded, clearing her throat as another middle-aged woman approached from the opposite direction.

"Eyes to yourself, hey?" she said just loud enough to break the women's fixation on Juliet's face. Juliet chuckled as the woman had to step off the path to let them pass.

"You want me to say that to every person that dares to look?" She gave Juliet a teasing poke. "'Cause I will."

"No," Juliet said softly, glancing up at Mia with a smile. "You might scare someone."

She held Mia's gaze longer than necessary, her expression slowly losing its lightness. Mia struggled to draw her eyes away, captivated. She wanted her own expression to portray everything that words seemed too difficult or too inaccurate to say. She wanted to press a kiss to Juliet and somehow communicate everything that was too early to declare—that she was safe and loving, devoted and sure. And in those few seconds, moving blindly along the sidewalk, she convinced herself that Juliet felt it too.

"Ouch, fuck!" Juliet's foot suddenly caught a slight rise in the footpath, and she stumbled, one hand immediately slamming against her ribs as she braced for the inevitable fall.

But Mia didn't let her fall.

She tightened the arm at Juliet's shoulder and rushed another to her elbow, easily stopping Juliet from falling further as she landed hard on the ball of her foot and her upper body jerked and folded forward.

"Ow." Juliet managed to fall back into a smooth step, but not before she released a childish whimper and her head lilted to the side, temple on Mia's shoulder. She squeezed her eyes shut.

"Are you okay?" Mia's fingertips grazed over Juliet's shoulder and the thick material of the jacket she wore.

"Ow, but yes."

Picking up on the frustrated catch in Juliet's voice, Mia released Juliet's other arm and brushed some loose curls away from her hair. "I'm sorry," she said. "I wasn't watching where we were going."

A few more slow, shallow breaths, and Juliet raised her head. "Neither was I." Mia was relieved to see a smile gradually tug at the corners of her mouth. "Jesus Christ, that hurt, though."

"I could tell."

"I could do with sitting down soon," Juliet said, huddling with an open palm still pressed to her injured side. "It's just here?"

"Yeah, yeah. Just up these steps. Careful, they're kind of uneven."

Straightening up a little more, Juliet winced and allowed Mia to direct her to a quiet booth towards the back but next to a wide window. The view stretched to the street they had just walked down and towards a green valley behind some shops and houses. A stream ran along a deep dip in the pastures.

"Better," Juliet said, blowing hair out of her eyes as she unknotted her scarf.

"Let me." Mia stepped behind Juliet and drew her jacket down from her arms. "I'll grab us a drink and the menus. I'm getting something hot, a coffee, I think. Do you want a coffee or hot chocolate or something else?"

"Is there ever a question? Coffee, please."

Reappearing and sitting down opposite her a few minutes later, Mia placed her handbag on the seat next to her and cast her eyes over Juliet. "You feeling all right?" she asked. "Breathing okay?"

"Yeah," Juliet said eventually. "It hurt, but it's okay. It's settling down now. I just needed to stop and sit."

Mia ran her fingers along the edge of the café table. She swallowed and looked up at Juliet, breaking her gaze quickly when she found Juliet intently watching her. "Was there..." Mia closed one eye and pondered her phrasing. "Was that a...*moment*, back there?" She tried to keep her tone light and jovial, but it came out more tortured and doubtful.

Juliet opened her mouth to answer, but seemed to pause as Mia continued to nervously examine the indentations on the polished wood. "I'm a little out of practise," Juliet said quietly, "but if my memory is holding up, I would have called that a moment."

"Really?"

"Mmm-hmm, I would."

Mia exhaled noisily and gave a tense chuckle. "I didn't mean to put you on the spot. Sorry."

"It's okay," Juliet said. "It's your eyes, you know. How have you ever managed to have a conversation with someone and not have them want to kiss you?"

An intense heat spread up Mia's neck and throughout her cheeks. Her gaze fell as she shook her head. "You haven't really...I mean, I wouldn't have thought you were...interested," she said, chastising herself for such awkward phrasing.

"Interest isn't an issue," Juliet said, one hand raking through her hair. "I could have had sex with you in the lounge bathroom in LAX or Dubai or Heathrow." She laughed and shook her head. "But Mia, that's not the kind of person you are."

"How do you know?" Mia teased. "I could be."

Juliet gave her a perplexed expression. "Okay, so maybe you are. I'm a little confused about where you're headed with that thought, though." When Mia didn't respond, Juliet continued. "I was flying to Europe. I was likely never going to see you again. And here I have to go back. I have a book to write. I don't want to mess you up. You've had enough shit to deal with without me letting you down."

"Why would you let me down?"

Juliet sighed. "Because I'll be leaving, Mia."

"I guess I thought that I just wasn't your type." She couldn't quite find the words to say that she didn't think that Juliet found her attractive, that she wasn't the kind of person Juliet would want to jump into bed with.

"No, that's not it. Not it at all. You are, well, you're something amazing. And you don't deserve to have me fall into your life like some broken-winged bird only to fly back out again."

"What if I wanted that? What if I wanted something that's just…brief?"

"Well," Juliet said quietly, "it's not what I want for you. Or for me right now. Besides, there's nothing fun about this body for the moment. It would be a very anti-climactic fling."

"Oh I didn't mean…" Mia rushed to tone down her intent. "I'm not pressuring, so please don't think that. I just, what happened out there, was, like, two seconds, but I'm not going crazy, so that's good."

Their coffees arrived, and two menus were placed on the table. Quickly, Mia grabbed a menu and focussed on reading it. "No idea what I feel like," she said, the heel of her right foot tapping nervously under the table. "Some soup, maybe. Do you know what you want?"

Pulling her coffee to the side by the saucer, Juliet reached across the table. She could only just tap the back of Mia's hand where it held the menu in front of her.

"Mia," she said gently, "I didn't take offence, and I don't feel pressured. And I want you to know that this is about me."

Mia rolled her eyes, and they both shared a soft laugh.

"Yeah, I know, terrible line. And honestly, if my entire life didn't feel so completely fucked up right now, things might be different. But I can't do this to you now. It wouldn't be fair. I don't want this to be awkward, but you and this place are the best thing for me at the moment. Is that okay with you?"

"Oh, of course." Mia shook her head in shame.

"Good."

Mia hesitated. "Can I just ask you one teeny tiny thing though?"

"Mmm?"

"Can we revisit this? In a few weeks, when things have settled down a little?"

"Mia…"

"I don't know how to explain to you how comfortable I feel. It's been so long—too long, actually—since I've felt whatever this is. And I know I'm not being articulate, because it doesn't all make sense to me either. But for the first time in forever, I want to spend time with someone rather than be by myself. And I'm not crazy. I mean, it's scary after all this time, and I keep telling myself that I'm probably wrong and that this kind of thing doesn't go my way. Or work out for me."

Juliet gradually nodded her head. "I do know what you mean," she said.

"So, yes? We'll relax and enjoy our time and talk about this again in a few weeks when you're feeling better and life is back on a bit more of an even keel, yeah?"

"Yeah." Juliet's eyes unexpectedly sparkled, laugh lines creasing. It made Mia wonder if despite her hesitation, Juliet was happier about that concept than she was willing to admit. Mia reminded herself that she needed to give her time, time to breathe and think. Let her do some processing and make a considered decision.

"You're too quick to get rid of me," Mia said with a deliberately inappropriate wink, somehow reassured that they had made it unscathed through that admittedly brief conversation. "You shouldn't write me off just yet."

Juliet just smiled and shrugged.

But a line had been crossed; Mia knew it. She caught Juliet glancing at her throughout the day, her eyes falling at times to the hollow of Mia's breasts. Each time, Juliet's face would distinctly flush. Similarly, when Mia touched Juliet's lower back with her palm, the pad of her little finger would tap at the curve of her buttock and Juliet would clench almost imperceptibly in a way Mia found deliciously muscular and inviting. Sometimes she would even dare inch her hand up higher so that it rested platonically on the waistband of Juliet's jeans.

This was exactly where Mia's hand lay when a couple stood just yards from their car. It took a moment of shared eye contact before Mia realised that she had been recognised; she hadn't even really considered the possibility, given her preoccupation on Juliet. Her hand dropped reflexively from Juliet's back, and immediately, she chastised herself. Old acquaintances shouldn't hold power over her now. She felt their eyes on her back as she and Juliet got into the car. She forced herself not to look up until she reversed the car out of the park. The couple still stood there unmoving.

"Someone you know?"

Mia startled slightly, then shot a brief glance at Juliet. Rolling her eyes, she nodded. "Yeah, sort of. From my old life."

The query ended there with Juliet quickly moving the conversation to talk about how good their lunch was. Mia could only presume it was deliberate. It certainly calmed her heart rate.

As they arrived home, Juliet accepted Mia's proffered hand at the side of the car. Outside the house, along the path where shade dominated and a thin layer of ice made it slippery and dangerous, she curled her fingers around Mia's knuckles and gripped tightly.

Days went by, and there was a sense of safety in their long-term togetherness, and gradually, Mia felt the invisible barrier pulsating between them slacken. They were genuinely free to take a deep breath and act fluidly, like they had all the time in the world.

It made for a very pleasant week.

Wearing knee-high sheepskin boots to keep warm in the old, draughty place, Mia slipped quietly into the office, mug of hot peppermint tea in her hand. She gave the open door a soft knock with the toe of her shoe, and Juliet spun around in the chair. Mia smiled at Juliet's image: hastily blinking, red-rimmed eyes and a messy ponytail with two pens poked through it. She had barely left the laptop in a week, just emerging for the occasional bathroom break and food. More often than not, she only stopped to eat or drink when Mia insisted. The desk was covered with scribbled notepaper, and stray sheets were scattered on the floor. Juliet insisted they were in a specifically ordered system; Mia wasn't so sure.

"I brought you tea," she said. "And cake. Janet makes the best pound cake."

Juliet released a satisfied-sounding groan of approval. "Awesome, thank you."

"How's the writing going?"

A grin slowly appeared on Juliet's face, and she nodded, eyes wide and tongue just nudging out between her teeth. "So good."

"Wow, you look pleased."

"I sent three chapters to my editor last night, and by all reports, they are loved!"

Mia clapped her hands and gave Juliet a quick, gentle squeeze around her shoulders. With her stitches removed almost a week ago, Juliet's face was finally free of bruising, and the swelling had gone. The lacerations were mostly healed. Just a slight red line remained that Juliet reported would occasionally itch or jab at her if she happened to catch it with her nail. Her ribs were still causing her trouble, although it would have been impossible for her to sit in a desk chair all day up until just a few days ago. She was doing better, and she hadn't once mentioned any intent to leave.

"Does that mean you might take a break tonight?"

"I think that sounds like the best idea you've had all week. And I've earned it, I really have."

"In that case, can I interest you in dinner and drinks?"

Juliet paused, a small broken piece of cake halfway to her mouth. "What, out?"

"No, no way. It's snowing again out there. It's freezing. I was thinking more here. We have things to celebrate."

"We do?"

"Absolutely. Aside from your writing, we need to celebrate the fact that you're starting to feel better. I know the side is still painful, but I think no bruises of any shape or form is something to drink to. And it's twelve months since I've been footloose and fancy free, sans husband, so I would like to take you on a date to celebrate. What do you think?" Her heart skipped a beat. She couldn't believe she had just dared call their dinner a *date*.

"We're celebrating the demise of your marriage?"

Mia chuckled. "That makes it sound very dysfunctional...but no, we're encouraging each other in our new focus and direction. It's about our future and new horizons."

"You sound like you swallowed a greeting card."

"Well, you're the writer. Help me out here. What should I say?"

"Ah-huh," Juliet said, pondering for a moment before leaning back in the chair. She cleared her throat. "Okay, you might say something along these lines." She tapped an index finger to her lips as she deliberated. "Say: Juliet, tonight at seven, I'm taking you to a celebratory dinner."

Mia did not miss the reframing of *date* into *celebratory dinner.* "That's not a request," she said, keeping her tone light.

Juliet shook her head. "Nope. If you want something, then I'm a big believer in making it happen. Besides, you're not asking me on a date. We're sharing a dinner." She took a sip of peppermint tea.

Mia's lips twisted with uncertainty. "Mmm, good point." It was sufficiently non-committal, she decided.

"So?" Juliet said.

"So what?"

"Are you going to say it?"

Mia rubbed her eyes. "Are you deliberately delaying answering?"

"Maybe a little."

"Mmm," Mia said again. She stepped back towards the doorway. "Well, now that you've asked yourself out on a date tonight, I better get some things organised. I assume you've accepted." She felt her heart quicken again as she pressed the *date* word again, even after Juliet's clear distinction earlier. She waited for another reframe from Juliet.

She got the complete opposite: "Does that mean I have to get out of my pyjamas?" Juliet asked, glancing down between her hands, where both were wrapped around the steaming mug. Dancing ducks stared back at her.

Mia laughed. "It's been a little while since I did the traditional dinner date thing, but it would certainly be unique if you came in...those. I've always wanted to *woo* a duck."

"I won't come in pyjamas," Juliet said jovially. "Hell, I might even shower and wash my hair." She ran a hand through her dirty and knotted hair. She really had found her muse, and everything else went out the proverbial window when the words were flowing, apparently. "But I might need to borrow some items, if we're going traditional. Clothes, hair straightener, heels…"

Tapping her fingers together, Mia formed a sly grin and pursed her lips. "Do you do dresses?"

"What do you mean do I *do* dresses?"

"Oh, I was thinking how I have one that would be perfect for you, but then I second-guessed myself. I mean, not everyone likes dresses. Do you?"

"Do I like dresses?" Juliet asked.

"Yeah." Mia rolled up on the edges of her feet where she stood.

"Of course I like dresses," Juliet said, breaking into a smile. Mia relaxed.

"Soooo," Mia said, "I'll leave some items on your bed? Is that okay? You're welcome to rummage through my wardrobe, but mostly my stuff will be too big. There are a few things that I think will fit, though."

"Sounds great—I'm in. I'll get a couple more hours of writing done, and then I'll do some prettying up."

"You could wear the ducks and still be pretty," Mia said quickly, another smile on her face as she disappeared out the door, pulling it half closed behind her.

She had some organising to do.

With a fluffy white towel wrapped around her chest, Juliet considered the items laid out on her bed. Mia had banished her from the kitchen and dining room, insisting that she would be knocking on her door at seven. Juliet had played along, distractedly typing and talking at the same time, teasing Mia.

But now that she stood in front of the dresses, a tumble of butterflies took flight in her stomach. She tried to calm herself with a series of reminders that she and Mia had shared countless meals and that there was no pressure or expectation.

Yet she had four dresses in front of her, and they weren't just outfits. They were subtle messages, carefully wrapped up in powder blue and cherry red. And she had to choose one.

She had no idea how to do it, really. Despite her assurance, it had been many years since she had worn a dress, and perhaps never one of the quality and cost of the options in front of her. It made her nervous, the dresses and the date.

Trying on each one, she examined herself in the full-length mirror.

The crimson strapless cocktail dress screamed, *tear me off.* It signalled nothing but wild sex against hotel room doors. Wearing it would evoke images of the red material gathered around her hips and lace panties discarded across the room somewhere, the zip at her back only half down. As tempting as it was, that message wasn't quite what she was going for. Besides, the bodice gaped at her chest, and the fitted waist was a little loose, meaning the thigh-high split lost its impact. Mia however—Mia would kill that dress, and Juliet took a moment to fantasise about the way the material would hug her fabulous curves.

At the other end of the spectrum was a simple black wrap dress with three-quarter-length sleeves and a conservative neckline. Juliet considered her reflection only momentarily, unsure what she was going for but knowing that this wasn't it either. Perhaps combined with knee-high red boots and a large pendant that drew eyes towards her breasts, it could pass as an emergency date night outfit, but she had neither to accessorise with. She carefully returned it to the hanger, practising taking some long deep breaths without flinching in pain.

That left two options: one was another simple black cocktail dress that was made out of a flimsy material. Thin spaghetti straps held the loose bodice in place. She tried it on, checking herself out in the mirror. It wouldn't look out of place in a semi-formal restaurant or an early evening celebration, something like an engagement party or birthday. Juliet deliberated, struggling to twist and see over her shoulder to examine the back.

Switching to the final option, Juliet pulled the soft blue dress over her head and shoulders. The straps were fine and had a thin and transparent cap sleeve that bounced over the curves of her slender shoulders. The neckline was similar to the black, loose and light, and it fell in place over the swell of her breasts. The blue followed the line of her waist and hips a little better—not snug but falling effortlessly to her knees. The skirt drifted slightly as she walked, and it gave off an almost bohemian natural look. In Juliet's mind, it whispered rather than yelled, *Hey, I'm beautiful and sexy, but I can hold a conversation too. It said, Kiss me, but don't put your hand beneath my clothes.*

Decision made. Checking the time, she grimaced. Ten minutes was not enough time to apply some basic makeup and do something with her hair. Perhaps she would be fashionably late. She tried on the two pairs of heels that Mia had left on her floor, discarding them both when an inch gap at the back made her slip with every step. She didn't think her body could cope with a spectacular fall into a piece of furniture.

When a knock at the door interrupted the quick makeup application, Juliet cursed, and her stomach flooded again with nerves. She opened the bathroom door and stuck her head out. "Come in. I'll be ready in a few minutes."

As she heard Mia step inside, Juliet hoped that she had tossed the black bra from the bed back into her underwear drawer.

When she walked out of the bathroom a few minutes later, Juliet giggled. "I've discovered something new tonight: my feet are a little smaller than yours."

Mia grinned, pulling one foot up to slip off the impressive heels she wore, tossing them to the end of the bed. She rested on bare feet and waited for Juliet to take a few steps closer. "So you look incredible, Juliet," she said. "Beautiful." One hand touched the inside of Juliet's elbow as she kissed her cheek.

"Thank you," she said, embarrassed. "You," she added hastily, "are gorgeous. How did you get so incredibly hot?"

They both laughed, and the awkwardness dissipated. "Just noticed, huh?"

"Definitely not."

"You ready? I'm…walking." Mia chuckled. "I was about to say driving, but that's not right. It's not a long way to the dining room."

"I'm ready." Juliet ran her hand down Mia's back, and the smooth material of the fitted black dress was thick under her touch. The pad of her fingertips traced down the inside of Mia's forearm, and she slipped their hands together.

They were off to an exceptional start.

CHAPTER 11

Despite looking slightly out of place sitting at the large wooden eight-seater table, Mia and Juliet talked easily as they sat next to each other at the table's far end. The lights in the dining room were dimmed, and a large white candle splintered a glow across their features. Their gazes stayed locked on each other as they sipped on what were not their first glasses of wine that night.

Mia had planned the menu with Janet that afternoon, ensuring that the food was all mostly prepared so that she could just go quickly into the kitchen and return with their meals. Janet had then made herself scarce, disappearing into the old workman's quarters from when previous owners had run a working property. Juliet noticed that she usually slept a few nights a week there, while other times, depending on the hours and days she was working, she drove back and forth from her flat in Inverness.

Mia took care of the wine, matching each dish with a specific blend from the cellar. The canapé starters were complimented by two generous glasses of a 1996 Dom Pérignon, and Mia and Juliet sat on a white double-seat recliner in an adjacent reading room as they drank and listened to music.

Mia directed them to the table for the first dish, a tasting plate of sashimi accompanied by a Chilean Semillon. Next came small slices of seasoned chicken breast with homemade cabbage salad; a glass of Sauvignon Blanc went down with those nicely. By the time the third main course was in front of them, the conversation had turned louder and more vibrant than ever, hand gestures eagerly supplementing the conversation.

"I'm not sure I can do it," Juliet said, examining the table with a groan, "but it looks amazing."

"You have to try it. It's a local lamb. Absolutely delicious, I swear. And the yogurt dressing is one of Janet's specialties."

"It's all been good, and I'm complaining about being full, but I'm pretty sure I've got room."

Mia nodded, cutting a small piece of lamb cutlet and coating it in the homemade mint and chives sauce. She slowly placed it in her mouth and emitted a moan of pure pleasure. "Mmm, so good."

Laughing, Juliet copied her, savouring the taste before sipping at the Merlot Mia had poured into two wide red wine glasses.

"We'll take a break before dessert," Mia said, leaning back, with her hands falling onto the linen napkin on her lap. "Work off a bit of this with some dancing," she added, winking at Juliet.

"Dance?" Juliet asked loudly, one open palm to her chest and the other reaching out to squeeze Mia's shoulder. She dipped her head and swallowed, buzzing with the copious amounts of wine consumed over the couple of hours. "I don't know if you've noticed, but these ribs—not so good for dancing."

"What kind of dancing do you do?" Mia teased.

"Awesome dancing." Juliet rested her hand on Mia's shoulder a moment before drawing it back. "I've spent a lot of nights dancing in bars...on bars, ordering drinks in a heap of different languages." Her voice dropped a little, and she drew in a breath. "But maybe not so much, now that I got the crap beaten out of me. Time to lay low."

"Have I ever mentioned how shit that was? I hate, hate, hate that guy for touching you."

"Whoever he was."

"I was so worried about you," Mia said softly, the words coming out mumbled. "But I didn't want to tell you 'cause I thought it would freak you out."

"It probably would have. I would have done a million head miles and then felt all insecure and smothered." Juliet squeezed her fingers around Mia's.

"Am I allowed to worry about you now?"

Juliet laughed, taking another long sip from her wine. "Why would you want to do that?"

"Oh, I don't know, Juliet, why would I?" Mia's tone was light, but still, Juliet didn't want to engage in the serious conversation that threatened.

"I'm fine, Mia, really. I'm not traumatised or some emotional wreck. You don't need to worry."

They quickly took the few remaining bites of the single lamb cutlet and settled their cutlery on the plate, washing the meat down with the remnants of their wine.

Mia stood and tucked her chair in, holding a hand out for Juliet to accept. "May I have this dance?"

Juliet nodded but didn't move.

Mia moved to the iPod docking station and switched playlists, playing a softer and slower collection of songs. "Better?" she asked, standing in the middle of the reading room and swaying her hips gently.

"Definitely," Juliet said, her gaze drifting down from Mia's face and sweeping across her exposed clavicles. "I could just stand here and watch you, you know."

Mia shrugged, holding her arms open and palms up in the air. "If you like, but I'll be gentle should you want to join me."

Juliet gingerly stepped forward until she could slowly slide her fingers in between Mia's. They stood momentarily connected by one hand, the space wide between them. Mia widened her eyes until they took on an earnest, childlike expression, as if inviting Juliet in. She folded their arms between them, their joined hands coming to rest in front of her shoulder. Slowly, Mia slid her other arm around the small of Juliet's back, fingers splayed over her hip. Ducking down, Mia inhaled, pressing a light kiss to the nape of Juliet's neck.

Juliet allowed Mia to lead them, just ever so slightly swaying, not quite in time with the music in the background. Not that either of them minded.

"Okay?" Mia asked.

Turning her face so that her forehead pressed into Mia's cheekbone, Juliet nodded, Mia's breath tickling her neck. "You know, I tried to convince myself that I just wanted to be friends with you."

"Is it such a bad thing if we're more?" Mia asked. "I already feel like we're more."

"It just wasn't my plan," Juliet whispered. Plans were important to her. They kept her in control; they kept her safe. But nothing about this working sabbatical had gone to plan.

Mia sighed and continued to slowly move them, feet firmly fixed as their upper bodies rocked together. "I won't hurt you," she said.

Juliet burrowed her face into the nape of Mia's neck. Mia released her hand as Juliet ran both hands around Mia's waist and joined her fingers behind Mia's back. "I'm not perfect," Juliet said. "I've got a past, insecurities."

Mia smiled. "You don't scare me. Intrigue me, yes. But scare me, no."

"I've had a lot of wine."

"Yes, we have. I like it. I feel relaxed."

Mia continued to sway their bodies, threading her fingers soothingly through Juliet's hair, rubbing her thumbs over the back of her neck for a number of minutes.

Placing her hands on Mia's hips and arching her back, Juliet leant her upper body away from Mia, and her face contorted in pain. She stepped backwards, straightening and relieving her tense abdominal muscles.

Mia gave her a sympathetic look. "Careful."

"Mia," Juliet said, scanning her eyes over Mia's face, "it's true that this wasn't my plan, but I do like you."

Mia immediately smiled, slipping a hand behind Juliet's neck. "Then do you trust me?"

Hesitating, Juliet half nodded. "I trust you more than anyone else."

"I'm going to earn an unambiguous *yes* to that question." Mia leant forward and gave her a searing kiss. It was tender and passionate, a little messy and tasting of red wine.

Breathless, Juliet stepped back into Mia's hold, placing her chin on her shoulder. "Do you trust me?" Juliet asked softly.

"I do."

"You do?"

"I have no reason not to. And Juliet, I have a past too. That doesn't matter to me, if mine doesn't matter to you."

"Then I want to try. But Mia—"

"Hey," Mia said quickly, "I'm in no rush. As long as you're not disappearing back to Belgium, we'll just go slow, okay? You'll have to be patient with me too." Juliet suspected that the last comment was for her benefit rather than Mia's. Mia seemed to have figured out that Juliet was much more comfortable when she perceived that she was being altruistic. And it was true. Juliet had always been that way.

"Thanks."

"I think it's almost time for dessert. What about you?"

"Ah, I think I have a little room." Juliet turned her body and awkwardly pushed off Mia just a little. "But before we do that, I just need to do one thing. 'Cause that kiss, that kiss was really nice."

Running her thumb along Mia's bottom lip, Juliet tugged her closer and promptly captured it between her lips. She sucked on it gently, running her tongue across the matted taste of lipstick.

They broke apart, and Mia grinned widely. "Now *that* I could do all night. But how about you sit down and I'll be right back?"

Returning, Mia placed a vintage dessert wine on the table but indicated for Juliet to move to the recliner. "I could get more comfy. You?"

"Sure, but do you need a hand in the kitchen?"

"I left some biscotti on the bench. Can you grab that?"

Juliet returned from the kitchen in seconds. "I didn't think I was hungry, but I definitely have room for that stuff. Tell me Janet didn't just whip up brownies this afternoon?"

"Mmm, no, actually. These she brought back from Ireland, but they are divine. They have macadamias in them and are all gooey. Fucking brilliant." She placed the items on the small coffee table and returned to collect the wine bottle and small sherry glasses. "I know we've had a bit to drink, but this is a tawny port—beautiful."

Juliet nodded and slowly lowered herself, controlled until she hit the cushion and slumped backwards. Mia rearranged a few items before scooping up Juliet's feet and placing them on the table. "Comfy?" She handed her a plate.

"Very." Juliet patted the space next to her. "Sit."

Taking two huge bites of brownie, Mia put the plate down and leant back onto the recliner, taking a sip of wine. She furrowed her forehead and licked her lips, taking another small taste. "Mmm, it needs to breathe a little. I should have opened the bottle a little while ago."

"How did you end up such a wine connoisseur?"

Mia gave her a half smile. "I'm not sure I could count the number of vineyards I've been to. And my ex-husband's family owned a couple of wine production companies around the world, one in France and one in California, and had vineyards all around the world."

"Whoa, no wonder you know your wine, then."

"Sorry. I don't mean to be arrogant. But I do kind of appreciate a quality bottle."

"No, I like it. Maybe I'll learn a few things." Juliet held out her plate, laughing when Mia took it without question and replaced it with her glass. "That was easy."

"You're still injured. I'm looking after you."

Juliet smiled and nodded, realizing that she hadn't accepted this kind of care and attention in a long time. She swirled the sweet, dull, red liquid around in her mouth. It was smooth and wood infused and tasted almost nutty. "Very nice," she said, and her body started to feel tired and heavy. She took another mouthful and, as she had with the mostly consumed brownie, held out her glass for Mia to take from her.

"You won't get away with me serving you forever," Mia said, relaxing back next to Juliet. They sat in silence for a few minutes until slowly, Mia crept her fingers towards Juliet's, which were resting on top of her thigh. She intertwined them. "You look tired." She pressed a kiss onto Juliet's shoulder.

"Mmm, I am. Too much writing, food, and drinking, I think."

"You want to go to bed? I'll clean up out here."

Juliet shook her head. "Nope, I'll help. But I kinda want to sit here awhile."

"Maybe we can finish cleaning tomorrow. I put most of the stuff in the dishwasher as we went along."

"Smart move."

Tenderly playing with Juliet's thumb, Mia eventually chuckled and trapped it. She dropped her head to the side, temple resting on Juliet's shoulder. "You okay, Juliet?"

Juliet nodded. "I'm good."

"Good. I'm good too."

"Will you be good in the morning?"

Mia laughed. "Not a chance. I'm going to have a massive headache."

"Me too. You know what would make it better though?" Juliet asked.

"Mmm? Water? Coffee?"

"Probably, but I was more thinking that waking up with you next to me in bed would be kind of helpful too."

Juliet hesitated even as she said the words. Not from regret but from wondering how Mia would interpret her request. "Oh, in your PJ's, I mean. Totally dressed. Just sleeping."

It took a moment for Mia to respond, and Juliet considered for a second that Mia was going to oppose the idea. Not for the first time, Juliet even found her own ability to panic relentlessly exhausting. "Well…only if you are sure."

"I am."

"Then, of course I would be incredibly happy to fall asleep next to you."

Juliet breathed a sigh of relief. "Good, because I am so exhausted." Her body deflated with her loud declaration.

Mia shifted her weight, sitting up and releasing Juliet's hand. "Go on, then. I expect to see those dancing ducks in less than ten minutes. My cupcakes will be waiting."

"Cupcakes?"

"Yeah, I have equally seductive flannels with giant cupcakes on them."

Juliet laughed. "Can't wait to see 'em." Any anxiety Juliet had over Mia's interpretations dissipated. Mia didn't seem to be in any rush at all.

Clapping, Mia stood, holding a hand out. Juliet took it, and Mia gently pulled her to her feet. They both stumbled slightly as they took a gradual curve in their path to the kitchen. Mia hastily shoved half-rinsed plates into the dishwasher and stained wine glasses into the racks as Juliet disappeared towards her room.

Mia was sitting on her bed when Juliet appeared at the door only a few moments later. Mia grinned. "I do love those pants."

Juliet blushed and played with the drawstring, retying it into a bow. "I can come in?" she asked hesitantly.

"Yes, yes, come in. God, you don't have to ask. Do you have a side preference?"

She shrugged. "Nope, I don't mind."

"I'll take this side, if that's okay…I often use the bathroom at night. Maybe it won't wake you if you're further away."

Juliet nodded. "Sure, I don't mind. I'm sure it won't." She closed the door behind her and crossed the room, sliding gingerly under the covers when Mia held them up. "It's cooler in here."

"Yeah, I had the heat up outside. I didn't want you to get cold."

"Nice." Juliet relaxed into the pillows, lying on her back as Mia settled in next to her. "This is a pretty good way to end an awesome day."

"Couldn't be better," Mia agreed, leaning up on her elbow and switching off the light.

"The cupcakes look super tasty too," Juliet said softly, turning away from Mia to her good side; she couldn't yet lie on the other. She dragged Mia's arm with her and wrapped it around her shoulder and chest. "Careful of the ribs," she murmured.

"Got it." Mia snuggled up behind her, sharing Juliet's pillow, nose pressed into Juliet's hair. "Good night."

Juliet smiled into the dark. "Night, Mia."

Mia could hear Juliet in the kitchen talking with Janet as she dragged herself in the next morning. She wordlessly accepted the offer of a mug of coffee. The microwave was going, and various bowls and pans were in evidence when Mia stood next to Juliet, whose wet hair lay around her neck. Her face was void of makeup.

"Good morning." Juliet pressed a chaste kiss to her cheek.

Janet did little to hide her wide grin.

"I can't handle you as a morning person." Mia caught her hand and squeezed it before sliding onto a stool.

"I got a head start."

"I see."

"Juliet wants to cook," Janet interrupted cheekily. "I provided some instruction."

"I can cook," Juliet said. "Reasonably well, actually, and breakfast—so my specialty."

"Made a few breakfasts for women over the years, huh?" Mia teased.

"Not at all. I just like breakfast—most important meal of the day and all."

"Yeah, yeah, likely excuse."

Janet laughed at Mia's banter. "I might leave you two to it," she said. "Give me a yell if the kitchen's on fire. Martin and I are going to clean out the barn today. Wish us luck."

"I might take one of the horses for a ride later," Mia said. "I've been a bit lazy, so they haven't had too many runs with you and Martin away."

"Sure, I'll give 'em a brush-down today too. Maybe have a second coffee first, though. You look like you had a few last night. And by the bottles I collected this morning, that's an understatement."

"I was going to clean up," Mia insisted, but Janet waved the weak protest away.

"Not a problem. It was cleaner than I thought it might be."

"Thanks, though. You didn't need to."

"Enjoy breakfast," Janet said as she pulled a thick waterproof jacket on. "Or should I say 'good luck'?"

"Hey!" Juliet threw a tea towel across the bench, though it only made it as far as landing on Mia's shoulder. "Whoops, sorry, Mia. You want some Turkish bread with your eggs? I can toast it."

"Sure." She sipped her coffee. "Hey, I heard your phone ring a couple of times just before I came out of the room."

"Oh, probably one of the card companies. Although I thought I had everything. It's just my US driver's license I don't have now."

"I can't believe how quickly you got most stuff. Having the police report seemed to help, right? And your passport, I guess, helped with the ID side of things."

"Thanks to you. If I'm remembering those pleasant few pain-filled days correctly, all I did was sign on the line when you shoved something in front of me."

"It was easy."

"Mmm, I doubt it, somehow. Time-consuming much?"

Laughing, Mia said, "All right, just a little."

"Maybe it's my turn to take you to lunch later this week now that I actually have money…"

"Oh, we should go to that B&B that I wrote to you about when you were in Bruges. It's so nice. I think you would really like it." She paused. "Hey, there's your phone again. You hear it?"

Juliet stilled, spatula held over a thick pan where she had just tossed the bacon in. "Oh yeah, they can just leave a message. I'll phone them back."

She manoeuvred well around the kitchen, Mia noticed, multitasking with speed and skill. She had two thick slices of Turkish bread toasting under the grill and two plates heating in the microwave. Every so often, she subconsciously rubbed at her side, and Mia could just detect the tiny grimaces in her expression.

"So, more writing today?"

"Yep, I keep having more ideas and thoughts. It's weird. When I wrote the first one, I spent half the time drunk and crying, a quarter of the time angry and swearing at the screen, and the other quarter of the time actually writing. Something tells me this one might have a different feel to it. My editor is thrilled."

"Sounds intriguing. Will I get to read it?"

"When it's finished."

"What?"

"Yep," Juliet said, but when Mia put on her best shocked and crestfallen expression, she relented. "Oh fine. Maybe I'll give you little excerpts to read, tasters."

Mia observed her quietly for a few minutes, watching Juliet plate their breakfast with a wry smile on her face. "Hey Jules," she said. "You look really happy right now."

Juliet placed Mia's plate in front of her. She fished out cutlery from the drawer and placed it onto the bench before leaning in to press her lips to Mia's. She cupped Mia's cheeks with her hands, and when she pulled back, Mia's tongue was still tingling.

"You're right. I really am," Juliet said.

Mia grinned with a hint of pride and waited for Juliet to slide in beside her before taking a bite of scrambled eggs. "There's your phone again," she said, her mouth full of food. "Maybe you should check it."

"After breakfast."

"They're persistent, whoever they are."

"Mmm." Juliet bit into a large piece of toast topped with bacon and eggs. "I don't know who would be calling me. No one really does. That's what e-mail and Facebook are for."

"Have I mentioned I hate Facebook?" Mia asked. "I refuse to be on it. I was once, but then it just became a bitch fest. I was quite the topic of discussion."

"Yeah, Facebook's good for stalking. Not so good for keeping your private life private."

"Not even remotely. And I can tell you now, I could not give a fuck what my friends from elementary school are doing, who they've married and how many kids they have. Oh, and of course, who got the most expensive birthday or Christmas gift from their dickhead husband."

"Mia, go ahead and tell me what you really think!"

Mia tried to feign a hurt expression, but in reality she loved that Juliet was comfortable enough to name her boisterous side. "I really need to work on that filter, huh? You've trained me too well. Now I just say whatever. And eat whatever too, apparently. Lucky I haven't put on two stone."

"You say whatever you like, and you are superhot with or without two stone."

"You wouldn't say that if I had to waddle instead of walk."

Juliet grinned. "I don't like this conversation. Have I mentioned that you're hot? That seems like a safe space to stay."

Mia dropped her fork to the bench and slipped her fingers through Juliet's damp hair. She pressed messy kisses to her cheek until Juliet squirmed. "You want me to stop?" Mia asked.

"You're tickling." Juliet said, screwing her nose up and taking another bite, her plate almost clean. She tipped the tall tumbler to her mouth and swallowed several mouthfuls of juice.

"Oh my God." Mia's body straightened vertically as she heard the familiar distant ringing again. "Go and answer that freakin' phone," she said.

Grunting, Juliet slid off the chair and hurried off. Mia continued to eat her breakfast, giving up on the cutlery and picking up the last section of toast, piled high with egg and bacon. She turned when she heard Juliet murmuring into the phone. Mia watched her go still near the television in the lounge, eyes on the ground.

Juliet seemed to freeze mid-movement, one arm held out in front of her and the other holding the phone to her ear. Her hair hung over her face, over her wide-open mouth. Mia tossed a piece of crust back onto her plate, continuing to chew. Her instincts were a little slow: she only slid to her feet when the phone in Juliet's hand tumbled to the ground. Juliet raised wide, petrified eyes and uttered just a small whimper as she stood in the lounge, motionless.

Mia stilled too, and she wasn't sure why. They stared at each other across the room until Juliet suddenly raked her hands through her hair and tilted her face to the ceiling. Mia rushed forward and cupped Juliet's elbows.

Juliet wheezed, squeezing Mia's fingers. A jumble of non-specific expletives burst forth from her until they morphed into a half sob.

And for Mia, it felt as if she were watching life itself fall apart in front of her.

CHAPTER 12

Juliet slowly drew her hands down from her hair, pieces now wayward and extending out at all angles. She accepted Mia's touch, fingers running up and down over her arms, but she could barely detect the sensation.

Staring at Mia, Juliet nonetheless had trouble focussing. Her eyes were fixed on Mia's, but her mind felt blurred and empty.

"What was the call?" Mia asked gently, but she might as well have asked in a foreign language. She took a step forward, but stopped as Juliet immediately jolted back from her approach. Panic filled her, and she shook her head. "I'm sorry."

"It's okay," Mia said gently. "What's happened?"

"I, umm, I have to go home."

"Home?"

"Ah-huh."

Juliet worked to catch her breath, her chest rising and falling rapidly. When Juliet looked over her shoulder, Mia stepped in again, this time holding her wrists, tenderly stroking over her pulse points.

"What's happened?" Mia repeated, but the words were nearly lost in mass of chaotic and confused feelings that preoccupied Juliet—the battle between an instinct to just stop and dissolve and knowing there were things that had to be done and done quickly. Falling apart was a luxury she couldn't afford right now.

"It's my dad." Juliet's voice was splintered. "He's died, and I have to go home. There are things to be organised, to do."

"Oh God," Mia said, her eyes closing briefly. "Juliet."

Juliet nodded and swallowed loudly. She stepped out of Mia's grasp and bent down to pocket her phone. "I just, I have to book a flight and make some calls." She forced herself into control. She needed to be focussing on something other than the complicated mix of feelings and thoughts this news had unleashed.

"Yeah, definitely. Let me help."

"They're going to organise getting him back," Juliet said, more to herself than Mia. "But I have to let my aunt know, and I should call Jack..." She put her hands on her hips, blowing air out of her lungs. "They're going to be devastated." Narrowing her eyes, she shook her head. "Should I call them first or book my flight? And I have to call Northwest…shit."

"Okay, let me sort flights, and you can make the calls that you need to. But Juliet, just take a second, okay?"

Nodding, Juliet tried to lose some tenseness in her shoulders, and she focussed on Mia. "I'll get you my card," she said softly, gritting her teeth when she felt a burn in her throat. "Umm, to Kansas City, just economy."

"I'm not letting you go on your own." Juliet didn't have the energy or focus to argue, but Mia's tone left little room for debate.

"I can't take you to my home," Juliet said sadly. "I just can't Mia. It's complicated. It's so fucking complicated. And now…this…"

Mia nodded. "Yeah, yeah, I'll stay in a hotel. Or if you need time, space, I'll disappear for a few days. I am not *not* going with you."

"I don't want to do this."

"Oh, I know. I know so much. And you can yell and swear and cry and punch things…and whatever else you need to do."

"I have to make these calls, and I don't want to." Her fingers trembled as she brought them to her lips, and her words came out muttered in one long, breathless drawl. "I have to do it, and I have to tell them and I have to get on a plane and I have to…and, and I…I need you to wait."

Mia shook her head, and even in the midst of the crisis, Juliet could see the confusion in her expression.

"Just wait until I can stop," she said. "Be ready when I stop." Again, a perplexed look crossed Mia's face. "For me…for us."

Nodding, Mia reached forward and squeezed Juliet's shoulder. "Okay. I'm going to sort the flights, and you go make your calls. I'm right here if you need anything."

Juliet turned away without another word; she was too overwhelmed to think about anything more than the next step. And her next step was to make a few impossible phone calls, the ones that you hope you never have to make. And she was making them for the second time.

"It's Juliet, Juliet Taylor," she said into the mouthpiece of the phone, rubbing her forehead as she leant forward on the sofa.

"Ah, Juliet, yes, how are you? Are you coming in to visit your mother?"

Juliet sighed; she would be now, she supposed. "Umm, yes, in a week or so. I have some bad news, actually."

"Mmm?"

"My father has died, and we'll be having the funeral later this week." The sentence sounded gentler in Juliet's head, the words less void of emotion. She couldn't change them now anyway. Words were like that: once they were said, they couldn't be retracted. Her father had always been good at saying things without filter, no matter the consequence.

"Oh, I'm terribly sorry." Juliet was grateful that she was on the phone as her eyes involuntarily rolled at the rehearsed response. "Would you like your mother to attend?"

"No," Juliet rushed to say. "No."

"We will let the doctor know and advise Mrs Taylor."

"Thank you, I appreciate that. Is there anything she needs at the moment?"

"No, not at all. Your father has always made sure there was more than enough in her account."

"Okay, well, I need to make some more calls, but please call me with anything else you need."

"Yes. I suppose you're the sole contact now."

Juliet clenched her teeth and drew air in noisily through her nostrils. The frustration was brief; it wasn't as if there were other options now. "Yes," she said simply. "Give Mom my love."

"Will do."

Juliet hung up the phone. She was done with pleasantries.

"How did the calls go?"

Juliet shook her head and slumped back, head resting against the back of the sofa. "Military life—word was already out, really. Not really a surprise, I guess."

Mia felt a pang of familiarity; it was same in her old life. Only the gossip wasn't always accurate. "Of course. Well, I have us on a flight tomorrow morning to New York. We just need to change at Heathrow. I wasn't sure what you wanted to do then."

"Thank you for organising that. I would probably have gotten our flights completely wrong. I'll just fly on to Kansas from JFK."

"Yeah, I know you said that you didn't want me to come with you, so I thought maybe I would go down to Florida. My family has their winter place there. Unless you want me to come, which I would much prefer to do." Mia was careful with her words. She knew that Juliet needed to do this on her own.

The idea of seeing her family filled Mia with endless anxiety and dread, but pondering Juliet's father's death had given her own need to get closure some momentum.

"I would like that. Maybe we can meet up somewhere after a few days?"

"That was what I was thinking too," Mia said. "Depending on how my visit goes, we could both be a mess."

"It's been a while for you, hasn't it?"

"Almost a year. And our last contact was fairly spectacular, I think *don't you ever bring this family into disrepute again* was the last thing my father said to me. So the reunion should go well."

The sarcasm was Mia's attempt at keeping the conversation as light as possible. Juliet had enough to deal with without her family dramas as well.

"What will you do if it all goes…well, crappy?"

Mia shrugged. Of course, Juliet didn't buy into her feeble attempt at humour. "See you in a hotel in New York?"

"Good plan. There better be chocolate and wine if that's the case, because I will need it too. A lot."

"There will be an endless supply regardless of where we are."

Juliet managed a small smile, and Mia could see her swallow heavily. "Aren't we too young to have so much shit happen in our lives?"

"Apparently the world missed that memo."

"I want to be twenty and carefree again." Tears pooled in Juliet's eyes.

"Only if I could have met you."

Somewhere mid-flight over the North Atlantic, Mia and Juliet sat quietly, earphones discarded after watching a movie and snoozing lightly. Painfully quiet for most of the day, in Mia's opinion, Juliet maintained a death grip on Mia's hand. Even when she curled away from Mia and stared out the window with a small airline pillow behind her neck, she kept a tight hold.

"Hey," Mia said after she was confident Juliet was staying awake. She pushed up the armrest between them. "Come here and lie on me for a while; I want to give you cuddles."

Juliet turned toward her with the hint of a smile. "I haven't stopped yet, you know," she said, tucking hair behind her ears. Juliet had continued to tell Mia that she would gladly fall apart later, when she could. And Mia respected that; sometimes you just do what you need to do, she thought, and then worry about the rest later.

"I know, and I'll still be around when you do. But I can still have you here, can't I?" Mia asked, tapping her chest with an open palm.

Juliet pulled her knees up and rested them over Mia's thighs, then lowered her head, cheek resting over Mia's clavicle, chin tapping the curve of her breast.

"I wish we were just back at your place and having meals and dancing and getting to know each other. Everything is crazy and chaotic. Why didn't we get to just start like a normal couple?"

"It has been a bit full-on, I'll give you that." Mia liked that Juliet thought they could be a couple, that the direction they were headed in was definitely together. She thought better of drawing attention to it though; Juliet had enough to deal with. "What's the plan when you arrive?" she asked instead, picking at strands of Juliet's hair. Juliet shrugged silently into Mia's body. "Your flight leaves JFK before mine, so I'll be able to wait with you until you have to board."

Juliet huffed. "Make sure I get on, huh?"

"I'll come with you. Just give me the word that you've changed your mind and I'll be on that flight."

"No. Thank you, but no. I just need to sort some stuff first. I'm not trying to be all weird about it." She nuzzled a little closer. "I didn't really tell you what happened to my father."

"I figured you would fill me in when you wanted to."

"He's in the army and based at Fort Riley, hence the Kansas destination," Juliet explained quietly. "He's been a soldier since before I was born. We moved around so much—whenever they changed his base. He loves it…loved it, I guess. I hated it. Mom hated it, though she never said that."

"I'm not surprised. It's a tough life for family isn't it? Always left at home worrying."

Juliet nodded, tapping her fingers that splayed over Mia's blanket-covered thigh. "In the last, maybe, ten years, Dad had been training teams to go over to Afghanistan and mentor the Afghan security forces. His teams started off doing some civilian stuff, just basic law enforcement and working with local officials—well, that was the section he was in. He used to say he was safe now, that it wasn't the front line."

"But he wasn't."

Juliet scoffed. "He had a heart attack, Mia. He might have been over there, but that's not why he died."

"Mmm, I know. But still…"

"It seems ridiculous. He would be pissed. He would be so pissed that after all our family has been through and all the deployments he's had that this is how it ended."

Mia pressed a kiss to her forehead.

"He was superhuman, Mia. How did he die from a fucking heart attack?"

"He seemed superhuman. None of us actually are, though."

"He always made me feel like I was nothing, like I was a failure because he was the hero, and no one ever lived up to his expectations. I wasn't good enough—my choices, my life was never good enough. My father was an awful man, and I have to go and say a eulogy that paints him as the…hero."

"You don't have to do anything, Jules. You have to do what's good for you."

Juliet's nails scraped at Mia's leg, and she felt the pressure through her jeans. Moving her fingers from Juliet's hair, she snaked her hand to wrap around the back of Juliet's neck, kneading the muscle. "I can't get up there and say what I think. I just need to get the funeral over and done with, play the game. I've been doing it half my life, I can do it for another few days."

"Family sucks, yeah?" Mia massaged her lightly, soothing and relaxing her in one gentle motion.

"So much. But distract me for a while. What are your plans? You're going to just go unannounced to your parents' doorstep?"

Mia groaned and hugged Juliet to her, rolling her eyes. "Did you have to bring it up?"

"You need to have some idea what you're gonna do, don't you?"

"I can't call them. They don't take my calls. Or they pretend to not be home. Daniela is the same. I don't have a choice except to just go to their house."

"What do you think they'll do?"

Mia shook her head. "Refuse to see me, slam the door in my face—something similar."

"Really?"

Shrugging, Mia focussed on Juliet, who looked ragged and tired. "I don't know. They'll expect that I've changed my mind, maybe. Accept that the divorce was my fault and that I've come grovelling back, to live by their rules."

"Fuck 'em."

Mia laughed. "Maybe I'll tell them that."

"Should go well," Juliet said with a light chuckle. "What are they like, your parents?"

"Evil," Mia said immediately but then laughed it off. "No, not really. They're just stuck in the world that they know and can't see out of it, which I guess I can kind of understand. How do you relate to people when you have never even remotely walked inside their world?"

"Mmm. I wouldn't quite be so forgiving, but keep going."

"Who will I tell you about first? Mom…my mom is absolutely gorgeous, she's a beautiful woman. And incredibly intelligent, up on current affairs and international politics. She reads like crazy and probably could have been anything at all that she wanted to be."

"Apple doesn't fall far from the tree…"

"Well, it kind of does. My mother might be all of those things, but she doesn't care about that stuff. What she cares about is charity fundraisers, balls, and auctions, about making sure she wears a new dress and a different designer, and about finding the perfect tie for my father to wear. She fires staff on the spot if they make the smallest of mistakes. We went through a million as kids because they were never good enough. Of course, we loved most of them. They were warm and nice. Our nanny once had her pay docked because she didn't match our hair ribbons with our dresses. We were just going into the city for lunch. Crazy shit."

"Whoa." Juliet wrapped her arm tightly around Mia's middle. "Staff? As in plural? I think I was like eleven when I was making my own school lunch, never mind having a nanny or anyone else."

"Yeah, I don't think my mom has a maternal bone in her body, and actually, Dad was probably better at the kid stuff. He at least would come home and read to us or play dolls. But he was strict. If there were other people around, we weren't allowed to speak. We were to follow his rules. And then, when we got older, Daniela and I could just run amok, really. We had platinum credit cards and spent weekends going from party to party, alcohol and drugs, whatever was on. It was how it worked in their world. As long as we weren't causing trouble to them, anything was acceptable. They all did it too when they were younger, I think."

"Rich kids gone wild, hey?"

"'Til a point, and then it all kind of stopped. Going through college was the same, but then you reach this age, and there are decisions made. You would think that the older you get, the more independent you become, but it doesn't really work that way. In these families—because it wasn't just mine, you know—you get this period of four…five, maybe six years of playing up. And then it's all shut down. You have to grow up and head into the family business or get married. Like you said, just play the game."

Juliet shook her head. "Dad always wanted me to go into the army, follow in the family footsteps. But there's no way. I didn't even entertain the idea for two seconds, but it was always the unsaid, you know?"

"Yeah, I get that. The unsaid. Man, my life has been all about the unsaid."

"So, what are you going to do if they figuratively slam the door in your face?"

Mia sighed. "Probably have a meltdown."

"Understandably."

"Yeah. What about you?"

Juliet tilted her head up. "What about me?"

"What if you're not okay?"

She shrugged in response. "I will be."

"You don't have to be."

"But I do, for a while at least."

"Well," Mia said, pressing a kiss into Juliet's hair, "as long as you know you don't have to fake being okay with me."

Juliet didn't respond, but she tightened her arm around Mia's waist, fingers pressing into the side of her back. None of it was simple, and they were both heading to that odd concept of home now, to face it all again. It was as if they were walking directly into a pit of fire, and then they would later wonder why they had gotten burnt.

If there were other choices, they both would have been taking them.

The moment the loudspeaker at JFK announced her flight, Juliet dropped her face to her hands.

"I don't want to go," she said. She only consented to turn her head when Mia tugged on her arms. She gave Mia a tearful, guilty smile. "But I know I have to."

"Up," Mia said. She stood up with both hands outstretched, waiting until Juliet reluctantly took them. She gently pulled Juliet to her feet.

"So, I will be in a motel tonight and will have my phone glued to me, got that? I won't call, 'cause I know that you'll have things that you have to do, and I don't want to intrude, but I'll be texting like a crazy woman. And you phone me, okay?"

Juliet nodded, and her lower lip slightly trembled before she bit down on it. "What time do you arrive?" she asked quietly.

"Just before you land. A half hour earlier, I think."

Leaning in, Juliet pressed a hurried kiss to Mia's lips; it was awkward and rushed. She wrapped an arm around Mia's neck and another around her lower back, clutching her tightly. "I'll call you." Her own voice was barely audible.

Mia enveloped her, ever so slightly rocking. "I know it's not okay, but you can do this." Juliet nodded into her neck.

A few more seconds passed and Juliet lifted her face and rested her chin on the curve of Mia's neck. "You don't let them fuck you over either, okay? They don't get to control you."

Smiling, Mia drew back and cupped Juliet's face. She met her in a slow, lingering kiss. And Juliet kissed her back. "I'll see you soon," Mia said. "And call me…"

"Yep." With what she knew was a defeated look, Juliet grabbed her worn backpack and hanging it over one shoulder, stepped away. She glanced back and waved. "Bye, Mia."

"See ya."

Juliet approached the counter and had her boarding pass scanned before she disappeared into the air bridge. She couldn't look back or she would never get on that plane.

～～

Standing in the middle of a barren lounge room, Juliet gratefully acquiesced to the distraction of her phone vibrating in the back pocket of her jeans. She had met with the required army personnel, though she was less interested in financial benefits and payments than she was with negotiating the funeral arrangements. But after hours of planning and completing forms and meeting up with extended family and friends, she was exhausted. And she was standing in the middle of a barely lived-in three bedroom house, with just a small amount of light from the low voltage bulb overhead.

Checking her phone, Juliet breathed a sigh of relief. It was a text from Mia.

Hey beautiful. How are things going on your end? I've checked in, been for a walk, gone to the shops, and tried to talk myself out of the family visit tomorrow at least twenty times. Been hoping you're doing okay.

Juliet slowly lowered herself onto a small sofa which had been pushed to the side of the room. It was the same old two-seater they had lugged from home to home throughout her childhood. Her mother had never liked the furnished army houses; she had always wanted her own things.

Have I mentioned how much I hate this? :-(No dramas, though, just full on. No talking yourself out of it—you're going. xo

Juliet's phone immediately indicated a return message from Mia.

You up for a call?

Juliet didn't hesitate to reply.

Call please!

It was only a few seconds before Juliet's phone started ringing, her text message box still open. "That was quick," she said into the receiver.

Mia laughed. "Just desperate to hear how you're doing?"

"Blech, I'm all right. Unless you ask me to sign a form, then I may just have to kill you."

"Oh, crap, is that all you've done all day? As if you don't have enough to be doing and thinking about."

Juliet swivelled around until she laid back on the sofa, head on the arm and feet hanging off the other end. "It was half the day. I had to go to the base and meet with some representative. I don't even know half of what I signed. The one good thing, though, is that they're organising most of the funeral stuff. I just spoke with the chaplain, and he's going to do it all. I suppose that's what happens when you've served for thirty-five years, even if half of it was, like, an office job."

"So that's good? Are you happy for them to do it?"

"Shit yeah, I don't have the energy. They probably knew him better than me anyway. Suppose that makes me sound like a bitch—there's just so much. I had to go and listen to my aunt sob for hours, and all these people I didn't even know kept coming to her house. I haven't even really been in his life. I mean, I have…I've known bits and pieces, but I haven't actually been *in* his life. All these people—they know him and I don't. Didn't. I don't know."

"Mmm, it sounds awful."

"I don't even know what to do next or what decisions to make. His closest friend, who I've known since high school, wanted to give me all this stuff to put in the eulogy. Stories to tell. So I said he could do it. And now I feel guilty— should I have? I'm his daughter. It's my job."

"Oh, honey, no. You shouldn't feel guilty—at all. That's exactly it. You're his daughter, so you do what's right for you, fuck the rest. You need to look after yourself."

Juliet released a shaky breath, pressing her thumb and index finger into her eyes. "Tell me I can do this."

"You can."

"My brother died." A choked sob escaped her, followed by a startled moan. "And my fucking ribs are still fucked."

Drawing her knees up, she rolled onto her side and slipped off the arm of the sofa, so that she was lying horizontal along the length of the couch and curling up with the phone still pressed with one hand to her ear. She cried into the phone, trying to elaborate multiple times, but stopping to gasp in mouthfuls of air and wipe at her nose with the back of her hand. "Ben died over there too, trying to live up to Dad's expectations. I spoke at his funeral…he was my best friend, and he died."

"Jules…"

"Do you know what Dad said at the funeral? He said that Ben *screwed up*, that it was his fault. Who says that? And what, I'm putting pressure on myself to stand up and paint that bastard as a hero who loved and supported his family? I have no family left because of him, and I hate him. And I can't hate him because he's dead. I'm not allowed to hate my dead father."

"You're allowed to feel whatever you feel."

Juliet cried more audibly. "I can't do this. I can't fucking do this again."

"Okay, Juliet you need to slow down and breathe. Just stop for a second. Take a breath."

A silence fell between them. Juliet tried to breathe, to settle. "I feel like crap."

"You think? It's a lot, too much."

"Yeah, well, life hasn't figured that out yet."

"You shouldn't be alone. Where's your mom? Why is this all on you?"

"She can't do any of this…she just can't." Juliet loudly sniffled, wiping at her face. "I have to do it."

"Okay, then I'll come, Juliet. Do you want me to? I want to."

She hesitated, genuinely considering the offer. "It's not that I don't want you to, I just need a few days."

"Okay. I'm trusting you to tell me if you change your mind, okay?"

"I will, I promise. And in a few days, I'll fly to you wherever you are, depending on what happens with your family. I don't think I'll want to stay here."

"Fair enough. Something tells me I won't want to stay here either. I hired a car at the airport, by the way. I'll drive out to see them tomorrow."

"You got your armour ready?" Juliet's throat was starting to relax.

"Yeah, absolutely. Full body armour, helmet, the whole lot. Bring it on, right?"

"And if all else fails, we have Scotland, huh?"

Mia smiled and chuckled. "Yes, *we* do."

It was familiar, and Mia hated that. She was being overwhelmed with memories, both good ones and the not-so-good ones. The road to the family winter property was relatively quiet, but the long driveway was simply deserted. The same trees that Daniela and she had tried to climb as kids lined the paved track, and when she looked out the window at the wide expanse of grass, she could almost hear Daniela's high-pitched childish squeals.

At the large iron gate, Mia leaned out her window and punched in the access code. To her surprise, it opened.

Driving around the large turning circle in front of the house, Mia parked under a shady tree. Her hands shook as she turned the ignition, and the keys fell to the ground as she stepped out of the car.

She drew in quick, anxious breaths, knowing that any word that left her mouth would come out in a pant and that attempting to calm herself would be futile.

Tears pricked at the edges of her eyes. She ducked back into the car and sat in the driver's seat, closing the door behind her. She needed to get a grip. Reaching into her handbag, she withdrew a small compact and examined her reflection. She tapped pressed powder to her chin and studied her eyes: they were unacceptably glazed with tears. Fishing out her phone, Mia checked for missed calls before clicking on the text message she had received from Juliet mid-route.

Good luck today. Let me know how it goes. xoxo

Mia quickly typed back.

Thanks—just arrived. Feel like a lamb to the slaughter. How are you?

Living the dream. Another meeting with the chaplain, about song choices and readings now.

Mia screwed her face up.

:-(No fun. Good luck to you too.

A message came back through quickly.

Stop procrastinating. Go. xo

Mia gave a nervous giggle and shook her head.

Okay! I'm going.........

Exiting the small rented Prius, Mia threw her bag over her shoulder and approached the house slowly. She walked to the wooden double door and pressed the doorbell. She waited.

And waited.

Glancing around her, Mia could hear movement inside, yet no one appeared. She rang the bell again, and it was almost a minute before the door swung open. Standing in front of her was one of their staff. The butler, maybe; he wasn't familiar to Mia.

Mia cleared her throat. "Good morning, I'm Mia...Mia Rev—" Mia said before being interrupted.

"I know. I have been advised to ask you to leave the property."

"Excuse me?"

"Mr and Mrs Revira have advised me to ask you to leave."

"Of course. Well, I would like to see them."

"That is not possible."

"They obviously know that I am here." Exasperation crept into Mia's voice, and she lost some of the forced control she had called up before leaving the car as the man squared his shoulders.

"I think it's best that you leave."

"What about my sister? Is she here? Daniela?"

He glanced over his shoulder then, and Mia followed his line of sight. Daniela stood quietly, watching from further inside the wide entrance.

She averted her eyes quickly as Mia's surprised gaze fell on her. "Daniela! Dani!"

Daniela glanced back once before shaking her head.

"Come on, Daniela. You could at least speak with me. What happened to you?"

"Daniela, do not." A slow deep voice emanated from inside, and Mia recoiled slightly. Her father was an impressive man, tall, with broad shoulders and a booming voice. Her mother followed dutifully behind, always the trophy wife, just as Mia was meant to be. "Christopher, arrange for the gates to be opened," her father said, voice seemingly void of emotion.

Mia stilled as her parents stood in front of her and no one said a word. Daniela took a few steps closer.

One by one, they each surveyed Mia, their eyes drifting from her face and over her body and back up again. Their expressions were united in clear dissatisfaction; jeans and a sweatshirt were not meeting their expectations.

"Hi." Mia's eyebrows widened at the clear, rounded swell of Daniela's stomach. She had to be at least six or seven months pregnant.

"Mia." She received a single nod from her father. It wasn't a greeting or a question. They didn't seem surprised to see her.

"I thought it was time that we talked." Mia cursed the hesitation and nervousness she could hear in her voice.

"Have you changed?"

"Excuse me?" Mia turned to her mother, feeling the glare before she saw it.

Daniela coughed. "They know, Mia."

"Know what, Daniela?"

"About you, everything—the women. They know. Stephen found out about the woman in the jazz club and made an announcement, and I confirmed it. They know."

"Are you kidding me? How? It's none of his…It's no one's business."

"You put it out there…" Daniela said. She crossed her arms and smirked, as if proud of her point.

"Have you changed?" Mia's mother asked again, each word pronounced slowly and deliberately.

Mia shook her head, forehead creasing and mouth slightly open. "No, I… no."

"Then you can stop there."

Without another word, the door closed heavily in front of her face. It wasn't slammed but gently closed. Mia heard the solid latch click into place and the distinct sound of a secured lock.

CHAPTER 13

Juliet was done. She was tired of placating relatives, engaging in crap conversations about how this was the perfect way for her father to have died. How he would have hated to get old and demented, how he wouldn't have coped if his body had slowly and progressively betrayed him.

It was bullshit.

And Juliet was becoming exhausted, her threshold for listening to false truths rapidly lowering. She had to walk away before she said something she regretted, especially to her histrionic aunt, who was rambling on yet again about what an incredible man her brother had been.

"It's such a loss...just such a loss for everyone. What will we do without him? He's always been the same, ever since we were children. Always the strong one, the protector."

Juliet's jaw hurt from clenching her teeth, and she was so tired. "It's funny, isn't it," she said, "how we immortalise the dead, even when they don't deserve it?"

Her aunt stopped mid-speech, and her mouth fell open. A few barely noticeable coughs and sniggers sounded from around her, from people who knew her and knew her father accurately.

"Juliet, that's a terrible thing to say."

"Accurate, Aunt Bev. Accurate."

"I don't think so at all!"

"Come on. He was a completely unforgiving man who had his own agenda, and if you didn't follow his rules, then you were nothing to him. You actually know that very well, Aunt Bev."

"He was just a proud military man, that's all. And that should be commended. He died in the line of duty and..."

"He had a heart attack."

"He was deployed."

Juliet shook her head and rubbed at her neck. She found her aunt unbearable, which at least was something she had in common with her father. *Intolerable drama queen* had always been his description of her. It was strange, though, how the living reflected on the dead: the musings were always so positive and inaccurate, lives seen through rose-coloured glasses and their poor, pitiful excuses for their untimely deaths too. It was as if painting a pretty picture would make it all better.

What was wrong with saying that someone had died and that it sucked, full stop? End of sentence. Nothing else was needed.

Her father wouldn't have been happy to die from an infarct; if he had had his choice, he would have died running through a barrage of gunfire, saving the lives of two innocent little girls under his arms. Or he would have taken some other similar grand gesture that would have earned him a posthumous award— the Medal of Honor, preferably.

"I have to go," she said quietly, though by that time, Aunt Bev had continued her conversation with a more willing ear. She slipped outside with a few mutterings of getting some air, skilfully avoiding the goodbyes. She left immediately, getting in the car and driving.

As soon as she returned to her parent's house, she slumped down onto the same uncomfortable small sofa. Juliet couldn't wait to give the direction to empty the house. Donate whatever to whomever, she didn't really care. She had the few small valuables, sentimental items, really, that she wanted, and her mother could keep the rest. Juliet would make sure her mom had her father's medals and wedding band, but everything else was fairly disposable. The family photos had already been distributed, and the house was cold and impersonal anyway. Her family had left her with enough metaphorical baggage; she didn't need it in the literal sense as well.

She didn't understand why they all had to sit around and talk about him as if this were something he wanted, as if the stars had aligned, and the world suddenly made sense; because it didn't.

But she only had to get through a few more days. The funeral was planned for the next morning, and then it would only take a day or two to sort everything else and she could disappear again.

She kept having a little battle with herself every time she went to phone or text Mia or to think about where and when they would meet up again. She told herself over and over that it was *new* and *complicated*. But other than that, her instincts were telling her *yes*. Right now, with Mia, everything was a *yes*.

With thoughts of Mia, Juliet checked the time and clicked her tongue. It had been almost five hours since Mia had messaged from outside her parents' house.

Withdrawing her phone, Juliet typed and deleted a text multiple times, rephrasing and adding hugs and kisses before reconsidering. She felt a little silly; it was her contact that was important, not the wording.

I haven't heard from you...all okay?

Forty-five minutes passed before Juliet received a response, though she was still sitting motionless and staring blankly at her feet. She jumped at the message alert tone.

Just sorting out flights to you. Late afternoon arrival tomorrow okay?

Juliet exhaled a sad sigh, obviously things hadn't gone well.

Of course. So, not great, then?

Fucked.

She knew she probably shouldn't, but she let just a slight smile pull at the corner of her mouth. Juliet didn't need to elaborate this time, the expletive was descriptive enough.

I'm sorry. What can I do?

Nothing, really. How are you? Funeral sorted?

Yeah, tomorrow morning thankfully, can't wait to get it over with. Do you need to talk?

All good. My hatred for Florida has grown, though. Can't wait to see you – you're the one good thing in my life right now, hope that's okay with you.

Totally okay, right back at you too. What are your flight details? I'll pick you up.

Nah, you've got enough to do. Text me the address before tomorrow, and I'll just come to your parents' place. Do you need me to book somewhere? A hotel?

Juliet looked around the vacant room. She had slept the previous night on a day bed in the spare room and hadn't really thought too far ahead. She wasn't prepared to sleep in the main room, despite the queen-sized bed. It all felt a bit strange and uncomfortable.

We'll sort it when you arrive, don't stress. Are you okay? I know you're probably not…

Okay at being disowned by my family? Not at all. You okay?

Not at all. Awesome, at least we're equally not okay. :-)

Juliet added the smiley face, though she knew it was a bit of a stretch. There was some ironic humour in their equally screwed-up lives. But even amid the loss, they still maintained some awareness of the absurdity.

And Juliet needed some lightness. The next couple of days were going to be horrendous. And light, *light* was something she was definitely not going to be.

In the end, Mia hired a car and drove the two hours from the airport to the address Juliet had provided. If she had thought in advance, she probably would have organised a private transfer, but given her distress the previous day, she considered herself lucky that she had even booked the right flights.

Predictably, Mia's level of anguish had dissipated slightly after a sleeping pill-aided full night of sleep. She had woken up and decided to be more angry with her parents than upset, which she felt was a good move. She despised the emotional response that her family usually elicited from her, that unguarded and raw flood of unfiltered sorrow.

Following the directions on the satellite navigation, Mia easily negotiated the suburban area until she pulled into the drive in front of a neutral, simple brick home. It was surrounded by similar buildings, all basically the same, with slight variations in roof colour and gardens out the front. Pulling her small suitcase from the trunk, Mia wheeled it to the front door, handbag over her shoulder. Knocking on the wooden door, the hinges creaked and it pushed open, clearly left slightly ajar and unlocked. "Juliet?" Mia called out, rechecking the address on her phone and matching it with the house number. "Juliet?"

Stepping inside, Mia settled her suitcase just inside and pushed the door closed behind her. She stepped slowly down a short corridor, eyes darting along the white walls. "Juliet!" she called again, louder this time and heard a slight bang from the lounge room, adjacent to the hallway. It sounded a little like a glass landing on a table.

"Hey, come in." Juliet sat on a sofa, a half glass of wine on the coffee table. Her eyes followed Mia when she dropped her bag on the floor.

"Hi," Mia said, leaning in to give Juliet a soft kiss before sitting down next to her. "How are you doing?"

Juliet was in a knee-length black dress and stockings with her shoes discarded, toes slightly visible through the semi-opaque hosiery. Even though she had a thick coat around her, Mia was still shivering; the house was freezing, and it seemed empty except for Juliet.

"Good," Juliet responded, staring at Mia wide-eyed and unblinking, voice empty and stable.

"How did today go?"

"Fine."

Shuffling, Mia turned her body further, pulling one leg up underneath her so she faced Juliet. She continued to stroke her back, slowly and rhythmically, while Juliet continued to just watch Mia, though she looked as if she were watching an ant crawl across the floor. "Have you been back from the funeral long?"

Juliet's forehead furrowed. "I'm not sure."

Running the back of her fingers up over Juliet's cheek seemed to elicit a few blinks from her. "Juliet? Are you all right?"

"Yes."

"You don't seem so good."

"I don't?"

"No."

"Oh," Juliet said, and her face creased in confusion again. "Did your flight go okay? And the drive?"

"Yeah, fine, no problems. I hired a car, so we're stuck with two, but that's not a drama, I can sort that," Mia said, dropping a hand down to Juliet's lap. She ran her fingers back and forth along the inside of Juliet's arm before squeezing her hand.

Juliet slowly looked down at Mia's touch. "Hi," she whispered.

Mia sucked in a breath. "Hi." She cocked her head to try and catch Juliet's attention before pursing her lips into Juliet's hair.

"Have you eaten today?" Mia asked.

"Yeah, an apple earlier. This morning."

"That's not enough. You need something to eat, some water."

"What time is it? You were arriving at five."

"Yeah," Mia nodded, twisting her wrist with Juliet's hands still entwined in order to check the time. "It's almost eight. Maybe something to eat and then some sleep, hey?" Her fingers lifted from Juliet's back to run over her head and down through her hair.

"I'm tired," Juliet acknowledged, though the lack of expression on her face was scaring Mia.

"Okay. Do you have any food here? I'll check the fridge."

"I got some bread," Juliet replied, but again, she looked confused. "I'm not sure where I put it. And I got some wine."

Mia nodded. "Yeah honey, I don't think you should drink that." She took the glass with her as she stepped into the kitchen, Juliet still in her line of sight. She found the bread untouched on the bench, still in a plastic carry bag. Opening the fridge, Mia screwed her nose up—just a few condiments and a UHT milk on the shelves. She quickly withdrew a jar of marmalade and made some toast, filling two tall glasses of water from the tap.

"Just have a few bites for me." She placed the plate onto Juliet's lap. Juliet reached for a slice and bit into it, screwing her nose up.

"I know. It's the only thing in the fridge to have on it." Mia said.

"Thanks."

Finishing hers quickly, Mia took a few sips of water and patiently waited for Juliet to finish. Juliet managed most of it before giving Mia a pitiful look. "That'll do," Mia said smiling. "And now some water."

Juliet drank it quickly and looked to Mia, appearing to await her next direction.

"Do you want to go and get changed?"

Glancing down at her dress, Juliet nodded. "Yeah, I meant to…"

Content that Juliet was capable, Mia went into the kitchen and quickly washed the two plates and the knife she'd used, refilled the glasses with water, and secured the front door before flicking off lights. This quiet and void version of Juliet wasn't something she had seen before—the way she seemed to be floating somewhere just below consciousness. She looked smaller and more timid, lost and confused.

Mia wheeled her suitcase into the spare room, noticing Juliet's backpack just inside the door. She left her bag next to Juliet's and placed the water she precariously balanced, on an old dressing table. Juliet was sitting cross-legged back on a day bed in the room, a thick wooden white frame that came to just under the window.

"I'm excited to see the ducks," Mia said, crouching down in front of Juliet, hands on her pyjama-clad knees.

Juliet nodded and politely smiled. "You need your cupcakes."

"I do," Mia agreed. "Can I get you anything? Anything you need." Juliet shook her head. "Do you want me to stay with you tonight, or do you want…I mean, I can sleep out on the sofa."

"Can you stay in here?" Juliet asked, but then cast her eyes over the single bed. "Oh, I guess it's small."

"Ah, it's fine. Good, just let me wash up, and I'll be right back," Mia said, rubbing her knees. "You get into bed and leave me a little space, okay?"

By the time Mia returned, Juliet was curled up on her side, facing the door. She was lying close to the edge, head propped up on a pillow and both fists curled up under her chin. Mia smiled and pushed the door. It tapped against the frame but didn't close. It wasn't important; there was no one else in the house but them.

Bracing herself against the edge of the daybed, Mia climbed over Juliet. "Gymnastics was never my strong point," she chuckled, fighting to get herself underneath the multiple layers of sheets and blankets. The heating in the room was completely inadequate. "Jesus Christ, this is, well, tiny."

"I can sleep on the floor," Juliet said simply.

"Not a freakin' chance." Mia wrapped her arms around Juliet and kissed her neck. "You're going to spend the entire night right here. Besides, I like it. It's very high school."

They laid in silence for a few minutes, their breathing settling in to a slow, even rise and fall, inhaling and exhaling in unison. Juliet's fingers uncurled and slipped around Mia's wrist, tugging her closer.

"I didn't ask about your family thing," she said, jerking Mia from her thoughts.

"Shhhh. Sleep tonight and talk later, okay? There's plenty of time."

"Okay," Juliet whispered, wiggling back as Mia showered her neck with tiny kisses. "God, I'm so glad you're here."

"Me too."

"I don't think I can do this without you. Is that insane?"

"Shhhh, it's time to sleep, not think. And I'll be right here in the morning."

As uncomfortable as the small space was, Mia barely moved all night.

The next morning, Juliet was only marginally more communicative. She answered questions but barely initiated a sentence, and Mia thought that she looked lost. It was as if she had built up these high walls around her, simply focussed on surviving whilst she presented a non-emotive exterior to the world. Mia was concerned but not overly worried. She figured that for the moment Juliet could self-protect however she wanted to. That's how people function in the most awful of circumstances, she told herself. They compartmentalise so they can get done what needs to be done. It's not dysfunctional or abnormal. It's just the way the mind has learned to function under stress. She would be worried if it went on and on, but right now, she was just happy that Juliet wanted her there.

Somehow, they ended up in the car, and Mia was driving, following the GPS-directed route produced when Juliet had punched their destination into the device. She knew that they were going to see Juliet's mother, and that the navigation system was taking them to St Joseph, just over the state border into Missouri. Other than that, she was completely in the dark. She wasn't a hundred per cent sure if Juliet had actually asked her to come along or had just expected it, but she certainly hadn't protested when Mia had opened the passenger door for her and slipped into the drivers' seat.

Despite being painfully quiet throughout the almost three-hour drive, Juliet would sporadically reach across the console and place her hand on Mia's thigh.

She would just rest it there, thumb slightly moving back and forth; at times, she would offer Mia a sad smile, but other times, she continued to stare straight ahead. Mia would briefly rub her arm and cover her hand, hoping to silently portray her consistent support.

Mia tried to talk at times, just idly chatting, but she only got the odd murmur from Juliet, short, one-word, distracted answers. She was only trying to fill the silence anyway and wasn't fazed at the lack of response. Eventually she needed direction, though, as they took the final few streets and Mia watched the distance to their destination count down.

"We're almost there...Am I looking for something in particular? Just a house number or..." the signs on all the streets since the main road had hospital symbols on them. "Juliet? What am I looking for?"

"Oh, umm." Juliet refocussed out the window, shaking her head and blinking a few times. "Just take the next turn and then follow it down..." She pointed in front of herself, indicating for Mia to turn right. The GPS announced their arrival. "Keep going, and in here, there's a car park out front, see?"

"Yep," Mia nodded, indicating and turning into the facility. The large sign left little mystery: *Northwest Missouri Psychiatric Rehabilitation Centre*. "Oh, a psych centre? Your mom isn't well, huh?"

Juliet exhaled heavily and shrugged. "The sign's deceiving. It's not really rehab. That doesn't work. She's been here for years."

They parked in a vacant space, and Mia turned off the ignition, unbuckling her seatbelt. Juliet didn't move. Reaching across, Mia pushed the release button on Juliet's belt and guided it off her. "All good?"

Juliet screwed her nose up; it was as expressive as she had gotten since she and Mia had started this drive. "You don't have to come. It's probably a duty that can wait for a few more years—girlfriend's mad mother and all."

Mia stifled a soft laugh. "Call me your girlfriend, and I'll visit anyone you like." She rubbed Juliet's arm. "If you're okay with it, I'd like to come in and meet your mom. You don't have to do everything on your own, you know."

Juliet slowly nodded. "We won't be here long."

Grabbing her handbag from the backseat, Mia got out of the car and walked around to Juliet's side, holding the door for her. Juliet still protected her ribs as she got out, guarding them with her open palm, her other hand holding a canvas shopping bag.

Taking Mia's hand, Juliet led her inside the main entrance, obviously knowing her way through the facility. They signed in at the front desk and then waited at a secure door when Juliet gave her name and the resident they were visiting. "Juliet Taylor visiting Barbara Taylor, please."

A young woman appeared at the door, ushering them through before giving Juliet a quick embrace. "I'm sorry to hear about Daniel. We all are."

Juliet's eyes widened. "Had he been visiting?"

The short, slightly plump woman shrugged, and a tinge of red blushed her cheeks. "Not for a while. He had been deployed, right? We got e-mails that we read to Barbara, much like with many of our other patients."

Nodding, Juliet was moving her head in a panoramic glance around the deserted hallway. Mia noticed the upmarket prints on the wall and the wide, freshly carpeted corridor. Rooms ran off the corridor before it curved to the left where there was a huge display of leaflets and booklets—military veterans' resources and general mental health information.

"How has she been?"

"Well, no big changes, but that's expected. The odd smile recently."

"Has she been told about my father?"

"Yes. There wasn't a lot of acknowledgement. Dr Kusak isn't sure she comprehended. But I suppose we can't really know." They all paused for a moment as if waiting for someone to make the move to Barbara's room. "And you've been overseas again?"

"Ah, yeah. I have a deadline." Juliet shared a glance with Mia. "Can we go in?"

"Of course, go on in. We'll be at the nurses' station if you need anything." The woman seemed to breathe a sigh of relief. For someone who worked in a psychiatric facility, she seemed incredibly inept at small talk.

Juliet led Mia along the corridor and to the left, curling an arm around to rest her hand on the small of Mia's back. Mia's hand found Juliet's, sticking with her closely. When they reached the correct door, Juliet knocked a few times before turning the handle. She waved Mia in as she entered, leaving the door slightly ajar.

"Hi Mom," she said softly, tucking her hair behind her ears and walking over to the recliner where a woman was seated.

The room had a single bed in the middle and an en suite bathroom off to the side. A small desk with a few framed photos, a tall wardrobe, and a television monitor lined the wall in view from the bed. Juliet crouched in front of her mother, whose long gray hair fell around her shoulders in neatly brushed lines. She had been dressed in dark slacks, a pink shirt, and an open black sweater.

"It's Juliet, Mom. I'm in town." Placing both of her hands over Barbara's, Juliet let them rest motionless in her mother's lap. Mia watched awkwardly at the foot of the bed. Barbara didn't seem to acknowledge Juliet's presence, blue eyes staring straight ahead.

Barbara spoke suddenly. "The walls are white. They painted the walls just white, see?"

Juliet squeezed Barbara's hands, and Mia's pulse raced, observing Juliet take in a slow breath. "I see, Mom. I brought someone for you to meet, I hope that's okay. See at the end of the bed? That's Mia Revira, Mom."

Again, Barbara's eyes didn't move, nor did she acknowledge Mia's presence.

Mia stepped forward. She moved to sit on the edge of the bed next to Juliet, fingers dragging across Juliet's shoulder as she lowered herself down. "Hi, Mrs Taylor, I'm so pleased to meet you."

"I've been staying with Mia in Scotland, and I've been working on my next book. I think it's going to be good." Juliet twisted her feet out from under her, resting down on her knees. She released Barbara's hands and sat back on her heels. "I, umm, I got you a few things that they said you needed. I didn't have much time, but I got you a couple of new shirts and some slippers. They tell me it's been really cold, so I got you a new jacket— it comes down to your knees, so nice and warm. Maybe you can sit out in the courtyard sometime when the sun's out."

Mia cleared her throat. "There are some seats out there, is that right?" she asked. It was a rhetorical question, of course. Barbara didn't seem to be electing to move anytime soon. Mia looked out a glass sliding door and beyond a security screen. "Looks like a nice area to get some sun or do some reading," she said anyway. "Probably a good place to have a snooze or be read to, actually."

Juliet turned and smiled up at Mia, who just shrugged and smiled back. Mia wasn't freaked out. Saddened, yes; freaked out, no.

"I brought you some snacks too. Do you still like coconut chocolate?" Juliet asked, turning back to her mother's inert body in the recliner. "And some fudge. I'm not sure you'll like it, since it's super sweet. Remember how you never used to let us have sweet things? It's backfired. I love sweets now."

Mia's thumb found the skin of Juliet's neck, stroking it between strands of hair. "You might have to watch out, Mrs Taylor," she said with a slight laugh. "You may not get any of that fudge."

Mia noticed a long blink on Barbara's expressionless face. And when she opened her eyes, they flittered a little, seeming to jump from Juliet to Mia.

"They took them down to paint the walls white. New white walls, and they took them down," Barbara said.

Juliet shook her head, confused, but Mia jumped in. "Oh, the frames, huh? Yeah, they can't paint around them, so they had to put them on the desk. May I look at them?"

Not receiving a negative or affirmative response, Mia stood after a couple of moments and walked the short few steps to the desk, bending down to inspect the few frames there.

"That's Ben, my brother," Juliet said softly. "We were what, maybe ten, Mom?"

"Man, you guys were alike." Mia checked out Juliet's features. "Blonde hair and blue eyes runs in the family, obviously."

Juliet nodded, standing up and walking over to peer over Mia's shoulder. "That was my Dad and Ben just before Ben's first deployment, and there's Mom and Dad on their wedding day." She pressed her lips close to Mia's ear. "Mom was four months pregnant with me."

Mia giggled. It must have been quite the scandal back then, she thought, leaning against the side of the desk, one hand on Juliet's back. "Do you think we can take her outside? It's pretty sunny, though I guess it's still cold. But maybe she would like some chocolate."

Juliet nodded. She pulled a lever and slowly lowered Barbara's legs. "Let's have a look outside, Mom, see how cold it is. How would you like to put on your new coat?"

Mia reached into the bag and withdrew the jacket, breaking the tag off with her teeth before she held it open before them. "Here you go, feels really warm—good choice, Juliet."

She guided Barbara's arms into the sleeves, and Juliet tugged the jacket closed, doing the buttons up. "Fits perfect," Mia said.

Taking her Mom's hand, Juliet led Barbara outside, opening the sliding door and stepping out into the courtyard. They were settled together on a bench seat when Mia walked out of the room, a medium-sized block of chocolate in her hand and a small plastic bag with a piece of fudge. Barbara looked at Juliet, confused, and seemed to hold her daughter's hand tighter.

"That's Mia, Mom, remember?" Juliet said. "I introduced you inside."

"It's so nice to meet you, Mrs Taylor." Mia, put on her widest, most placating smile. "I would like to take credit for the chocolate, but it was your daughter. She has a bit of thing for junk food."

"Mmmmm." It was almost a logical and appropriately timed response.

"Would you like some?" Mia asked, breaking off a line of three squares and holding it out. Barbara took it and bit into it, sucking slowly on a single piece.

"Thanks," Juliet whispered, and Mia nodded.

"You warm enough?" Mia asked Juliet. "I've got another layer on. You can use my coat..."

"Nah, I'm good. I've missed the sun."

"Yeah, not a lot of sun in Scotland, or Belgium for that matter." Mia stood in front of them, rolling on the balls of her feet and holding her face to the sun. "How was that chocolate, Mrs Taylor? Not too bad, huh? So I'm guessing you might be keen for this piece of fudge."

Barbara's hand was out before Mia had negotiated the plastic wrapping. Barbara offered another murmur of approval as she took the fudge. "I got a few pieces, Mom. I'll have the nurses put them in a jar. You can keep it in a drawer. I hope they get you the things you need. We always pay extra for anything else."

Juliet sighed. Her mother released her hand to place both of her own on the piece of fudge and was soon nibbling slowly at it. "Guess there'll be more money now..."

She glanced up at Mia with a helpless expression. Mia gave her a sympathetic look. "You know, Mrs Taylor, your daughter's been pretty amazing these last few days. Weeks, actually, but particularly the last few days."

Barbara paused, looking between them, just a split second of passing awareness in her eyes before she resumed working on the square of fudge.

"Do you remember, Mom?" Juliet said. "Dad won't be visiting anymore. Is there anything you want to know?"

Not giving any indication that she understood the question, Barbara finished the sweet and dropped her hand back to her lap. Reaching into her pocket, Juliet sighed and then reached for her mom's hand. She produced a simple gold band, sliding it over Barbara's thumb; it fit securely over the woman's knuckle but was loose towards the base. But it wouldn't fall off. "I thought you would want Dad's ring," Juliet said.

Tearing her hand away and standing up suddenly, Barbara returned quickly to her room and settled back on the recliner, rocking slowly. Juliet bowed her head, and her hands fell to her sides. She rose to her feet, her eyes glassy as she looked at Mia.

"You're doing really good," Mia whispered, placing a hand on the back of Juliet's head and kissing her temple.

"I can't stay much longer."

"Sure. I'm ready whenever you are. This must be really hard."

Mia kept a hand wrapped around Juliet's hip as they walked back inside, both sitting on the edge of the bed as Barbara continued to rock. They stayed for another fifteen minutes, but it was tough to have a three-way conversation when only two were really present. They persisted though, mostly thanks to Mia's ability to talk gently and fluidly, as if Barbara was following and commenting on her small talk.

When they finally left, Barbara placidly allowed Juliet to press a kiss to her cheek and to squeeze her hands. Juliet stopped at the door. Turning back, she said, "I'll see you again soon, Mom, okay? I love you."

Barbara's eyes blinked once, and her fingers turned the ring on her thumb over and over. She just stared ahead.

Leaving some paperwork at the desk on their way out, Juliet had a quick discussion with the manager in regards to continued financial commitments. Her mom would be the recipient of her father's life insurance and various army payments, which, along with her brother's, were more than sufficient for lifelong care.

Juliet gripped tightly to Mia's hand as they walked out.

"You just want to go?" Mia asked quietly. "Or do you need a few minutes?"

"I just want to go, if that's okay. You good to drive?"

"Yeah, of course. I could do with a coffee stop, though."

Juliet nodded, tipping her face up and kissing Mia's cheek. They stumbled a little, and Mia laughed. "Careful."

"I have to thank you," Juliet said quickly. "You're better with her than I am."

"It's easier to be a stranger."

"She wasn't always like this," Juliet said before Mia closed her door and walked around the car.

"I figured she wasn't," Mia said, "but what happened? I mean, is there not any treatment? Or is that the result of medication or something?"

"I don't really know the specifics, as in what initially happened. Dad always brushed over the details and focussed on her recovery. It was after Ben died, though, that this happened. There was one time before, years and years before, when we were kids. Dad got injured, and she had this breakdown, I guess. But she got better. This time she didn't."

Mia started the car and pressed at the GPS before reversing out. "She's been like this since your brother died?"

Juliet nodded. "They just thought it was shock at first, and then later a type of depression. They gave her ECT for a while, and she would talk a little more, have conversations. But they couldn't keep doing it forever, and it didn't seem to work as well the more times they did it." She rested her head back, examining Mia. "Dad never really visited. They said he did, but he didn't."

"Mmm," Mia said. "There's this part of me that gets that, but then this whole other part that says, 'Hey, it's your wife, and your career is probably part of what's causing the issue.' I mean, did he ever think of retiring, that it might help to even just be around?"

Mia glanced across to the passenger seat and saw the despondent expression on Juliet's face.

"His career was everything, so much more than family."

"Seems like family comes second a lot of the time in this world." Mia had also once thought that family was always the number-one priority, the one thing that came first, no matter what.

The conversation quietened down after that, and they drove most of the way with only the occasional observation or random thought and a brief comfort stop. Juliet slept some of the way, obviously spent from days of heightened stress. Mia was almost grateful for the silence and content to be with her own reflections for the drive. With soft music playing on the car stereo and just the expanse of highway in front of her, Mia could lose herself in her deliberations.

They were almost back to the military-issued house when Mia broke the silence. "You feel like talking?"

Juliet drew her lower lip into her mouth and pulled her knees up close to her chest. "Not really."

"You sure?"

Juliet drew in a rushed breath of air through her nose. "I don't want to talk," she whispered as tears welled and pooled under her lower eyelids. Mia made a split-second decision: she would push just a little.

"We don't have to," Mia said, placing her hand on the edge of Juliet's car seat. Juliet didn't move, but watched her closely, her eyes suddenly fixated. "You don't have to talk, and you don't have to be okay."

Nodding, Juliet allowed a tear to slowly slip down her cheek. Mia glanced frequently from the road to Juliet, watching the teardrop tumble from her cheekbone. She gave Juliet a few long seconds, then moved her hand to rest on Juliet's knee. "I know you're not okay."

Squeezing her eyes shut, Juliet's face contorted and her shoulders shook. She took Mia's hand, held it between both of her own, and placed her forehead against her own knees. A slow, drawn-out sob emanated throughout the car.

She cried for a long time with sporadic hiccups and soft whimpers. As soon as they arrived home, Mia pulled into the driveway and held Juliet as best she could across the console.

Mia cried then too, just a few tears that toppled from her eyes as Juliet's feelings of loss morphed with her own.

When Juliet finally lifted her blotchy, stained face, Mia gripped her tightly, bowing her forehead to Juliet's. They both sniffled and released a final spent cry. Then Juliet licked her lips, murmuring in a hoarse, broken voice, "There's no one left. I'm alone."

Mia curled her fingers, and they scraped lightly against Juliet's skin. "Me too."

CHAPTER 14

The next morning, Juliet ushered Mia into the car and to a nearby row featuring small shops and cafes and a few restaurants nearby that were closed until lunch. They settled into two comfy leather lounges opposite each other in a small cafe, a table in between, and sipped coffee from large mugs. Reaching across the table, Juliet wiggled her fingers until Mia grasped her hand.

"What?" Mia finally asked. "Have I got chocolate on my nose?"

Juliet shook her head. She made a deliberately serious face. "Nope, and I would tell you if you had anything on your nose, just so you know."

"Well, you're staring at me."

"Mmm, 'cause you're pretty amazing." Mia clearly needed to hear this more, Juliet had decided.

"Oh I totally am. I know that." But she was blushing.

"So I've been going over this speech in my head for the last half an hour, and it's crap and completely tangential and lacking in any kind of eloquence that you might expect from someone who supposedly writes for a living." She stopped and drew in a breath. "You wanna hear it?"

"Ah," Mia said with a nervous smile, "should I be worried?"

"Oh no, sorry. Not at all, I don't think. Unless you're freaked out by me or something. But no, I don't think so. I'm not about to tell you I'm crazier than my mom or anything."

"Maybe you should go with direct rather than this lead-in. I'm completely confused…"

"Okay, I can do that. I ramble a lot when I'm nervous, more than usual anyway."

"Rambling is good. It's quiet that freaks me out."

"Oh yeah, which is kind of part of the speech. I know I've been out of it, almost since we met, and I'm not like that. That's not me, really. But I've started at the end…this wasn't what I practised in my head. Right." Juliet took a long gulp of coffee and smiled. "You are amazing. Let's go back there. I was on track there. I've been trying to figure out a way to thank you for what you've done, to say how incredible and supportive you've been, but saying 'thanks' doesn't go anywhere near what I…well, feel."

"Juliet, it's nothing…it's…"

"No, it's not nothing. Please don't downplay it, because it's so much more than nothing. I don't do this, Mia. I don't meet someone and then cling to them and fall apart. I don't ever." Juliet paused and sighed. "It's always been the criticism. I keep everything locked up—my greatest flaw or whatever. I put on this act of being all calm and in control, even with people who don't deserve it, with whom I shouldn't." She swallowed, and Mia squeezed her hand. Juliet smiled. "But I don't with you. I don't feel like I have to."

"And no way. You don't have to. But isn't that good?"

"Yeah, I mean yeah, absolutely. And a bit scary…"

"I get that," Mia said. "And I can say that you should trust me, but I realise it's not that simple. It takes time."

Juliet sipped at her coffee, taking a quick look around the room to give herself a moment. "I don't want to stay here. I'm ready to leave this town for a while. But I want to stay with you, Mia. I want to go where you want to go. There are no ties for me anywhere, and I hope that, well, I hope that you want me to tag along."

Mia grinned, and Juliet could almost see relief wash over her as she exhaled. But still, Juliet hesitated. Was she putting pressure on Mia?

"I don't want you to *tag* along, Juliet." Mia planted her palms down on the table and fixed a gaze on her. "But I do want us to go together."

"You do?"

"Ah-huh. But where? I mean, do you want to head back to Scotland, just settle for a while? Or are you keen on somewhere new? A fresh start?"

Juliet shrugged. "It's up to you. I think it's time that you get to do what you want to do. I'm flexible. There's nothing holding me back, no reasons."

"That's clearly too much power," Mia joked.

It was Juliet's turn to roll her eyes. "You have had a really, really crappy time in life because of people making decisions for you, so I'm putting you in the driver's seat. Anyway, I have a feeling that whatever makes you feel good will make me feel good too."

"I don't suppose you meant that to have a double meaning."

A slow grin spread across Juliet's face. She shrugged. "Well, that too."

"I guess I want to go back to Scotland…but does that suit you? It's my place these days, so it's kind of home."

Juliet nodded, though she could see Mia's forehead creasing suddenly. "I'm good with that. You look worried though."

"No, sorry. That's just my mind running a million miles ahead. I just went straight to visas and shit, 'cause I've got permanent residency from all of our business stuff, but what are you travelling on—a tourist visa?"

"Yeah, they allow six months, I think, so I'm all good."

"But is that what you want to do? Are you sure?"

"Mia." Juliet's voice took a stern tone. "Yes, I'm sure, completely sure. But, there is something else that we need to talk about, and that would be the whole flight thing."

"Hmmm? Flight thing? I don't get it."

"I have money, as in, I have money to live on and travel with, at least until my book is published and that starts coming in. But, I'm not, I guess…I don't have the money to fly business class, and that's totally okay that you do that. But if we're going back to Scotland, I can't have you keep *sorting* the flights and…"

Mia halted Juliet with a gentle hand on hers. "It's not important, Juliet, it's just…money."

Scoffing, Juliet sighed. "The only people who ever say that are people with shitloads of it."

Mia gave what appeared to be a brief guilty glance and then a nod to concede Juliet's point.

"And that's not a criticism, really it isn't. I've always paid my way. I'm crazy independent, and it makes me, well, uncomfortable, I suppose."

"But it doesn't bother me." Mia's voice turned soft. "I wouldn't ever expect anything in return. You know that, right? God, really, I don't expect anything at all."

"I know, but what if one day you do? What if I really, really piss you off and you want to make me as miserable as humanly possible? I've seen worse."

"I won't."

Juliet squeezed Mia's hand and gave her a sad smile. "The truth is, it's more my issue than anything to do with you. I can't accept that kind of gift from you, it's too generous. And I'm not paying you back or giving you anything in return. It's not fair."

"Not giving me anything in return? Are you kidding me? Juliet, my entire family just slammed a door in my face, literally. They closed a door right in front of me. But I'm okay, and that is because of you, and only because of you. Can't you let me thank you too?"

Juliet slowly shook her head. "Not like that. It's too much. You don't need to thank me, and definitely not with cash. I feel like I'm taking advantage of you."

Smiling, Mia said, "Is it just me, or are we debating the same concept? I don't want to insult you, but this is something that I can do for us. And honestly, I'm not just talking shit. I have got so many perks and points and contacts that flights are like you going to the supermarket and buying a Diet Coke. It's nothing. So the way I see it, there's a few choices: One, we both fly economy, in those ridiculously small seats, no leg room and cabins filled with smelly men. Or, two, you let me take care of the flights and in return, on this trip, you tolerate a bit of a detour."

Juliet cocked her head. "Detour?" She leaned back with her fingertips just meeting Mia's across the table and they hooked together by the first knuckle.

"Yeah," Mia said, exhaling. She looked away and back again, licking her lips. The expression on her face was unreadable, and Juliet wasn't sure whether she should patiently wait or press for more.

"Well, sure," Juliet murmured softly.

"Yeah?"

They were interrupted by their breakfast—two large plates spread with toasted Turkish bread, eggs, mushrooms, bacon, and tomatoes. "Thank you," Juliet said, sliding the coffee mugs to the side to make room. "Looks great."

"Yeah, thanks," Mia said, smiling at the waitress.

"So, do you want to tell me about our 'detour' before I start arguing the fare?" Juliet said.

Mia took a mouthful of scrambled eggs and tapped her lips with a napkin. "Mmm-hmm," she murmured, swallowing. "You know how I mentioned that Christmas was an anniversary for me?"

"Yep, just a bit over a year ago now, right?"

"Yeah, right. Well, Dubai is where she was…is…*was* cremated—whatever the right phrasing is. And I haven't been back. I've wanted to but haven't. And I know that it might be too much after everything you just went through with your dad, but you wouldn't have to come with me to the umm, memorial place thing." Mia stopped and sighed. "Now who's rambling?"

Juliet kept her breathing light. When she spoke, she made her voice almost lyrical, what she hoped was completely non-threatening and soothing. "That's why you were going through Dubai from LA."

"Yeah, but then the thought of it made me a little crazy. I lost it and changed my flight. And I still might panic…"

"Okay," Juliet whispered. "Consider it done."

"I think it's something I need to do, should do."

"Yeah, makes sense. And of course I'll be there, right beside you."

"I wouldn't normally have made the trip now, and it doesn't have to happen now. Not really. We could go back home, back to Scotland, and then do a separate trip later, if you don't feel okay with it. I don't want to upset you or make things harder for you."

Juliet dragged her eyes away from Mia to cut a piece of toast. She added a small piece of bacon and dipped it in the bright yolk of a poached egg. Chewing, she looked back up and knew that Mia would see the tears filling her eyes. She swallowed heavily, sliding the food down her slightly aching throat. "My dad died," she said simply, "and my brother. And I got to be there, to say goodbye to both of them, in my own way. It's not easy, and it doesn't always make sense, especially now. But you lost someone too, and I know you'll tell me about it when you're able to, and that's okay. But Mia, I can see it written all over your face, this is something you need to do, and I'd like to be there for you in whatever way you need. And I certainly know, and I'm sure you do too, life is too short to put off the important things."

Dropping her knife to the plate, Mia reached an open palm across toward Juliet, pressing her hand lightly to Juliet's cheek. Juliet closed her eyes on contact, absorbing the gentle stroke of her thumb. "And that's why you're a writer," Mia said, "I could so be crying right now."

"Ha, fortunately, I'm a little more concise when writing." Mia's hand went back to her cutlery. Juliet continued, "I know this is a bit of a change in subject, but what do you think of staying in the city in a hotel rather than staying another couple of nights at…*the* house?"

Looking up, Mia paused. "You mean the single bed isn't really working for you?"

"No, it's not. Amongst other things, anyway. I think my mental health might be greatly improved by a bit of space, a change in scenery."

Mia smiled and nodded. "Sure. We can just go back and grab our things. Once we check in to a hotel, we can sort flights and stuff. I mean, I'll sort flights, because that's what we decided, right?" She thrust out her chin.

Laughing, Juliet held her hands up in the air. "It's one argument I'm never going to win, am I? Should I just concede that now?"

"Yeah, definitely, you might as well." She leaned back, wrapping one arm in a casual way around the back of her chair as she gazed at Juliet. "I do get where you're coming from, you know. And I can totally promise that this is the one thing that I'll be all obsessive over. Can I have that?"

"Fine," Juliet declared with sarcasm, hopefully too overdone to be interpreted as real. "Okay, so we have a plan: book into a hotel, sort flights to Scotland via Dubai, and that's it, I think. Anything else?"

"Nope, not from me. I'm dragging you around the world, so I think that'll do." Mia grinned. "Is there anything you need to do while you're here?"

Juliet shook her head. "Nah, just a few calls to that army rep, and that's it. You probably think I should see Mom again before I leave, hey?"

"No, no, not at all." Mia's tone sounded vehement. "To be honest with you, I can't imagine how hard that must be. Seeing her, but not really seeing her; and it's not like it's just new. This has been a couple of years."

"Yeah, it's shitty, actually. If I thought being with her made a difference, or it did actually make a difference, then I would do it. But it doesn't. It really doesn't. I've tried everything I can. Mental illness is just…well, crap."

"Mmmm, it's weird. In my circles, everyone is on antidepressants. It's like they're taking breath mints. But being there and seeing your mom... Wow, it blew my mind, actually. It's full on."

"Everyone takes antidepressants?" Juliet's pitch rose.

"Maybe not everyone. That's probably an exaggeration. But yeah, heaps of people. I was once. On them, I mean. Not now, though. Definitely not now."

"You've really been through some crappy times, haven't you?"

They both paused, gazes locked on each other. "Yeah," Mia whispered before her mouth slowly widened into a grin. "But things don't seem so bad right now."

"Good." Plate half finished, Juliet pulled out her phone and scrolled through her contact list. "I tend to stay at the same place when I'm in town. Are you happy to just go with that?"

"Absolutely. Whatever suits."

"An old friend is the manager, a family friend, kind of. He was buddies with Ben. They were inseparable for a long time." Juliet pressed the phone to her ear, pulling up her shoulder and holding it in place as she finished her cooling coffee.

"Hey," she said into the phone, her voice deliberately quiet so as not to disturb the patrons around them. "It's just me. How are you?" She lapsed into silence for a few seconds. "A couple of nights, maybe, I'm not sure. You guys aren't booked out, are you?" She laughed, playing with her fork as she looked off into the distance across the cafe. "Nah, not twin bed, queen." She looked up at Mia as he excitedly pumped her for more information, and she thought she could just make out a blush on Mia's cheeks.

"Shut *up,*" Juliet said. "We'll be there in a couple of hours, probably, and yes, I will introduce Mia to you."

Finishing up with a few pleasantries, Juliet hung up the phone, shaking her head. "He seems to think that since he's declared himself my pseudo big brother, the fact that I mentioned you a couple of days ago means he has full access."

"I'm happy to be interrogated."

Juliet could only interpret her reply as confirmation that the single-room booking was a good thing.

Mia didn't mind that the motel was simple; it was more than adequate, given their reason for being in town. Mia noticed a restaurant on the ground floor as they ascended in one of the two elevators; there were six levels of rooms. Juliet's childhood friend Harry was in a meeting when they arrived, but he had arranged a spacious room on the top level, complete with a bottle of champagne and a cheese platter on a coffee table by the window. There was a queen-sized bed along one wall and just two wooden chairs against the window with the coffee table between them. The wood was scratched and chipped, but the cushions were clean and bright.

"How long has he had this place?" Mia asked, groaning with effort as she lifted her suitcase onto the metal stand. "It's nice."

Juliet dropped to sitting at the edge of the bed and then slowly lay back. "He's managed this one for probably three or four years now. I always stay here when I come back. Before this, though, he worked his way around the world. He starting off with pulling drinks on party islands and moved his way up."

"Impressive. And he provided champagne and cheese goods, so he's already won me over."

It gave Mia a warm feeling to see the way Juliet's hands folded themselves behind her head, the picture of relaxation. "It's your job to pour," Juliet said. It was something between a declaration and an order.

"Really." Mia arched her eyebrows, crossing her arms across her chest.

Juliet gave her a single, emphatic nod. "Yep, under the logic that you're standing and I'm not."

With a chortle, Mia crossed the room. She paused at the end of Juliet's bed, facing her, and then letting herself plummet onto the bed over Juliet, landing on the bed with both palms on either side of Juliet's prone body. Juliet smirked up at her, hooking her index fingers over the waistband of Mia's jeans.

"Don't think this gets you out of pouring." She tickled the soft skin and jutted her chin, an obvious request for a kiss. Mia indulged a long exchange of them; they broke apart with wide smiles.

"We haven't gotten to do that enough," she said, adding another quick series of kisses to Juliet's cheek before struggling back into a standing position. "Ooomph." She could see Juliet's visible amusement. "Sooo, drink, flights and cheese—somewhat in that order; what do you think?"

"Yep, do you need my laptop?"

Mia shook her head, fishing her phone out of her handbag. "No thanks, I'll just give a call to my travel agent." With the phone pressed to her ear, Mia went about uncorking the champagne bottle, giving a sheepish look as the cork rocketed across the room, provoking a giggle from Juliet. Crawling back up the bed, Juliet repositioned two pillows to allow her to sit with her back against the wall. Staring at her phone's screen, Mia quickly mentioned some flights and various dates, patiently waiting for availability.

With a shrug, she turned to Juliet. "Late tomorrow night or mid-morning the day after?"

Juliet held both palms in the air. "I don't really mind. Tomorrow night gets us moving, I suppose."

"True." Mia's face tightened in concentration as she turned her attention back to the phone. "What? Are you serious?" She shook her head, more to herself than to Juliet, and huffed into the phone. "Well just start a new account under my details. You have it all on file."

She paced across the worn carpet. "Yes thank you. You have Juliet's details from last week as well." Muttering a curse goodbye, Mia placed her phone on the bedside table and repeatedly tucked little strands of hair behind her ears.

"Everything okay?" Juliet asked.

"Yeah, just the start of many cut-offs from my family, I suppose. It's not a big deal, but I could do without the attitude from someone I've spoken to on the phone probably a hundred times." Mia sighed heavily, walking back to collect the cheese platter and placing it on the bed next to Juliet. She carefully climbed the bed to mirror Juliet's position. "Nothing this won't fix." She resolved to not let her family's bullshit ruin this hard-won moment of quietude and peace.

Juliet sagged backward and rubbed soothingly at Mia's shoulder. "I'm sorry."

"Eh. How's the champagne?"

"Mmm, not bad. It was about time the cheese came over, though." She placed a slice of Brie onto a water cracker and into her mouth.

"Oh really?" Mia asked, taking a few long, very necessary gulps from her glass and placing it back on the bedside table. She rolled onto her side and slid down the bed slightly, taking Juliet's hand and holding it to her chest. Opening her mouth, Mia waited with a half grin until Juliet dropped a square of Gouda inside. "Mmm, better."

"You're beautiful, you know that?" Juliet said suddenly.

"Flattery will get you everywhere," Mia said, swallowing and kissing Juliet's fingers. "How have your ribs been?" The pads of her fingers pressed at Juliet's side.

"Mmm, okay." Juliet glanced down at her stomach. "Still annoying and sore, but okay. They're not hurting right now."

"Just when you move, huh?" Mia walked her fingers slowly down to Juliet's hip, focussed on finding the soft skin under her shirt.

Juliet watched her quietly. "Yeah, something like that."

"So," Mia said, "if you weren't to really move, then they might cope okay. Am I interpreting that right?"

Juliet chuckled. "I'm sensing you have some ideas, Mia?"

"Mmmm, maybe a few." Mia continued to crawl her fingers up Juliet's abdomen now, under her shirt, hand splayed out so her thumb just scratched the underwire of her bra. "But we did say we would take things slow."

"We did." Yet she slipped her leg to fall over Mia's, calf running over Mia's shin. "But, that said, we've hardly had the smoothest start."

"True." Curling her upper body, Mia pressed a kiss to the curve of Juliet's shoulder through her shirt's fabric. "And there has to be a limit to our self-restraint, doesn't there?"

Juliet hastily turned her head, her lips moving towards Mia's mouth. They kissed deeply, warm tongues pressing into each other, fighting for space. Mia's hand gradually edged further until she breathlessly palmed Juliet's breast. She moved her hand under Juliet's arm and gripped tightly, breaking away and nuzzling into her neck. Panting, Mia chuckled, and Juliet smoothed some dark hair away from her face. "I think we spilt some cheese," Juliet whispered, and Mia jumped back.

"Whoops." Mia rebalanced the plate and swiftly picked up nuts and cheese that had spilled onto the duvet cover. "Here," she said with a smile, spreading some Brie over a cracker and handing it to Juliet.

"You taste better." There were traces of a petulant whine in Juliet's voice. Mia needed no further enticement. She moved the plate from the bed, and they both took a few more mouthfuls of champagne, finishing off their glasses.

Settling onto her stomach, Mia tugged Juliet down the bed. "I want you down here," she said as Juliet shuffled down, hands slipping around Mia's waist. "But, so you know, I'm happy just being here with you. We don't need to…"

"I want to." Juliet had one hand pressed to the small of Mia's back, whilst the other traced the neckline of her shirt. Mia shivered. "It's just been a crazy few days…weeks even."

"And waiting is perfectly okay."

"What I actually want to do is tear your clothes off." Using her little finger to pull Mia's shirt away from her skin, Juliet made no bones about peering into Mia's cleavage, offering an overwrought groan that smacked of frustrated desire. "But can you put up with waiting just a little longer? 'Till we get back… back home?" She went quiet.

Mia nodded, kissing the corner of Juliet's mouth and lingering there, feeling Juliet's fingers dance over the bare skin of her chest. "Oh honey, anything you need."

"I have a bit of a track record of jumping into bed with people whom I don't care about, usually in the midst of some crisis. But you…" Juliet said, fingers curling around the pendant at Mia's neck until she formed a fist, "you I care about."

"So the ones you don't care about get to sleep with you, and the one you do doesn't?"

But Juliet was already shaking her head before Mia finished her sentence. "No, that's not it. And that makes me sound fucked up. When you and I, well, when *we* get together, I don't want to be distracted. I don't want to be thinking about anything else but you, because you are amazing."

"I was only teasing," Mia said. "Good things come to those who wait."

"Yeah, something like that." The kiss Juliet planted on Mia's lips came in slow and deliberate, like Juliet wanted to savour it. "Or rather, an ability to move comes to those who give their body time to heal."

"And hurting you is not on my list of things to do." Gripping Juliet's hand, Mia leaned forward and kissed her back softly. "We have a half of a bottle of champagne left and the cheese that didn't end up all over the bed. Maybe we can order some room service too. What do you think?"

Juliet nodded, but she held Mia in place, the pads of her fingers on one hand creeping inside the waist of Mia's jeans. "You always wear this, don't you?" she asked, carefully rolling a thick gold pendant between her other fingers.

Mia nodded but didn't elaborate. "Mmmm, I do."

Juliet continued to examine the piece of jewellery. Mia watched her finger it lightly, the smooth edges of the cylinder-shaped pendant warm as Juliet let it fall back to her chest.

"It's pretty," Juliet said eventually, her eyes narrowed. "Different but pretty."

Mia sighed. "Don't freak out."

"What do you mean?"

"No one knows about it—what it means, what it is—and I don't want to freak you out."

"Lucky I don't freak out easily then."

Mia smiled, brushing some blonde hair away from Juliet's temples. She smoothed the messy curls back with her thumbs. "It's a memorial pendant," she explained softly. "It has some ashes in it."

Juliet exhaled heavily.

"I know," Mia muttered. "Weird, right?"

Gripping Mia tighter as she moved to untangle herself, Juliet stopped her with a shake of her head. "Not weird," she whispered, carefully resting the cylinder in her palm and bringing it to her lips, where she kissed the smooth gold before falling back to the pillow and pulling Mia along with her.

"Definitely not weird." Juliet's voice was barely audible as she smoothed Mia's hair and curled into her.

"Thanks." Mia rested her face on Juliet's shoulder, her temple settled just below the collarbone, while Juliet picked up a rhythm as she ran her hand back and forth over Mia's hair, soothing her. Mia wasn't sure why words escaped her, but she couldn't manage to identify to Juliet the important person whom she carried every day around her neck. Of course, she knew that Dubai would offer the context and the detail, and even if she lost the words, everything would be obvious then anyway. Her loss would be raw again, exposed.

Death had an uncanny ability to do that.

CHAPTER 15

Everything I wanted that never was
Just dust and shattered dreams
Amongst the grass.

Mia talked more than Juliet when she was nervous and stressed. Where Juliet had a tendency to withdraw, to disappear into her own thoughts and the revolving door of her own mind, Mia seemed to externalise her anxiety. As the flights progressed and their day of arrival ticked over, Mia talked more and more, about her childhood and her family, about the schools she went to, and about the friends she'd had. She pointed out the best shopping malls in Dubai, giving Juliet a rundown of which shops were which and in what order she should visit them.

She talked about anything except the reason they were in Dubai to start with.

That is, until they were standing in an air-conditioned room—a quiet comfortable and reflective space that would have been a pleasant reprieve from the heat had it not been adjacent to a crematorium and a memorial garden.

"You want to sit for a while?" Juliet asked gently, leaning her body into Mia's so that their arms pressed together.

"Mmm-hmm," Mia murmured, nodding. Juliet would have liked to hold Mia's hand tightly were it not for the conservative culture.

Juliet led her to the corner of the room, where there was just one other couple at the opposite side quietly talking to each other. It was a waiting room of sorts, a place for grieving people to gather their thoughts and energy. Fortunately for Juliet, the environment was different enough from the army burials she had experienced to not be a rush of overwhelming sensory cues. Mostly. The flowers at these kinds of things always made her chest feel heavy. There were the same boxed arrangements in funeral homes the world over. Always the same.

"Sometimes," Juliet said softly, sitting down next to Mia with one arm draped along the back of the two-seater chair and the other resting in her lap, "I think we don't really do death that well in western cultures."

Mia raised her eyebrows. "Why do you say that?"

"Do you often wonder what I'm going to come out with next?" Juliet chuckled at herself. "Who starts a conversation like that?"

"You do." Mia's head rested back against Juliet's forearm, her thick hair loosely bunching over Juliet's arm "And I like it…so keep going."

"I know everyone experiences mourning differently. And of course, there are differences from family to family, and there's religion and all that. But I think that generally, western cultures are more removed from death. When someone dies in our culture, they're taken away and, I suppose, dealt with, and everything else is planned away from that. Sometimes we don't even see someone after they've died. That's not really unusual."

Juliet articulated her words slowly and deliberately, since she didn't know Mia's exact experience with death. But Mia was nodding at her words. "When I've travelled to other places," she said, "I've been kind of lucky to see how other cultures experience it."

"Like what?" Mia asked.

"I don't know exactly, and I don't mean to generalise…But when I was in Nepal, I was there to do the Everest Base Camp hike and ended up staying a little while, going into some towns up in the mountains. I stayed in Kathmandu for a few weeks. They have all these rituals there when someone dies, and it was just the most amazing thing to see."

"Yeah?"

"Yeah, the family stays with someone, and there's this process of getting the body ready for cremation. The rituals happen along the river in this really public place. The family does washing rituals, and it's all very hands-on. They even carry the body from wherever the person died to the river, and there's a totally normal outpouring of emotion from the family and friends. Everyone is supportive, almost like a group grieving."

"As compared to us. We're just pretty much expected to just hold it together," Mia said, "because God forbid we make anyone else uncomfortable." She sounded enthralled by Juliet's descriptions.

"Right," Juliet said. "We're expected to be able to deliver eulogies with no more emotion than a contained tear or something. We're criticised for being cold if we don't cry, but then we're melodramatic if we cry too much. It's crazy."

A bitter-sounding laugh ejected itself from Mia's throat. "Yeah, my ex-husband used to tell me all the time that I was a drama queen."

Rolling her eyes, Juliet gave a quick glance to ensure they were unobserved and pressed a kiss to her temple. "Ridiculous."

"Mmmm, maybe. But you do recall that Christmas phone call, right?"

"And what was melodramatic about that? Completely normal," Juliet soothed. "What I really like about the Nepalese way though, is their post-death stuff. I can't quite remember the exact days, but I think when someone dies, their wife or child or whoever it might be, gets maybe something like twelve days off, or is it seventeen? I don't know, something like that. And then they have these rituals that start off as daily for those days, and then it goes to monthly, for up to one year, and then yearly for, well, forever, I guess. So on those days, they do particular things and remember or celebrate the person that has died."

"Really?"

"Yep, so there's a real connection to the person. While we're just expected to almost forget that they even existed. Like I spoke about my brother when I was planning Dad's funeral with the chaplain, and my Aunt just about threw something at me. She asked me why I would want to remind everyone that Ben had died too."

Mia shook her head. "Are you serious?"

"My aunt is a little eccentric, but still, that's not exactly surprising. My point in this very long story is that we don't give people an opportunity to grieve, to talk about this super important person that has died. We're all so desperate that everyone *move on* that we don't let them *move with*."

Juliet stilled for a moment. She could feel herself getting slightly fired up. It was something that completely frustrated her, and if Mia wasn't so distracted, she probably would have made the links with some parts of her book.

"I like it," Mia said softly, hand falling to rest on top of Juliet's, fingers brushing together. "We should do it, start some rituals."

"We should," Juliet agreed, "we definitely should. Starting with you not feeling all this pressure to not be upset."

"Although, that said, maybe it would be good, if people we loved stopped dying."

Juliet nodded, jutting out her thumb to scrape softly over the back of Mia's shoulder. "Yeah, that would be good too."

They sat in silence for a few minutes, just the soft sound of doors opening and closing in the background. "When we were back home, did you go into the spare room at all?" Mia asked.

Juliet jumped slightly at the sudden break in quietness.

"Sorry," Mia said.

"No, no, I was miles away. Umm, no, not at all."

"Oh," Mia said. "Well, it's a nursery. A little girl's room."

Images of the brief opportunity she'd had to see into the room came flooding back. The large teddy bear that had disappeared from view as the door closed. She felt a fleeting wave of nausea. Juliet stilled and calmed her voice deliberately, containing her emotion. "Mia...you had a baby girl? Is that...is that who we're going to see here?"

Mia nodded yet shrugged at the same time, tears burning her eyes. "Sort of," she managed to scrape out from her constricted airway. "She was stillborn, but yeah, she's here."

Sighing, Juliet shuffled a little closer. "That's...that's just horrific," she murmured, although she had to admit she was lost for an appropriate response, if there was even such a thing. "What was her name?"

Mia blinked a few times, a couple of rogue tears escaping. "Her name?"

"Yeah, what did you call her?"

"Umm, Zalia...Zalia Millie."

Juliet smiled, ducking her face to murmur into Mia's ear. "Beautiful," she whispered. "But I was expecting something entirely traditional, for some reason."

Responding with a tearful laugh, Mia sat up a little straighter. "She would have," Mia explained, "but *he* didn't care so much when she was...when she wasn't, when she didn't live."

"Of *course*." Juliet couldn't quite hide the bite of her anger. "Excuse the lack of filter, but your ex-husband? Complete ass."

Again, a small laugh escaped Mia's lips. "Yeah, he was. Still is, no doubt. Did you know that no one has ever asked me her name? Not once. Not one person in my family or friends. All I heard was *Oh, well, you can try again*. Or a number of variations of that, anyway."

"People are stupid."

"And anxious. I guess the last thing they would want is to make me cry."

Juliet shrugged. She had no tolerance for people taking out their own insecurities on someone else. She just wanted to yell at them to grow the fuck up and think about someone else for a change. "Yeah, God forbid, they might have to show some humanness."

"Ah, for that, they would have to be human."

Juliet chuckled. "Love it, and so true. I can't imagine, Mia. I just can't even remotely imagine what you've been through. But I'll listen, to anything at any time; whatever you need."

Mia nodded. "You get it. You get what it's like to lose something so important. The most important thing in the world."

"Mmmm, maybe. There's no worse or anything, but I don't think it gets much harder than what you've been through. And hey, I won't ask questions or anything, but really, I hope you can feel like you can tell me anything."

Mia turned and pressed a kiss to Juliet's cheek. "Maybe ask me things sometimes. It helps. It helps me to talk about stuff."

"Okay," Juliet said, observing Mia take in a deep breath before she stood.

They paused, watching each other before Mia held out her hand. "Come with me?"

Juliet breathed a sigh of relief. "Of course."

Weaving through small paths, Mia and Juliet followed some basic instructions on a card. The heat was sweltering, and sweat beaded quickly on their foreheads. They unbuttoned collared shirts to expose cotton camisoles, their shoulders still respectfully covered. Juliet silently debated at first whether to idly chat or to allow Mia's silence to settle between them, finally deciding on some gentle touch and the occasional neutral comment.

She tapped at Mia's back with her fingertips, keeping each movement platonic in the more public space.

"Left, Mia," she said, catching Mia's elbow when she took a step down a pebbled path to the right.

"This place is a maze," Mia said, her shoulders rounded.

"Not sure who's worse with directions, you or me. Hey, did you come here after the funeral ceremony? Or is this your first time?"

"First time. Stephen had our flights booked back to Edinburgh, so we left literally straight after. He was on the phone in the car, making business meetings. I still can't believe that." She met Juliet's eyes with a distant stare, as if she were experiencing the pain all over again.

Juliet felt her nails biting into her palms and realized she had closed her hands into tight fists. "I get that people grieve differently but there's a limit. And he should have been supporting you."

"Leopards don't change their spots do they? It took me a long time to learn that. He was never there for me. Not sure why it took me as long to notice as it did, actually."

"When you want something to work..." Though Juliet knew that concept intellectually, she didn't keep working at something that was broken; even when it was working, she tended to be half-gone anyway. Always better to bail first and save oneself the heartache of something falling apart in front of your eyes.

"Yeah," Mia said. "I always thought that what I had was the best it would ever get—not the only thing I was wrong about."

On either side of the path of the specific children's section were tall cemented structures with elaborate murals across the expanse of slightly greying structures. Amongst the water theme were large whales and dolphins, sea turtles and fish, and a boat that glided through the water's surface. Arranged in perfect lines were small glass squares with names and dates on them; there seemed to be an endless number of them. Some still were blank, presumably not yet holding the ashes of a tiny human.

"Should be here," Mia whispered. Juliet watched as she held her hand out in front of her, drifting through the air in front of the small plaques; it was shaking uncontrollably.

Juliet nodded, standing a step behind Mia with her gaze running along the rows. She was still looking intently at the wall when Mia stepped back, forcefully crashing into her.

"Juliet, I can't breathe."

Juliet gripped both of Mia's arms. "You can," she said, her voice low and even. She moved one arm to wrap around Mia's abdomen, the other hand holding tight to her bicep.

"I think we should leave." Mia's voice was barely a murmur.

"You're panicking, it's okay. Just stay here with me and breathe—slowly."

Juliet stood like a pillar that Mia leaned heavily against. "It's just you and me at the moment, see? It's just us here."

Drawing in an audibly shuddering breath, Mia tilted her head back a little, eyes casting skywards. "I should never have agreed to this."

Juliet squeezed her tight to reassure her. "Agreed to what?"

"To keeping her here. I wanted to take her back home, or even to Scotland. We were mostly living there anyway."

"Did you really have a choice?"

Mia shook her head and gave a soft cry. "No, not really." She continued to shake her head. "I was meant to move on, to forget. But it's made it harder, her being here. I want to remember." Her uneven breathing took short, sharp inhalations interspersed with the occasional deep sigh. "What am I meant to say now when people ask if I'm a parent, if I have any children?"

"I don't have the answers either, Mia. That seems so hard." What does the death of a child do to someone's identity, she wondered? To whom they are and who they planned to be?

"My marriage was fucked—just years of lies and make-believe—but I wanted a baby. I really did, but I didn't deserve her. Things happen for a reason, apparently. And clearly, I wasn't meant to be a mom."

"I don't believe that." Juliet quickly kissed the back of Mia's shoulder and ran her fingers down Mia's arm until she stroked the inside of her wrist with her thumb. "I understand why you'd want to rationalise such a huge and substantial loss, so that it has some greater meaning, but shitty things happen all the time with no reason."

"It's not fair," Mia whispered, turning in Juliet's grasp, immediately hiding her face in Juliet's blonde hair as she cried into the nape of her neck. "It's not fair."

Juliet nodded. Indeed, life had a strange habit of not being fair, everywhere and all the time. All you had to do was walk through a hospital to know that: drug addicts shooting crystal meth in the car park whilst professors die in the oncology wards; fertility clinics full of desperate childless parents when teenagers have children placed in state care straight from the maternity wards; people jumping off cliffs and surviving with the odd broken bone while loving families riding in a car for their daily commute ended up in a morgue.

Young men serving their country to please their fathers and never coming home.

Life was anything but fair.

Sitting back in the cool comfortable waiting area after they had returned from Zalia's gravesite, Mia sat slumped in a chair. She was light-headed from the heat and rushes of emotion were still hitting her in waves. She watched Juliet tying her blonde hair up off the back of her neck.

When she finished her task, Juliet turned to face Mia, placing a hand on her knee. Mia offered what she could feel was barely a weak smile. She was oblivious to her own tears until Juliet wiped tenderly at her cheeks. She rushed to pull a tissue from her purse and blew her nose.

"You okay?" Juliet asked, rubbing her leg.

"Mmmm, okay. Though I doubt I look it."

"You look beautiful," Juliet said, smiling, "like always."

"I needed to do this," Mia said, exhaling heavily. "But I never would have done it without you."

She leaned into Juliet, elbow jutting out slightly. It had happened almost without conscious thought, but they now moved together as if they fitted. The small movements, like a jutted cheek pecked with a kiss and the knuckles that grazed each other twice before intertwining. These tiny actions that seemed so natural, that *were* natural—these were the things that made them a couple, not corny declarations.

"Then I'm glad I could be here."

Mia tried to smile again, but it fell away before it was even formed. She avoided Juliet's eyes. "I feel guilty," she blurted out. "And I still do, leaving her here. God."

"You have nothing to feel guilty about," Juliet said. "There's nothing I can possibly think of that you should feel guilty about."

Mia shrugged and crossed her arms over her chest. "I must have done something wrong. Babies are born in freakin' forests and third world countries and…I must have done something."

"Like?"

"I don't know, I should have noticed that she wasn't kicking. I should have…mother's instinct or whatever." Mia lolled her head back. "No. It still would have been too late." She'd been through this a thousand times in her mind, and it never did any good.

"I don't really know much about this stuff, but from what I do know, there's little that you could have controlled."

"The logical me gets that, but most days I find myself apologising to her. For failing her." She squeezed her eyes shut. "For killing her."

"Mia, no." Juliet pulled Mia into her chest again and enclosed her in tightly-wrapped arms. "I can't imagine how that feels."

"If I could make it go away, I would."

"You can't punish yourself. You didn't do anything wrong."

"What if I did?"

Juliet's fingers dug in to Mia back, shaking her slightly. "Did anyone say that to you? Did anyone say that you could have done something different?"

"No." Her voice had become strained.

Pulling back, Juliet cupped Mia's face. "Then what makes you the expert, huh?"

"I have to blame someone, and who else is there?"

"It's hard not to blame anyone. It's hard just to say that it happened and that no one had control over that."

"He said that he was relieved. Stephen, he said that he was relieved because it meant he didn't have to be tied to me. That he could fuck off and live his own life again."

Juliet shook her head, mouth slightly ajar as she dropped her hands to the small space between them.

"Who says that?" Mia said. "Who says, 'Hey, you are such an awful person that I'm glad our daughter died, now I don't have to see you ever again.' Fuck."

"An awful person says that, that's who." Juliet shot up slightly, a hint of anger edging her voice. "You were grieving and probably crazy hormonal, and he was treating you like you were trash. He should have been sharing your grief, comforting you, each other. Instead he was firing off insults and hurtful comments. And I don't care that he had his own stuff going on. You never treat people like that, no matter how bad you're feeling."

"See?" Mia sniffled, covering her face with her hands. "I am so fucked up. Do you know what you're getting yourself into?"

Juliet tugged at Mia's forearms. "I figure we cancel all the fucked up-ness out, so we're all good." Mia couldn't help but laugh. "You wanna go?"

"I want to go shopping." It was random and tearful and brimming with the ridiculous. Mia took Juliet's hand, and with a quick glance around, pressed a chaste kiss to her fingers.

"Well, okay then." Juliet agreed with a cheeky smile. "If that's what you want."

"Yeah, it's that or I'm going to spend the rest of the day curled up in bed crying into you, and that's no fun for either of us."

Juliet rolled her eyes. "I'm good with whatever. I could do with some food whatever we decide, though, and a cold drink. Alcoholic preferably."

"You'll love the shopping. We can buy clothes, have lunch, go to a million different cafés and bars, and not once leave the AC of the mall."

"Mmm, so now probably isn't the time to tell you that I suck at shopping?"

"What?" Mia asked with disbelief.

"Yeah, I walk into a shop, glance around, and make a split second decision whether there's anything I like, and then I'm back out again. I shop like a man."

Mia laughed. "You're going to hate shopping with me then, I never get tired of trying on and buying." She hesitated, red-rimmed eyes clearing slightly. "Actually, Manolo Blahnik has the most incredible boots this season. You will love them and…" She brightened as she leaned in to whisper into Juliet's ear, "you would look so hot in them."

"Hmmm, I don't know a lot, but doesn't he do those crazy heels that no one can walk in?"

"Hey, not no one. But yes, he designed those boots…I've seen them in a catalogue. Freakin' amazing."

"Okay, okay. If it gets that kind of smile from you, then they must be good. Should we go?"

Mia nodded and they both stood, straightening their clothes. Mia tapped at her lower eyelids. They were puffy and with dark rings, but the compact she had in her handbag would conceal most of it. She glanced back as they left, sighing and closing her eyes in a prolonged blink. She'd done it. She'd come back.

Mia was more than happy to return to Scotland a couple of days later despite the freezing Edinburgh weather they flew into. Doing a mad dash from the airport building to the car, they had both hastily greeted Martin before tumbling into the car's backseat, a range of nonsensical complaints emanating from Juliet's lips. It made Mia laugh.

The drive seemed longer, though Mia had only managed to stay awake until a little after the comfort stop halfway home; she outlasted Juliet, though. When they returned from the comfort station back to the vehicle, hot coffees consumed, they settled in, engaging in a passionate embrace that shut out the rest of the world. It began with Mia seeking a simple kiss, before it grew in intensity. Juliet's cold hand slipped under Mia's shirt and Mia had giggled at the touch, trapping Juliet's fingers by the elbow.

Afterwards, Juliet had rested against her, ear to her chest as she closed her eyes. Only seconds later, it seemed, she was sleeping soundly, her head slipping down to the rise of Mia's breasts. Mia had gently eased her to her lap, seatbelt half undone where Juliet curled along the seat.

They were still in that position when they arrived home and Mia slowly eased Juliet awake, despite the adorable peacefulness that she exhibited in sleep and the tiny amount of tongue sticking out at the corner of her mouth.

They stumbled inside, Juliet still half asleep and disorientated. Slumping onto the couch and rubbing her eyes, she asked, "Is it morning or night?" Her voice resembled that of a sullen teenager just awakened for school against her will.

"It's night-time, sweetheart," Mia said. "Lucky for you."

Martin's lips clamped together with just a hint of a smile threatening to break through his professionalism.

"Humph. I feel like hell."

"It was only a seven-hour flight, Juliet," Mia teased, scratching at her head as she slipped past.

"You two want any food?" Martin asked. They both shook their heads.

"I think I'll just get this one to bed." Mia shared his grin, holding her hands out to Juliet and hoisting her up. "Come on, grumpy."

"Hey, I'm tired, not grumpy."

"Sure you are."

Mia dragged her into the main bedroom and plonked her on the side of the bed, tossing her a loose tee to change into. A cursory glance at the bedside showed that Janet had turned on the electric blanket, and the room was heating up. It felt nice to be cosy warm and not sweltering, Mia thought.

As Juliet went about blindly changing, Mia pressed the messages button on her answering machine. She moved to undo her suitcase as she listened. The first was a distinctly British-sounding woman confirming something about the electricity company reading. Mia shrugged at Juliet. "Remind me to ask Martin about that. Maybe we changed companies."

A familiar masculine voice resounded through the crackled speaker, and Mia froze, her hand held in mid-gesture.

Mia, it's Stephen. I need to speak with you. Call me on the cell. The number's the same. Please.

The message cut off with a distinct beep, and the room fell into a haunting silence. Juliet looked at her across the room, her T-shirt just barely hanging over a pair of black panties. She opened her mouth to speak but shook her head instead, walking directly out of the room.

"Juliet? Juliet!" Mia sprang into action to follow her, tripping on the edge of her suitcase when her little toe caught on the corner. "Ow, fuck." She hopped twice before falling back into step. "Juliet! Come on, I don't know why he's fucking calling me." She reached Juliet's door just in time to catch a pained expression before it shut gently in her face.

Mia groaned. *Shit.*

CHAPTER 16

Mia stood at the door, bewildered. She had caught a glimpse of Juliet's expression as she closed the door, and Juliet's eyes were wide, and she shook her head slightly, though it didn't seem directed at Mia. She had been calm but definitely retreating from the situation—at a rate of absolute knots. Mia's knuckles rested against the door frame.

Even after she rapped on the door, Mia heard no sounds at all from within the room. "Can I come in?" she asked, trying to keep her voice at a gentle, respectful tone. She leant in close to the door, opening it when she got no response. The sight of Juliet sitting on the edge of the bed, head bowed, provoked in Mia an involuntary sigh.

She hadn't even reached Juliet's side before she heard the murmured, apologetic "I know. If it helps, I know."

"Know what? There's nothing to know." Mia sat next to her, the mattress dipping with her weight. Juliet's hip tapped against hers.

"No, I know what it is that I'm doing," Juliet said. "And I'm trying not to. This is me trying not to do what I do—what I always do."

"Right." Mia tried to give herself time to think of her next words. "I haven't known you very long. Can you catch me up? What is it you do, exactly?"

"Expect the worst."

"You know you're overreacting, right? It was a phone message. I don't have any control over who leaves me messages." All the muscles in her face tightened and she tugged repeatedly at her right ear. It seemed to Mia as if all that they had shared had had no impact on Juliet at all, as if they really were still strangers in an airport who meant nothing to each other. How could she act like this? They had shared so much in their short two months.

"But he still did," Juliet said in a monotone.

Mia exhaled noisily, unable to keep a distinct edge of irritation from her voice. "You're actually being completely irrational. It was a fucking phone message."

Juliet nodded, but it still didn't make any sense to Mia. It wasn't as if she hadn't been clear with Juliet about who she was and who she had been. She had an ex-husband, and she had always been honest about the fact that she had no contact with him.

"I'm sorry," Juliet murmured, shoulders hunched and her hand pressed to her side. In any other moment, Mia would probably have asked if she was in pain, but her fury was growing.

"You realise you just walked out? We were about to go to bed, and you just walked out of my room like a… *Like a freakin' teenager.*"

"Yep," Juliet agreed. "I know, okay?"

"Can we just go back to bed?"

Juliet hesitated, and Mia yanked herself up into standing.

"Oh, come on." She paced the floor a few steps, to the door and back, hands on her hips. "Are you kidding me?"

"Just give me a second, okay? I know what I'm doing, and if you stop jumping down my throat for a minute, I'll sort my shit out."

"All this from a phone call, Juliet? What the hell is wrong with you? I won't even phone him back if that's what you want, okay? I don't care. I don't want anything to do with him or anyone from my old life. My family has made that easy for me, at least. Whatever it takes for you to not do…" Mia said, gesturing a hand between them, "whatever this is."

Juliet shook her head. "I can't ask you not to phone him back, and I don't want to. It could be important."

"Then what do you want?" Mia asked, the volume of her voice rising.

"I just need you to be a bit patient." Juliet groaned as she raked her fingers through her hair.

"And I can be, you know," Mia said with a grimace. "But what I can't be is this person that stands by while you get up and walk out for no reason. How about you stop and talk? Form words and tell me what you're freaking out about before you just walk out of my room without a word. All I wanted was to snuggle in bed with you tonight." Her voice softened. "I kind of hope I still can."

Juliet patted the bed next to her, and after a moment of hesitation, Mia sat, letting Juliet take her limp hand and entwine their fingers.

"You scare me, you know." Mia could hear how careful, how tentative Juliet's voice was, even with just those few words. "'Cause I have all these feelings for you. That scares the crap out of me. I was determined not to do this again."

"Is it a *good* scared? Because I need to know that you're in. I'm in love with you, Juliet, and I really need to know that you're in."

Juliet nodded, but then she closed her eyes for a long time. Mia sat there next to her, trying to stop her mind from making assumptions.

"I'm in," Juliet whispered. "But I'm not perfect. I'm not anywhere near that."

"I don't need perfect. I just need you with me in bed tonight."

Juliet nodded slowly.

"I'm not so scary, okay, Juliet? I'm really not."

"You should call him back." Juliets eyes were glazed with tears. "It's not what I'm stressing over, and you can always talk to whoever you want to. I would never expect you not to."

The idea of talking to him made Mia nervous. Her last conversations with Stephen had been full of accusations and derogatory names. "I don't want to talk to him. I'm not even remotely interested in talking to that asshole. But realistically, it could be something to do with the house or something— I don't know—paperwork I didn't get. Or maybe it's about someone we know. I don't really have any idea."

"The house?"

"Yeah, this house. I got this property in the divorce and an apartment in LA. He kept the businesses. He did have to pay me out a reasonable amount still, not that he cared. It all settled a few months ago, though, and it was through lawyers. But he always tried to speak to me outside of them. I don't know what he wants."

Juliet shrugged. "I'm sorry." She pressed her forehead into Mia's shoulder. "I'm trying not to be a crazy person."

I don't do quiet, you need to know that. The passive aggressive, silent treatment sends me insane, stresses me out."

"Okay."

"Did I tell you that it was Stephen who told my parents about the women? Daniela confirmed it, but he revealed it. That's mostly why I've been cut off. It's not like they were happy about the divorce, but they would have come round eventually. I guess he was trying to get back at me or something. Ironic, given that it was him and not me who was cheating throughout our marriage."

Juliet raised her eyebrows and smirked. "Guess it was bad for his ego."

Mia scoffed. "Yeah, men do wear their ego in their pants."

Laughing, Juliet rubbed at her eyes. "I wouldn't know."

"You've never been with a guy? Even when you were younger?"

Juliet shook her head. "Nope."

"Not that it matters. I was just curious." Mia squeezed Juliet's hand in her lap. "Now, can we go to bed?"

Nodding, Juliet stretched her neck. "I have a massive headache."

"Really? I know a good cure for a headache," Mia said, bending her voice into a sultry flirtation.

Juliet deadpanned. "Paracetamol?"

Mia grinned. "Yeah, that too." Standing, Mia led Juliet back to her room.

It wasn't particularly late in the morning, but Juliet was wide awake. She was turned on her side, head just on the edge of her pillow. In the stillness, she could feel Mia's breath on the back of her neck and legs curled around her backside. Considering how long it had been since either of them had been in bed with another person, they had slept soundly and comfortably together. Juliet could hardly wait until her ribs were completely healed and Mia would be able to rest her hands on her waist.

The oversized T-shirt she wore to bed was gathered around her stomach, a gap between the elastic of her panties, low over her hips. Mia's stomach was pressing almost imperceptibly against the small of her back with each breath.

Juliet closed her eyes, a feeble attempt at willing sleep to return. She was distracted, though, by the conversation she knew she needed to have with Mia at some point. The warmth of Mia's body kept drawing her back from her perpetually analytical headspace. Mia's hand lay motionless over her breast— thumb and forefinger against the bare skin above the low neckline of her T-shirt. Her little finger was just below Juliet's shirt-covered nipple, and a deeper breath would be all the movement it would take for Mia's fingertip to brush the oh-so-sensitive tip. With the slightest focus, Juliet felt arousal tightening her nipple and tugging at the pit of her abdomen. She sighed quietly.

She wanted Mia—physically. Desperately.

Juliet wanted to explore every possible inch of Mia's body, to slowly remove her clothing and kiss the exposed skin. She wanted to find the random places—like the inside of her thigh or the small of her back—that would make Mia squirm and demand more. Though she had experienced only hints of Mia's sexual appetite, she imagined her to be vocal and tactile and perhaps a little assertive. If she wanted Juliet's fingers deeper inside of her, Juliet bet she wouldn't hesitate to ask. Maybe she would just take her by the wrist and demand it.

They were adults, and they were consenting. Did it really matter if they hadn't talked everything through? Juliet was tired of thinking and processing. For once, she just wanted to do what felt right. She had made a mistake the previous night, but things hadn't fallen apart. Mia had still snuggled in bed with her despite her moment of crazy, and that was new for her. It was complicated, but she was trying to move with it and not against it. She was trying to grow and be brave.

And she so wanted to know what it was like to have Mia's fingers inside of her and her mouth devouring her breasts. She wanted to know if Mia liked being touched lightly or firmly, if she wanted to be licked or sucked, and whether she preferred to be on top or on the bottom.

She swallowed, and Mia murmured in her sleep behind her, as she tightened her arms and then relaxed them again. Mia pressed her hips into Juliet's back, rolling them slightly.

The neurons under Juliet's skin were firing, each touch that grazed her body sending little messages of growing heat to her centre. She closed her eyes and smiled to herself; clearly it had been a while. She paused a moment, calculating in her head: It had been months since she had had even a sporadic one-night-stand. And with the assault and the trip back to the States, she couldn't even recall the last time she had slipped a hand between her legs and brought about her own release.

No wonder she was a little eager.

Sliding an open hand along the mattress, Juliet splayed it over her hip and across her body, slowly moving over the curve of her thigh until she could rest it on Mia's. She ran her thumb tenderly back and forth along Mia's thigh, and it seemed to provoke Mia to press tighter against her. She felt a soft squeeze at her breast, and she stifled an exhalation.

For almost ten minutes, she stroked Mia's skin, working her hand until the tips of her fingers edged underneath Mia's panties, earning the first touch of her perfectly firm and rounded buttock. A delectable moan drifted to her ear and she felt wet lips on her neck. "Mmm, morning." That sleep-filled voice of Mia's—barely managing itself into a husky whisper—Juliet wanted to devour it.

"Hi," she said, not stilling her fingers. "Did I wake you?" Teasing amusement played at the edges of her words.

"Mmm-hmm," Mia said. When she nodded, her nose brushed back and forth over Juliet's shoulder. "But you can wake me like this anytime you like."

"Really?" Juliet's hand crept further beneath the material.

"Really," Mia said, moving her fingers in a back-and-forth motion over Juliet's breast.

"It's your fault I'm awake," Juliet said after a few moments, her breathing becoming slightly heavier. "You were feeling me up in your sleep."

Mia laughed, chest wobbling at Juliet's back. "Whoops."

"And then you wouldn't wake up, and I had all this time to think about where else I wanted that hand."

"Mmm." That hum was pure seduction. Mia's fingers started roaming Juliet's breast with more intent, lightly scratching at her nipple beneath the shirt material. She lifted her arm and focussed on the other breast. "Well then, I like this thinking you were doing."

Softly moaning, Juliet shifted her weight and edged her hips back to press even closer to Mia; there was swelling between her legs, and she noticed her labia felt damp. The thought alone elicited another half sigh. "You brush you fingers by me in your sleep, and I'm more than ready to go," she said with a rueful air. "Pathetic, really."

"Nah-ah, and I'll tell you one day just as proof."

She traced Mia's hand over her chest, as Mia's fingers focussed on her tightened nipple. "Tell me what?" Juliet asked slowly, and her voice was lower than usual.

Mia sucked lightly on Juliet's ear. She ran the length with the tip of her tongue before nibbling at the lobe. Its small earring felt cool where it was drawn into her mouth. "Noooo," Mia whispered, and her hot breath elicited a shiver.

"Please?" She ran her hand awkwardly up the front of Mia's thigh.

"Hmmm," Mia tugged Juliet's shirt up and slipped her hand underneath. She used her fingernails to lightly tease over the now-accessible nipples. "I'll just say that I've done my own thinking about the places where I would like your hands."

Juliet responded with an initial soft laugh that merged into a lengthy groan. "That's hot," she said, and her index finger padded down Mia's underwear until Mia dropped one leg back allowing access. She pulsated against the nylon material between her legs, lace waistband under her wrist. "I'm hoping here was one of those places."

"Absolutely. Absolutely there. No question about that."

They both continued to tease. Juliet's complete focus was between Mia's legs, but she deliberately remained outside of the thin material. Juliet could feel the sporadic tensing under the base of her palm, accompanied by the occasional sharp groan escaping Mia's mouth. Juliet's own arousal grew as Mia's underwear gradually became wet and Mia's hips jolted.

Similarly, Mia paid careful attention to Juliet's breasts, at times rolling the nipples between her fingers and squeezing them and at other times flattening her palm and making large circles with her hand. She pooled some saliva and dipped her thumb in her mouth, returning to wet Mia's taut nipples and slide hastily back and forth. Juliet was squeezing her thighs together, managing to gain some pressure against her throbbing clitoris.

"Juliet," Mia said, and Juliet could hear her continue to pant. "I don't want to hurt your ribs."

"My ribs," Juliet said flatly, "are not where I want you to touch me."

Dragging her hand from underneath Juliet's shirt, Mia's hand slipped down Juliet's body and over her hip, pausing to press Juliet's hand against her centre for a moment. Rocking her hips and mumbling a few expletives before sliding her underwear down her thighs, not bothering to kick them off, instead pushing Juliet's fingers back into place.

"Ohhhh," she muttered as Juliet slipped a long middle finger into her folds. "Fuck yes."

Mia's entire hand gripped Juliet's breast, and Juliet gasped.

A few seconds passed before Mia snaked her hand over Juliet's hip and down her leg, sliding back up between her thighs as Juliet tilted more onto her back. Juliet hoped the immediate groan from Mia was as a result of finding Juliet's fingers on top of her panties. "You mentioned hot," Mia said. "Well, that is hot."

Too aroused to blush or hastily remove her hand, Juliet continued to work on Mia with the other, lightly pressing and rolling Mia's clit between her fingers.

"Just so you know," Mia said, "I had planned to be all slow and sensual."

Juliet shook her head. "That can be next, but right now, I just want to fucking *come*."

It was enough to inspire a quick movement from Mia, and she slipped her hand beneath the waistband of Juliet's cotton panties. Her finger entered Juliet briefly, just slipping inside of her a few times before moving to where Juliet knew she would quickly and easily climax. "You're so wet," Mia whispered, barely audible in Juliet's ear.

Juliet tipped her head back. "And so are you."

"And very close," Mia said.

Juliet covered Mia's hand and wrist with her palm, which at the moment, rested at her curls. "Fuck, Mia," she gasped and felt Mia shiver against her body.

"Say it again," Mia demanded.

Juliet turned toward her, mouth open, which earned her Mia's hasty, hot breath against her temple. "God." Juliet's voice caught. "*Fuck*, Mia." Her voice fell a register deeper. Her words slowed, as her desire nearly completely hijacked her ability to articulate. A protracted moan met her ear. Both their fingers were flying without care or coordination as they edged each other closer and closer to climax.

"Fuck, Mia." Juliet dug her fingernails into Mia's wrist, and Mia stroked her three more times before stilling her hand, cupping her but not moving anymore.

At the sudden change, Juliet paused too. Mia drifted one finger up the length of her before pausing yet again.

"Make me come," Juliet said, moving her free hand up to toy with her own breast, while Mia's fingers still intermittently played with her other breast.

Mia dragged her finger painfully slowly along Juliet's slit again—two circles around her clitoris before stilling. "I will, I definitely will." There was a catch in her voice as Juliet mirrored Mia's fingers' actions.

"I really, *really* need to," Juliet said, her face contorting slightly as Mia repeatedly tapped the pad of her finger against her for a few long seconds. She was so close. The small of her back arched as she strived to gain more pressure; unfiltered moans and mutterings escaped her throat constricted with anticipation. "*Please*." Juliet drew out the word, and she felt Mia's hips jolt back.

Mia bowed her head and pressed an open mouth onto Juliet's shoulder. "Whoa," Mia gasped. "You're...you're too hot." She began sucking at Juliet's skin.

Juliet moaned in response. "You really do want me to beg, huh?" she whimpered, her words coming out completely unfiltered. In this moment, she would do anything for the woman behind her; absolutely anything. "Faster," she whispered, yet Mia didn't alter her pace. "Faster, please?" The pace changed momentarily and Juliet felt her stomach start to tingle. "Fuck, Mia," she said and stroked Mia's clitoris. "*Please.*"

Only a handful of seconds later, Mia gave a moan before her teeth dug into Juliet's shoulder and her body vibrated as she finally came in a tumbling of rapid jerks against Juliet's hand, fluid dripping between her thighs and onto the bed. "God!"

Juliet followed quickly, just as Mia seemed to be riding the final moments of her own peak. She reached between her legs to firmly hold Mia's hand in place, shuddering in a series of climactic waves. The two of them trembled in fits and jolts for nearly a minute, their hands still firmly in place. Mia finally giggled, and Juliet dropped her hand away.

"Best wake-up ever." Mia pressed a series of feather-light kisses to Juliet's shoulder, then blew at the mark. "Sorry. I don't think I broke skin."

"Oh," Juliet said, glancing over her shoulder at the redness. "I didn't even notice." She snuggled back into Mia, entwining their fingers where Mia still had one hand at Juliet's chest. "Really," she insisted.

Mia slowly removed her fingers from Juliet's folds, slipping them out from under her panties and running her palm slowly up and down her thigh. "That was completely unexpected," she said, kissing her way up Juliet's shoulder, "in the best possible way."

Juliet smiled. "Good." A wave of relief hit her. They were compatible in another area of their life, comfortable with each other and able to please each other in the bedroom. It wasn't the most important thing, but it was still significant. Juliet really didn't believe that a relationship could work without mutually gratifying sex. And it wasn't necessarily about skill, though that helped. It was about not being completely guarded or, at least, not holding back. She'd had good sex, great sex, even—hours long and with strangers—but it didn't go close to the brief thirty minutes she had just spent with Mia.

Of course, for a relationship to work, they would also need to share similar ideas about the future. Juliet shuddered and pushed the thought away. It was still too early for that conversation.

"Cold?" Mia asked.

"No. I'm all good." Juliet moved her neck and a crack sounded from each side.

"Mmmm," Mia said. "Good, 'cause I want to stay right here with you."

"Me too." They fell into silence, and Mia dragged lazy fingers over Juliet's leg and stomach, tracing patterns. She kissed over her shoulder and up her neck, dipping behind the messy blonde hair. Juliet smiled and turned, laughing at the mischievous expression on Mia's face. "Hey, Mia," she said softly, and Mia's eyes widened. "I'm sorry about last night."

"Shhhh, it's okay. I'm sorry I snapped too."

"No, no, it was all me. I'm a little complicated."

"Complicated can wait for later in the morning. We haven't done slow and sensual yet." Mia's hand slipped back beneath Juliet's shoulder and between her breasts.

"That's true."

"Because I really want to do slow." Mia said as her fingers lightly traced the swell of Juliet's breast in wide loose circles. "Is that okay with you?"

Juliet grinned. "That's totally okay with me."

Yes, complicated could definitely wait until later.

CHAPTER 17

Pushing the door to the office open, Mia balanced a steaming cup of coffee and a small plate in one hand. She had spent the morning in the kitchen with Janet, talking and cooking whilst Juliet continued to write. Juliet had disappeared with her laptop for almost a week, barely emerging, and when she did, she looked nothing short of amusingly eccentric.

Mia was respectful, not intruding on Juliet's space, yet ensuring she drank water and continued to eat. She could imagine Juliet fading away for months on end and emerging, text complete but a shell of who she was before she started.

When she stepped inside the office, the image that greeted Mia was similar to that she had found each day before—blonde hair matted over rounded shoulders, back hunched over the small laptop. Truth be told, the computer was a little archaic, and Mia had some secret plans to give Juliet a gift of a new one; it was her birthday coming up. Although Juliet's face had scowled at the acknowledgement. She would be thirty in a couple of weeks, another milestone that Juliet wanted to forget and yet another reason to celebrate, in Mia's opinion.

"Just your coffee delivery," Mia announced softly, resting the items on a table behind Juliet. She placed an open palm between her shoulder blades and Juliet glanced up, eyes slightly bloodshot and glazed from staring at the screen. Mia wasn't sure how she did it. The mere thought of focussing on a computer all day made her twitch. She much preferred to be outside or at the very least, moving around. She was a little attention-deficit perhaps. "You know, you may actually become one with that computer one day."

"Oh hey," Juliet said, face forming a wide smile. "Where did you come from?"

Mia laughed. "I teleported in, and you missed it all." She leant down and pressed her lips to Juliet's cheek, grinning when Juliet grabbed her by the collar and demanded a more passionate kiss. "And for that," Mia said, "you get a brilliant coffee."

"Not just a coffee, but a brilliant coffee? And hey, I have very good awareness that this computer is an inanimate object, and I'm not planning on becoming it."

"Ah-huh, whatever you say. The coffee though—I've been practising on the espresso machine. So far, I've mastered the milk frothing, but my espresso shots are still being worked on. They're a bit hit and miss."

"As long as it has caffeine in it, I'll be incredibly happy."

"Oh, it definitely does, a double-shot, in fact. I thought you could do with a decent cup." Mia placed the mug and plate next to Juliet's laptop. "And Janet has been doing some baking, so you have a selection: there's a caramel slice and a stereotypical British scone that is to die for. That's a strawberry conserve that Janet's daughter made, and those little chocolate things are homemade fruit and nut creations. They're made with Swiss chocolate, pretty good." She picked up a small jagged piece of broken chocolate and popped it into Juliet's mouth, standing up straight and smoothing Juliet's hair down.

"Mmm." Juliet chewed as she nodded. She leant her head back so that it rested on Mia's stomach, casting her eyes up. "While you're there…" she said with a stretch of her neck.

"Oh, so I bring you coffee and food, and you still demand a massage?"

"I'll repay the favour," Juliet replied with an innocent smile.

Mia laughed again. "Okay." Her thumbs kneaded the muscles leading to the base of Juliet's skull. "Writing going well?"

"Yup, I'm almost halfway, and it's actually going okay. I love this space of completely submerging myself. I'm always the most productive when I'm like this."

"Again, any hints for me on themes?"

"Umm. Not really, I'm starting to think that there is more of me in this one than the last, which is always a scary thought."

"Eeeek. Does that mean 'us' or just you?" It concerned her a little how Juliet seemed to do more of her thinking through her writing than actually sharing with her. Or anyone really. Mia wondered if there were things about both of them in there; things that Juliet couldn't bring up and discuss openly.

"Oh, all me. You're clearly perfect, useless for a character."

Mia pressed her thumbs harder into Juliet's shoulders, working at relaxing the tight muscles. "Not exactly," she said.

"That feels amazing." Mia didn't miss how she had successfully steered the conversation away, though, as Juliet closed her eyes and took a large bite of caramel slice, gooey filling dripping down the side of her mouth and lower lip.

"You're making a mess." She crouched down beside Juliet. While keeping one hand working at her neck, she kissed the side of her mouth.

"Well, it should be enjoyed, right? Anyway, what have you been up to today? Been out riding?"

"Hmmm, I should have, but the weather isn't great out there. There's been another dusting of snow, but it's meant to clear up over the next few days, so I'll go out then. You should come out with me…"

Juliet laughed. "Yeah, I'm sure the free summer 'Kids in the Military' activities, which included an entire summer of riding lessons when I was eight, are really going to hold me up well out in the snow."

"You'd be surprised. I hadn't ridden for years, but it all came back to me. It's like riding a bike, and honestly, the weather is meant to clear up, so some of the snow might start melting, particularly if it warms up a little. I could take you on a nice easy trail."

"I'll think about it," Juliet said. "So, if no riding, have you been helping bake?"

"I have. Janet has been introducing me to the concept of tray bakes. I'm not sure if I'm a help or a hindrance, but she's been tolerating me well." They both laughed, and as Mia stood, Juliet wrapped an arm around her waist and pressed her cheek against her stomach in a tight hug. Mia smoothed her hair and sighed. "If I run you a bath tonight, will you soak in it?"

"Hmmm, I could be convinced." An embarrassed look crossed her face. "Oh, do I smell? Have I not showered? I swear I have…Oh, maybe my hair needs washing. It's not good, huh? This is what happens when I'm in the writing zone."

"It's not so bad…A little in need of a shampoo, perhaps, but I was thinking more that your neck is so tense that a hot soak in the tub would do you good."

"And I might smell a little better, always a good bonus." She lifted her arm to give a slight whiff, smiling as she screwed her nose up.

"On the plus side, there's a range of bath oils that you can choose from."

"You can choose for me. I don't mind."

"And," Mia began slowly, "I was kind of wondering if I could talk something through with you. I know you're busy with writing and things, but yeah, I just thought maybe we could talk tonight."

Visible panic flashed across Juliet's expression. "Have I missed something?" she hastily asked. "Are you okay?"

"Yes, yeah, of course. I'm fine."

"Umm okay, sure. I mean, yeah. Are we not okay?"

"Hey," Mia said, crouching back down again. Pressing her cheek to Juliet's, she kissed her ear. "We're fine. I didn't mean to worry you. It's not bad, I promise."

Juliet audibly exhaled, though her forehead remained creased and tense. "Okay."

"I'm sorry," Mia said. "You stress too much, you know that? Which is weird, given how carefree you are about travel. Why do you worry about everything else so much?"

Juliet shrugged. "Travel is easy. Nothing is really that disastrous." She paused. "Except I wouldn't really recommend being assaulted in a foreign country."

"I guess." But Mia couldn't ever imagine being as free as Juliet when it came to travel. Other things, yes, but that particular kind of one-way-ticket style travel, not likely.

"I just wish you didn't get that stressed look on your face when I say something like that." Mia said. "I don't want to make you stressed. I want you to be relaxed."

"I am. You make me relaxed," Juliet said, raising an open palm to Mia's cheek. She kissed her lips. "You really do. You see this document?" She pointed to her screen, and Mia nodded. "Can you read what page I'm on?"

Squinting, Mia tilted her face closer to the screen. "Ah, yeah. Is that one hundred and fifty?"

"Yep."

"Is that good?"

"Yep, that's good. That's a hundred and fifty pages of awesome, which was about twenty pages of crap before I came here. Thanks to you."

"I help?"

"You do." Juliet stifled a sudden yawn. "And you bring me coffee, and that makes you more than helpful. That makes you my saviour, in fact. My editor may want to shower you in kisses when this is finally freakin' published."

"I would probably rather you shower me in kisses."

"I think that could be arranged. If you play your cards right and keep making coffee like this."

"You're gorgeous," Mia declared, hoisting herself back to her feet by the back of Juliet's chair. She gave Juliet's neck and shoulders a final squeeze before stepping back. "I'll give you a couple more hours and then come and interrupt you for a bath and dinner, okay?"

Juliet nodded. "And to talk," she said. Mia nodded, smiling.

"And it's nothing to worry about. Okay?"

"Okay. Thanks for sorting dinner."

"You're welcome. Although I can't take full credit. I'll let Janet know too."

Juliet grinned and turned back to her laptop as Mia slipped out the door, pulling it closed behind her.

In the corner of Mia's bathroom was a large triangular-shaped spa, though Juliet had adamantly declined the powerful jets, preferring to soak gently. Bubbles gathered on the surface of the water and just Juliet's head and the tops of her shoulders peeked through. She had initially gathered her hair in a loose tie, but now the strands lay wet over her neck. They were still dry, though, at the top of her head and around her face.

"How's the relaxation level going?" Mia eased her way through the door with two glasses of champagne.

"Mmm, exceptionally," Juliet said, smiling as she opened one eye.

"Here you go. It's always better with a drink."

"Thanks," she agreed, reaching a wet hand up to take the glass, water lapping under her arm.

"You look much more relaxed than earlier."

"Are you joining me?" Juliet asked, looking Mia up and down. She could admire Mia's body for hours.

"I was just going to sit here, actually, let you have all the space to yourself," Mia said. "And this way I can refill our glasses."

"Oh." Juliet looked away. "Sure. Well, you're welcome to come in if you feel like it." Her fingers splashed restlessly in the bath water as the determined mantra in her mind reminded her that it was far easier to run then to let someone hurt her. Breaking a habit that had developed over a lifetime was more difficult than she ever imagined. More difficult than she had portrayed in her book, that was for certain.

"I like watching you when you're all calm, you know," Mia said softly, perching herself on a leather stool that was backed against the wall.

If only you knew, Juliet thought. When Mia dangled her fingers over the edge and into the spa, Juliet could feel her fingers tap at her calves.

"On second thought," Mia added, "that makes me sound strange." Her tone made it sound like a joke, but she was looking at Juliet intently, focussed and unwavering. Juliet coughed and squirmed under the concentration, but she remained silent. "Did you get some more writing done after your coffee?"

Juliet nodded. "Yeah, yeah I did. I've had no problems getting stuff written, it's good. Really good."

"How long until you think you'll be finished?"

Shrugging, Juliet sighed and placed her glass on the corner of the tub, making a light clinking sound against the marble. "Technically, I could have it finished in maybe two months. But I don't have the ending sorted at all. I thought I did, but the further I get into it, the more I develop the characters, the less sure I am." She bit her tongue. "So it might never get finished, and even if it does, there's a hundred back-and-forths from my editor."

"Can I ask again for hints what it's about?"

"You can," Juliet said with a coy grin, not elaborating and giving herself a little time to articulate what she was writing about without actually disclosing it. It was an art she had developed quite well over the years.

"Sooooooo…" Mia ran the tips of her fingers through the water, just breaking the surface and creating swirls in the bubbles. "I'm only kidding. You don't have to tell me. I can always read it when you publish it."

Juliet laughed. "So true. Hmmm, how can I explain it? I suppose it's about trying to lose the façade. The main character, she's this person that she created. It's not someone she was born to be. A lot of it's just an image…But that said, there's parts that she doesn't want to change and some she does. The pretending is the main thing, even though it's not always conscious. So, yeah. It's about finding a way to be authentic."

"Okay." Mia appeared to contemplate the concepts. "So, the issue with the ending? What? She can't do it? She spends her life being this shell of a person?"

"I don't know yet. I can't seem to get her there. It's a process, and a lot of hard work. But stories don't always have happy endings, Mia."

"Sometimes they do."

"Mmmm, yeah, they do. But life doesn't, so why create a book, this entire massive story that doesn't reflect reality?"

"Life doesn't have happy endings?"

"Not really."

"Ever?"

Juliet stilled. Did she really think that things never had a positive outcome? Surely she couldn't be that jaded. "They do," she conceded softly, and the look of relief on Mia's face didn't go unnoticed. "I just have trouble believing that sometimes, and it makes me a little crazy to think that after all you've been through, you still have 'the glass is half full' thing going on."

"Well, yeah. Giving up isn't part of my plan. You never know what's around the corner, what's waiting for you in the middle of an ordinary day. *Who* might be waiting when you enter an Emirates Lounge."

Juliet laughed, but she sunk a little lower in the water, clavicles covered. "You wanted to talk to me, Mia…" It was an abrupt change of topic, but some things had a now or never kind of feel to them.

"I did. I do, actually." Mia drew in a breath, and her fingernails grazed Juliet's shin, fingers visibly shuddering. "I kind of told you about what happened when I went to see my family, right?"

"Mmmm," Juliet said, one eye half closing, thinking. "Kind of. You said that Stephen had told them about the whole girls…*women* thing and that they wouldn't talk to you. Which reminds me, have you phoned him back?" She paused. "Oh, is that what you wanted to talk to me about?"

"No. I haven't called him back yet. When I'm ready to not scream down the phone at him, I'll do it, but I don't want to give him that satisfaction right now. And besides, there's someone who is so, so much more important around right now."

Juliet felt her cheeks warm, and her eyes fell to the water for a moment before she could look back up again. "Did something else happen with your parents?"

"Not especially, but I want you to know my past, my situation. And when I went to see them, I still had some access to the family finances and business and stuff, you know, on top of my divorce settlement. But that all changed after they closed the door in my face, literally. I mean I was standing on their doorstep, and my parents and sister were all there, and they closed the door."

"I know. It must have been…crap, just awful."

"Yeah," Mia said, shrugging, "but it is what it is. Anyway, after that, they cut me off. And I guess I just want you to know my situation, what I have and what I don't have."

"Mia, I really don't…" She had some resources herself, but nothing compared to what Mia had. And she certainly didn't think she was entitled to know the details of Mia's financial situation.

"Just listen, please?" Mia gave her a pained stare. Juliet's hand flew to her lips, and eventually she nodded, wide-eyed.

"So they signed over my trust fund, and it's all in my name now. They sent me a copy of their will, which shows Daniela as the sole beneficiary."

Juliet stifled a gasp, shaking her head at Mia's wan smile.

"I know, it's fucked, but what can I do? It's not like the trust fund wasn't sizeable. And with the payout I got in the divorce, there's no issue. I'm all good…and I have this property and the LA one."

Juliet creased her forehead. She wasn't sure she was following. "You know, I don't have a property portfolio, right?" she said. "And fortunately, my bank account has some money in it, and I have some bits and pieces in investments. But if you're thinking we're…Well, if you think we're both bringing equal finances to whatever this is or isn't, you're really wrong."

Mia was shaking her head all through Juliet's announcement. "Sorry," she said, "I'm not explaining well, and I'm really not meaning to offend you, though I seem to do that without even thinking about it. I just, Juliet…This is kind of me. It's me, and there's no one else. I have a past, a crazy, fucked-up past, but right now, it's just me and enough cash that I can do whatever I like."

"Soooo, that's okay? I don't know what you want me to say. It's not like money matters to me, not really."

"I know. I do. And it's more about what I don't have…I don't have any important people in my life anymore. I did once. Well, I thought I did. I had a family and a husband and a…a baby on the way. I thought that I had it all worked out."

"You had a plan, huh?" Juliet said, trying to summarise the meaning of what Mia had said. For once, the normally talkative Mia was clearly having difficulty articulating what she wanted to say.

"Yeah, exactly." Mia nodded emphatically. "I had an entire life plan mapped out, but it was so stupidly flawed. And it fell apart a long time before I actually realised or accepted that it had. There are still lots of screwed-up bits and pieces, and I'm not all Zen with it. I mean, the world is pretty cruel if it takes away an innocent little baby because her mother was clueless."

"Mia…"

But she shook her head. "You see, I haven't been okay for a long time—a really, really long time. Now something has changed, and it's you. It's because of you, and I want you to know that. I don't know what this thing between us means, because I'm only talking from my perspective. But I feel okay with you, Juliet. I feel like the rest of it all doesn't matter when I'm with you." She took a deep breath. "I am, so…" she paused again with a nervous laugh, and the words tumbled out. "I am so in love with you."

Mia closed her eyes, and she put her glass down to wipe at her tears.

Breathing in and out, Juliet focused on keeping the air from whistling from her lungs. She had to avert her eyes momentarily from Mia's; they were so full of honesty and openness. Mia was everything Juliet was trying to be but failing at. Mia was sitting opposite her, heart displayed on the outside and inviting Juliet in, wanting to have the conversations that Juliet so feared. What if she didn't live up to Mia's expectations? What if she wasn't able to do the very thing she wanted?

But she had always wanted *something* more than she wanted *someone*; so what did she do now?

"Mia," she whispered, drawing her wide eyes up to meet the tearful ones waiting patiently for her response.

"It's okay," Mia said. "I just needed, wanted maybe, to tell you how I feel. I hope that's okay."

"Of course, of course it is." Juliet leant forward, drawing her knees up to her chest, and Mia's fingers dropped away from her skin, treading through the water. Tapping her chin to the bony curve of her knees, Juliet reached out her hand and dragged it along the rim of the bathtub until her wet knuckles tapped at Mia's bicep.

"Do you know how incredible you are?" Juliet said.

Mia rolled her eyes and smiled. Juliet knew there wasn't a chance she was going to accept a compliment without sarcasm or direct protest.

"Hey, he was a fucked-up arse to treat you like he did," she said before Mia could get a word in. "And your family, they have no idea what they're missing out on—your attitude, your perspective, your intelligence, your openness. After how you've been treated and what you've had happen to you, you're still here, laying it all out. I wish I was more like you, because you really are everything."

Splashing droplets as she weaved across the surface in a distracted fashion, Mia remained silent for a long time. "Everything you want?" she finally asked, the words barely audible. Juliet could see the slow well of tears gathering in her eyes.

"*More* than everything I want." Her own voice was a whisper. "But sweetie, I don't deserve you."

"What?"

Sighing, Juliet reached her hand to linger over the sleeve of Mia's shirt until her damp fingers could move up to press to her neck. "I'll hurt you." She tried to put as much steel into her words as she could. "And I don't want to hurt you. I want to love you, but I know I'll end up hurting you."

"How do you know?" Mia asked. A tear tracked out the corner of her eye and down her cheek

"Because it's what I do," she said. "There are even a few who would testify to that fact." She shrugged and sighed heavily. "Maybe not deliberately, but does that matter?"

"I think it does."

"Why, though? You still get screwed over."

"It matters because there's always a chance that this is different, we're different, that I'm enough."

Mia's body shuddered under her palm's touch. "You are," Juliet said, and she made sure to articulate and emphasise each syllable this time: "It's me that's the problem. I bail. It's what I do. The closer I get, the more I feel that I have to run. And I know I told you that I'm trying, and I am, I really am. But the closer we get, the more I feel like I can't live without you. And then my mind runs like a million miles ahead, and I think to myself that I can't stay, because I can't possibly be everything you need or want me to be."

"Juliet, I just need you to be you."

"Mia, I barely know who that is. Like I said, I'm trying, I really am—you have to believe that. But I'm not there yet." She scraped her thumb along Mia's jaw line, and Mia leant into the touch. "I have this history, and I'm fucking ashamed of it. I'm like Forest Gump. I run like the wind as soon as I feel myself getting closer. It's warped and crazy."

"You haven't run, though," Mia said.

"Yet." The one word made her chest tremble. She was airing her weaknesses like dirty laundry. "But I do. There isn't anyone I haven't run from in a long time. Surely you know this, Mia. I was on the other side of the world when my dad died, and Mom, well, I've left her in that place forever. And I phone, but haven't visited nearly enough. And my brother. Ben. I saw his grave for the first time when we buried Dad. How fucked is that? He was more than my brother, he was my best friend, and I never went back."

She folded her legs underneath her, hunching her body so that she stayed hid beneath the water. "I'm just so scared I will hurt you, and you're so resilient and strong. I don't want to be the one to take that away from you."

"I won't let you. We can make this work. You promised to talk to me, to communicate. You said you would do that."

Juliet nodded feeling the emotion bubbling in her chest. She had never wanted to protect anyone as much as she wanted to protect Mia. Even keeping her own heart safe seemed to pale in comparison. "And I am, I will. But Mia, you read my book, right? You asked me how much it was about me, yeah?"

"Mmm-hmm, yeah."

"Well, it's all crap. It was me, it was all me. Everything in that fucking book was me except the outcome. There's no epiphany; it doesn't exist. My journey of self-discovery and all that shit, it's not true. I didn't make it, I don't know how."

"So what? You never try? You're giving up on everything?"

"You're too important to me. I should practise on someone who is not…" Tears started escaping from her eyes. "I think I'm irreparably broken. I'm just… yeah. I'm broken, Mia. And I don't want to break you."

It was perhaps selfish of her, but she wished Mia wasn't crying right now. It was taking everything Juliet had in her to say these things, and this didn't help her get the words out. Nor did it help when Mia pried Juliet's hand away from the back of her neck where she was rubbing at it over and over and clasped it between her own hands as if it were her prisoner.

"You're not broken. You're not. You're hurt, and you've had all these reasons to not trust anyone but that isn't the end of the story."

Juliet stifled a cry, shoulders trembling; she gripped Mia's hands back. "Remember, I don't know *how* to end it."

"We can try. Tell me that we can try. Because I love you. I'm not falling for you. I'm not falling in love with you. I love you, Juliet."

They entwined their fingers into a death-like grip and held on. With tears trailing down their cheeks, they stared into each other's eyes.

And held on to each other and cried.

CHAPTER 18

Days ticked by, and neither Juliet nor Mia had brought up their bathtub discussion. Mia found that they were being polite and supportive with each other, even more communicative than before in many ways, but still, there was something strained between them. It was as if they were both scared of the consequences if they did turn the conversation to their relationship, to their future.

But that didn't mean that Mia didn't spend time thinking about it. At random moments, she found herself mesmerized at how naturally beautiful Juliet was, even now, as she padded into the kitchen in thick socks and a loose sweater hanging low over her faded jeans. Her hair was tied back with a single hair tie looped twice, two pens pushed through the ponytail. Blonde strands had already long since fallen loose around her face. She smiled at Mia and it felt so good, familiar. She even trailed her fingers along the small of Mia's back as she slipped past her and stood at the espresso machine, frowning at it and rubbing the corner of her eye.

"Coffee time?" Mia asked softly and Juliet nodded.

"I might just have instant."

"Don't be crazy," Mia said. "I'll make it for you."

Fluidly working around the coffee machine, Mia watched Juliet out of her peripheral vision. She kind of loitered as if unsure of whether to sit or stand, to help or not. When the appliance stirred into life and noisily started heating water, Juliet surprised Mia by coming up behind her and pressing herself to Mia's back, hands wrapping around her middle. Mia tensed at the sudden affection and then relaxed in her embrace. "What's this for?" Mia asked quietly, tracing circles on Juliet's forearm.

Juliet shrugged and tightened her grip. Mia felt Juliet's nose press to the centre of her shoulder blades. When a few more moments passed without a response, Mia untangled the arms enclosing her and turned around, wrapping Juliet in a tight hug.

"You okay?" She swayed them slightly.

Juliet nodded, drawing her head back and bringing glazed eyes to meet Mia's. She tilted her chin up and kissed Mia deeply, warm tongue slipping past her lips. When she drew away, Juliet offered a shaky smile before pressing her forehead into the nape of Mia's neck. Mia made gentle movements over her back, trying to soothe her.

"It's all right," Mia whispered, lips to Juliet's temple. "You don't need to say anything."

They must have stood that way for ten minutes, barely moving.

Lost in thought, Mia sat on the sofa across the room from the large dining room table. She had a small bowl of pistachios untouched on the table in front of her, and the coffee she had made earlier was half consumed but now was cold and bitter. She was mildly aware of movement around her as Janet went about her routine, wiping down furniture and preparing meals in the adjacent kitchen.

Mia still hadn't phoned Stephen back, but knew at some point that she needed to. But her energy for the moment was focussed on trying to progress things with Juliet. Mia wasn't sure how to convince her to take a chance on her, to convince her that even if Juliet did hurt her, it wouldn't be anything she hadn't survived before.

"Can I get you anything, Mia?" Janet's fingertips squeezed at her shoulder. She was smiling kindly when Mia turned to glance up at her.

Mia shook her head. "No. Thank you." She glanced at her watch. "I thought you were off today?"

"Yes, that's right, but not until this afternoon. I'll leave some time after lunch. Just getting some meals frozen for you and Juliet. Is there anything else you need done before I go?" She was leaving that afternoon for a week, returning to her apartment where some family were visiting.

"No, not at all. And honestly, we can cook. You don't need to do all that."

Janet shrugged. "I find it a bit difficult these days. I do half the work for the same pay. You're too kind to me."

"If you had been here before, my husband would have treated you like his personal slave, but that's hardly my philosophy. And be grateful you were never on my mother's staff."

Janet gave a small smirk. "I have heard some things…"

"Mmmm, her reputation precedes her, huh?"

"Possibly," Janet said diplomatically, although Mia was more than aware that her family had a terrible reputation and that many service staff had avoided them over the years. "I hope you don't mind me asking," Janet said after another moment, "but is everything all right? You've been staring at that coffee cup for over an hour."

Mia smiled. "That obvious?"

"Hmmm, a little."

"It's a little complicated."

Nodding and smiling, Janet stepped back. "Things always are," she said. "I'm sorry, I didn't mean to intrude. Just thought you might need an ear."

Mia drew in a deep breath. She certainly did need an ear. "Oh, it's okay. Really. I'm just sitting here trying to figure out how to, well, what to do about… Juliet. I guess."

"What to do?" Janet said.

"You've probably heard some things, right? Picked up on them. This place is hardly huge."

"Ah, not really, not a lot. I thought things were going well between you. You both seem fairly content here. Juliet is looking better, I thought."

Mia nodded. "Yeah, physically she's much better now." She offered a half smile. "And things are okay between us. It's just…She keeps implying that she can't stay here—with me—that she can't or won't stay with me, even though she wants to."

Forehead creasing, Janet crossed her arms. "She's scared?"

"I guess. I'm not sure. She says that she has to protect me from herself, that she'll screw me over." She realized she was blushing slightly at her choice in words; normally, she kept her language relatively respectful.

Janet waved at her with a dismissive gesture, as if she found Mia's sheepishness unnecessary "Do you think it's an excuse? I mean, what's her track record? She doesn't seem like the vindictive or dangerous type."

"I don't know. I don't think so either. She's gentle and caring, and I don't think there's anything *mean* about her. But she's so insistent that she'll hurt me. Apparently she has a bit of a history of running from relationships…people."

"Oh," Janet said slowly nodding. "Which is what people do when they're scared, no? I've seen it before. When you get too close and it all becomes too serious and difficult, then it's easier to leave. It doesn't hurt so much if it all messes up—if it all *screws up*—if you're not as close."

"Yeah, exactly," Mia murmured. "But what do I do? I don't know how to convince her that some things are worth the risk."

"And she is, for you? Worth the risk?"

"Yes, absolutely. I have no question about that. In fact, that's the only thing I'm sure about."

"Then you fight, Mia. Do whatever it takes to convince her."

Mia gave her a pitiful look in return.

"Anything. Tell her every day or show her how trustworthy you are. Reassure her that you're not going to leave too. Maybe she just wants to get in first."

"Yeah, I guess. I can do that."

"She's scared. How do you treat people who are scared?"

Mia shrugged. "I don't know, be there. Be constant and supportive, reassuring."

Nodding, Janet smiled. "Exactly."

Slowly returning the smile, Mia leant forward and hugged Janet tightly. "Thanks. So you go in a couple of hours?"

"Yeah, there's been no snow for days so the roads are cleared. I'm not worried about driving later, and Martin was out earlier. Apparently it's quiet and no problems."

"That's good. It can be pretty crazy out there when it's dark and icy. Actually, since it's cleared up, I might go for a ride. Do you know if Martin has had any of the horses out today?"

"I think he took them for a run yesterday, or maybe that was the day before. He said it was a bit slushy with some of the snow melting."

Mia smiled. "Good. A ride in the sun is exactly what I need."

"Sun? Well, I suppose it's out, so that counts. It's hardly warm though."

Laughing, Mia stood up. "Thanks," she said. "And I hope you have a good week. Don't rush back if you need more time, okay? Just let me know."

"Sure, thank you. And good luck yourself." Her eyes indicated to the other end of the house where Mia knew that Juliet was huddled over her laptop.

Mia half grinned and disappeared, heading towards her bedroom to layer up for a midday ride. She tugged some long underwear from a bottom drawer and put them on, pairing them with a thick pair of jodhpurs. She added a vest and a long-sleeved shirt before zipping up a wool middle layer and hooking a thick thigh-length coat over her arm. Adding socks and boots, she pocketed some gloves and a hat before walking down the hallway to the office.

Juliet was sitting back on the chair, arms crossed at her chest and staring at the wall behind the computer, oblivious to Mia weaving a path through the papers spread across the floor. In comparison to Mia, her coffee mug was bone dry, just the remnants of foam and chocolate sprinkles remaining around the rim.

"Hey," Mia said as she entered, tossing her jacket on a chair just inside the door as she made her way to Juliet. "I'm just heading out for a ride. You want to come along?"

Smiling, Juliet shook her head. "I need to work through a bit of a block."

Pressing a lingering kiss to her cheek, Mia crouched next to her, both hands on Juliet's thigh. Juliet watched her silently. "When I come back from my ride, I'm going to cook us dinner, pour a wine…maybe give you a massage. What do you think?"

"Mmmm," Juliet murmured quietly. She sounded melancholy. "And what did I do to deserve that?"

Mia smiled. "Nothing at all, and you don't have to do anything. That's just how it's going to be between us: I get to show you how awesome you are and how lucky I am to have you in my life whenever I like."

"Mia…I'm not…" She smiled. "I'm okay," she whispered.

Mia thought she looked anything but okay, but she maintained a forced lightness despite her worry. "Of course, but I still want to take you on dates and ask you loads of questions about your favourite Disney movie or whether you played with dolls or trucks as a kid. And I want to rewind time a little, kiss you properly, and pretend that it's our first kiss. Or I could lead you to my bedroom and just spend hours showing you how incredibly beautiful and amazing I think you are. We skipped the middle, Juliet, and that's okay. But I just really want to let you get to know me. I want you to trust me."

Juliet's open hand reached up to cup her face. Mia leant slightly into the touch and playfully kissed her palm. "Honestly," Juliet said, "I'm okay. And you're taking responsibility for something that isn't yours…I don't want you to excuse my trust issues. That isn't fair, but can't you see how I'm already doing this to you? I'm making you feel like you have to change, and that isn't right. You're…Well, you're perfect Mia."

Mia couldn't help but release a soft laugh. "I'm so not perfect," she said, relieved to elicit a tiny smile from the corner of Juliet's lips.

"You should go for a ride," Juliet said after too long a moment of silence for it not to be a bit awkward. Mia squeezed at her leg. The muscle moved under her touch, and she wondered if Juliet had lost more weight undetected beneath the loose winter clothing. She seemed to be literally slipping away.

"I will," Mia agreed, straightening her back and extending her neck to engage Juliet in a kiss. They both allowed their tongues to meet and explore, and the kiss felt long and passionate, though it wasn't how Mia had intended it to be when their lips met.

"There'll be some more of that tonight," Mia said when they finally separated. She stood up, and slipped her hand around the back of Juliet's neck, stroking her skin softly. "I'll see you in a couple of hours, okay? Martin is around somewhere, but Janet is leaving for home soon."

"Sure, have a good ride. Be careful, 'kay?"

"Always." Mia grinned, clapping her hands. "It's the perfect day for it, you're missing out. But I'll take some photos on my phone for you."

"Next time." And again, her eyes filled with tears. Mia sighed and left the room, pulling the door half closed behind her. Maybe she needed to get Juliet someone professional to talk to. Maybe she was struggling more with her dad's death then either of them realised.

If only Juliet would talk properly to her.

Tossing her small daypack over one shoulder, Juliet smiled at Janet as she approached the kitchen. "You still good to give me a ride into town on your way?"

"Yes, of course," Janet said, fiddling with the clasp on her handbag. "You know you could just take the other car, right? Make it quicker for you."

Juliet shrugged, and her eyelids flickered as Janet's eyes rose to meet hers. "Yeah, the whole driving in snow and on slippery roads…freaks me out a little."

"Martin was out earlier. The roads are great. It's a nice break from what we've been having."

"Mmmm, Mia went out for a ride a while ago. She said it was a good day for it."

"So have you organised for Martin to pick you up?"

"Ah, yeah, he's umm, going to collect me from outside the post office around four."

Janet pulled the leather flap over her bag and tucked it under her arm. "Stupid thing," she muttered at it. "You feeling okay?"

"Me?" Juliet asked, straightening up.

"Yes, you look a little tired."

"Too much writing, I guess, I have a bit of a headache. Nothing a break to pick up a few things in town won't fix."

"Of course. Well," Janet said, checking her watch, "should we go? I thought Mia would have been back by now. I was hoping to let her know about the meals I put in the freezer."

"I'm sure she can figure it out," Juliet said. "And I can let her know," she added almost as an afterthought.

"Well, I've left a list of what I've put in there. And there's plenty of fresh food in the fridge and pantry, so if you want to do some cooking, then go for it. Mia's been getting into it, she's quite the connoisseur."

Juliet heard the words but she was processing slowly. "No problem."

She followed Janet outside and towards the car. The day felt quite bizarre, beautiful clear blue skies but with a biting coldness that made her wrap her coat a little tighter and stuff her hands into the pockets.

Janet groaned as if on cue, shuddering. "Cold," she said, seeming void of anything else to say. Juliet wasn't really listening anyway, glancing back at the house and around the adjacent paddocks, looking for Mia.

"Can't see any sign of her," Janet said.

"No," Juliet agreed, opening the car door and sliding into the passenger seat. "Enjoying the dryness, I guess."

They were almost half a mile down the driveway when lights flashed at them from Mia's Jeep, driving directly towards them from the gate. Janet slowed the car to a stop and wound down the window, waiting patiently as Martin jogged from the car, door ajar. "Have you been out with the fences?" Juliet's ears pricked at the confusion in her voice, thinking she could hear just a tinge of worry there too.

"Yeah, and I just saw Oscar running across the south paddock fully saddled. Mia isn't out, is she?"

They all froze for a second, processing, and Juliet felt a wave of nausea spread through her.

"Yes." Janet's eyes widened. "She's been out…for how long?" She turned to Juliet, who blinked a few times and glanced at her watch.

"Umm, I don't know. Maybe three…four hours? She went well before lunch."

"It's two thirty now," Martin said gruffly, raking hands through his hair. "Okay, I'll start looking. She tends to take those trails out the back of the house. There's three or four. I'll have to go on horse."

Janet glanced at her watch. "My family are arriving tonight, but I can stay for a while. I'll help you look…I can't ride though. I'll take the Jeep."

Martin was shaking his head before the words even fully left her mouth. "You *have* to go on horse." His breath came out in short, sharp inhalations.

Mobilising, Juliet opened her door and stepped out, reaching back to grab her backpack. "I can ride," she said with far more confidence than she felt. But technically, she could ride with some capacity. "You go," she directed Janet. "We'll let you know, I guess. Maybe umm, well, should you call the paramedics or rescue or something?"

Janet and Martin shared a glance, as if both waiting for the other to make a decision. Martin cleared his throat as he glanced at the sky. "Yeah, call the paramedics. In this cold…"

Juliet stifled the urge to vomit. This wasn't how the day was supposed to end—traumatic in itself, but not in this way. "Right, you come with me," Martin told Juliet, waving at the car. "We really don't have a lot of time."

Juliet worked at calming her racing pulse. "But we'll find her, right?" she asked. "She uses the same trails, so it'll be one of them, right?"

"Did she say where she was going?"

Racking her brain, Juliet felt suddenly helpless and inadequate. She had no idea, really, but she didn't think Mia had said where she was going. But then, she had been so wrapped up in her own shit, thinking and panicking, that she hadn't concentrated on the details. How could she have been so self-absorbed?

"I don't think so." She swallowed at the heavy lump in her throat.

Martin grimaced. "Then we hope like hell it's one of the two we pick, because we don't have a lot of light left."

Juliet nodded, and they silently raced towards the barn. Juliet tried to help, but ultimately allowed Martin to saddle a horse for her and hand her the reins. She fumbled in her backpack, pulling out a cylinder of water and a bag of sweet jubes, tucking them into the saddle bag. She also gripped an extra jacket and her phone, forcing her arms inside the jacket before checking her phone.

"Martin!" she shouted as she pulled up a message from Mia. "It's a photo! She sent me a photo…umm, a while ago. Two hours?"

Rushing over, Martin squinted at the small screen, muttering a few expletives. "Get yourself a better phone." He snatched the phone away from her and scrutinized the image.

"Sorry."

"I don't know…It looks like the dam, but I'm not sure from what angle. Ah…it narrows it down though. So, we'll head south, but you go to the west of the dam and I'll go east." Juliet gave him a helpless look. She had barely been outside of the house, let alone orientated herself to any direction.

"The right side," he muttered. Juliet nodded shakily at the obvious anger in his voice. She hoisted herself onto the horse and nervously settled, placing her feet in the stirrups and trying to balance her centre of gravity. She held her phone to her ear, trying to call Mia; it went straight to voicemail. She pulled the phone away and stared at it in frustration.

"No coverage past the dam," Martin said, "so keep riding further. And don't fall off. I can't find both of you."

"Umm, Martin?" Juliet trotted after him and out into the open. The cold air hit her again, and she shivered. "What do I do, I mean, what do I do if I find her?"

"Get her back here." His tone left no room for alternatives. "The ambulance service will be waiting."

"Okay," she whispered, tears pricking at the corner of her eyes. The ground was wet and slippery, and even the surefooted horse felt incredibly unstable with each step. Her fingernails dug into her palms where she gripped the reins, and she knew her legs were straining against the leather saddle—everything she wasn't supposed to be doing when riding. Disappearing into the foliage, she felt like she was entering a movie about a gruesome fight for survival which culminated in a ghastly murder. It was dark under the trees, just the occasional sunlight breaking through. The ground was still snow covered, particularly to either side of the path. She startled each time a lump of gathered snow fell from a tree branch. Luckily, the horse was not at all skittish. Nor did it react to her uncertain sense of command.

She kept holding her breath with each slight incline or decline, releasing a loud, shuddering breath each time she arrived at even ground again. She even stifled a sob at some point, wiping at her face with a wet glove. She hadn't brought her waterproof ones. She wasn't meant to be outside. Outside was not where she had intended to be that afternoon and evening.

Where the hell was Mia? Why hadn't she paid better attention when Mia had told her what she was doing? And would she ever forgive herself if something had happened to her?

After almost two hours, Juliet was panicking. She hadn't discussed with Martin how long to go before she turned back, though she knew the sun would be falling below the horizon soon. The light was already fading. She had passed the dam thirty minutes before and hadn't seen any sign of Mia, although she had thought at some point that some broken branches and prints in the mud could have been made by Mia's horse. Or any wild animal, she had muttered to herself. Eventually, she started calling out, yelling Mia's name over and over until her voice started to croak. Martin could have found Mia by now and could be back at the house with the paramedics or following them to the hospital.

Lost in thought, with images of Mia's body on a gurney filling her mind, it took Juliet a moment to notice that her horse had stopped. She kicked her heels into the horse's flank before she actually looked and saw Mia's limp body resting just to the side of the path against the wide trunk of a tree.

"Mia!" She slid stiffly off her horse and rushed the few steps towards her. "Mia!" She knelt at Mia's side, casting her eyes over the length of her. Her jeans were soaked. There was no mass of blood; that was the first thing she noted before gently placing a palm under Mia's jaw and realizing that her head was hanging in a limp way. She looked like someone who had fallen asleep on a plane or bus seat.

"Fuck," she murmured, pulling Mia's face up and noticing the abrasion over her forehead. Blood had dried down the side of her face and neck. "Mia, *please*."

Leaning in close, Juliet pressed two fingers to the pulse point in Mia's neck and bent down, lingering with her cheek close to Mia's lips. She nearly cried at the warm sensation she felt on Mia's skin as Mia blew air out of slightly ajar lips. A faint but pulsing beat throbbed under Juliet's fingers. She was alive.

"Mia, please. Please wake up. Talk to me." Juliet had no idea what to do. She didn't have first aid training, and she definitely hadn't done pre-med at college like Mia had. She had never felt more helpless in her life.

A long, barely audible groan escaped Mia's lips, and her eyelids flickered a few times. Her tongue poked over her bottom teeth, just tapping the inside of her lip.

"Mia?" Juliet discarded her gloves. "Can you hear me?"

A string of poorly pronounced words fell from Mia's mouth, and she kept sticking her tongue out as if it were bitter and swollen. She wasn't making a word of sense, but she was one step closer to lucid consciousness, and that was something. Breathing a slight sigh of relief for a moment, Juliet ran her bare hands over Mia's face and neck. Her skin was freezing. She glanced down Mia's body and noticed her hands lacked gloves and her usually warm, soft fingers were white. Her skin was taut. Mia muttered another string of random phrases as Juliet fought to slide her gloves over Mia's hands.

She removed her jacket, and pulling Mia away from the tree, she draped her own jacket around Mia's shoulders and neck for warmth.

"Are you hurt, Mia? Is anything broken?" she asked, although she wasn't expecting a logical answer. She just wanted any response, any more signs of life.

She squeezed each of Mia's shoulders and arms and her thigh and her calf, watching her carefully for any sign of a grimace. Nothing. Repeating the process with her ribs and hips, Mia again remained unreactive. "Okay, we have to get you back, okay? You hear me? You're going to be fine. I just have to get you back."

Juliet glanced over to her horse. It was patiently waiting in the middle of the path, almost standing guard. She looked back to Mia and stifled a sob. She had no idea what to do.

"I'm sorry," she declared suddenly, crouching over Mia's legs, hands cradling Mia's pale cheeks. "I'm so sorry." She felt hot tears trickling down her face. She felt Mia's eyelashes as she blinked, and when Juliet pulled back, Mia's eyes were now tracking her. The most incredible, unnatural shade of crimson on her lips looked even more so against her ghostly pale face, which was chapped with flakes of skin. It truly frightened Juliet.

"I need to get you up," she said, shuffling her feet to plant herself firmly on either side of Mia. She knew her ribs were going to push a wave of pain through her, but she had no choice, and she didn't care. Hooking Mia's arms around her neck, she pulled Mia close against her chest and braced herself, standing up in one motion with a loud cry. Once on her feet, Mia seemed to hold her weight, and her eyes again kept track of Juliet. As Juliet worked at supporting Mia whilst manoeuvring the horse, Mia slowly started to shiver.

"I'm going to get you home, okay? I promise, okay, Mia? You hear me?"

Mia nodded as she raised a gloved hand to press against her head. "Humph."

"I know," Juliet said, both arms still hooked under Mia's. "It's okay. The ambulance is back at the house. You're okay. We just...I just, I just have to get you on. I'm so sorry."

Stepping closer to the horse, Mia leant against its warm body. Juliet kept trying to problem-solve, her mind racing but not coming up with any easy solutions. Reaching for Mia's leg, she placed it limply in the stirrup and guided Mia's hand to the saddle. On autopilot more than any sign of strength, Mia tensed and lifted herself up though Juliet had to grab her jacket to stop her from sliding off the other side. Mia looked back down at her with a mournful expression, and her entire body was starting to tremble. Juliet didn't know anything about medicine, really, but she had done enough research over the years for her writing to know that by now, Mia's body would have started pushing blood to her extremities, and her muscles would be working hard to use any energy Mia had. Her body temperature must be dangerously low, but Juliet did at least know that each shiver meant she was slowly warming. Still, they needed to be back at the house, and now.

With one hand gripping Mia to keep her upright, Juliet took a few steps along the path until she found a fallen tree to step up on. Awkwardly sliding one leg over the saddle first, Juliet somehow shuffled onto the horse, not that she was concerned with grace. Pushing at Mia's legs, she settled into the saddle, replacing Mia's feet with hers in the stirrups.

Mia moulded immediately to her back, cool cheek flush against the back of Juliet's neck, nose creeping inside the collar of her coat. Both of Mia's hands snaked around Juliet's waist, and she limply held on, heavy as she conformed to Juliet's back.

"Just hold on," Juliet whispered tearfully as they slowly started to walk down the path. The light was fading quickly. "We're going home, okay?"

Mumbling over and over, Mia deliriously mumbled out nonsensical sentences as they gradually made their way closer to the house. Eventually, the path seemed to have become instinctual for the horse. Juliet occasionally used the light in her phone to ensure they were still on the trail but could tell the horse knew where it was going. It rhythmically plodded them towards home.

They were past the dam, and lights were starting to sporadically appear through the trees in the distance when Mia uttered her first sequence of logical words: "Please don't leave."

"What?" Juliet gasped, turning her head slightly. Mia tugged her limp arms markedly tighter.

"You were going to leave. Please don't leave me."

"Mia." She gasped out her name. "How did you know?"

CHAPTER 19

Despite Juliet's initial reservations about the small community hospital, she had eventually relaxed during the hours spent waiting and being ushered in and out of Mia's bay. A CT scan had cleared Mia of any closed head injuries, although they were still awaiting a report from a more experienced radiographer who was examining the images at a larger hospital. The laceration just below her hairline was small and didn't require any sutures, just a couple of neat butterfly plasters. She would have nothing compared to Juliet's scars.

Mia's main issue, as had been explained multiple times to Juliet and Martin, was the hypothermia. Her core body temperature was hovering around 32 degrees Celsius on arrival, and her consciousness kept drifting in and out. They were experienced at rewarming people like Mia, hypothermia not being an uncommon patient presentation in the highlands of Scotland, particularly since their location was close to some spectacular winter hikes. A cannula pushed warmed saline infusions into Mia's arm, and as she lay oblivious on the gurney, air was circulated around her body by specific blankets and devices.

She quickly became a less exciting, more mundane patient as her level of consciousness improved, and she began responding to painful stimuli and some verbal commands. With a nonchalant shrug that annoyed Juliet, the doctor told Juliet that Mia hadn't had a cardiac arrest, so it could have been much worse. Perhaps it could have been, she thought, but that didn't make her feel any better. Any less guilty.

After she was allowed to return to Mia's bedside, she watched Mia sleeping and repetitively ran her fingers along the thin mattress of Mia's bed. Juliet found the gesture comforting. The steel frame of the gurney was cool against her wrist, but when she located Mia's hand beneath the plastic airflow cover, it was warm to her touch, a stark contrast to the freezing hands she had touched out past the dam. Mia's lips were pale now, and a small amount of colour was returning to her cheeks, all a welcome sight.

Juliet closed her eyes and blew a slow exhale of air through pursed lips. She was trying to calm the knots that hadn't left her stomach all day. Even before

Martin had stopped their car, the indecision had been haunting her. Every fear and concern for her and Mia's future had snowballed, gaining momentum and becoming something unbearable. She supposed it had been cowardly to pack up her small backpack and laptop and throw in her passport, as if that document gave her the option she was looking for. She still had no idea whether she would have gotten on a bus in town and travelled to the nearest airport, but she had made sure that she'd had everything needed to do so.

She had asked herself a hundred times over the last few hours, *would she have gone?* Honestly, she wasn't sure. Fear definitely made her indulge irrational and self-damaging decisions—decisions like walking away from the one person who loved her so unconditionally and without any expectation.

Juliet felt even more ill: she had left a note on Mia's bed—a confusing, hesitant note that Mia would probably have understood in two seconds flat.

She felt stupid and immature and ashamed.

And ashamed again.

Coaxing Mia's hand to the edge of the bed, Juliet held it tightly and bowed her head, resting her forehead on the curve of Mia's wrist. She kissed the skin there, finding it warm but dry, and she knew that Mia would turn up her nose as soon as she properly woke up, asking for her favourite moisturiser—and to go home probably. Juliet couldn't imagine she had a great love of hospitals after Zalia's birth.

She wasn't even sure how Mia still got up every morning and smiled and laughed and oozed love and affection. It was the way Juliet did too, until she allowed the insecurities to start messing with her head. Then she just became inconsistent and confusing. She knew that Mia had been tolerating the way she drifted closer and backed away with more patience than Juliet deserved.

Where Juliet had gone wrong—and she was more than willing to admit this to Mia—was that she hadn't done what she had promised to. She had assured Mia that she would talk with her, that she would communicate what she was feeling, and that she wouldn't run without having that discussion with her first. And then her mind had messed her up—again.

And maybe it was too late; Mia had known, after all, even lost in the peripheries of her altered level of consciousness that Juliet had intended on leaving her.

Mia would have to be almost superhuman to forgive that, wouldn't she?

"Excuse me?" Juliet felt firm fingers squeeze her shoulder, but she shrugged them away; she wasn't ready to wake up. She wasn't sure why her back was aching, and she could only feel one foot. Where had she put her pillow? "Excuse me?"

She jerked awake, blinking hastily to clear her hazy eyes. She sat up and peeled her face off Mia's bed, her chair creaking as she slumped back. A pale green wall came into view, and a sea of blue swayed to the right of her. "Sorry," she muttered, wiping her mouth and licking her dry lips. "Oh, sorry," she said again, recognising the nurse from when Mia had been moved from the trauma area into a long row of bays.

A soft laugh emanated from the bed, and Juliet turned her head quickly towards Mia. "She needs to take my vitals, and you're inconveniently sleeping on my non-cannulised arm."

"Mia…" Juliet pulled her wrist into view, trying to ascertain the time from the blurry-looking hands on her analogue watch. "How…how are you? How is she?" She focussed with expectant eyes on the perpetually bemused young nurse.

The woman smiled. "She's fine. Body temp is up, blood gasses have normalised."

"Seriously, I'm fine." Mia repositioned the pillow under her head and shuffled to sit up.

"Well, we're keeping you overnight, but yes, you are fine and very lucky."

"Hmmm, I shouldn't even be here, right? Just a warm blanket and a hot bath would have done. I didn't need to come to hospital." Mia grinned wildly.

Juliet opened her mouth to speak but found herself sucking in air instead.

The nurse chuckled. "Yeah, that's right. Look at your girlfriend's face, Mia. Does that look like the face of someone who could have just wrapped you in a blanket? Sometimes I wish we took recordings of patients when they came in, just as a reminder of what a difference a few hours make. Particularly the young drunk teenagers, those delightful things."

"What?" Mia asked innocently. "I do feel fine."

"Now you do. You were a rambling mess hmmm…six, no seven hours ago."

"Oh." Mia glanced at Juliet with a gentle expression as Juliet stepped away from the bed to allow the nurse access. "Right, so I have to stay until tomorrow?"

"Yes," Juliet said, and she had to cough to clear her voice. "Listen to the experts."

Mia's eyes looked off into the distance. She raised her eyebrows. "What was my temp?" she asked the nurse.

"Low. Too low, unless you're a hibernating lizard."

"I like you." Mia laughed again. "It's Sam, right?"

"Good memory. That's right."

"Well, what was my temp, then, Sam? I was pre-med once. I need to pretend I have some knowledge here."

"Really. Pre-med, huh? Well, you were around thirty-two."

"Thirty-two?"

"Celsius," Sam countered, rolling her eyes. "S'pose I can't make a judgemental comment about Americans and their stubborn insistence on living in the Dark Ages? Nah, I'll be nice. Translates to about ninetyish Fahrenheit...I think, if my memory is serving me correctly."

"Ah, that makes more sense. Shit."

As Juliet silently watched the exchange, it occurred to her suddenly that Mia could probably have anyone she wanted. She was confident and articulate, so communicative and effortlessly flirtatious, even when she had no intention of being any of those things. In comparison, Juliet spent so much time in her head, like the author she truly was, that it felt as if she were two different people sometimes: there was the one who disappeared inside of herself and wrote for hours, days, months on end, and then there was the one who tried to engage with life and people. No wonder she wasn't great at either one.

"So I was cold...to put it mildly," Mia said. "Soooo you used that air flow thing that you took off before. Anything else?"

Juliet forced a smile onto her face while Sam took Mia's blood pressure and temperature and redid a check on her heartbeat.

"Warm fluids, and we kept you in the trauma room. Well, as much of a trauma room as you get here. But they can turn the heat up, so we had it warming up when the paramedics phoned through. You were a bit combative for a while. But after some oxygen and some time, you settled. You maintained your airway but kept kind of drifting in and out. We had to kick Juliet out a few times."

She flashed a kind smile towards Juliet, who was now leaning back against the wall. Despite her relatively recent hospital experience, Juliet felt out of her depth in this setting. She felt like she had when her mother first went into the psychiatric ward. It felt like when Ben died. She was feeling the weight of responsibility of a family member.

But then, she *was* family, wasn't she? Mia's family. Was she ready for that?

"Guess I am right, huh?" Mia said, sounding sheepish as she glanced at Juliet.

Looking down awkwardly at her muddy shoes and back up again, Juliet said quietly, "Better than when you got here."

"Getting here was no easy task from what I heard from the paramedics," Sam said, jotting a few readings into Mia's chart.

Juliet felt a blush coming on as she ran her fingers through her hair and found them stuck in a range of knots. "There was just a horse…and you and… me…and an ambulance waiting at the house…"

Sam patted Juliet on the arm and slipped out pulling the curtains closed behind her.

Mia shifted her weight again, tugging the blanket over her chest. "I don't really remember," she said, "though I remember falling, sort of. And then sitting against a tree. I was going to just use my gloves to clean my head up and then walk back."

"Mmmm, good plan, that. You may have happened to have sat in snow and had a bit of a concussion." Juliet slid back into the vinyl seat next to Mia. She placed her arm on the bed and curled her fingers around Mia's elbow, their forearms pressed together.

"How did you possibly find me?"

"I'd like to take all the credit, but really, it was Martin that knew. Your horse came back, and then I had that photo you texted. He figured it was one of two trails, and yeah, that's how I found you."

"And you rode? And you rode us back?" Mia hesitated for a moment before whispering, "Yeah, right. I was behind you, wasn't I?"

Juliet nodded. "Mmmm, yeah, I rode us back, with no skill and completely petrified, but yes. You were…you were out of it."

"Oh my God." Mia emulated the way Juliet was holding her elbow. "That must have been awful. I'm so sorry. If I hadn't thought it was all right, I never would have gone out. The trail was heaps more muddy and icy than I thought it would be. I'm a complete idiot."

Juliet sighed and dropped her gaze, feeling overwhelmed." I couldn't leave you out there, Mia."

"Well," Mia's fingers trailed across Juliet's skin, "I'm really, really glad that you couldn't."

"I umm," Juliet dragged her fingers away from Mia's arm, and she stood, leaning over Mia's blanket-clad body and ever so softly kissing her, "I love you," she said, closing her eyes.

Mia drew in a breath and reached up to tug Juliet into her, arms around her shoulders and fingers entwined into her hair. Mia smelled distinctly of dampness and mud, the remnants of horse sweat still lingering on her skin. "Thank you." Her whisper tickled Juliet's ear.

"I'm sorry," Juliet said, pulling away. She sat at the foot of the bed, precariously hanging halfway off its edge, her left foot planted on her chair as a counterbalance. Her hand trailed across Mia's stomach and stilled at her side.

Mia frowned and shook her head at Juliet.

"No, I am," Juliet insisted. "I've been...umm, I've been pretty awful to be around." Mia shook her head, but Juliet pressed on before she couldn't get it out. "Let me apologise to you," she said, "because I have been...I've been completely unlovable...but you've still been, well, amazing."

Mia's expression was one of sadness, as if she hadn't even heard the compliment in Juliet's message. "You're anything but unlovable, Juliet." It didn't surprise Juliet. Mia was endlessly giving and focussed on her.

"I was leaving," Juliet said simply and suddenly found Mia's index finger over her lips.

"Shhhh, I know. I know. But we can talk later. Because you'll still be here."

They settled on a lingering glance, eyes locked until Juliet slowly nodded. "I will."

"Then we can talk later."

"Okay."

"Hey," Mia said, glancing over her shoulder as she was wheeled out of the hospital, the culmination of a long debate over hospital policy and Mia's need to independently walk to the car park. "I know I asked, but Oscar is okay, right? No injuries or anything?"

Juliet shook her head, "Nope, all fine. Martin got the vet out, just to triple-check, but other than a scrape on the side of his neck, which was probably just from a branch, he's all good."

"He would be spooked. We've never had a fall like that, the poor thing."

"Mmmm. I think he came out of it better than you, so Oscar will have to cope with my lack of attention."

"Does that mean I get all your attention?"

It seemed as though all their conversations eventually came around to the topic they still needed to talk about. Juliet hadn't left her side for the twenty-four hours Mia was in hospital, even showering in the patient bathrooms and changing into one of two shirts she had bought in the small hospital store. The other shirt was for Mia, along with a few tabloid magazines for her to read. But her efforts to find a complete change of clothes and some decent shampoo and conditioner were futile. Mia had complained, clearly feeling well enough and not at all tolerating the hospital-issue gown she was forced to keep wearing until Martin arrived to collect them both.

Juliet laughed. "You will be resting, completely and utterly. Any questions about that?"

"I know." Mia groaned. "You've lectured me all day."

"You need to, Mia. You heard what the doctor said. No pressure on your body, it needs time to recover, get back to the status quo."

"I was listening, I just don't like it. I'll get bored. Surely I can do some cooking, and maybe I can clean out some of the office and spare room, I've been meaning to do that for ages."

"That isn't resting at all, actually."

"You'll have to entertain me, then," Mia said, reaching over the arm rest and moving the small strap from the bag on her lap that was tapping against the wheel. "For a while at least."

Juliet rolled her eyes. "I have some books you can read. It'll be good for you."

Mia tried to give her best scowl of disgust. Despite often sitting down to read novels, the idea of having to relax was not something she was appreciating. And she really did feel fine, a little tired maybe, but mostly well.

"Maybe you can read mine," Juliet offered, and Mia thought for a moment that she hadn't heard her correctly.

"As in the one you've been writing?"

"Mmmm."

Excitedly, Mia clapped her hands and looked up at Juliet. "Are you serious?"

"For the moment," Juliet said. "But don't ask too much, or I might take the offer back."

"Yay, I would love to read it. I will definitely stay in bed for that, the whole time. I will not get out of bed until I've read it all."

"That sounds a little weird, you might want to shower or something. Eat maybe; but you can also help you know. Maybe you can help with the ending. I'm, I'm stuck."

Mia nodded slowly, lifting her hand to wave at Martin as she noticed him standing next to the car. She had to resist the urge to make a sarcastic comment or even a slightly annoyed one. Were their lives so paralleled with Juliet's storyline that she had to bail on them as well? She had to create some traumatic ending to her novel because of a jaded disbelief in happy-ever-afters? Mia was quietly pissed off at Juliet's intention to leave, and she had good reason to be. It didn't mean her feelings for Juliet had changed, because they hadn't, not one little bit, but it did mean that she was human too. She wasn't someone who could just be pushed around without feeling the effects of that.

Part of the reason she had fallen was because she hadn't been concentrating on where she was going; she was a little too busy crying. And then the trees blurred and Oscar's footing slipped, and she responded with a jerked reaction rather than the calm and smooth response that was needed. She didn't even see the branch that hit her in the head, or rather, that she half rode and half slid into; and by the time she was being knocked off, it was too late. All because she was thinking about losing the most important person in her life, and accurately so, it seemed.

"I have a feeling we can write the ending together," Mia said softly. Subtlety had never been her strong point.

Juliet let the comment slide as they came to a stop aside the car. Taking the bag off her lap, Juliet tossed it in the middle of the backseat and stood back as Martin guided Mia in. She slid along the seat with only a small grimace. "Thanks," she said as the door closed and shut her off from the hushed, terse exchange between Martin and Juliet, even though she could still hear them talking.

"You joining us?" Martin asked curtly, leaning towards Juliet with both hands on the arms of the wheelchair.

"Umm, yeah," Juliet answered.

"You better give some thought to how long that's for." Even from the car, Mia could make out the anger in his voice. He was protective of Mia, particularly since she had returned. He seemed to feel it was almost his duty. God knows he had seen how everyone else in her life had treated her. Mia wondered if he knew or not that she could hear everything he was saying to Juliet.

"She didn't need to come home to this," he was saying now, thrusting an envelope at Juliet's chest that had been folded multiple times in the palm of his hand.

"Ah…"

"You make her happy," he uttered with a low growl, taking the chair out of Juliet's grasp. "Who knows why, with the way you seem to have treated her." There was no end to what both he and Janet were privy too, just by their daily presence in the house. "Listen, I think I could really like you. I'd like to see you two work. But that girl in the car, she's like family to me, so if you screw her over like that bastard husband did before you, I'll…let's put it this way, I'll look after that girl as I would look after my daughter."

Mia could see Juliet visibly swallow, straighten up and shove the envelope into her jeans pocket. She tossed the small duffel bag over her shoulder and nodded, eyes falling to the bitumen.

"I understand," she said so softly that Mia barely heard her. "Wish I had someone to back me up too. Mia…she's lucky to have you."

Martin gave a stern nod, and that was the last Mia could see, since he took a step back towards the hospital entrance to return the wheelchair. Juliet stood motionless, watching his retreating back. Juliet was hardly dangerous or aggressive; stupidly armoured to protect herself, maybe, but deliberately harmful; no.

"Sometimes if you stick around long enough, you earn the right to have people go to bat for you." Martin had returned. "I would never turn down another daughter, but not if she's going to disappear every time she feels frightened." Mia noticed how his voice was lower and gentler as he pointed towards her pocket. "My girls are more than that," he said, tapping at his chest. "More guts, more heart."

He walked away then, leaving Juliet to hopefully contemplate his words. He waited in the driver's seat for her to join Mia before placing the car in drive and slowly accelerating away.

CHAPTER 20

Sitting up in bed, Juliet sunk back, surrounded by pillows. She had gathered them behind Mia and against the bedhead, obsessing about moving them around for minutes despite Mia's insistence that she was already comfortable. Then Juliet had joined her in the bed. The thick duvet was pulled up high over their laps, and gathered around their stomachs. Soft music played in the background from Mia's phone attached to a dock on her bedside table. Juliet cast her eyes over the small cut on Mia's forehead, just to the side where she was sitting. It was hard to comprehend that the abrasion was the only lasting injury that Mia had walked away with. It still had two white butterfly plasters in place, but they would be discarded in the morning. The possibility of what could have been made Juliet's stomach drop.

When they arrived home, Juliet took some pasta and sauce from the freezer and prepared dinner. She liked having something to focus on while Mia took a long bath and settled into bed; it gave her time to think and relax and give herself a bit of stern self-talk as she replayed Martin's short but direct words over in her mind. She hadn't given much thought to the fact that her issues would translate to something observable, that she was so hesitant and indecisive, that her behaviour would be obvious. It had clearly been, though, and for what it was worth, she appreciated Martin's directness.

It elicited a few pangs of jealousy, though, knowing that Mia had someone playing a pseudo-family member when she had no one. He had picked up on that too, apparently, since he had invited Juliet into his world with just a couple of conditions. Juliet had always considered herself to be fairly emotionally mature, intelligent, and independent, and she was probably all of those things to some extent. It just seemed like her need to analyse and be self-reliant had compromised her ability to sustain an emotional connection.

As always, the knowledge wasn't the issue; it was action she struggled with.

So, they chatted easily over dinner, eating from trays on their laps and playfully chiding each other about Mia's horse riding and Juliet's writing mode. Mia seemed to be patiently waiting for Juliet to initiate their more serious discussion, ensuring the ball was in Juliet's court. And as subtle as it was, it shifted the dynamic, something that Juliet knew was needed.

Still, Juliet remained casual, until they both held steaming hot chocolates in their hands.

"Mia?"

"Mmmm?"

Juliet's eyes fell momentarily to the sheets, out of habit. She forced them back up and offered a shaky smile, then nervously laughed. "This is hard, huh?"

With a nonchalant shrug, Mia took a sip of her hot chocolate. "Lots of things are, aren't they? I mean, the important stuff usually is."

"Yep, ah-huh," Juliet said, tracing the mug in her hands distractedly. She was only marginally aware of her movements, just one of those simple soothing actions that she did when she was uncomfortable. "So, I should have been out there with you…"

Mia gave her a confused look in return. "Why? I go out all the time on my own. You were writing. There was nothing strange about that, was there?"

"I guess I freaked out when I saw you on the ground. You could have died out there."

"I know. Really I do. Guess we're becoming masters of close calls, but that doesn't make it your fault. I can probably imagine what it was like for you." She grimaced a little. "A bit like when I saw you in the airport, all bruised and beat up."

Juliet smiled softly. "Yeah, fun times. Maybe we're like cats and have nine lives or something."

"Can we not test that theory out?" Mia asked.

"Mmm, okay." Juliet took a sip and placed the cup on the bedside table before shifting and pulling up her knees, settling more on her side so she faced Mia. Her side gave a small pang of pain, a little reminder that her stomach muscles had worked hard to keep her and Mia upright on the horse. Her legs were just as sore. "Sooooo." She drew out the word as if she were stalling for time, and Mia smiled, trying to calm her. "So, I umm, I don't *want* to go. I don't *want* to leave you. I guess I wanted to say that first."

"You were about to, though, weren't you? Leave?"

"I was, I think. I mean, I gave myself the option. I don't really know if I was going to use it, but yeah, maybe."

"I think you were, Juliet." Mia's voice, though not at all angry, left little room for challenge.

"You're probably right. You usually are." Juliet's head turned upward with her eyes shut tight.

"I feel like this is Groundhog Day, Juliet." When Juliet opened her eyes again and looked down, Mia was waving aimlessly at her. "You're telling me you don't want to leave, but you are…Is that where you're going with this?"

Juliet shook her head. "You should be angry with me. I told you that I'm not good for you."

Mia drew in a sharp breath. "That's just an excuse. Well, it feels like an excuse. You have this reason that you hold onto for why you can't get close to people. Well, look around—we're close. We're already there. You don't need to be constantly stressed out, we're good together. We're fine. If you just stop running."

"I know. I fucking know." Why did she have to feel so exasperated at herself all the time? "It's not like I want to, but yeah, I get how stupid and childish it seems."

"I'm not saying that, okay? I'm really not. But you're worried about us never being what we already are. It doesn't make sense to me."

"It barely makes sense to me."

Sighing, Mia dropped her voice and shook her head at the room. "You weren't even going to tell me."

Silence fell between them, awkward and lingering. "I left you a note…a letter. I would have called." It was a feeble offer, she knew.

"Do you know how that feels? And I'm not trying to blame you, and I don't want to, but the fact that you would have left and I would have come back to a note? God, Juliet."

Juliet grimaced. "And if this is too hard for you, if I'm too much work, not worth it, then just tell me, please. I don't want to do this to you. If you want me to go, tell me and I will."

"Are you kidding me? If you want to leave, you can look me in the eyes and tell me that. You don't get to use me as an excuse, okay? I am here, and I am willing to work this out with you, to support you."

"But?"

"But nothing. There's no huge conditions. I've told you I love you, and I don't even want to imagine my life without you now. There is not a chance, though, that I am going to live every day petrified that when I get home, you're not going to be here. And that all that you will have left behind is a...is a note." Mia's voice stayed calm and unwavering. "That's your choice, not mine. Yours. You need to be accountable for your decision in this, because this isn't me. I'm not pushing you away. You're tearing yourself out of my life."

"I'm not blaming you Mia. I know this is all me."

She had this splintered shell that she disappeared behind when it came to relationships. Juliet knew she accepted this inability to deal with her emotions without even considering fighting it. That side of her, the side of her that hid, was a far cry from the person she was when she spoke about travel or writing. She was animated then, excitable and passionate, brave. Such a stark contrast.

"What do you want?" Mia asked. "If you forget everything else, what do *you* want?"

"What do you mean?"

Mia dragged a hand through her hair and drew in a breath. "If you stop and just pretend that you can have whatever you want in life and there's a complete guarantee that it will work, what do *you* want? Not what you think you should want or have, but what you actually want."

"I want to be with you," Juliet said without missing a beat. "But without the constant running commentary in my head."

"What? The commentary that says I'm going to turn out to be some psychopath?"

Juliet laughed, lifting her hand to slide down Mia's arm before pausing and dropping it back to the pillows. "That you'll realise that I'm far too complex, too screwed up, and not worth the hassle."

"Not gonna happen," Mia said nonchalantly. "I already know you're screwed up," she teased, "and totally worth the hassle." She drank a few more mouthfuls of the hot chocolate before settling the cup to her side. "And to be serious for a second, I just want to see that I'm worth it too, that I'm worth you fighting whatever it is that you need to fight to stay with me."

"You're the only one that has ever been close to worth it."

"I'm not so confident either, Juliet. I need to hear and be shown that I'm kind of important too."

The guilt tore at Juliet, washing over her in a wave of regret. "And I'm so very sorry that I haven't done that, been doing that."

Mia nodded. "It's important to me that you show me that." She was silent for a moment. "What do we do?"

Juliet sighed, and when she spoke, she could barely get her voice above a whisper. "Can you help me?"

"Oh honey, I have no idea how. But yes, over and over again, yes."

"When I was twelve," Juliet said quietly, sinking further down the bed and into the pillows, "I saw my father in bed with a woman, in bed with someone that wasn't my mom."

Mia screwed her face up. She looked immediately disgusted.

"I never told her or Ben or anyone. But he knew. My father knew I saw him. On the surface, they had this supportive marriage, but underneath, it was fucked. I'm sure he had more affairs, probably a crapload of them."

"And I know what it's like to find that out and to see that as a kid, almost a teenager. Makes sense that you think all relationships are doomed."

"Not this one." Mia's hand dropped to lay palm up between them. Juliet pointed her index finger and traced lazy circles over the skin. "And, for the record," Mia said, "when it comes to cheating, I could not be more anti that if I tried."

Juliet smiled slightly.

"I just, well, I think I've experienced a fair few things, mostly bad stuff." Mia trapped Juliet's finger in mid-circle, pulling her arm to hug it to her chest. "And if I based the future on that, I'm not sure I would ever do anything now. I may as well have called it quits."

"What you've been through," Juliet said, "God, I couldn't compare. Wouldn't."

"It's not that. It's more about making a decision not to base the future on the past. Which is easier said than done, but I think making that decision and naming it helped me a lot."

"That worked for you?"

"It did. I mean, I'm not naïve and I don't think it's that simple. But honestly, the place I was in, how low I was…I really could have just given up and figured the entire world was out to get me, so why even bother? Really making that conscious decision and telling myself that, it did kind of work. I still tell myself it sometimes, in my head, that is, although I do talk to myself frequently." She grinned.

"I think I feel more sane when I'm on my own and people aren't privy to all this crazy," Juliet said.

"Mmm," Mia said, nodding and smiling. "The sex is a little different though."

Juliet gave a laugh, she appreciated that Mia could give her brief reprieves from the intensity of the conversation.

Mia continued, "It's easier because you don't have to open yourself up to anyone...It's all surface level. And that might be fun and yeah, easy, but is that really how you envisaged your life to turn out? Alone just so you didn't have to deal with the important shit?"

Slowly, Juliet shook her head. "Not really, I used to imagine spending my life with someone when I was really young. Having the house and the backyard, two big dogs that we would play with. But then life happened, I suppose. That got harder and harder, further out of reach."

"Mmm, until it wasn't. Until it was actually a reality."

"Yep. And then I go all super-crazy."

"Crazy doesn't have to be bad, but what it might mean is that you try this whole new strategy and prepare, 'cause it's pretty out there. You ready?" Mia asked.

Juliet rolled her eyes.

"Yep," said Mia." You *talk*. You talk to the person who is head over heels obsessed with how hot and awesome you are. Tough, huh?"

"Very funny, Mia."

"I know. I should have been a comedian..."

"Mia?"

"Yesssss?"

"What if I can't give you what you want, later on...in the future?"

Mia narrowed her eyebrows. "I don't get what you mean." She squeezed Juliet's hand.

"Well, I don't really know what I want, down the track. I never used to want...Well, I didn't really want kids for a long time, and I know, I really know, how important that is to you. And it should be, it really should be, after everything. I shouldn't be the one to stop you from having kids."

To Mia's credit, she seemed to absorb Juliet's words calmly and carefully considered them before responding. "Is that what you're worried about? That I'll want kids and you won't?"

Shrugging, Juliet finally nodded. "Do you?"

"Want children?"

"Yeah." Juliet felt Mia shudder a little. Maybe it was something she just perceived, but it felt like Mia's heartbeat began to race.

"Maybe," Mia said. "Probably." She glanced up to the ceiling. "Life doesn't always give you what you want, though, and that doesn't necessarily mean it's a bad outcome."

"What if I end up not wanting a family?"

"Why do you worry so much about *what ifs*? I had my life figured out, planned and sorted, like tick boxes. But here I am, a world away from where I started."

"Mmm, guess I like to have it all sorted, different contingencies figured out." But as she heard herself say it aloud, it hit her: how could she possibly cover every different scenario? She couldn't.

But Juliet didn't have to. She ran instead.

Mia slowly drew wide eyes to Juliet. "You're a control freak...with yourself."

Juliet stared back at her. Of all the things she had been called or labelled in her life, a control freak was not one of them—the opposite, in fact. People usually called her a free spirit, occasionally brave and adventurous. Mia had just seen through all the layers, and no one ever had, not once.

"I think the thing is, Juliet, that shit in life will always hurt, no matter what. And as much as you try to protect yourself, all that effort that goes into controlling what comes your way and avoiding it won't work."

Juliet slowly nodded; she didn't trust her voice.

"So, kids? Yeah, sure, but I've given up on having something abstract become more important than what is in front of me."

Clearing her throat, Juliet looked to the wall and back to Mia. "I'm not anti-babies. I'm just not sure."

"And in a few years, that might be an important discussion. But who knows what else might be important then too? Unless you've been carrying around a crystal ball in your backpack, we don't know." She tested a small smile. "With your passport, that is."

Tears burned her eyes, and Juliet blinked hastily at them. "I'm just," she paused, taking a slow breath. "so sorry. It seems ridiculous right now, but I know it was me and what I was doing…"

"I haven't been pushing you, have I?" Mia asked suddenly, but she earned a shake of the head in response.

"Nope. No."

Mia released an audible sigh of relief. "Good, because yeah, not what I want to do."

Juliet smiled and sunk a little lower under the covers, edging closer to Mia's side.

"And I really don't, okay, Jules? I don't want to push you, yet there is a tiny *but* in that. I guess I need to know what you want to do, because I can't be stressed all the time that you're going to disappear. That's something that I can't do, yeah? I'm just, when it comes to that, I'm just not strong enough to live with that…with wondering constantly."

"Yeah," Juliet said, drawing her face up when Mia interrupted.

"Because that's worse, having that in the back of my mind. That's harder than actually having you go."

Despite the calm demeanour Mia had been exhibiting, her voice trembled. It wasn't quite an ultimatum, but it felt close; a blatantly necessary question that had to be asked. There was no negotiation around that; Mia couldn't keep up her patience, because the uncertainty and the constant fear was something she said clearly that she couldn't live with. And it was okay that she asked; a moment of growth for Mia too, as she was recognising that she was important as well.

Juliet opened her mouth and made a few sounds, just half formed words and stilted syllables; she couldn't get her words out. Juliet lifted back the covers and silently slipped from the bed. Her bare feet met the floor, and she walked away slowly, without glancing back at Mia.

When she returned, less than a few minutes later, Mia was curled on her side crying. She had shifted down the bed and her head had slipped off the pillows, knees drawn up under the duvet. With one hand pressed to her face, she collected the wet tears while her other arm stretched out into the space that Juliet had silently left.

"Mia," Juliet whispered, climbing onto the bed and hastily tangling into the sheets rather than easily sliding under them. "Mia," she repeated, leaning in close and kissing Mia's forehead, "I just wanted to get something for you. I'm sorry." Her voice was shaky too, nervous and heightened with emotion.

It took a few additional shudders and quiet strangled sobs before Mia dropped the hand from her face. She kept her eyes squeezed shut for a moment, sucking on her bottom lip before exposing her glazed eyes and wet cheeks.

"I'm..." Juliet said slowly, pausing, "How did you put it? *In*. I'm in."

Mia gave her a nearly blank expression. "But I want you to trust me...and that, well, I've got some work to do on that. Right?"

Mia shrugged. "Mmmm." She acknowledged that with a sniffle.

"I want you to keep my passport, just as...what, security maybe? I don't know. Because I want you to know that I'm serious, and maybe I don't want an easy out either."

"No Juliet, no. I can't keep your passport, I won't. I get the offer, and I appreciate it, but I won't do that. That's what crazy, violent people do. I won't take away your right to leave."

Juliet considered for a moment, then crawled up to her knees and leant over Mia. She pulled the drawer out on her bedside table and threw her passport in, feeling Mia's hand wrap around her hip as she held her weight over Mia's chest. Awkwardly moving back, she fell next to her. "We both know where it is this way," Juliet said. "Is that okay?"

"Yeah, that's okay." Lifting her arm up, Mia silently encouraged Juliet to lie against her. She waited for Juliet to wrap an arm around her middle and to share her pillow before dropping her hand to splay on Juliet's back.

"Ummmm," she drew out slowly.

"Ummmm," Juliet confirmed.

They both laughed quietly. "You're doing okay with all this?" Mia asked.

"I am," Juliet replied, with a hint of conviction and honesty. "It's tough to change something that has taken forever to develop, as dysfunctional as it might be. But you're not like everyone else, and maybe I can be someone...hmmm, maybe I can be the person I want to be, with you, rather than the person I've had to be."

Mia nodded silently and Juliet kissed her cheek chastely, dried tear tracks still apparent.

"Are you okay?" Juliet asked.

Though barely a smile moved her lips, Mia murmured, "Yeah, I think so."

"You can tell me if you're not or if you need to be upset or angry with me some more, I deserve that."

"I'm not sure we should mess with this very mature conversation—no one has yelled or thrown anything."

Juliet could tell that Mia was only minimally joking. Still, Juliet's grip tightened a little around her side. "You're pretty hard to be mad at."

"I'm not sure that's a good or a bad thing."

"Good, I think; you're just trying to find your way, that's not something I should get frustrated at."

"Even when it affects you?"

"Mmmm, I guess. The more I understand, the easier it is, and that negative stuff that I feel, goes away."

Juliet didn't quite understand, but Mia continued. "You told me about your dad, Juliet, and it helped things make sense. I want to know you. I want to know more about what you've been though. It's like I've told you everything about me but I barely know your past."

"Some of it isn't that exciting," Juliet said. "And some of it…Well, I haven't been angelic or the victim in everything. I've made plenty of mistakes."

"Haven't we all?" Mia asked, and Juliet had to agree. She always felt like less than others, that she was less moral, less intelligent; just less. "I'm not going to judge, you know. But I want to know, because I want to know you, everything about you. I want to be your go-to person."

"You are my person," Juliet said. "Who did I call when it all turned to shit in Belgium? And I want to tell you…everything, if you want. I'm just not great at doing that, at knowing what you want to know or are interested in. Sometimes things seem unimportant in my head, like I would be making you listen to something boring."

"Oh God, no, no way. Honey, I hang on every word you say. And when it's about you and your life, what you've seen—I'm like a dog, lapping it up."

Juliet laughed. It did seem a little incredulous to her that Mia could be interested in these things. She could still see the glazed look in her father's eyes when she won a state writing award at age eleven and the way her mother brushed over it and dropped her off at the ceremony on the way to her brother's baseball game. Or when she told them of the college she had been accepted into and they breathed that obviously disappointed sigh before murmuring a brief string of empty congratulations. She had a whole lifetime of baggage.

"What do you wanna know, then?" she asked. She was always better at answering questions than starting conversations.

Mia shrugged and moved her hand slowly to trace up and down her spine. "Whatever you like."

Juliet squirmed, pressing her face into Mia's shoulder before settling back on her pillow. She snaked her fingertips under Mia's top until her palm was flat against the warm skin of her abdomen; the contact relaxed her. She stilled for a minute, just quietly thinking and breathing evenly, and Mia didn't press at all, content in the silence. Eventually, Juliet withdrew her hand and held it up in front of Mia. She made a fist and jiggled her wrist, beaded bracelet moving loosely. "I got this when I was in Asia doing my retreat thing. I had just had a crazy, messy breakup and it was all awful and then I got news that Ben was being sent to Afghanistan. So I bought this, and by 'bought' I mean paid all of about twenty cents or something, and I sent it to Ben because I couldn't get back before he left." Pausing, Juliet puffed her cheeks before continuing. "He was wearing it when he was brought back, so I took it off and kept it. Now I wear it all the time. I never take it off. It's knotted on; I'd probably have to cut it to get it off. Guess it'll fall off one day."

"What was he like—Ben?" Mia asked.

Hours later, they were still sharing sibling stories, exchanging their diversely different childhoods—where Juliet and Ben had built swings off tree branches and made go-karts out of old car parts, where Mia and Daniela had swapped party dresses and snuck coloured hair ties under their ribbons.

Then, somewhere, not long before the sun would start edging up behind the mountain ranges, they let themselves sleep in peace.

CHAPTER 21

With her fingers at a standstill after having been flying over the keyboard, Juliet gave an audible cheer and sat back, arms crossed at her chest. She had spent multiple weeks in a rush of motivation and writing energy, culminating in a very rough ending to her book. Rough or not, the shell was completed from beginning to end. Now she had weeks, months maybe, ahead of her of editing, rewriting scenes and restructuring chapters, which was almost as difficult as writing the initial version. She would spend the time second-guessing herself and changing miniscule details. She could toy with the notion of a simple adjective change for hours.

Still, she felt a sense of achievement. Six months ago, she had been giving up and strategizing ways to refund her advance.

Things had certainly changed.

She clicked *save* and then went about ensuring her USB stick and external hard drive backups were up to date. No way in hell was she losing it now.

With a satisfied smile, Juliet rolled her shoulders and stood up, leather office chair wheeling back behind her. She leant over the desk and shut down her laptop, bouncing up and down on the balls of her feet. The sense of relief was like nothing she had ever felt before, likes bricks being thrown off her shoulders.

Juliet was good, now that she and Mia had slowed down. They were gradually building up their relationship, as weird as it was to do that, given everything they had already shared.

At times, they took it as far as Juliet sleeping in the guest room, particularly on the nights where she was up writing until the early hours of the morning. There was something enjoyable about the affectionate cuddles though, and the long, drawn out kissing sessions, with hands that roamed on their own accord. It meant they were building up to something important, rather than jumping right in at the end.

With a small, uncoordinated jump, Juliet stumbled over some papers on the floor and walked out of the office, poking her head down the hall to see if Mia was in her room before heading to the living room. Mia was sitting on the sofa, iPad on her lap as she squinted in concentration at the screen. She looked up, smiling at the interruption. "Hi," she said.

Juliet grinned, placing both hands on Mia's sides as she leant in and kissed her enthusiastically, tongue sneaking playfully over Mia's lip. She smiled into the kiss before pulling back, turning and collapsing dramatically onto the cushions, legs falling over Mia's lap and knocking the iPad to the side. "Whoops," she said, "but hi!"

"You're in a good mood," Mia observed, leaning her head back and placing her hands over Juliet's legs. She massaged the muscles loosely through casual sweats.

"I am. The first draft is done."

"Seriously?"

"Yep, now is the really fun bit. I get to ignore it for at least a week and then start again with fresh eyes." Juliet fell backwards, hands behind her head, wiggling her toes for Mia to continue. "We should do something to celebrate, go away for a few days or something. Up for it?"

"Am I up for it?" Mia asked, jokingly. "Do you even have to ask? Of course!"

"Good, I'll organise something, maybe a spa retreat or something, we can get pampered. Good idea?"

Mia nodded eagerly. "Excellent idea."

"So what were you concentrating on? I completely interrupted you."

Rolling her eyes, Mia stilled her hands and smiled. "I was doing some research into med schools here. Crazy, huh?"

"Oh, the thought hasn't gone away then? You're really thinking seriously about it?" Juliet asked, eyes wide.

"I think I am. It's not like I can go on doing nothing for the rest of my life. And it's what I was good at and interested in, so why not?"

"I'm all for it. If it's what you want to do, than I think you should go for it. I'll happily be your patient to practise on too."

Mia laughed. "You might regret that when I've taken your blood pressure and listened to your heart for the hundredth time."

"I just draw the line at having you put those things in my arm, a line."

"A cannula? Yeah, that's probably fair enough. I promise not to give you needles then." Mia pointed her index finger and jabbed at Juliet's arm until she earned a playful swipe and a childish giggle. Amazingly, being happy wasn't so scary. "It's different here, though," Mia continued, chewing at her bottom lip. "It's a five-year degree, because they don't really do pre-med, and I don't think I would get any or much credit for what I've already done. Maybe."

"Wow? Five years. After what you've already done, that's huge."

"I know. It would be four years back home, so it's just an extra year; but there's other stuff to consider right? I mean, your visa is one hurdle. That's even if you're keen to stay here, for this to be home."

Juliet nodded and shrugged. *Home* wasn't a big concept for her, and hadn't been for a long time. Her attachment to places had historically been even worse than her attachment to people. Which even she had to acknowledge was saying a bit.

"I can write wherever if I get another publishing deal," she said. "So that would come down to where you prefer. To be honest, I'm not really desperate to settle back in the States, but if you wanted to go back to Harvard, than I would. And," she added sheepishly, "I've been kind of toying with the idea of trying to get into some teaching, even at a community college or uni here, running some writing classes."

"You haven't mentioned that." Mia said with a wide smile. "But I like it. Sounds fantastic, actually. You would make a great teacher."

"There is the visa issue…"

"Mmm, not something I know anything about, really. I do know a migration agent; or I did. I could get her contact details if you want."

"A normal job seems pretty appealing right now."

"Doing something is appealing to me. I think I've reached my limit of relaxing. I need a plan."

"A plan? Five years at med school is a bit more than a plan!" Juliet said with a chuckle. The idea of going back to grad school or to do her doctorate sent Juliet into a state of panic. She had survived college on the barest of incomes, trying to balance work and study while still keeping her grades up.

Mia's hands stilled where they worked on Juliet's feet, and she screwed her nose up. "Am I being crazy? To think of going back now? There's school and then my intern year, then residency. I'll be geriatric before I even get completely through."

Struggling to sit up with her legs outstretched over Mia's lap, Juliet cupped her cheek and stared into her eyes. "Screw it. Screw the long-term plan or how long it might take. If it's what you want to do, I think you should do it." She earned a slow, hesitant nod from Mia and a slight smile. "You know, when you talk about that kind of stuff—medicine, you get all...smiley."

Mia laughed. "Smiley?"

"Yeah," Juliet eagerly said, shaking her head shyly. "That was meant to be a compliment. I just think that if it makes you happy, then why not? Don't worry about me and what suits me. I'm good wherever. Honestly."

"Maybe I should get my transcripts then..." Mia's fingers tapped at Juliet's legs.

"You should. And while you organise that, I might get something booked for us. I'm so desperate for a big spa and a few massages and leaving my laptop back here."

"Your *laptop*?" Tilting her head back, Mia laughed. "You're really going to leave it behind?"

"Yep!"

Picking up Juliet's legs, Mia laughed as she plopped them down on the cushions and straddled her. "I don't have to share you with a Word doc...your e-mail...the Internet?" Mia held herself above Juliet, her eyes comically wide.

"Ha ha," Juliet murmured, hands trailing over Mia's shoulders and down her arms. "You're so funny."

"I totally am."

"I might book you a separate room for that."

Mia forged a shocked expression, mouth forming a wide circle. Her eyes sparkled, her dimples on display. "I'll be good, I promise."

Juliet cocked her head. "You sure?"

"I'm sure."

"Okay then," Juliet conceded with a cheeky grin; she was feeling so playful and relaxed. She sought out Mia's lips, making a series of air kisses that Mia resisted, laughing as she tapped her nose back and forth against Juliet's. "You're so beautiful," Juliet murmured, the words coming out unfiltered and spontaneous.

Mia reacted quickly, devouring Juliet's mouth with fervour, resting her lower body against Juliet's. "I so like this you, the you that has just finished a novel and has a week completely stress free."

246

"Ah-huh," Juliet agreed, fingers sliding around the back of Mia's neck and drawing her back in. "I like this me too," she said, before returning her lips to Mia's. "And bring on a week's getaway," she added breathlessly.

"This is really where you got my book?" Juliet asked, small backpack over her shoulder as Mia wheeled a suitcase behind them. She glanced at the small café and bookstore next to the bed and breakfast, hesitantly winding her way down a small pathway to the side of the building where they had just checked in for their holiday. The young woman who had checked them in had seemed especially friendly and deferential with Juliet, which had nevertheless done little to improve Mia's grumbling as they proceeded towards their room. Tall, dry grass and a handful of flowering weeds lined the sandy, rock-filled path along which Mia struggled behind her, case bouncing sporadically. "Why didn't we bring your large pack instead?"

Juliet reached the large wooden veranda and awaited her with an amused expression at her complaining. "You want me to take it?"

"No." Mia looked up at her. "It's not that bad. I'm just being grumpy."

"We're here to unwind for a week, remember?"

"There's champagne waiting for us, right?" She yanked again at the case's handle to straighten its direction. "That drive was fucking ridiculous."

"My turn, I'll lift it up the stairs," Juliet insisted, taking the extended handle off Mia. "Oh, smile, Mia. And yes, there is champagne and wine and a cheese platter. Will that cheer you up?"

"Maybe."

She lifted the case up seven steps, turning away from Mia so she could wince freely. She had been insisting for the past week that her ribs were completely healed, that they weren't bothering her any more, but the truth was, if she twisted the wrong way, then a quick pull made her notice them. It was merely annoying now, more like a pulled muscle or a sprain, just enough to annoy and frustrate her, to pull her back a little, a reminder not to get too confident.

"Come on, the drive will be a distant memory in about ten minutes," Juliet said, puffing as she stopped at the top of the stairs, "and, I want you in a good mood."

Mia scoffed, hands on her hips and a handbag over her shoulder. "Well, if you want me in a good mood…" she winked.

Shaking her head, Juliet laughed. "Now, that was attractive. Can you taste the champagne yet? I think you'll approve of the request I made." Stepping inside the door revealed a large room with a four poster bed of dark wood against the far wall. Juliet dumped the heavy case onto the sofa closest to the door, next to the large wide windows. There was an open-hearth fire already lit. "Oh shit," she said. "You were right. This place is divine."

"Whoa." Mia's eyes creased, and she exhaled with a lengthy breath. "What did you do, promise to do a book signing or something? This is stunning."

"Hmmm, well, you mentioned that she was a fan, so I may have made sure that she knew who I was. Is that bad?"

"Bad? This is all good." Mia walked into the room. It was cut off from the main area of the establishment where the rooms with water views were. But it was quiet and inaccessible to other guests, so it was their own sanctuary in an already decadent area. And the extra touches—fresh fruit in a bowl, a range of food on the bench, a tiny kitchen against the far wall with a fridge, made it only more so.

Juliet poked her head through two double doors that led to a bathroom with a huge open shower in one corner and a spa bath in the other. A shelving unit held a range of organic body products and plush towels and robes were folded with precision. Back by the bed were two pairs of slippers, despite the fact that the hearth warmed the wooden floorboards.

"Seems almost a shame to mess this up," Juliet said quietly, indicating loosely to a line of rose petals that littered the top of the duvet.

Mia slipped behind Juliet and rested her chin on her shoulder. "Is it in the shape of some kind of bird?" She indicated towards the petals.

"A dove, maybe? It looks like wings right? Angel wings?"

"I don't think we should be too concerned about messing it up."

"A traditional heart shape might have been easier."

"Ya think?"

Juliet laughed. "It's kind of cute, whatever it is."

"Mmm, like you're cute," Mia said, nuzzling into Juliet's neck and kissing along her jaw.

"I thought you wanted some champagne?"

"I do, but I can multitask."

Tilting her head back to rest on Mia's shoulder, Juliet briefly closed her eyes. She felt peaceful, and she wasn't so sure about the last time that she could have used that term to describe herself. Never, probably. "We should fill some glasses, unpack a little, and fill the tub."

"Ah-huh," Mia said. "I'm all for those things, with the exception of the unpacking." Sliding her hands back to rest on Juliet's hips, Mia kissed the corner of her eye.

"But we might need some clothes and…*stuff*," Juliet placed a childish hint in her tone.

"Nope, clothes are definitely not going to be needed. Besides, we have robes. That's all we need for at least a few days, until we get bored."

"Bored of…?" Juliet teased.

"Playing Scrabble. I put a travel version in the suitcase. Why? Did you think I meant bored of nakedness and brilliant sex?"

"I do like a girl who can play Scrabble."

"I'm having bad flashbacks to teenaged drinking games."

Juliet laughed and turned around in Mia's arms, hands joining behind Mia's neck. "Drinking games with Scrabble?"

Grinning, Mia nodded, pulling Juliet tighter against her pelvis. "Yep, did they not teach that at writing school?"

Juliet rolled her eyes. "So I'm thinking something to do with shots and… what? Certain words? Scores?"

"I'll admit the rules were a little flexible. But generally, yep, double or triple word score equalled double or triple shot. Or dirty Scrabble: if you couldn't make a *dirty* word, then you had to drink a shot…or whatever was going."

Juliet screwed up her face, and Mia laughed. "Is it bad if I'm too old for that shit?" Juliet asked. "I just want to drink wine—more than a bottle preferably—all afternoon and night. But still…I'm old, aren't I?"

"You don't look old to me." Mia gave her a long kiss. Her eager tongue found a willing recipient. "If it makes you feel better," she said, "I think I'm too old for drinking games too."

"Not too old for this though," Juliet insisted, tugging Mia closer, her fingers splaying across the back of Mia's neck, applying pressure and keeping Mia in place. "And, you want to know what else?"

Mia nodded, pupils dilated. "I'm thinking *you* in the spa—candles, champagne, some music…"

"*Fucking* awesome idea." Mia grinned and stepped away from Juliet, who grazed her fingertips over Mia's shoulder and down her side, trailing lightly across her stomach as they parted. "I'll sort the music, and you sort the drinks."

Licking her lips, Juliet nodded her approval, smiling too as she turned away. "Done."

With her head resting back against the porcelain rim of the tall tub, Juliet had a hand towel folded comfortably under the back of her neck, and her eyes were closed. Mia was settled in between Juliet's legs and flush against her chest, long wet dark hair drifting loosely under the surface of the water, brushing against Juliet's bare breasts.

Mia sipped quietly on her champagne, glass precariously close to empty as she hummed along to the soft music that emanated from a dock out by their bed. Juliet's fingers sporadically stopped and started working at her neck for a few minutes until she felt them slacken and come to rest on Mia's arms as Juliet drifted into a blissful state of semi-consciousness.

Mia tried to close her eyes and relax too, but the drive still had her wired from the concentration that it had taken and the strange amount of road works they'd had to negotiate, not to mention a few overenthusiastic drivers who'd insisted on sitting right behind her, then overtaking her with the smallest of margins.

She sighed. That was all behind them now. She had nothing but a week of relaxing and spending time with Juliet, who not only seemed happy but calm and light too.

Nor could she stop touching Mia. After the weeks of Juliet withdrawing and them slowly edging back to a good place, even the random, platonic touches Juliet gave her mid-speech filled Mia with a sense of belonging, as if things were finally right.

Pointing her toes to just touch the other end of the expansive spa, Mia braced her body to allow herself to sit up slightly. The movement made Juliet jump, sending her elbow flying and her champagne glass tapping the tiled wall before tumbling straight into the bath.

"Was just going for a refill," Mia explained sheepishly, looking back at Juliet's quickly blinking eyes. "Guess you need another now too, probably without the oils."

"Crap, was I just asleep?" Juliet raked a hand through her loose hair. When she dropped her hand to scoop out her glass, her bangs pointed haphazardly upright, making Mia grin.

"I would be going with 'yes.'" Mia took the glass out of Juliet's hands and leaning forward, turned on the faucet and rinsed the glass. She paused as Juliet's hands cupped warm water and trickled it down her exposed back.

"Sorry," Juliet said.

"For being relaxed? I was quite happy. My glass just got empty. I tried to hold off on a refill."

Chuckling, Juliet rolled her neck before leaning back, hands still outstretched and trailing down Mia's spine whilst Mia twisted and refilled their glasses from the ice bucket on the small table next to them. Differently sized candles on wooden frames flickered, casting intermingling shadows. Juliet drank a couple of gulps from the glass Mia had handed to her, her fingertips still exploring the ridges of Mia's spine. "You have, the most beautiful skin, you know that?" she said after a moment.

Brushing the tender compliment off, Mia felt heat blush her cheeks. She placed her glass on the corner rim, slowly lowering herself back into Juliet's embrace. "It's nice to hear you happy," she said, turning her face and kissing the wet skin at the front of Juliet's shoulder. "I was worried you wouldn't be."

With her arms wrapping around Mia, Juliet smiled as water lapped and spilled over the rim of the tub. Her fingertips grazed Mia's abdomen, muscles tensing as she reacted to the ticklish sensation. "I feel..." Juliet paused, "weirdly settled. And yeah, happy. Without the book deadline looming and all the family crap becoming a bit more background noise, it's good to be able to just live in the moment. I'm not really trying, but that's sort of how it is. I'm just trying to enjoy the now."

Mia grinned. "So maybe I'm a little bit wise?"

"What? You mean all that rambling about not stressing about the future? Maybe."

"I'm totally wise." Mia's chest jiggled with laughter under Juliet's arms. "I'm pretty proud of you," she said after a moment, "for having the guts to, well, to not be all crazy-like but to actually confront your fears. How many people can say they do that? Or say that they will but never do? I wasn't so sure you would, to be honest."

Juliet's eyes drifted up to the ceiling, and she sighed. "I wasn't so sure either. But you were...You are too important not to. I just clearly needed a shove—a reality check. I didn't really think through what it would be like to not be with you."

"Completely boring, right?"

Laughing, Juliet bowed her head and kissed the curve of Mia's ear. "Completely. And, you know, lonely, painful." She pressed a few more scattered kisses into Mia's hair and onto the side of her face. "Besides," she said, her voice deliberately lighter and teasing, "you're the only one I want naked and between my legs." She pressed at Mia's thighs as if in evidence.

"Mmm." Mia exposed her neck as if to encourage Juliet's ministrations. "Let's see what else you want."

"Ah-huh. Let's."

CHAPTER 22

"I think we should rock, paper, scissors for it," Mia said, her voice muffled as she unburied her face from the pillow.

"I'm not sure I can move." Juliet lay prone on the bed, arms limp by her sides. She groaned. Her muscles felt like they were made of rubber—rubber that had been stretched to nearly its breaking point. "It's hard to say what hurts most, my head or my muscles. Everything aches. I genuinely think I've pulled a hammy."

"Really?" Mia reached across the space between them and dragged her hand over Juliet's bare stomach and down her leg, which sent all Juliet's nerve endings into a fabulous tingle. "I don't remember you complaining last night."

"Hmmm, I think it was the shower session. Or maybe it was the time against the fridge."

Mia curled into Juliet's side, pressing her forehead to Juliet's shoulder. "Oh God, we fell from the bed. Do you remember that?"

"We fell from the bed? That could explain the bruise on my arm."

"It's possibly not the only one," Mia said.

"So, I'm never drinking again. You?"

"Moderation has never been my strong point. Yeah, definitely never drinking again—until maybe tomorrow."

"Water and paracetamol and, umm…fried goodness. That's what we need. Recovery breakfast and coffee. Words cannot describe how much I need coffee."

Mia just offered a series of prolonged blinks and then said, "Yes, we're rock, paper, scissoring for it, and the winner gets to laze in bed."

Juliet dragged a weak arm out from under the thick duvet, holding a fist up in the air. A distinct inch-long bruise lined the underside of her forearm. "I always lose. All right, one…two…three."

They both pumped their fists, Juliet's hand flattening to become *paper* and Mia's staying curled in *rock* formation.

"Shit," was all Mia had to say about the results.

Grinning, Juliet relaxed back into the pillow with a heavy sigh. "Thank fuck for that. I'm not convinced I can stand yet."

"I thought you always lose rock, paper, scissors."

"Maybe it's like billiards—I improve with alcohol."

Mia laughed, curling up a little and nuzzling into Juliet, nibbling at her neck. "Hmmm, you smell good."

"You know what else will smell good? Coffee and bacon."

"Okay, okay. I'll get up."

Juliet pulled her in for a long kiss. Mia grinned when they finally broke apart.

"God, I'd die for those kisses."

"I think we just about did," Juliet said with a short, surprised laugh.

"Ha ha," Mia mocked, running a hand through her matted hair. As she shuffled up into a seated position, she rested back against the bedhead, and the sheets fell down to expose some very pleasing, full breasts. "Now I know we didn't unpack, but I did have clothes on when I arrived."

"I think those cute lace panties of yours are hanging over the lamp."

Mia clapped loudly and then quickly winced. She stood up. "When we're old, I still want to be having mind-blowing sex where we have to find our underwear in the morning. Deal?"

"When we're wearing those gigantic white cotton things? Do you think that will have the same effect?"

"Oh yeah, completely. I find white cotton very hot."

Juliet tried crawling upright a little before slumping back against the bedhead in defeat. She stared at Mia as Mia walked barefoot and naked across the room. Images from the night before flooded her mind, and one side of her mouth crooked up with pleasure.

She could explore that body forever.

Pulling on her panties, Mia put her hands on her hips and scanned the room doing a search for the rest of her clothes.

"Ah, I'm actually happy for you to stay just in those," Juliet said, at which Mia immediately swayed her hips and then rubbed the bridge of her nose. "But I think your clothes are still in the bathroom. Oh, there's a robe over there on the chair."

Mia nodded, slipped it on, securing the tie at her waist.

"Okay. Let's start with water." Mia balanced carefully as she walked across to the kitchen, feet kicking a number of items presumably swept to the ground in their intoxicated passion the previous night. "So we're going to stay in bed all day, right? Watch trashy DVDs or talk shows?"

"Absolutely, there's no fucking question about that. What time is it anyway?"

"Ah," Mia mumbled. "Umm, oh, microwave." She gazed at it. "Twelve thirty."

"We had an awesome sleep-in."

"I don't think we were in bed early…" Mia said, pouring two tall tumblers of water and bringing them back to the bed. She placed one next to Juliet, leaning in to kiss her forehead, the back of her fingers trailing briefly over her cheek. "Okay. Bacon, eggs, tomatoes, umm…" As Mia slowly opened the fridge door, Juliet smirked at the memory of gripping the top of the fridge with her legs hooked behind Mia's back. "Is toasted Turkish bread okay? Hang on, let me check the basket. That's right, muffins and croissants, yum."

"That all sounds good. Whatever you like. God, I'm hungry all of a sudden."

"I can't believe we have a whole week of this. This was the best idea you've ever had."

"Ever?"

"That and the shower head thing last night. That was definitely one of your bests."

Juliet covered her face with her hands. "Nothing like going from zero to a hundred in one night, huh?"

"Hell, I'm not complaining!" Mia whisked some eggs in a bowl and set the pan on the stove. "It's been a long time since I had a night of what, three orgasms? Four? I lost count. Let's just say a number of times."

"A number of *good* times," Juliet said, blowing a kiss when Mia glanced over at her.

"God, you're cute…And does this mean I don't have to keep my hands to myself now? I've been trying to be well behaved."

Juliet threw her palms into the air. "You didn't have to be well behaved, Mia, I'm no prude. Nor an angel, as you now know."

"It's not that. I just wanted you to get to choose, to pace things. I didn't want to be all smothering."

Her narrowed eyes locked onto Mia. "Has anyone ever told you that you're too nice?"

"I'm far too hung-over for this conversation."

Juliet giggled. "Well, if it makes you feel any better, you can put your hands on me whenever you like. Hands, fingers, tongue…"

"Oh, stop!" Mia placed some bacon in the pan that sizzled loudly, sending a delicious aroma throughout the room. She leant over the bench, flopping down on the countertop with a hefty whimper. "We need some recovery time, and words like that are not about recovery."

Juliet shook her head and laughed, taking a number of long gulps of water. How had she ever hesitated about Mia?

"Hey, Juliet?" Mia said, waking Juliet from her nap.

The day was incredible, with blue skies and soft clouds in the distance, the sun on full display. They had rugged up in thick hoodies and jeans with woollen socks pulled over their feet and ventured outside to lie on two recliners on the wide patio, crocheted blankets tucked up under their chins.

"Mmm?" Just one of Juliet's eyes opened. She held a book limply against her chest.

"You sleepin'?"

"Nooooo."

"You did ask me not to let you snooze." Mia held her fingers up in the air in playful air quotes. "And I quote: *Otherwise I will never sleep tonight.*"

"Clearly, I was joking." Juliet leaned into Mia's palm with her eyes closed as Mia tenderly stroked her forehead and hair.

Mia couldn't believe how the days had passed in a blur. It felt like their week had been a haze of long nights, bottles of wine, and countless hours of amorous foreplay and long, drawn-out climaxes. Even if she tried, Mia couldn't have figured out the sequence of days and activities. She would miss the mornings, where they slept for as long as possible, tangled together until one of them slowly roused into consciousness.

Afternoons were a mix of slow walks, hand in hand, loud chatter, and good coffee down at the café. Juliet had befriended the owner, talking about various contemporary authors and engaging in some polite debate about where the reviews had positioned her and how she viewed her own writing. Critics, she explained one afternoon to Mia, she enjoyed. She loved an educated discussion with someone in the field. She hadn't had that since she worked in an office with her editor. It elicited a similar sparkle in her eyes as when Mia spontaneously kissed her temple and the same blush of energy in her cheeks as when Mia discovered *her* spot.

"You want me to do another coffee run? I can bring them up here."

Juliet shrugged sleepily, squirming. She took Mia's hand and entwined their fingers. "I'm good. You?"

"Not as sleepy as you."

Juliet tugged on Mia's arm. "Come join me, I'll help you get sleepy."

"That sounded kind of seductive, but not quite right."

"Come on," Juliet insisted, creating space for Mia to lie next to her. "It wasn't meant to be a dodgy invitation. I was after hugs." She grinned, and Mia melted. Those dimples would be the death of her. "Sleepy cuddles," Juliet said childishly, voice like a toddler.

Mia eagerly conformed, slipping out from under her blanket and carefully moving until Juliet wrapped an arm around her waist and pulled her hastily into her body. Juliet inhaled slowly, nose buried in Mia's loose hair before breathing out a rush of warm air against Mia's neck. She kissed the curve of her ear. "I really don't want to go home tomorrow," Mia said, sorting the throw over them and covering Juliet's arm around her waist.

"Ack, I know. Back to reality."

"Yeah, I guess. Back to decision-making time."

"About study?"

"Mmm, not really. I think I know what I want. There's really nothing to lose, and it was always my dream. So I should, don't you think?"

Juliet nodded slowly, chin moving over Mia's shoulder. "I think that your dreams are the most important thing in the world, and you should do whatever it takes to make them happen."

Mia hesitated for a moment. Juliet had slowly been making Mia believe that what she wanted should be a priority, that she shouldn't be spending her life putting everyone else first, that she was important. It was a new concept, delightfully new. "You're not the most important," Juliet had told her, "but equally important."

"I used to think that I was giving up something by being…you know, all in. But I'm not," Juliet said. "I haven't, I've only gained. So, your dream, Mia? That's awesome, and I'm right beside you, because my dream is both of us being happy."

Juliet's lips worked tiny patterns against the nape of Mia's neck, blowing hair out of the way and soothing her skin. It sent Mia's breath racing and elevated her pulse.

"I might be fucking up this moment, but I've spent ages trying to find the right time to ask. I'm not even sure why I need to know, but I do."

Breathing in and out three times, Juliet nodded. "I'm sorry you're scared of me," she whispered, "of asking me something. That's not what I want, so please ask anything and I'll answer."

Mia shakily released a long breath that she wasn't even sure why she was holding.

"It's okay," Juliet soothed, and Mia tipped her head back to determine if Juliet's expression was matching her words.

"It's just about your book—the first one."

"Yeah?"

"It's all built around the character, right? From that catalyst where she disappeared?"

Juliet smiled. At least Mia had interpreted her storyline as intended; many hadn't. "That's right. That's what I was going for."

"She walked out on her wedding day. She got up in the morning and checked out of the hotel and never came back."

"Ah-huh."

"Was that you?"

Juliet released an odd sound from her mouth. "Would it change things if it was?" she eventually asked.

Mia sighed. "So it was?"

Visibly swallowing, Juliet nodded just once. "Yes."

"Shit."

Juliet clicked her tongue. "Yep."

"It doesn't change things," Mia said softly. "Sometimes I wish I had done it before or even on my wedding day. Everything was already crap, and then everything I touched turned more to shit."

Sighing, Juliet relaxed a little, taut muscles physically releasing against Mia. "I left a trail of destruction, and I should never have done it. As you would have read, there's a lot of truth in that book. I should have had the guts to say what I felt a long time before that day. No one really deserves that."

"Maybe it was better than marrying someone you didn't love."

"Mmm, maybe. I loved her, though—just not enough for me or for her."

Mia drew in a shaky breath. "I didn't love *him*."

"It's hard when you look back, but I'm guessing you did a little. Or you thought you did. It doesn't matter so much now, does it?"

"Hindsight's a bitch."

"Yep, surely is," Juliet said quietly. "Come here," Mia smiled, resting her face on the inside curve of Juliet's shoulder and draping a leg over hers. "So I have a snooze, and you go all reflective and sad, huh?" Juliet snuck her fingers inside Mia's hoodie, warm fingers rubbing soothingly against the back of her neck and between her shoulder blades.

"Whoops," Mia said.

"Any more questions for me?"

Mia shook her head, but swallowed against the burn in her throat, a brazen tear quickly absorbed by Juliet's clothing. Slowly, Juliet sustained a soft, even flow of touch over Mia's back and arms and through her hair. She assumed that Mia had more to add and that the question about her was just a subtle segue.

After a few minutes filled only with the odd bird chirp and distant sounds of people talking, Juliet asked, "Is today something, Mia? That I don't know about or haven't remembered?"

"No," Mia answered quickly, sighing, "not at all. I just...Can you be all super calm for me? 'Cause I'm not feeling super calm, and I really, really need you to be."

"Look at me. I'm a picture of serenity."

Mia tearfully laughed. "I'm sorry."

"For?"

"For having my crazy backpack on today."

Juliet didn't quite stifle the laugh as she lowered her face and pursed her lips into Mia's hair. "You'll need a bigger pack to be competitive with my crazy, you know."

"Okay, I know. I'm catastrophising." Mia took a deep breath. "All right, okay. I had another message on my phone today. Actually, I had two."

"Ohhhh," Juliet said. "From Stephen, hey?"

Mia nodded. "Yeah. Am I that obvious?"

"Just explains the freak-out. It's okay, and I'm good. So what did the asshole say?"

The easy way it rolled off Juliet's tongue was perfect, and Mia felt the first semblance of relief. "Two assholes: one was my dad and the other Stephen. Or *the* asshole."

"Asshole One and Asshole Two. Got it."

"Yep. So *the* asshole is apparently landing on our doorstep in a few days. He seems to think he has some belongings left at the house. Reckon he got tired of waiting for my call back, so he contacted my dad."

"What?"

"I know, fucked up," Mia said, her throat burning again. "Anyway, it's a long story, but Dad has managed to get a set of house keys that I keep in a security box in the States and has given them to Stephen."

"*What?*" Juliet's mouth was agape.

"I know."

"What?" Juliet repeated yet again, voice much higher pitched than usual.

"It's not even the keys…" Mia squeezed her eyes shut. "It's the fact that he just backed Stephen. It's not enough that my family ignore me? They wrote me off, but they actually helped him. Why the fuck would they do that?"

"I have no idea." Juliet softened, shaking her head. "That doesn't make sense to me."

"They're insane, aren't they? Normal people don't screw over their own kids. They stand up and they back them. They look after them, and they hate… they hate the people who hurt them. Why? Why can't I have family like that?"

"I wish I knew the answer to that one." Juliet continued her calming movements.

"And now he's just going to show up whenever he likes, Juliet. He's got a key. He doesn't have to call or make sure we're home or that someone's home.

And he didn't say when on the phone. He's just coming whenever the fuck he likes, like the controlling prick that he is. Just one bit more power."

"I know, it's…it's just so typical." With her thumb, she brushed at Mia's cheeks, which were half-hidden in her hoodie. "Honey, I'll be there, and we'll have Martin and Janet, maybe. We won't let him fuck around with you, okay? We won't let him. *And* we'll change the locks."

"I just don't want to see him." Mia bit at her lower lip. She wasn't scared of him. He wasn't violent or aggressive, but she had put so much time into managing her emotions towards him, containing it all. She just didn't want to see him; she didn't want to have that twisting of her stomach, the nervousness, the anxiety. "There's nothing there that's his anyway. There's nothing."

"Then he'll see that, and we'll send him on his way." Juliet paused. "After we make a small incision in his fuel line…"

Mia laughed loudly, a cry catching as she did so. Shaking her head, she lifted herself up and shuffled over a bit before slumping against Juliet again, half lying on top of her and burying her face in Juliet's neck. "Can we do that?"

Juliet pulled her arms tight around Mia's back. "Absolutely."

Following Mia with her eyes as she paced the length of the lounge room, Juliet rubbed at the bridge of her nose. A few muttered phrases of Spanish sporadically emitted from Mia's mouth, which Juliet had come to learn were distinct curses. Even though Juliet didn't know the words, Mia's body language left no room for misinterpretation. Who needed to know Spanish when Mia was as expressive as she was?

"Okay," Juliet said calmly, standing up and halting Mia's path. "You really need to take a breath. Martin has given us the heads-up, so you just need to try and relax."

"He's only a few minutes away, Juliet. I don't want to do this."

"Yeah, I get that," Juliet said, rubbing Mia's arms, "but you don't really have a choice."

"And that isn't working out so well for me right now. Gah."

Cupping her face, Juliet stepped in and pressed a chaste kiss to Mia's lips. "Just stop and breathe."

"I know. I really do."

"Shush."

Mia smirked, taking Juliet's hands from her face. She held their arms down between the two of them and met Juliet's eyes, matching her breaths as well.

A slow smile spread over Juliet's lips. "Good," she said softly.

Nodding, Mia ran her thumb over Juliet's knuckles. "Stay with me, okay?"

Juliet tried to portray a look of disbelief. Mia would have to give her a swift kick to get her away; she didn't trust this man one little bit.

"Just making sure," Mia said quickly, closing her eyes at the sound of the car approaching.

"You're fine, and you're in control," Juliet said, though it didn't matter if Mia was in charge or if she was; there was no chance the *asshole* was going to be.

"I am?" Mia asked.

"You are."

"Right."

"You ready?" Juliet asked. An engine stilled outside, and she heard a door slamming.

"Maldito bastardo."

"Yeah, Mia, yep. He is." Juliet's hands tightly gripped Mia's until the doorbell chimed. Mia whimpered before drawing in a long breath and hardening her features.

"Perfect," Juliet observed, dropping one hand and leading Mia to the entrance.

Opening the door, Juliet stood firmly beside Mia, proud as Mia contained the tremble in her hand. Juliet wasn't sure what she expected, but Stephen looked perfectly normal and somewhat dissatisfied, arms crossed defensively at his chest. The suit he wore was clearly worth more than Juliet had earned in a year during college, and a pair of unnecessary sunglasses sat on his head, protection from the dismal weather, Juliet sarcastically guessed.

She stifled a smirk at her initial impression, aware suddenly that neither Mia nor Stephen had muttered a word, and they were all still standing on the doorstep.

He cast his eyes from top to toe over both of them in a sweeping expression of obvious disgust. Juliet squeezed Mia's hand.

"What do you want?" Mia said through gritted teeth.

He grinned, although it didn't even go close to reaching his eyes. "Mia, it's been a long time."

Mia shook her head. "Not long enough."

"You look well." His gaze flickered to Juliet. "And I've heard quite a bit about you."

Juliet raised her eyes, and he coughed away an arrogant-sounding laugh. "My condolences for your father," he said to Juliet. "I do hope your mother is doing better."

With an immediate step backward, Mia shook her head before Juliet could react to his bait. "Get out." Her voice had gone low and gruff. "Get out." Reaching for the door, she gave it a hefty shove, and Juliet braced for the sound of heavy slam that didn't come.

Foot in the doorway, Stephen pushed the door back open and rolled his eyes. "No," he said sternly. "Not until I get what I came for."

Fuming, they all stood stuck in the doorway and waited.

So it's a standoff, then, Juliet thought.

CHAPTER 23

Mia and her ex-husband stood face to face, staring just over each other's shoulder, waiting, she supposed, for the other to make the first move. Juliet considered being the one to do it, considered saying anything that would break the bizarre power struggle playing out in front of her. *No one wins these kinds of games,* she thought.

Releasing Mia's hand, her fingers slipped out unguarded, though she noticed Mia's breathing hitch. Her nostrils were flaring too. Lowering her palm to the small of Mia's back, Juliet found the bare skin under her clothes and rubbed the pads of her fingertips against Mia's tensed muscles.

Mia exhaled. "What do you *want*, Stephen?"

Juliet looked him over, seeing even more clearly how his arrogance exuded from him like sweat despite his appearance: his abdomen hung over the suit pants, his belt hid somewhere beneath the fold of indulgence.

"In the spare room," he said, arms crossing at his chest, "are some of my things. I need them back now."

A pinched expression crossed Mia's face, and Juliet hoped the annoyance was easier to manage than the anxiety that she knew was underneath. Juliet stroked at Mia's back to keep her grounded. She felt Mia press back into her open palm. "I could have sent them to you. You didn't have to come here."

Stephen rolled his eyes again. "I doubt that. Sharing was never your strong point, Mia."

"And it was yours?"

"Are we really going to do this?" Though his fingers curled sporadically and he shifted his feet constantly, he affected a bored tone.

"Why shouldn't we? I have plenty I have wanted to say to you." Mia spat her words out.

"Let me save you the time," he snapped, and Juliet snaked her hand around Mia's side, pulling her back towards her. "I'm evil, you were perfect, and that was our marriage. I've heard it all before."

Mia's cheeks reddened, but not from embarrassment. Her eyes were cold and hard as she kept her gaze locked on his. "I was far from perfect," she slowly articulated, each word careful and deliberate like they all needed emphasis. "But you, *you* are a disgusting, revolting excuse for a human being."

Looking briefly wounded, Stephen forced the false smile back on his face. "I'm not the one playing around with…" He looked to Juliet, and she gritted her teeth, daring him. "With a timid little toy."

But the weak insult merely splashed over Juliet like a sprinkle of light rain, and her nonchalant glance was accompanied for effect by a slight shrug.

"You want me to call the police, Mia?" she asked. "He is trespassing." She kept her voice light and relaxed, unfazed.

Mia gave her a strained smile. "That's a hint, Stephen. Get your shit and leave, because we're not going to put up with this in our own home."

"You're the one who wanted to start something," he tossed back.

"And you're the one that is standing on my doorstep."

"Are you going to let me in?" he asked after a moment. Mia stepped back slightly, bringing Juliet with her and creating the smallest of margins for him to walk through. "I knew you would," he muttered. "Always so accommodating." He squeezed past them and strode without pause or permission in the direction of the bedrooms.

Mia audibly hissed, and Juliet placed her chin on her shoulder from behind. "I love you," she said quietly, and Mia deflated, resting her cheek on Juliet's head for just the briefest of moments.

"Don't say that." She stepped out of Juliet's hold and closed the front door. "I'll cry."

Juliet smiled, squeezing her forearm. "You're doing awesome."

Shaking her head, Mia indicated to Juliet to follow her. They walked through the house. The door to the guest room and the office were closed as Mia and Juliet had left them to conserve energy. Mia stilled at the entrance to the fourth bedroom, where the door was now widely ajar.

"What the hell are you doing?" Mia's voice was more of a growl, low and uneven.

"Getting what's mine," Stephen voice emanated from inside the room, though Juliet could only see the back of his feet from where he was kneeling on the carpet, appearing to be searching underneath a piece of furniture. A few seconds later, the sound of wood scraping echoed through the room, and he grunted in effort before standing and walking across to lean the adjustable side of a crib against the wall in front of Mia. He was slowly dismantling it, the small mattress discarded on the floor and an embroidered blanket balled up and thrown at the large teddy bear in the corner.

"What do you mean 'mine'?" Mia asked breathlessly. "That's not yours… That's, that's *not yours*. What do you think you're doing?"

"It is mine," he shot back, uncensored and cutting. "In fact, it was literally mine. My parents gave it to me."

"To us!" Mia's voice escalated for the first time. "For our daughter!"

"It's a family heirloom, or whatever, and now I'm taking it back."

Juliet watched this scene unfolding. She wasn't sure whether she should pull Mia back and away or encourage her to scream endless abuse. She waited instead, watching their movements carefully and trying to trust her instincts. Juliet needed to not think and just act, and she wondered if that was exactly what Mia needed as well.

Stepping into the room, Mia gripped the side of the crib where Stephen was working with a screwdriver. "I spent hours, days on this," she said. "I scrubbed it, and I peeled it back. I stained it. It was ready for the trash when your parents gave it to us, when they told me that I *had* to use it."

Stephen grunted. "Move."

"No, I won't move. Get out of my house. This is not yours to take. This is our daughter's. *Our* daughter's!"

"Have a look around. It's in an empty room, you mad bitch."

Mia's nostrils flared, and she leaned backwards before moving her body weight forward again, rocking the wooden frame.

"I need it now," he mumbled, and Juliet wondered at the way his voice suddenly dropped to a milder, less confident-sounding tone. "I have a baby, and if I didn't come and get this, then my parents were going to. And I assure you, you don't want to see them right now. They think this…" He waved his hand towards Juliet, who was standing in the doorway, "is sickening."

Mia had stilled, and her eyes stared at him wildly. "You have a what?"

He exhaled, hands on his hips. "What? Did you think I would be celibate?"

"Say it again."

"I have a daughter, Mia, and I'm taking this crib for her."

Mia's open palm raised and slammed across Stephen's cheek with a loud slap. A sharp gasp flew from the back of her throat, and she covered her mouth, staring, unblinking at the bright red mark her action had drawn. Stephen stepped back, rubbing his face and muttering under his breath. Juliet knew immediately what to do.

She appeared beside Mia, throwing a visceral glance at Stephen before stepping in between them. She pried Mia's hand off the top of the frame and directed her out of the room with a gentle push before turning back to Stephen.

"Hurry the fuck up and get out." She licked her lips. "And don't ever contact her again, or that slap will feel like a hug, asshole." She had to work at unclenching her jaw as she swallowed the verbal rant quelling in her gut and guided Mia down the hall to the main bedroom, pushing the door closed behind her. Seating Mia on the edge of the bed, Juliet knelt in front of her, hands running down her arms and thighs, before encasing her hands in her own.

"Honey," she said softly, bowing her head and kissing Mia's knuckles, hands trembling in her hold.

Wide eyes stared back at her, and Mia opened her mouth a few times to no avail. She shook her head before eventually murmuring, "I don't know what to say."

"Oh God, no," Juliet whispered. "Don't say anything. You don't have to say a thing."

Mia nodded, and she let her gaze lose some intensity. Their eyes fixed onto each other. Mia shrugged her shoulders and loudly sucked in air.

Closing her eyes in a long blink, Juliet crawled to her feet and sat next to Mia on the bed. She enveloped her, pulling Mia close to her body. Mia limply conformed to Juliet's contours.

"You don't have to see him anymore," she said after a number of minutes. "I'll get rid of him, okay? You just stay here, and I'll take care of it."

Mia nodded, fingers grasping at Juliet's jean-covered thighs as she kept her eyes closed. "I just want him gone."

"Yep," Juliet said. She could hear pieces of wood brushing together and scraping on the floor through the adjacent wall. Stephen was still working at dissembling the crib.

"I'm okay," Mia said distantly, as if she were reassuring herself more than Juliet.

"Yeah, you're okay," Juliet said. "This was all him, not you. If he can live with himself, then let him. This doesn't change anything. This doesn't change you."

Mia shuddered. "She was his too. I don't get it. Zalia was his little girl too."

Sighing, Juliet rubbed Mia's back. "I don't get it either."

"I want him out."

Leaning back slowly, Juliet held Mia by the shoulders. "You stay here," she said gently. "I'll be right back."

Offering a small sad smile, Mia nodded. "Thanks," she murmured, and Juliet leant back in to linger over a long soft kiss to her cheek. She squeezed Mia's hand before she stood up.

"I got it," she repeated to herself as she slipped out the door, securing it in place behind her.

After wordlessly waiting at the door for Stephen to complete multiple trips to his hired car, Juliet made one sole demand for Mia's keys. She was direct, concise, and assertive, locking the door immediately behind him when he stepped out.

Then she breathed a long sigh of relief.

Returning to Mia via the kitchen, she drew a plastic water bottle from the fridge and swallowed a number of mouthfuls.

That whole episode sickened Juliet. She could almost get her mind to a place where she understood his desire for the crib, sort of, if she made a very long mental stretch. But that kind of arrogance and superiority complex, *that*, she would never understand.

When she headed back, water bottle hooked between two fingers and swinging at her side, Juliet stopped at the door to the nursery at the sight of Mia sitting in the middle of the room, cross-legged, an infant's blanket in her hands. It was the one that Stephen had balled up and thrown against the wall.

"Do you have some sewing skills that I don't know about?" Juliet asked softly, one hand on Mia's knee as she sat down, mirroring her position.

Mia looked up from her lap, her face noticeably more relaxed and her eyes glazed but clear. "Definitely not." She spread the blanket over her lap so that the detailed image of various wild animals was on display. "My mom has. She made this. Amazing, huh?"

"Incredible." Juliet ran her index finger carefully over the fine stitching, tracing a number of animal shapes. "That giraffe is gorgeous."

"She wanted to do fairies, but I didn't know I was having a girl when she started."

"I wish I could do stuff like that. I think it's beautiful."

Mia nodded. "I'm going to keep it."

"You should. You could bring it out when we celebrate Zalia's birthday this year. I'll, ah, bake a cake. Or buy one."

"I'd like that," Mia said, folding up the blanket up and tucking her loose, dark hair behind her ears. "I like that you make me feel that it's okay to remember," she said. "Did you have any dramas with him?"

Juliet shook her head. "No, and I got your keys back. They're just on the kitchen bench. I didn't want to make things worse, so I didn't say anything to him. But the way he treated you, that's not okay with me."

Slowly nodding, Mia morphed it into a shrug, and she glanced to her side. A few chips of wood and some noticeable dust were on the carpet where the crib had been. "It's just an object," she said eventually.

"An important object. This whole thing isn't about stuff, it's about what the stuff means. To you." She paused. "Not to mention, this came with a little extra unexpected news as well." Juliet's hands trailed over her crossed legs.

"Yeah. That was a nice touch, I thought. She was probably already pregnant when he was still here, and I'm apparently the bad guy."

"From my end, for what it's worth, there's no question of who the bad guy is." Juliet resisted the urge to toss in a few extra terms. It was her softness that Mia was really responding to.

"I'm not going nuts then?" Mia asked. "I didn't make him act like that?"

"No, no way. Is that what he was like? When you were together, I mean?"

"I don't know. You look back and see things differently, right? That thing he did, putting me down? I realise now that he was always like that."

"Yeah, it's always different looking back." She couldn't imagine why Mia hadn't fired up and told her where to go during that period in their relationship when Juliet had lost herself in her head and threatened to run. She couldn't beat Mia down when Mia had worked so hard to build herself up. "He always put you down?"

Mia nodded. "It was little things at first, and it took me a while to notice. As it does, I guess. I remember going out to dinner with his friends, just after we started seeing each other, and he laughed with his friends because I listened to country music. And then I put an egg roll on my plate, and he took it and ate it, joking that I didn't need it."

Juliet reached across the space between them to press her palm to Mia's cheek, waiting until Mia lifted her eyes, now brimming with tears. She made sure Mia didn't shrug her away in embarrassment.

"You know I'm pretty crap at speeches, even though I can write awesome letters," she said with a small smile. "But I want to make one, I want to somehow make my mouth say everything you deserve to hear and haven't."

"You don't need to, Juliet." Mia's voice was barely audible.

"Shhhh," she said. "You have some listening to do. You have to believe me when I say that you are the most amazing, caring, and strongest person that I have ever, ever met. You are gentle and patient and so full of love. And I know that you've been through hell more than once, but the idea that you could still be with that man and not here with me...Well, that is just impossible to me. Everything he said, every derogatory comment and stupid thing he said to you was wrong. Do you hear me? He was wrong, every time."

Mia blinked, and tears spilled from her lower eyelids. She closed her eyes and grasped Juliet's hand from her cheek and held it to her mouth. "I'm sorry about what he said, about you and your family."

"It's fine," Juliet replied softly, wiggling her fingers slightly. Mia gave her a tearful smile. "But you didn't answer my question. You know he's the asshole, right? You are everything that he is not."

Dropping their hands to her lap, Mia clasped Juliet's fingers tightly, lowering her gaze to focus on them. She shrugged. "It's not always easy to remember."

"Fortunately, I'm pretty good at reminding."

"Is that right?"

"Yup, awesome, actually." Juliet sighed. "Honestly, Mallania, you are so close to perfect, it's insane. And I'm not naïve enough to think that relationship breakups are all one-sided and that it's always one person's fault, but I know you. No one I have ever met in my life has shown me the same patience and understanding that you have. You need to know how rare that is. I mean, when I pushed you, and I know I pushed stupidly hard, you didn't push back like everyone else. You didn't tear me to shreds and blame me for being nuts. You waited and you listened. If that's not being an amazing partner, I don't know what is."

"Ack, too many compliments. You have to stop. I'll never stop crying at this rate."

"You cry as long as you like," Juliet said quickly, and Mia gave a small sniffle in response. They sat quietly for some time, hands together and surrounded by the heartbreak of an empty nursery. A sombre heaviness settled in the air, the giant soft teddy bear a witness to it in the corner. The bear sat alongside a set of drawers filled with newborn onesies and tiny pairs of socks and mittens. A set of open shelves in the corner still displayed packs of disposable diapers and wipes, not to mention a range of wraps and blankets—everything that was needed to bring a baby girl home from hospital.

It had a surreal feel to it, for Juliet at least. It was a testament to the time that had passed and the massive changes that Mia had lived. A year and a half ago, she had been busy planning the nursery and choosing colours and wall decorations. She'd had a husband and a network of friends; she'd thought she was happy; she'd thought it was what her life was meant to be.

As Mia had repeatedly explained, it had all been false, of course, the façade of a happy marriage and friendships that were all cheek-kisses and strained hugs. It hadn't been perfect; in fact it had been toxic and damaging. She could only imagine the shell of a woman Mia would have become had she stayed in that marriage, slowly losing everything that made her the kind of person that Juliet was choosing.

"I hate him," Mia said suddenly, interrupting Juliet's thoughts.

"Good."

"I don't know whether to feel sorrier for him, his new wife, or that poor child."

"I'm not sure that's where your energy should go, hon."

"You know he'll be a shit father. He might go to the kid's soccer games, maybe, if it doesn't clash with his business meetings or poker afternoons. Maybe he'll even go to a school recital or play, if he isn't fucking their schoolteacher."

"It's their life now, their problem, not yours."

"Leopards don't change their spots."

"Some don't," Juliet said, smiling meaningfully.

"I know we turned out right," Mia said, her voice sounding strained. "There are so many things in my past that I would change if I could, and if it was even remotely possible, I would have her here with us. Zalia. But it doesn't work like that. Time can't be reversed and life can't be changed. It just is."

Just like Juliet couldn't change who she used to be. But she could sit silently, unwaveringly calm, with strong hands. People forget sometimes, she thought, that only the present is in their grasp and that tomorrow is their only hope. Everything else doesn't matter.

So Juliet barely blinked when Mia finally looked up, drew in a deep breath, and asked, "Would you be upset if I wanted to move from here? Sell and live somewhere else?"

She just gently shook her head, smiling. "Of course not."

Mia nodded and fell silent again.

"It took me a while to realize it," Juliet said, "but as long as I'm with you, I'll be happy."

"I didn't think I could be happy. And even if I could be, I wasn't sure I was allowed."

"You're allowed, honey."

Tears welled up again, but Mia smiled through them. "Yeah, I don't remember a time when I was. Not really. Not even Zalia would have fixed me or my marriage. Not that I've admitted that to anyone, but I know that. Maybe this protected her from…whatever damage I was going to cause her."

Sighing, Juliet slowly shook her head *no*. "I don't believe that. You would have been the most incredible mom to her; I know that. We can look for reasons for shitty things all the time, but in the end, it doesn't stop crap from happening to good people. It just does, and it isn't fair. It's okay to think that it just isn't fair. Not every shitty thing has to have a silver lining."

"I guess," Mia said, leaning back on her arms and tapping her knee to Juliet's. "And I suppose it's me kind of saying that my life wasn't what I wanted it to be. And I know that you're not sure about kids and all that. But one day, if that's something we want, then that will just make us happier; it'll add to our happy." She smiled, shrugging. "It won't be about trying to make something work that was never going to work." Mia's eyes scanned around the room again. "I can't believe I've never been back in here."

"Pretty hard, huh?"

"Yeah, hard; and kind of good too. It hasn't destroyed me, coming in here. It hasn't made me lose it. I've avoided this room for so long. It took so much to get myself off the ground that I didn't want to go back to feeling like that."

"That I get," Juliet said gently, shuffling herself back to lean against the wall, fingertips trailing over the leg of the oversized teddy bear. Mia followed, settling close to Juliet, their elbows touching as she lolled her head to rest on Juliet's shoulder.

"I have a little box, just umm, maybe an enveloped-sized box. It sits at the bottom of my pack inside a bright-red waterproof travel sack. It has a few things from home, but I haven't looked at it since I put it there. I even keep a pair of hiking pants on top of it that I never wear or move so I don't even have to see it." She laughed. It sounded ridiculous as she described it.

"Don't laugh," Mia murmured, moving her face so that she could kiss Juliet's neck. "I have one like that too, but it's in the cupboard up there, behind a box of old vinyl records and two boxes of my fat clothes."

"Maybe," Juliet said after a moment, tracing patterns on Mia's leg, "that's all we take of the past when we move. Just our boxes and the things that are important to us."

Mia exhaled quickly. "Whoa, that sounds oddly liberating. And we build our life together."

"As corny as it sounds, yeah."

"I can take my clothes, though, right? And my boots!"

Juliet laughed quietly. "You're going to need your own wardrobe, aren't you?"

"Of course. That goes without saying."

Chuckling, Juliet said, "Whatever you like. I think it's the symbolism of it all rather than the actual stuff."

"I like it," Mia agreed, curling into Juliet and draping an arm around her middle. "Can I show you my box?" she asked, ever so quietly.

"Hmmm," Juliet murmured. "Can I show you mine?"

CHAPTER 24

Mia found the apartment leasing process in Dundee simple and carefree, though the move had taken almost two months in the end. The timing was perfect, as the move ended up happening just a few weeks prior to Mia's enrolment in medical school at the University of Dundee and Juliet's temporary appointment there as well to a few junior teaching roles in English Studies and Creative Writing. One of the professors would be going on maternity leave midway through the semester, and the expectation was that Juliet would step into that role if all went well.

They had methodically packed up the Highlands house, designating a pile of furniture and random items to donate to charity and another pile of things that they took either to their new apartment or put in storage. Mia was particularly proud to admit that the charity pile was by far the larger of the two.

And then the house was on the market.

Entering their new apartment, with the door swinging shut behind her, Mia jumped in place as she untangled herself from her satchel, hair and jewellery tangled in the strap. "Juliet!" she called out from the doorway.

Finding Juliet waiting expectantly in the kitchen, dishwasher open and dishes lining the bench, Mia skipped a step towards her. "I'm so glad you're here!" she said.

"Did you get them?" Juliet asked immediately.

"Yep," Mia said, grinning and tumbling into Juliet, knocking her backwards two steps before they hit the bench together. "I didn't just pass, I aced them. First exams, Juliet, and I kicked ass!"

She engaged Juliet in a passionate kiss, leaning back and lifting Juliet, spinning her in a full circle. They stumbled together, laughing and grasping at shirt material and the table top.

"You did? That's so awesome, Mia, freakin' amazing! I'm not surprised. You knew that stuff inside out."

"This week is…It's so good. This decision, coming here—best decision we ever made."

"I agree," Juliet responded, untangling herself to place two open palms to Mia's cheeks. "I'm so proud of you," she said, her blue eyes bright.

"I'm just relieved and excited, and we still have your launch to do. Fuck, we're amazing! We're, like, successful and happy and…"

"Whoa," Juliet interrupted with a smile and a chaste kiss. "Let's not be too loud about that. Things are likely to come crashing down in some apocalyptic disaster."

"Oh Juliet, stop it. Celebrate, dance, jump up and down, because we're *that* couple."

Eyebrows rising and falling, Juliet nodded. "We are," she said, pushing at Mia's shoulder. "Now, go get sorted. We have to leave in an hour. You need to pack some clothes and whatever else you need."

"Yep, on to it." Mia rolled up on her toes, jumping a little with a wild grin. "Have you heard how the invite response has gone? Got the interest you were hoping for?"

"Mmm, and more. There're even reps from the States and a couple of publishers from Europe. And apparently that gorgeous bookstore woman from Durness has a whole heap of independent store owners who are loving on me and coming along. And, if you can believe it, they're doing some Internet podcasty thing. Apparently, this second book has created a bit of a stir."

"Does this mean I'm going to get to read it now?"

Juliet grinned. "I'll even sign you a copy."

"See how good we are?"

"Shhhh, stop it." Juliet playfully touched an index finger to Mia's lips. That earned her a kiss against the underside of her knuckle.

"Do we have to go right away?" Mia asked, fingers curling coyly around Juliet's wrist.

"Ah, kind of. We don't want it too dark when we arrive. Why?"

Mia laughed. "You're so adorable sometimes. In that case, I'm booking you in for a marathon sex session tonight, agreed?"

"Ah…" Juliet stumbled, looking confused.

Mia waved her hands between them. "Well, with all my studying and your midnight meetings with your publisher, I am insanely desperate to devour your body."

"Ohhh, yes…yes, yep. I, ah, I wholeheartedly agree. Your body, I want to do more than devour your body."

Smiling at Juliet's quick change in demeanour, from confused to pointedly keen, Mia stepped away with a slight spring. "Glad we agree."

"Oh we do. We definitely agree."

"I should get ready."

"I'll umm, finish the dishwasher."

Mia nodded, and walked towards the bedroom, calling out over her shoulder, "I'll pack that cute red bra and panty set you bought me."

After a lengthy drive, they arrived to the now-familiar seaside bed and breakfast where the book launch would be held the following afternoon. Juliet stumbled into the open arms of her editor, publisher, and the publishing company's media representative. She was showered with praise and complimented a thousand times over.

Juliet didn't hesitate to include Mia in her every move. She introduced her to each person slowly and carefully. She draped an arm over Mia's shoulder at every chance, replacing her wine glass as soon as it was close to empty. Juliet was balancing the different aspects of her life, and it was all falling together. It all fitted in an effortless kind of way.

They were chatting easily as the night progressed, a countless number of wine bottles consumed between the group of nine or ten. Mia listened and laughed at stories of Juliet's procrastination and complete disregard for deadlines, not to mention her refusal to change a range of scenes in her books. They talked. They smiled. They drank. They celebrated something unidentifiable, something that felt a lifetime away from the past.

At the sound of a gruff male voice, Mia and Juliet both turned, and the table fell into a muffled distant laughter and monotone speech.

"Juliet Taylor."

A wide smile spread over Juliet's face, and she stood quickly, chair grating back across the floor behind her. "Jack," she gasped, fingertips running along Mia's neck as she gained momentum into a quick run towards him. "Jack," she repeated, voice cracking as she tumbled into the middle-aged man. Juliet had to stretch onto her tiptoes to even get close to wrapping her arms around his neck. When he stretched upward, still holding her, her legs hung limply off the ground.

"How did…? I haven't been able to get hold of you." Juliet's words scraped through a constricted throat. "How did you know?"

"Sweetheart, I'm sorry. I missed the funeral, and then when I got back, you were gone. You are, as always, impossible to track down."

"*I'm* impossible to track down?" He returned her to her feet, and Juliet shook her head, one hand cupping her mouth and the other resting on his chest. She bowed her head, tears pooling in her eyes. "So much has happened."

"Your second book, darling," he said, placing two fingers under her chin and drawing her gaze up to meet his eyes. "I hear it's a good one."

Juliet shrugged and slipped her hand into his, turning back and beckoning Mia with a wave. "I want you to meet someone," she told him. "Mia! M, come over here."

Fingers curling around Juliet's elbow, Mia slipped in behind her.

"This is, ah, this is Jack. Jack is, well, like family. Umm, and this is Mia, my partner."

A wide smile spread across Jack's face, and he dropped Juliet's hand, reaching out to shake Mia's before leaning in to kiss her cheek and briefly embrace her. "It's an absolute pleasure."

"Likewise," she said, squinting slightly, and Juliet realised that Mia would have no idea who he was.

"Sorry," she said. "Jack lived near us at a few bases when we were growing up. He's Harry's father. He used to house us when Dad was shipping off or when we needed somewhere to crash for a few days."

Mia nodded, smiling. It was all making sense. Juliet and Jack were clearly close, and it was almost a relief to see someone from Juliet's past who didn't fill her with angst and hurt.

"Ah, Harry," she said. "The one who manages that great motel we stayed in for a few days."

"Yes," Jack said. "He's already moved on, though. If I could get that boy to settle down, I would."

"He will," Juliet insisted.

"There's still hope." Jack's eyes darted from Juliet to Mia. "After all, if I'm judging right, it looks like *you* ah…might have…settled down?"

Juliet pressed a kiss to Mia's cheek before wrapping her arms again around Jack's shoulders. "I have," she whispered. "I really have." Pulling back, she rubbed at her eyes and glanced around the room. "Umm, can I get you a drink? You're staying, aren't you? I really want to catch up."

He nodded. "Yes, I am staying. But I'm actually going to check in and get some sleep. What the hell made you have this launch in the middle of nowhere?"

Juliet felt the heat rise to her cheeks. "Sorry, I know—insane right? You didn't have to come. I mean, I'm so, so happy to see you, but yeah, it's so far from anywhere."

"Juliet?" He placed a hand on Mia's shoulder. "I would have travelled anywhere to see you this happy. You…You're like my daughter."

"I remember when you first said that," she whispered.

He grinned at her and Mia, dropping his hand to scratch at his beard. "She was this little eight-year-old girl running after the boys. They kept hiding from her. She said that she hated them, but I told her that one day she would like boys and marry one and that I would be at her wedding, just as proud as her father."

Mia scoffed, and Juliet laughed.

"Well, I was wrong about some things."

"Including my dad," Juliet murmured, leaning into Mia. "You were a more supportive father than he ever was."

He nodded slowly. "Your father was a damaged man."

"Yeah, yeah, he was."

"I am sorry about missing his funeral."

Juliet shrugged and shook her head. "It's fine, really. We can talk more tomorrow. I'm just so glad you're here. You have no idea."

Mia pulled Juliet close, kissing her temple. "We should get to the room too. It's lovely to meet you, Jack. I look forward to hearing more about this cute little Juliet. How about we meet down here for a late breakfast? Ten?"

"Great," he responded, leaning forward and kissing Juliet's cheek. "Go on. You go and get some sleep."

Juliet nodded and let Mia lead her away, up along the side of the café, treading the same narrow path that they had used during their last stay. Their room was the same too in all of its isolated and decadent glory. They chuckled as they walked, stumbling and swaying from the alcohol.

Juliet rambled initially, as they walked. "I can't believe he would fly all this way. Seriously, this is the stuff that my father was supposed to do. It's so strange when I look back. Jack was everything that Dad wasn't or couldn't be or didn't want to be. Can you believe it? We don't even always stay in touch. I think I disappeared for a year once, backpacking, and then I ran out of money and ended up on his doorstep."

She shook her head. "Insane. I remember that afternoon, Jack's wife, who was so nice and died way too young, didn't even look surprised when she opened the door to me. She just gave me a hug and asked me if lasagne was okay for dinner. Like I had been away for a weekend. I was always welcome there, the complete opposite to Dad's place. They really were the family I never had."

Until Mia had bowled into her life with the biggest heart she had ever known. Juliet had built her own family now too.

And by the time Juliet was aware of it, Mia was standing opposite her, still nodding as Juliet talked and talked. Mia was dressed in the stunning red underwear set, and she was slowly peeling layers of clothing off Juliet's body. Kissing each miniscule section of exposed skin as every item was discarded to the floor. Juliet moaned into her touch, arching her back and enveloping Mia, their legs tangling together and moving in a symbiotic rhythm.

"God, you've driven me crazy all night." Mia sat on the side of the bed and tugged at Juliet until she sat on her lap, breasts falling to Mia's mouth.

"I was so hoping you had this underwear on," Juliet spoke into Mia's hair. "It looks amazing," she whispered, slowly spreading her hands until they smoothed down Mia's back, thumbs hooking into the waistband of her panties and fingers kneading at her backside.

"You have exceptional taste."

Glancing down between them, Juliet asked, "Does that go for these too?" Her own simple black hipsters paled in comparison.

"Mmm, they're practical, and you look hot in anything."

"You only care about what's under them."

Mia shrugged, tonguing one of Juliet's nipples as her fingers slid into Juliet. "True," she murmured as she stroked underneath her breast.

"Mia." Juliet rolled her hips. "We should move up the bed."

Continuing her onslaught, Mia made a few encouraging sounds. "Okay," she eventually whispered, as Juliet lifted herself slightly and rode her hand. "These need to come off." She flicked at Juliet's cotton panties.

Grinning, Juliet slipped off the bed, her feet landing hesitantly on the cold floor. She slowly pushed her underwear down her legs and stepped out of them, palms falling to her hips as Mia cast her eyes up and down. Exposed, she stood in front of her.

Sliding back along the bed, Mia unclipped her bra, tossing it aside. Pressed back against two pillows, Mia lifted her lower body and slid the red lace down her legs, then spun them around her finger until they flew off. Juliet grinned, eyes still locked intensely on the darkness of Mia's irises.

Slowly tucking her hair behind her ears, Juliet crawled up the bed, straddling one of Mia's legs before lowering and meeting her mouth. She slowly built momentum, thumb flicking at Mia's nipples and fingers tangling in her hair.

Fluid pooled across their thighs as they rolled their hips slowly and evenly at first, then in increasing urgency, before becoming rapid and plain erratic. Mia knew Juliet's body intimately now, and she responded on instinct. Gone were the hastily moving fingers desperate to find the right spot or the sudden position changes out of some misguided, altruistic need to please the other first.

Juliet's shoulders rolled back. Mia cupped her breasts and traced patterns with her index finger. And when Mia's pelvis shuddered, Juliet pushed her thigh firmly against her. Her mouth opened slightly as she held herself just inches from Mia's face.

They stared at each other, unblinking, their expressions mirrored in rushed breaths and jagged urgent whimpers. "Juliet," Mia finally rasped out, and Juliet pressed her lips together.

They emitted primal grunts and moans, their lips sporadically touching as they rode out a prolonged climax, hearts racing and fingernails pressing into skin.

They sought each other's lips for more extended kisses as the adrenalin rushed over them, beads of sweat sending their entangled limbs into shivers.

With that kind of connection, once was never enough.

There were things that Juliet was good at, exceptional even. She was a writer—confident and skilled even in teaching the art and science of putting words on a screen. She was elaborately verbose. Excitable and tangential, yet incredibly passionate and competent.

Announcing to the world how amazing she was, though, pushed a lead weight into her chest and made her fidget with anxiety.

Even wedged securely between Mia's knees as she sat high on a bench in their boutique hotel guestroom, Juliet's fingers flicked and scraped and tangled with each other. Her body moved restlessly with each tap of her feet. Mia quietly soothed her, massaging her neck and smoothing down the softly capped arms of a simple dress over her biceps.

"Why can't I just write it and let my publisher market it? I don't want to do this."

"They want to see you, honey, and hear from you. Not some pompous guy in a cheap suit. You're the amazing writer who they love and have come here to see."

"But I'm not. I put words on a page. I haven't cured cancer. I'm just a chick who hated nine-to-five jobs, so I wrote a couple of books."

Mia dropped her face to press a kiss to the crown of Juliet's head. "Should I mention the Pulitzer now or later?"

"Shush," Juliet replied quickly, turning in Mia's hold so she stood facing her, hands flattened over her thighs. She sighed, giving Mia a sorrowful look and dropped her chin against Mia's chest.

Mia's firm hands grasped the front of her shoulders. "Your makeup and hair is done. No smudging it, or you're going to miss this launch."

"I think I want to miss it."

"Just think: in a couple of hours, it all will be over and done with and you can get started on the next one…" The comment earned a loosely closed fist against her leg, and Mia giggled.

"I have two things for you Juliet. Would you like them now or after?"

"Things?"

"Hmmm, yep. One is a bit of a, how should I say it, a kind of good luck message from back home." Juliet raised her eyebrows in a confused expression. "The States. From *home*. Your home."

"Ohhh," Juliet said slowly, although Mia wasn't making sense to her.

"You want to see?"

"Yeah, I guess. Do I?" She was uncertain, hesitant. Good things had seldom come her way from *home*.

"You do, trust me."

"I trust you."

Mia's feet hooked around the back of Juliet's legs as she reached across the bench. She fingered an opened envelope, then reached in and withdrew a photo. Juliet gasped as Mia rested it on her palm. She looked up at Mia, then back down again at the photo. She repeated the motion a number of times before she could speak.

"Amazing, hey?" Mia picked up the photo and held it out towards Juliet as if to make her finally believe in what she saw there.

"Is she really reading it? They haven't just set it up?"

Mia shook her head, thumb rubbing at Juliet's side through the fabric of her dress. "I phoned them, and yes, she's actually reading it. And saying some words, just a few, but the occasional phrase too."

Juliet shook her head in amazement, blue eyes fixated on the image between them. It was a photo of her mother, thin and emaciated, but sitting relaxed in a recliner. Her feet were stretched out in front of her, and an old-fashioned, pale, pink knitted blanket was spread over her lap. In her hands was Juliet's new book. Her mother had it on her lap, opened midway. There was a smile on her face.

"Glad you sent that advance copy?"

Juliet opened her mouth to articulate words, but nothing came out; it was the last thing she had expected Mia to give her.

"You okay?" Mia asked.

She earned another nod in response. "She's said a few things?"

"Yeah, apparently. A few things about the book, and when people come in, she holds it up and says 'my Juliet.' The staff were so excited, I was almost in tears. They were all grabbing the phone and telling me the phrases she had said to them. I couldn't keep track."

"Mia…"

"I know. We'll go and visit before school starts up. I've already started planning."

"I never let myself think," Juliet said. She worked at swallowing the emotion that was bubbling up inside.

"Yeah, I get that." Mia leaned forward tipped Juliet's chin up by her fingertip, kissing her tenderly.

"It's hard to top," Juliet said, "but I got you something else too. Just to say that I think you're amazing and I'm so proud of you and that I love you."

Juliet blushed. "You didn't need to do that."

"Oh, come on," Mia declared. "You showered me with a crazy number of gifts when I started med school. How can I not return the favour?"

"You deserved them all." Juliet cocked her head to the side.

"And you," Mia said, sliding off the countertop and padding across the floor to her handbag, "deserve a little more spoiling." Rustling a little, she eventually returned with a small velvet bag with a tie. She dropped it into Juliet's hand. "It would have been in a box," Mia explained sheepishly, "but I thought you might freak out that it was a ring."

Juliet laughed and closed her eyes. "Probably would have."

As Juliet slowly untied the ribbon and dipped her fingers in, Mia, her voice low and serious, said, "I love you, Juliet, and I am so incredibly amazed—honoured, even—to be your partner."

Juliet blinked hastily. "How do I even respond to that?" she asked, a little bewildered by the intensity of Mia's conviction.

"Oh, you don't."

"Oh, but I do," Juliet countered. "Because I love you too."

"You do?"

Juliet laughed, drawing a long chain out of the small bag. "I really do." Slowly, she held the fine chain up in the air and dropped its pendant against her palm. "Mia, it's…it's gorgeous."

Shrugging, Mia traced Juliet's fingers. "I didn't want to be too full on," she said softly, "so I hope that's okay."

The pendant, a flat, oval-shaped gold plate, had tiny diagonal cursive writing engraved. *Yours*.

"I kept thinking up all these phrases about family and choosing family and some long, complicated thing. But honestly, you're everything to me…You're my family, my best friend, the hot, hot woman I get to have amazing sex with. So yeah, I'm just yours."

"Mallania." The word was exhaled rather than spoken.

"We should go. You have a crowd waiting and Internet feeds, and it's all set up and ready for you. You should go."

Juliet drew in a deep breath and raised a slow-moving hand to cup Mia's cheek. "Thank you," she said, rising up slightly on her tiptoes to kiss her. "Thank you."

Mia watched quietly from the side of the small conference room with a glass of champagne in her hand. Juliet, despite her earlier protests, spoke eloquently and almost poetically, the epitome of exceeding expectations. She was softly spoken and casual, bohemian in her sensibility, and she oozed that persona of being everyone's favourite friend and next-door neighbour.

But her eyes kept drifting to Mia, seeking her out even when Mia switched from a chair at the back to standing to the side by a bookshelf. Mia tried to relax Juliet from afar with an endless supply of encouraging smiles and nods in her direction while Juliet read out a lengthy excerpt, then invited questions. During the Q&A, there was a flurry of hands and gestures, and Juliet squirmed in her seat, staring from Mia to her publisher and back again.

"Juliet, given that this book is well past the original release date, can we infer that it was a difficult journey to write?"

Juliet offered a small smirk to the journalist. Mia knew there were various theories, mostly that Juliet had disappeared and had no intention of ever completing her second book. Mia hoped that they were pleasantly surprised.

"I've found that writing a novel is as much about me the author as it is about the characters on the pages. It's a challenging process."

"There are some distinct similarities between *Things My Mother Should Have Told Me* and this," another journalist rushed to ask. "Would we be correct in assuming that there are some autobiographical elements?"

Juliet glanced down, flicking the end of a pen with her thumb. "As I said, for me, writing is as much about self-discovery as it is about getting the words out. I wouldn't say either novel is autobiographical, but I've drawn heavily on the people I have had the displeasure and pleasure of knowing in my life."

An arm flew up from the midst of the crowd, a writer for a review website, perhaps, or another magazine journalist—Mia had lost track. "Your previous story was about solidarity. Would you agree that this is a story of love?"

Mia observed how Juliet's finger stopped playing with the pen. "Perhaps a story of learning to love despite a flawed sense of solidarity," she said after a moment of silence.

She continued to field questions for more than an hour and then spent another hour signing books with meticulously personalised messages.

Finally reaching the end of the queue and watching people slowly leave, Juliet reached Mia, who was waiting patiently on a stool, champagne glass in hand. Juliet moulded straight into her.

"Exhausted?" Mia asked gently, leaving her champagne on the table and closing her arms around Juliet.

"Ah-huh." Juliet's voice was muffled from nuzzling into Mia's neck. "But I just want to stay like this for a few minutes."

Mia flattened her palms to Juliet's back and moved slightly, just enough to rock her almost imperceptibly. "You were amazing."

"You think?" Juliet asked. "I felt like I rambled, and the questions were full on."

Scoffing, Mia kissed her temple. "Seriously, you were so good."

"Thanks."

"Did you sign me a copy amongst that mass out there?"

Tilting her head up, Juliet engaged in a prolonged blink. "You got a dedication on the first page. I think that trumps a crappy signature."

"True. Made my head swell."

"I never would have finished it without you, you know that."

Juliet nodded, smiling widely with dimples on full display. With a softened expression, she said, "Everything's going so well with us lately. I wish things were better with your family, though. I mean, that would be awesome for you, for you to have things with them fall into place."

"I wish that too," Mia said. She kept her features neutral, rather than worry Juliet. "But I would rather them not be in my life than in it and causing us problems. You're my family, Juliet, and if one day they want to be too, then fantastic. But if not, you and I are totally enough."

"Totally, huh?"

"Totally." Mia confirmed, sliding off the stool and steadying herself with Juliet's arm. "Sorry, those Moëts have been going down a little easy."

"Coffee back in our room?" Juliet asked softly, one hand on Mia's hip, steadying her.

"We're like an old married couple."

"But with more sex." Her eyes sparkling, Juliet tugged Mia in a weaving path through the chaos of discarded chairs and tables towards the exit. Mia laughed with delight as she followed behind Juliet, feeling warmed by the glasses of champagne and the undeniably settled feeling she carried with her these days. It wasn't hard to see that they were both incredibly content. Happy.

They passed a poster just before they left through a staff door at the back of the bookstore. It was an enlarged version of Juliet's book. She had deliberated for some time over the cover, working with the design team to get it right, e-mailing proofs back and forth at least ten times. When Juliet had finally showed it to Mia, the impact on Mia had been a rush of humbled and touched tears.

Two abstract hearts were centred on the cover, various colours and cracks evident on both. They were splintered, broken, shaded, and simply imperfect. They were connected by interlocking items, and it took the viewer a few moments to identify what they were. One was an identical representation of Mia's necklace and pendant, and the other, the old frayed bracelet that Juliet wore. They looped around the hearts and then twisted into the gap between, around and around.

The simple title was positioned below.

And I love you
So I stay

"Yeah," Mia whispered to herself as they slipped outside and onto the narrow track to their room. "She stayed."

About hp tune

hp tune is a travel addict. You name it, she has been there on a donkey, or a camel, or snowshoes.

Born by the beach in Australia, she grew up catching waves and endlessly typing out elaborate stories on her prized possession – an electric typewriter!

Somewhere along the way, her typewriter got upgraded to a Mac Air, her backpack to a suitcase, and her hostel to four star hotels. hp still travels the world with the love of her life — her partner, not her Mac – though it is always packed.

CONNECT WITH HP TUNE:

Webseite: www.hptune.wordpress.com
Twitter: www.twitter.com/hp_tune
E-Mail: authorhptune@google.com

Other Books from Ylva Publishing

www.ylva-publishing.com

All the Little Moments

G Benson

ISBN: 978-3-95533-341-6
Length: 350 pages (132,000 words)

Anna is focused on her career as an anaesthetist. When a tragic accident leaves her responsible for her young niece and nephew, her life changes abruptly. Completely overwhelmed, Anna barely has time to brush her teeth in the morning let alone date a woman. But then she collides with a long-legged stranger.

Bunny Finds a Friend

Hazel Yeats

ISBN: 978-3-95533-499-4
Length: 204 pages (55,000 words)

Cara Jong's bad day doesn't improve after a run-in with Jude Donovan, who's playing Santa in a department store in Amsterdam. When Cara finds out that the woman beneath the Santa suit is a children's book writer, she's intrigued. But she doesn't trust her luck in love. Can Cara's meddling sisters and a hilarious road trip convince her to go after her happily-ever-after with the writer?

Coming Home

Lois Cloarec Hart

ISBN: 978-3-95533-064-4
Length: 371 pages (104,000 words)

Rob, a charismatic ex-fighter pilot severely disabled with MS, has been steadfastly cared for by his wife, Jan, for many years. Quite by accident one day, Terry, a young writer/postal carrier, enters their lives and turns it upside down.

A Story of Now

Emily O'Beirne

ISBN: 978-3-95533-345-4
Length: 367 pages (128,000 words)

Nineteen-year-old Claire knows she needs a life. And new friends. Too sassy for her own good, she doesn't make friends easily anymore. And she has no clue where to start on the whole life front. At first, Robbie and Mia seem the least likely people to help her find it. But in a turbulent time, Claire finds new friends, a new self, and, with the warm, brilliant Mia, a whole new set of feelings.

Coming from Ylva Publishing

www.ylva-publishing.com

Collide-O-Scope

Andrea Bramhall

An unidentified woman is found murdered on the North Norfolk Coastal Path and newly promoted Detective Sergeant Kate Brannon and Kings Lynn's CID have the task of figuring out whom, how, and why. A job that's made more difficult when everyone of the forty residents in the village has something to hide and answers her questions with a string of lies.

Georgina Temple has her own secrets to keep, and her own reasons to keep them. But her growing attraction to Kate makes it increasingly difficult to keep them.

Kate's investigation into the woman's death brings delves into the heart of the tiny fishing village where nothing and no one is quite what they seem.

Welcome to the Wallops
(The Wallops - Book #1)

Gill McKnight

The villages of High Wallop and Lesser Wallop have graced either end of the Wallop valley since medieval times. And competition between the two has never ceased since, especially over the famous Cheese and Beer festival.

As head Judge of Show, Jane Swallow has always struggled to keep peace, friendship, and equanimity within the community she loves, but this year everything is wrong. Her father has just been released from prison and is on his way to Lesser Wallop with the rest of her travelling family and their caravans.

Her job is on the line, and her ex-girlfriend from a million years ago has just moved in next door.

Her life is going down the drain unless she can pull off some sort of miracle.

Rewriting the Ending
© 2016 by hp tune

ISBN: 978-3-95533-503-8

Also available as e-book.

Published by Ylva Publishing, legal entity of Ylva Verlag, e.Kfr.

Ylva Verlag, e.Kfr.
Owner: Astrid Ohletz
Am Kirschgarten 2
65830 Kriftel
Germany

www.ylva-publishing.com

First edition: 2016

Credits
Edited by Michelle Aguilar & Joanie Bassler
Cover Design by Streetlight Graphics

www.ingramcontent.com/pod-product-compliance
Lightning Source LLC
Chambersburg PA
CBHW030940260626
47169CB00002B/546